Escaping on the Danube River | Shmuel David

Producer & International Distributor
eBookPro Publishing
www.ebook-pro.com

Escaping on the Danube River
Shmuel David

Translation from the Hebrew: Noel Canin
Contact: shmuelik7@gmail.com

ISBN 9789655751437

Dedicated to my father, the late Shlomo David, who continued to be troubled by the Kladovo-Sabac affair until his last days.

This book was inspired by his vision and his insistence on not allowing this obscure affair to be forgotten.

This book is also dedicated to all the heroes of the group, members of Youth Movements and families, who knew pain and disappointment and never lost hope.

ESCAPING *on the* DANUBE RIVER

SHMUEL DAVID

ACKNOWLEDGMENTS

Thank you to Professor Dalia Ofer, from the Institute of Contemporary Jewry at the Hebrew University, authority on the Kladovo-Sabac Affair, whose research on the subject and helpful comments guided me during the writing of this book.

Anat Shen, literary editor, who counseled wisely and went through the final writing stage with me.

Noël Canin, for her wonderful translation, professionalism, devotion to the project, and emotional involvement throughout all stages of the work.

Mara Juvanovic, for her incredible witness journal – "We are Packing, We are Unpacking", translated into Hebrew from Serbo-Croatian, by my father, Shlomo David.

My father, the late Shomo David, whose stories of the journey, excerpts from his diary and, above all, his determination to immortalize their story, inspired this book.

Nina Rimon Davis, writer, editor and translator. Although not involved directly, her good advice and deep insights hovered above this book all the way.

My mother, Varda David (Lotte) who, in her quiet way, and without knowing it, inspired the writing of this novel.

And thank you to all the survivors, heroes of the Kladovo-Sabac Affair, who still wish to share the memories they hold in their hearts. And to the second generation, who continue to honor and preserve old cardboard folders of letters and journals from that period, which shed light on the Kladovo-Sabac Affair.

PART I

NEW YORK, NOVEMBER 1998

The picture had been ingrained in his memory since childhood. A stately, beautiful woman leaning against the wooden banister of a staircase in the foyer of a mansion, a small smile on her lips as she gazes at some distant point. She is elegantly dressed, as if about to go arm in arm with her husband to see *La Traviata* at the Grand Opera House. Draped over her shoulders is a fur shawl, and her dress falls almost to the floor.

She was the grandmother he'd never met. The gilt-framed picture hung in his parents' home on a *moshav* in the Galilee next to a bronze statue—the head of a stern man with kind, intelligent eyes and a jutting chin—his grandfather, Emil David, a renowned Belgrade architect in the 1930s.

He got to thinking about the picture that morning on the bus to work when a photograph in the fashion section of the *New York Times* caught his eye. It was titled "Women on *Váci Utca*—How Women Dressed in Budapest During the Twenties." Even the geographical location was right, and for a moment, he thought the woman in the photograph could be his grandmother.

The passengers on the bus were quiet and subdued, some absorbed in their morning newspaper. A whiff of fresh newsprint ink drifted on the air. Others stared out the window, wrapped in remnants of a dream reluctant to make way for reality. In recent years, since moving to the neighborhood Rachel had yearned for, he no longer remembered his dreams. Life had become more pressured ever since the option of returning to Israel had been dismissed. Through the bus window, he noticed the pale light from windows of early risers, the lawns around their houses dipped in morning mist.

Two years previously, they'd considered moving to another neighborhood but worried that the transition to a new school might upset the girls. This was when Alan began to deeply miss Israel, summer especially, the smell of fresh earth after plowing, and the sound of the Hebrew language. In Queens, you could still hear Hebrew here and there, or go into a local pizzeria to eat falafel.

The yearning had kept him awake nights, and when he finally fell asleep, his dreams were swamped with nightmares and anxiety. Once or twice, Rachel shook him awake when he screamed in the depths of a bad dream. She suggested he see a therapist.

"Everyone goes to a therapist these days," she told him. "Only Israelis with their dumb sense of pride think they don't need one."

Alan, of course, refused, but these reflections tortured him for months.

Rachel was adamant in her refusal. Born and raised in New York and a staunch supporter of Israel, she nonetheless wanted to go on supporting the country from a distance, from the comfort of her beautiful home in the luxurious neighborhood she'd dreamed of.

After getting off the bus on Thirty-Fourth Street, he was sucked into a bustling swarm of humanity. Men in coats, briefcases in hand, morning paper tucked under their arms, were swallowed up into the tall buildings like target-guided robots. Salvation Army bells were heard from every corner, and the earthy smell of burning chestnuts filled the air. Alan pushed his way through the throng descending into Penn Station.

In the commotion of the subway, he suddenly worried that the presentation he'd prepared for today's meeting wasn't clear enough. He was supposed to present Charles, Vice President of Computer Resources at the investment bank he worked for, with a project progress report and his plan for making up the schedule delays.

He'd been working hard lately and hadn't spent enough time with his daughters. When he'd arrived home the day before, the girls were ready for bed, and the eldest, eight-year-old Nina, asked him to read her a bedtime story. He read her *The Giving Tree*, and toward the end of the story, a tear rolled unashamedly down his cheek. Nina noticed it and asked if he also liked climbing trees.

By eight o'clock in the morning, Alan feels as if half the day has already gone by. This routine of commuting to work was beginning to get to him. Each morning at five thirty, groping about in the darkness, he dresses quietly and leaves, collects the newspaper from the mailbox, and buys a cup of coffee next to the bus station. Same old faces, same old stories every morning.

He's been absent from the gym for too long now and it definitely showed. Various aches and pains bother him now. He used to play basketball with friends on Tuesdays and Saturdays. But getting home at eight in the evening meant he had to give it up. A coworker urged Alan to join him at a nearby gym during their lunch breaks.

"You catch two birds with one stone." He smiled. "Skipping a meal you don't really need and getting rid of your paunch at the same time."

"And why not?" he muses. He needs to take himself in hand.

The doors opened. People squeezed in. Alan was so self-absorbed he didn't notice he'd reached Rector Street. Leaping out just before the doors closed, he hurried along the platform toward the exit. The platforms shook as a train going in the other direction roared into the station. Exiting the station, he was greeted by the cold November air with its aroma of coffee and fresh pastries coming from the stands on the sidewalk.

The skies seen from the office window were deep blue, giving no hint of the bitter cold outside. As he hung up his heavy wool coat, he recalled the newspaper photograph. How could he be certain it wasn't Grandmother Louisa?

He remembered the strange telephone call he'd received one evening a year ago, in the middle of family dinner. The phone rang and he heard a Hebrew accent in the energetic, authoritative voice on the line.

"My name is Efraim Lahav. I'm a journalist for the *Jerusalem Post*. I'd like to schedule a meeting with you to discuss a highly important matter."

Alan was surprised and intrigued. They scheduled a lunch meeting at Alan's favorite Italian restaurant, next to the downtown Trinity Church. Efraim Lahav told him he was about to publish an article about the Kladovo group's failed emigration from Europe during the 1940s.

"Your father and I were in the same group, even on the same boat—one of the three boats there. 'The two princes and a queen,' we used to call them. Eventually, both of us were lucky enough to get to Israel, but most of the people in the group didn't make it."

"Yes, I know the story. Father told us several times about the boats and the Danube River that froze during the winter. He used to get very emotional, talking with real nostalgic longing. Which was a little strange, considering the fact they were stuck there without basic living conditions and unable to move for a very long time. Hundreds of people died in the end, including his parents."

"The article I'm writing will make waves," said Efraim. "It will finally expose what really happened back then and remove the veil of silence and secrecy that has surrounded this entire affair for dozens of years. The piece will point a finger at those responsible for that failure. Unfortunately, when I spoke with your father, I got the impression he wasn't really interested."

"As far as I know, he thinks it's pointless to expose the responsible parties because it isn't going to help anyone at this point. It certainly won't bring the dead back to life, just more grief and sorrow."

"I know your father. He's afraid. But something must be done. He says 'failure is an orphan,' but one can and should find the fathers of that failure. Your father is a member of the Kladovo-Sabac commemoration and research committee, and as such, I'd like his support in exposing the responsible parties. I only need the support of a few people."

Alan had promised to see if he could convince his father to support Efraim's initiative but didn't commit to any period of time. He recalled the telephone conversation with his father right after that meeting with Ephraim and his subsequent letter a few weeks later.

All these thoughts passed through Alan's head as he aimlessly stared at his presentation. The meeting was scheduled for ten, so he still had over an hour. A few final touches wouldn't hurt…

But on second thought, why make last-minute changes? He still had to prepare answers regarding the late schedule and had already begun putting them together. Absorbed and focused, he was startled by the ringing of the telephone. He had specifically asked Sarah, his secretary, not to put through any calls.

Sarah apologized for the interruption. "It's from Israel. They said it's urgent."

What could be so urgent? he asked himself, calculating the time difference. Maybe it had something to do with his father. He hadn't spoken with him in two months. The last time they'd talked, his father mentioned coming for another visit, which had aroused mixed feelings in Alan because of the inconvenience involved in such a visit.

"Should I put the call through?" asked Sarah, bringing him back to reality.

The troubled voice of his sister, Bracha, was heard on the other line.

"Alan, Father's in the hospital. He's had a stroke."

Five years ago, his father had undergone cardiac catheterization. Back then, he was told it was a simple procedure. He hadn't gone to Israel to visit him then because of his work. But when it came to his father, things almost always got complicated. A year later, bypass surgery was required as well. That time, he'd visited his father at Haifa Rambam Hospital in Israel.

Now what?

He'd always preferred to keep his distance from his father because he saw him as a defeated man. Even when he'd been healthy and active, fighting a quixotic war against management corruption on their *moshav*.

He could recall few moments during his childhood when he'd actually felt proud of his father. It was mainly when he beat all the youngsters on the *moshav* at table tennis, landing killer smashes in each corner, to the enthralled whistles of his friends. Not everyone had a tennis champion for a father. During his childhood in Belgrade, his father had participated in table-tennis tournaments.

His father had spent several years in various hospitals, but in recent years, his condition had improved. And now, of all times, a stroke. Out of nowhere. Alan wasn't ready for it. He needed to speak to him. They still had so much to discuss. Maybe that's why he'd emigrated to America. He'd always believed there'd be time to talk about the things they'd never quite managed to address. That he would find a convenient time, go to Israel for a long vacation, sit comfortably with his father under the mulberry tree in the garden, and talk about everything.

So why did things have to get so complicated? Why now of all times, when he was under such stress at work?

When Bracha, his sister, told him he'd better book his flight as soon as possible, he realized his schedule was about to change.

***

The monotonous sound of the jet engines, and perhaps the Bloody Mary he'd drunk, dimmed his uneasy thoughts, replacing them with a drowsy sensation of comfort. He placed the sleeping mask over his eyes and tried to fall asleep. It was going to be a long flight. But every time he was about to drift into sleep, troubling thoughts resurfaced in his mind.

For years he'd worked hard, taken risks, advancing from one position to another, from one office to the next. That telephone call had come at a decisive moment, a possible springboard to the great career he'd always dreamed about.

The seatbelt light came on and the captain announced that the plane had hit an air pocket. The guy in the next seat ignored the announcement and burst out laughing. His screen showed Mr. Bean dropping numerous cereal boxes on the floor. His neighbor's cheerful laughter reminded Alan how long it had been since he himself had enjoyed a hearty laugh. Not that he'd ever been one to laugh easily.

The jolts and bumps of the airplane gradually intensified, as if to remind the passengers it could all end in catastrophe, but his neighbor just kept on laughing. Alan continued to feel sorry for himself and think about the work opportunity he was about to lose. But what could he possibly do? Charles would never wait for him. He'd made that perfectly clear during their last conversation.

Alan had gone to his office before the trip, expecting a "Don't worry, we'll wait for you," declaration from him, but that just didn't happen. Charles grimaced and spoke of the project's importance, and in the same breath said there were more important things in life.

"A man must make his own decisions." He used the same worn-out expression Alan himself occasionally used.

The air pockets subsided, and the flight became less bumpy. Most of the people around him had already sunk into sleep. Once more, he recalled the letter his father had written him following his conversation with the journalist. For the first time, he heard his father openly speaking of the affair he'd so rarely referred to over the years. Efraim Lahav and his efforts to find the culprits had aroused his father's anger.

And this was what he wrote:

Efraim told me about his interview with Ruth Klüger.[1] This is nothing less than slander. She can't possibly recall all the details of a conversation with Spitzer twenty years later. Making Spitzer out to be a lunatic? Spitzer dedicated his life to aiding and trying to save the group. True, there were difficulties, numerous difficulties, and you had to be an acrobat not to come crashing to the ground. He did everything in his power. My father knew him well. He served as chairman of the Yugoslavia Federation of Jewish Communities and lived not far from us in Belgrade. They were friends. It's true that he was the one who suggested my father join the group, but who could have predicted what would happen? And who could have known that the Germans would take over Yugoslavia so quickly? It's easy to be wise after the

---

1 Ruth Klüger Eliav was a Jewish Zionist activist who helped with *Aliyah Bet* and did much to assist in the saving of European Jews between 1938 and 1941. Her autobiography, *The Last Escape*, is the turbulent story of her life, which includes many details about the period, as well as details related to the Kladovo-Sabac Affair.

event. But foresight is a rare quality few are blessed with.

Not even the *Darien*, the ship the Mossad[2] bought in Piraeus in a complicated, convoluted operation, could possibly accommodate the entire group. Only eight hundred people could board it. But then we received word about the disaster that struck *Salvador* in the Sea of Marmara at the beginning of December 1940, just as Spitzer was deliberating whether or not to have us board the *Darien*.

I repeat, I will have nothing to do with Efraim's foul accusations against Spitzer.

Even the stories Ephraim has been spreading about youngsters having no bread to eat, and how he and a few of his friends had to steal bread from the wealthy people in the group, are complete fiction. I was right there with him, and I have no memory of any shortage. Spitzer kept us supplied with food even after the river froze over. When he couldn't make it, Naftali Bata or Elli Haimbach were there to connect us with the outside world. They'd pass over the money to buy provisions, post letters, and later on, they were emissaries for the National Israeli Office in Zagreb. I can testify to the fact that we never went without food. Not the youngsters. We lacked for nothing.

---

2   *Mossad* – here throughout the whole book, the word Mossad stands for The Mossad le-Aliya Bet which was an arm of the Haganah organization to organize for the Yishuv leadership all the illegal immigration to Palestine (which was illegal under British Mandate laws).

Alan was curious and wanted to hear more about the affair. He thought he'd try to get additional details from his father but wasn't sure he'd be able to talk. Fragmented memories flooded his mind. He and his father had never seen eye to eye. There was always such an air of seriousness about his father, lightheartedness and laughter not a part of him. Alan always seemed to make him angry.

As he grew up, the atmosphere between them gradually changed. He remembered how happy his father was to hear that Alan planned to continue his studies and get a master's degree. For the first time in his adult life, his father had actually hugged and warmly praised him.

"You've no idea how important this is to me. You couldn't possibly understand."

No one was happier than his father as he sat among the guests during the graduation ceremony at University Stadium at Givat Ram. He listened attentively to each and every speaker, wiping away a tear when Alan was declared an honors student. He constantly snapped photos with his ancient Minolta camera. He photographed Alan on stage shaking hands with the dignitaries, then leaving the stage with his diploma. Finally, he made sure he himself was photographed while proudly holding his son's diploma.

When Alan accompanied his parents to the bus, his father mentioned the Minister of Education's speech during the ceremony.

"We must listen to the nine o'clock news tonight. They'll probably broadcast part of the speech," his father declared solemnly, pulling out the transistor radio that served as his constant companion. "Just in case the driver doesn't put on the nine o'clock news for us," he said triumphantly.

The laughing neighbor had fallen asleep, his head tipped back, a contented expression on his face. The stewardess came by with the duty-free cart. Perhaps he'd buy a carton of cigarettes for his sister, Bracha. He couldn't remember what brand she smoked and finally bought a carton of Kent cigarettes.

He returned his wallet to his pocket; his mother had given it to him years ago for his birthday, together with her blessing that his wallet would always be full. Years later, when she came to visit him in New York and witnessed the opulence and grandeur of his life, she said it wasn't quite what she'd intended. She hadn't meant for money to blind him so much he'd forget where he came from and choose to live in a foreign country.

"This isn't the Zionist dream your father and I cultivated," she said reproachfully.

His father, on the other hand, simply admired everything he saw on glittering Fifth Avenue, and Seventh Avenue, with its illuminated restaurants and dimly lit clubs.

"Here I am in a big city again, a real metropolis," he said enthusiastically as they slowly explored the avenue and side streets, Alan recalling his father's stories about his childhood in the large city of Belgrade.

His father wasn't bothered by Alan's luxurious lifestyle. But he didn't like the career change Alan had made a few years earlier. His father had come all the way to Jerusalem to see him, a four-hour journey on three buses and a train, to try to dissuade him from abandoning his PhD studies in physiology. How surprised he was to see his father suddenly appearing at the door to his laboratory, right in the middle of his physiology session for sophomore students.

"And for what?" his father demanded. "This modern computer stuff? Another passing fad like my transistor radio? Is this what you're throwing away an academic career for...?"

Alan tried to explain he'd been offered better conditions and a much higher salary.

"You don't realize how important this is," his father continued angrily. "I never had the opportunity you've had to study and advance at university. You're throwing away the chance of a lifetime!"

That sentence echoed in his mind for a long time. Just like the story his father had told him about the beautiful villa on the hill in Dedinje, Belgrade. He'd seen the large house with its spacious garden in an 8-mm film Grandfather Emil had shot; an avid photographer, he was up-to-date with all the innovations in the field during the 1920s and early 1930s. The photographs of the large house in Belgrade ran through his mind as he thought of his father's missed career when he left everything behind to go to Israel. A distinguished student and literary man, fluent in several languages, he was a man who appreciated literature and poetry. All his teachers predicted a bright future for him. But then, in 1939, he'd found himself on a boat, on his way to Israel to fulfill the Zionist agricultural dream of cultivating the land of Zion.

Half the flight was behind him. Alan thought about his missed work opportunity, but realized his father had missed far more opportunities than he had.

As a child, he saw his father's inadequacy, witnessed how people took advantage of his innocence and honesty. Dishonest merchants would try to swindle him, divert his attention while he was weighing poultry or vegetables. His mother was the vigilant one, discovering deceptions right under his father's nose and trying to correct them at the last moment. All the *moshav* officials and heads of committees with their promises of help failed to do so. They all spoke of assisting the hard-working farmers but ended up making the situation much worse.

Alan found it hard to see his father's weakness. He wanted to help but was powerless to do so, deciding instead to try his luck out in the wide world, embark on an independent career, and leave everything behind. He visited rarely, only coming when something happened. Like now.

Were these his father's final hours? Would he get there too late? But surely his condition might also improve, stabilize for months, even years. So why had he been in such a hurry, then? Why had he been so eager to sacrifice his career?

The pressure in his ears indicated the plane was dropping in altitude. The saccharine voice of the stewardess requesting them to "please fasten your seatbelts" brought him back to reality. The captain announced that the temperature in Tel Aviv was ninety-one degrees, the skies were clear, and a light easterly breeze was blowing.

HAIFA, NOVEMBER 1998

Bracha was waiting for him at the airport, her face flushed with heat and tears in her eyes. She gave him a big hug.

"I'm so happy you came," she said, starting up the old Volvo that was as neglected as it had been five years ago, on his previous visit.

"Father is recovering nicely from the operation, but the situation is still complicated," she said as they exited the parking lot.

Once again, he wondered if he hadn't been rash to come so quickly. He looked into his sister's tired face and saw the additional wrinkles around her eyes.

The same avenue of eucalyptus trees still lined the road leading to Petah Tikva, as if nothing had changed since he left.

"Well, how was your flight? Did you get any sleep?"

"Too many thoughts to sleep."

"I can imagine," she answered. "How are Rachel and the girls? I heard Nina got another award for excellence at school."

"Yes, she's a good student. Not like me at all," he said and immediately changed the subject. "Has he asked about me?"

"He was very confused at first. Spoke in a language I didn't recognize. Who knew he still remembered Serbo-Croatian?" she said, adding after a brief pause, "I only knew he spoke German, French, and

Hungarian. Lately, he's been studying Arabic.".

"Why Arabic?" asked Alan.

"He said something about 'a citizen of a Middle Eastern country needing to learn the most commonly spoken language in the region.' He's always had a remarkable gift for languages."

A bus shot past them, dangerously close to their vehicle.

"Bracha, has he asked about me?" he urged again.

"Since the stroke, he hasn't asked about anybody. It's impossible to understand him. He just mumbles half-sentences, some in Hebrew, and some in Serbo-Croatian. He did ask about you before the stroke, though."

"I thought he was mad at me for drifting away from the family."

"Just so you know, he really enjoyed the letters you sent him. It's a shame you stopped writing."

"I stopped writing him letters because my life there is a race against the clock. I need to keep up the pace, get things done, and move on. Work, career, I don't have a moment to myself."

A silence followed. Alan looked up at the sky and saw a flock of birds flying south in V formation.

"So, what does the doctor say?"

"Dr. Paritzker sounded optimistic after the operation. He gave me a real fright at first, said that many patients never fully recover, and if they do, it's only for a limited time."

"Well, we happen to live for a limited amount of time," Alan answered and scratched the back of his head. "So he isn't really telling us anything new."

"You know, you're starting to sound and act just like Father," she said. "The way you moved your hand to the back of your head, he does the exact same thing when he's bothered about something."

"What do you mean? We couldn't be more different," he answered. "I've always regarded him as the symbol of everything I don't want to become…"

"You just don't get it, Alan." She smiled at him. "The fact that you keep running away says it all." She quoted the psychology textbooks from her university days. "Deep down, you're very much like him, but you don't want to be. So you intentionally go on doing the exact opposite of everything he's done. He came to Israel to become a farmer because of his Zionist ideology. So what did you do? You refused to hear anything about farming, left the country, and ran away to the biggest metropolis in the world. Right?"

"It's got nothing to do with him. It's just who I am," he said.

The first houses of the Bat Galim neighborhood could now be seen up ahead.

"It's subconscious, Alan. You can convince yourself all you want, but bottom line, you're very much like him. You're fulfilling all the dreams he had to put behind him when he decided to come here."

They took the elevator up to the seventh floor. The Bay of Haifa in all its splendor was visible through the windows. The sight of green banana plantations, the red-tiled roofs of *moshav* houses along the beach wrapped in the blue of the sea, stirred up childhood memories for Alan.

"Prepare yourself, Alan. Don't expect to meet the father you remember. They shaved his head, and he's hooked up to tubes. He may not even recognize you."

They walked down the hospital corridors between grim-faced nurses, inhaling the odors of medication and disinfectant.

"Trauma room," said Bracha. "Everyone here has suffered severe car accidents or heart trauma. They don't let everyone in."

She turned to one of the nurses, "My brother just arrived from New York to see our father."

The nurse admitted them, adding, "Only for a minute. You can't stay there too long."

In the room, people were lying in a blur of personal identity and form. A plastered leg suspended in the air, tubes attached to chests or heads and ventilators. The nurse led them past the beds, through groans and cries of pain, bandages and towels soaked with blood. Alan looked at each patient, seeking his father.

He lay at the far corner of the room and looked exactly as Bracha said he would. The gleaming surface of his shaven scalp exposed fresh sutures on the left side of the skull. Transparent tubes drained liquids into a drainage bag hanging beside him. His deep-green eyes were open, yet expressionless. He lay quietly, eyes vacant, but his face was tranquil and his skin looked youthful.

Suddenly, he focused his eyes and tried to pull himself up in bed.

"Pauli. So you finally remembered to come?" A stream of words sounding like curses in an unfamiliar language erupted from his mouth.

He reached out with his hand and tried to touch his son. Alan briefly recoiled, then quickly regained his composure and bent toward him in a clumsy embrace.

"It's me, Father, Alan. Your son," he tried to break through the veil clouding his father's mind.

"What about Inge? Where is she?" his father asked in an outburst of fluent Hebrew.

"Who?" asked Alan, thinking perhaps he might have misheard, or his father had merely mixed up a familiar name. "Who are you talking about, Father?"

"Inge, Inge," he said in a weak voice, sinking back on his pillows.

On the way to the car, Bracha said she hadn't seen him so agitated or trying so hard to say something since the operation.

"Who is this Inge? And Pauli, why talk about him now?"

"It's true. He hasn't mentioned him since he passed away. How long has it been?"

"Seventeen years," Bracha prompted.

"But who is Inge? I've never heard that name before."

"Me neither," she said. "He's never mentioned her. I don't think she's family. Perhaps someone from his distant past," she hazarded a guess. "Lately, he's started talking about the group."

"What group?"

"The group on the transport boats on the Danube. He's started mentioning names of people there."

They got into the car and began to drive.

"You look tired, Alan. Your eyes are closing. You could do with a rest after twelve hours of flying," she said. "Come, I'll take you home."

"What home?" he asked, half-jokingly. "I didn't know I had one here."

"I've made up a bed for you in Father's house," she said.

***

Alan made himself some tea in the kitchen where every tile and cupboard handle was familiar to him. It was the house he'd grown up in. He opened the kitchen window and heard the rustling of eucalyptus trees swaying in the wind. They didn't seem so threatening now. When he was a child, he was certain it was the trees themselves that produced the strong winter winds, and he dreamed of living in a place without trees. By the time he was a teenager, he loved them, and later, in America, the avenue took on the image of his native landscape, revisited in many of his dreams.

The whistling of the kettle broke into his thoughts.

The kitchen was almost the same. The only addition was a tiny microwave, a token of the times. He sat in the old armchair with its wide wooden handrests. His father used to sit there with a book or a newspaper. His eyes flickered over the headlines of the newspaper lying on the table. It appeared that his father had been reading when he had the stroke.

Again, he recalled the name Inge, a name he'd never heard before. Now he couldn't get it out of his mind.

He got up, opened the cabinet, and took out the envelopes of old photographs from his father's house in Belgrade. He hadn't looked at them in years. His grandfather had taken them with his fine Kodak camera. In one of the photos were two children with shorn heads; they were tanned and smiling, about eleven or twelve years old. On the back, written in German: "Pauli and Hanne, Belgrade 1934." Hanne was the nickname his grandmother Louisa had given his father in tribute to Goethe, her favorite poet.

In the photo, they were standing next to a swimming pool, dressed in bathing suits. They were so thin that the hollow between shoulder and collarbone seemed too deep, although it may have been the light and camera angle.

A large, plain-looking envelope from Migdal Insurance containing many documents. He took out a folder bound with a blue ribbon. On the first, slightly stained page appeared a charcoal portrait of his grandmother Louisa. Above it was the title:

DIARY ENTRIES, BELGRADE 1931–1939 (HE-
BREW TRANSLATION, 1962)

He opened it, and began to read:

> Today, when I came home from school, Mother gave me this
> smart notebook as a present, my first diary. It was packed in
> a cardboard box and wrapped with scented paper. The pages
> have gold margins and that nice smell of paper. Mother said
> I can write interesting things that happen to me in this diary
> and anything else I think about. She says I should think of
> this diary as a new friend. I'm already in second grade, but
> I've known how to read since I was four. Mother always tells
> everyone her son has a gift for writing. She probably wants
> me to grow up to be like one of the writers that sometimes
> come to lecture to her and her friends on literary evenings
> she holds in our house.

Alan turned the page and went on reading, captivated by the images
of life that emerged from the pages.

BELGRADE, JULY 1931

Today, Father brought me lots of new stamps for my collection. Klarie helped me sort them out by subject and country. But in the afternoon, Klarie's friend Frenzie came to visit again. I don't like it when she comes, because Klarie tells me to go to my room, even if we're in the middle of something important. Klarie told me to go to my room this time, too, and sort out my stamps on my own.

Klarie is a good sister, maybe because she's ten years older than me, not like Pauli, who's always picking on me and taking my stuff. Klarie showed Frenzie photos Father took on Saturday at our swimming pool. They laughed, then Klarie closed her door and I went down to my room to sort out my new stamps.

Klarie helps me with my German lessons, because she knows German almost as well as Mother. Mother is always busy, and Father isn't home all day. In the evenings, when he comes back, Lord and I stand next to the gate and wait for him to drive his car through the gateposts. Lord always begins to bark with joy, even before we see or hear Father's car. Almost right after that, we see Father's broad shoulders inside the car, his head almost reaching the roof of the car, and his elbow sticking out the window. Father promised he'll open the car top again next week, just like he did last summer. We took a trip in the Žirovnica forest and saw the Danube winding through the trees. Mother kept humming "The Blue Danube," then she suddenly stopped and cried enthusiastically, "Look, look children. See how blue it is? Just like Strauss's music."

Then we parked the car and Mother took out the basket, spread a beautiful cloth on the grass, and we had a picnic. Pauli and I went to look for berries and butterflies. When we came back, we saw Father sitting with his back against a tree, and Mother lying on her back with her head resting on his knees.

Pauli stole some of my photos of the Red Star Belgrade players. I have photos of all the players. I have a notebook with newspaper clippings about all the team's games. Father once took me and Pauli to see them play against Dinamo Zagreb at our Beograd stadium. Milošević scored a goal with a massive kick, and the crowd all stood up, screaming, "*Hyda* Milošević! *Hyda* Beograd!"

After the game, Father invited all the players to our house for a bottle of *slivovitz*. But he told me and Pauli to take Lord out for a walk because he'd been inside the house all day. I got really mad at Father for not letting us be at the victory celebration, but he still refused. I wanted Milošević to sign his photo for me. We were dressed in the team uniform Father bought us, red and white shirts with the team's logo in black and yellow. Father took a photo of me wearing the uniform, with a soccer ball under my foot, just like a real player. Father takes photographs all the time. He walks around the house with a camera hanging around his neck and keeps telling us to pose and smile for the camera, then the flash lights up the room. Mother complains he's getting on her nerves with his constant photography. The whole house is full of photos, especially of Klarie with her blond curls. Father always boasts about how beautiful Klarie is. I once heard him tell Mother that sometimes he thinks Klarie doesn't belong to our family, because Pauli and I have thick, black hair.

Every summer, Father invites Simon, the barber, to our house to shave our heads. Simon is a funny man. He wears suspenders to hold up his pants so they won't fall off his fat belly. Mother calls the suspenders *shleikes*. He also has a funny little mustache. He always reminds me of the fat cat from the Mickey Mouse cartoons who wants to catch Mickey, though he never does.

It always makes me laugh when he arrives, opens his black bag, and takes out the haircut instruments in that funny way of his. There are all sorts of scissors and colored combs in his large black bag. The razor is the most dangerous instrument. It's a folding knife, and it's very sharp.

One day, he came and started with his funny movements. He took a kind of gray sleeve, wore it over his arm, and said he had a surprise in his bag. Then he took a black instrument from his bag. It looked a little like the flashlight Father bought Pauli last year. Simon waved it in the air and announced, "Surprise! Surprise!"

Pauli and I looked at him as if he were a magician. Next, he took a long, black electrical cord from his bag and looked for an electrical socket. When he plugged the instrument into the wall-socket and pressed a button, we heard a loud buzzing sound. Simon told us the machine shaved hair quickly and evenly all over the head. It was his first day with the machine. Simon promised it wouldn't hurt; on the contrary, it would even be pleasant. So I volunteered to be first, even though Pauli is normally first. I could tell that Pauli was a little afraid of the machine. He even tried to open the main door connecting the garden with the living room so he could escape, but changed his mind and stayed to see Simon removing all the hair from my head with just a few movements. I wasn't afraid at all. My head even felt nice, and I sat quietly, till suddenly, I saw Lord running across the path into the garden and trampling all of Mother's flowers on the way. He was chasing the ginger cat that belongs to our neighbor, the angry Mr. Pops, who hates everyone.

I wanted to save the cat, because I knew if Mr. Pops thought

Lord had hurt his cat, something really bad would happen. So I immediately jumped up from my chair with the blue apron still tied around my neck. The chair fell over on Mr. Simon's foot, and I heard him yell out in pain. I ran, shouting at Lord, who had meanwhile knocked over the round tea table with the white cloth that Sophie, the maid, had set just a few minutes before for afternoon tea. All the cups fell on the patio floor with a big noise, and the cat managed to climb on a very tall branch. Simon was very frightened by what had happened and shouted for me to come back. He explained the danger and how fortunate it was that he was using the shaving machine and not the razor. He didn't even want to think about what might have happened if it had been the razor. Meanwhile, Mother heard the commotion as well and came outside in a panic. She was also very angry when she had heard from Simon about my dangerous stunt. She told me to go to my room, because at five o'clock, Mr. César, my French teacher, was coming, and I'd better be prepared for the lesson, or else…

I just don't understand why it's so important for a child in second grade to learn both French and German, in addition to Serbo-Croatian, which is our principal language at school. But Mother thinks that the world of German literature and poetry is so rich that a cultured man simply can't live in the world today without knowing German. She once taught me German herself, and we used to read aloud poems by Goethe and Heine. She loved listening to me reading aloud, but now she's too busy. She has too many things to take care of in the house, most importantly the five o'clock tea with her reading-club friends. Mother is very active in the club. Once a month, she organizes a big literary evening at our house and invites lots of people. Everyone comes dressed very elegantly, the men with broad hats and the women in long dresses.

Mother always plays some sad piece by Schubert in honor of such a serious occasion. She won't let me and Pauli stay up and makes us to go to bed so we won't get under her feet. She calls me "my little spy," because I love eavesdropping on adults' conversations. When she thinks I'm already asleep, I go down very quietly and stand behind the staircase post; sometimes, I even go down the stairs and listen to their conversations. If I hear someone coming, I quickly run upstairs and hide under the blanket in my room. Most times, someone reads a poem, and Mother accompanies him on the piano. Then everyone talks about it.

Sometimes, they talk about what's going on in the world, and then it gets really interesting. Last time, they spoke about the Zeppelin that reached the North Pole and everyone got excited, except my father, who declared he wasn't surprised at all, then he spoke about the German Zeppelins again, about how, when he served in the Kaiser's army during the Great War, the Germans used their Zeppelins to discover whether the enemy was approaching their ships.

Father once brought me an American stamp with a Zeppelin for my collection and explained how it worked. He showed me a photo of a Zeppelin hovering above skyscrapers, the tallest towers in New York. It's a very big city, even bigger than Budapest in Hungary. Father travels to Budapest sometimes because of his work, and comes back after a day or two. The name, Zeppelin, made me laugh. Father explained it was named after a German count, Ferdinand von Zeppelin, who invented it, but he wasn't the first one to come up with the idea. There was someone else who planned a model of it before him, a Croatian called David Schwarz. I thought it would have been even funnier if that puffed-up airship had been called a Schwarz, or perhaps "Zeppelium," because of the gas that makes it lighter than air.

That night, I dreamed I was sitting in a Zeppelin, holding a wheel, just like the one in Father's car. I was flying the Zeppelin to the North Pole. In the morning, I told Mother about the dream and that I'd like very much to see a real Zeppelin rising into the air. Perhaps Father could take me to Germany to see a real Zeppelin going sky-high? And Mother said, "You've been listening to adults' conversations again. Instead of getting a proper night's sleep, you're running around, listening to adult matters. I can tell by your eyes you haven't slept enough. You must sleep at night, otherwise you won't grow properly."

I also like listening to Father's stories about the Great War.

He told us about the bridges and railroads he'd built over rivers and valleys so the army could cross over. Other times, he had to do the exact opposite, destroy enemy bridges to make it more difficult for them to advance. When Klarie was a little girl and the war started, Father was an engineering officer in the Kaiser's army, and he fought for the Hungarian side.

On the living room wall, behind the piano, there's a large photo of father. In the photo, he's sitting in a chair, wearing a hat that looks like an upturned flowerpot with two red stripes at the top. He's wearing high boots and a very long sword. He has a mustache, and his expression is very serious. Klarie told me that when she was five, Mother took her to visit Father in the trenches. Father put her on his horse and then left her on a cot next to his tent while he and Mother went to one side and kissed. Klarie showed me a photo Father had taken of her on a horse that day. She was wearing a wool hat pulled down over her ears, because they were freezing from the cold.

When I asked Father about Klarie's photo on the horse, he answered, as always, that I ask too many questions. He doesn't like talking about that time, the time of the Great War, and only says war is a terrible thing and we must never allow it to happen again.

Father wants me to be an engineer, too, when I grow up, but my history teacher told him I'm his best pupil, and he believes I'll be a great researcher or writer when I grow up. Mother was very pleased to hear that, but Father told her it would be better for me to be good at arithmetic and geometry, like him as a boy, because engineers make a lot more money than writers. Mother was mad at him and said that lately he was only interested in work and money, and that he no longer took an interest in her literary evenings, that he used to read books and love poetry just like she does. Suddenly, she saw me standing at the door, listening.

"Little spy," she said, frowning. "Is it polite to eavesdrop on adults' conversation? Off you go and do your homework."

Instead of going to my room, I went to visit Lord. I missed him. I lay next to him in the corner of the patio and stroked his head from his ears to his nose. I whispered to him that he was my best friend, and that he should keep me safe and I'd protect him from the neighbor, Mr. Pops. He hates dogs and has already told father that if he ever catches Lord in his yard again, he'll kill him.

***

Exhausted, Alan stopped reading, despite his fascination. His curiosity and desire to discover who Inge was urged him to keep looking at the photos. He was hoping to find a photo of a girl his father had met in Belgrade, in the youth movement perhaps, or at summer camp, or one of Klarie's friends who used to come for a swim in their pool, as he once told him. Three photos seemed worthy of further examination.

Two of them were taken by the pool. In each, Klarie appeared with a different friend. The third photo was of a curly-headed teenager with beautiful eyes and a sad expression. She wore a long skirt and a plaid vest and held a bag in her hand. Could that be Inge? She appeared older than Klarie and her friends from the other photos, which made him wonder if she even belonged there. He placed the photos in his inner jacket pocket. Tomorrow, if his father was clearheaded, he could ask him about the girls in the photos.

The following day, when he returned from the hospital, he took out the envelope with the photos once again, finding a postcard photograph of the entire family: the two boys, Pauli and Hanne, their parents behind them, all wearing the one-piece swimsuits of the time, with shoulder straps and bathing caps. They all seemed very happy.

On the back was written "Summer vacation in Opatija, August 1931." Then he turned his attention back to the diary he'd discovered the previous day and continued to read with increasing interest.

JUNE 1933

Today, Mother suggested I do my homework early, because Mrs. Garai was coming for tea with her daughter, Branka. I quickly finished my calculus and geography homework. I'm really bored with calculus but love geography. Today, we learned about South American Indians and Aztec temples. I was so excited that I went to the school library during recess to look for a book about the Aztecs.

Branka has golden curls and sad eyes; she's even shyer than me. Last time she visited, we barely spoke to each other. It was only when her mother was standing at the door that she started talking to me. She's a year older than me, but already talks about grown-up things and told me she's learning to play the piano and had even been to a real concert. I told her we'd be going to a summer house in Opatija, by the sea. But she told me she hated the sea and didn't like swimming.

When they arrived, I invited Branka to come and see how Lord was, because today, when I got back from school, he didn't run to me as usual, but just lay in the shade. He panted a lot, and his nose was all dry. Father told me a healthy dog's nose should be wet. I brought him some water, but he hardly even drank. It turns out Branka doesn't like dogs. She doesn't even like the two cats in her own house.

I don't understand people who don't like dogs. Even though Lord is a dog, I feel so close to him, as if he were a real member of the family. I spend more time with him than I do with Pauli.

I thought that if she doesn't like swimming, she probably wouldn't want to get into my swimming pool either, so I suggested showing her my stamp collection, especially the new stamps, the ones Father had brought me from Mexico and Guatemala. I told her about the rainforest in Brazil and the Aztecs and the Maya people the Spanish discovered during the sixteenth century, but she was still bored. So I told her about our last train trip to visit Father's aunt in Budapest and about the long tunnels under the mountains and how you suddenly go inside them and hear a great noise and everything turns dark and you can't see anything for over fifteen minutes.

Branka told me they don't have any family in Budapest, but that she's been studying ballet for two years with a very famous teacher in Belgrade, and she wants to be as famous as Anna Pavlova when she grows up.

Then Mother called us to join them and asked Branka to play the piece she'd performed at her end-of-year concert at the conservatory.

Branka obeyed, confidently going over to the piano and pulling up the chair; Mother brought her a cushion to sit on.

"I've just told Louisa about your concert. She asked me if you could play one of the pieces," said Mrs. Garai.

It was a movement from Schubert's piano sonata that Mother especially likes. Branka played perfectly, and Mother wiped away tears of emotion. When she stopped playing, they both clapped their hands. I felt lost and embarrassed.

Mother and Mrs. Garai discussed the latest news—the burning of books written by Jewish authors at the Bebelplatz square in Berlin.

"Ever since that fire in the Reichstag at the beginning of the year, Jews and communists are being blamed for everything under the sun," Mother said.

"I've heard that Hitler on the radio. He just won't stop screaming. It sounds awful. Leo, my husband, says that ever since the Nuremberg Laws they've become a dictatorship."

"But burning books? That's simply barbaric. I've heard that books by Jewish authors were burned in Munich and other cities as well. It's simply terrible."

"I can't even imagine where all this is leading," said Mrs. Garai.

"Heine already said over a hundred years ago that 'where they burn books, they will ultimately burn people as well.' It is a powerful prophecy. If I were living in Germany, I would start packing."

"It's not so simple to just get up and leave your home. You have to leave your friends, language, and culture as well. Another advanced culture like the one in Germany isn't so easy to find."

"You'll get no argument about that from me," said Mother. "As far as culture, literature, and music go, Austria and Germany are unparalleled."

Then they rose to leave, and Branka asked me if I'd enjoyed her playing. I said I had, but I didn't really, and I don't like her either.

1935

These are the last days of the summer vacation, and I'm already missing school. Pauli says I'm a freak of nature. He's never heard of a child who misses school. The school year starts in a week, and I'll be going into fifth grade. Father says I should play more sports and that there's nothing like tennis or swimming. A good school report card is important, said Father, but it's not enough. A teenager like me should be more athletic. He promised to train me, but after a while he no longer had the time and suggested that Klarie do it. She's more patient with me, anyway.

Today, when I got back home, I noticed something was wrong as soon as I saw Mother.

"They've taken Uncle Albert away," she said, choked with tears.

I couldn't understand who had taken whom, or what she meant by saying someone had taken him. Did criminals come to his house and kidnap him for money? Albert is Mother's elder brother. He lives in Munich and is very rich. Henrick, his son, had visited us during the last summer vacation, an annoying kid who thinks the whole world belongs to him. He cried every time he lost at table tennis or came last in swimming races.

"Who took him, Mother? Where did they take him?"

She gave me a sad look and said, "To Dachau. They're imprisoning all the Jews in Dachau now."

I remembered what Father had told me—that perhaps we should all leave and go to Israel, become farmers and sit under our vines and fig trees instead of hearing about new decrees every day.

"Could they take Father away one day, just like they've taken Uncle Albert?" I asked.

"No. They'll never get here. There's no Nazi Party here and there won't ever be one," said Mother confidently. Maybe she was just trying to reassure me.

Klarie promised to take me to play tennis again that day. My game has really improved lately. At first, I didn't even know how to hold the tennis racket. But after playing with Klarie a couple of times, I was already able to pass the ball and improved my serve. Klarie is an excellent player and has already won several championships.

I waited for her for half an hour at the court in my white tennis clothes and hat that Father had bought me, but she didn't show up. I began to worry, because Klarie is always punctual. I thought she'd show up in a moment or two. Meanwhile, I practiced diligently at the training wall.

The sound of the ball beating against the wall woke Lord, who was lying sleepily outside and enjoying the sunlight. Lately, he's been spending a lot of time sleeping. Father says he's starting to get old. Time moves faster with dogs. Every human year is like seven years for a dog, so I guess Lord is actually seventy. He's a German Shepherd. He has a black back and a light-colored stomach, and his eyes are as smart and understanding as any human. Sometimes, I'm sure he understands every word I tell him. He loves sitting beside us while we're playing tennis, moving his head from side to side and following the ball with his eyes. When the ball falls, he runs to get it and even brings balls back to the court when they fly really far. He also knows who to give the ball to.

Minutes went by and Klarie still hadn't shown up. Something must have happened. I decided to go back home and ask Mother. I put the racket back in its bag and ran through the patio. Today, Mother is hosting her friends for tea, and they'll be here in half an hour. Perhaps I should spend the afternoon finishing my geometry homework. Anyway, Father doesn't have time to help me with my homework now. He comes home very late in the evenings, because he has a lot of work. I liked it when Klarie used to help me with my math homework. She's a good teacher, a good friend, and a good sister, but now she's married and left home and doesn't have time for me and Pauli. She lives in the city with Lazar, who has a photography shop called Photo Lazar. She works as a lawyer at the De Mayo law firm. Father is very proud of Klarie and calls her "the pride of the family." He never says that about me or Pauli, perhaps because I'm not very good at math. I'm considered a pretty good student in other subjects, and the history and language teachers have praised me for achieving above and beyond what is required of me, but I just can't get numbers into my head. Father has never understood what's wrong with his son who can't even manage the basics of mathematics. Klarie not only excelled in all subjects, she was also an accomplished athlete—school champion in the hundred- and two-hundred-meter dash, a good swimmer, and a gifted tennis player. Father keeps all her medals and tennis league trophies in his office.

I found Mother sitting in the large armchair in her room with a small wooden box in her hand. There was a photo of Klarie on the inner lid. Father had taken the photo when Klarie was little and had all her beautiful golden curls. Inside the box, wrapped in blue velvet, were two bright locks of Klarie's hair. Mother sat in front of the open box looking worried.

"Where have you been?" she asked. "I've been looking for you for an hour."

"At the tennis court. Klarie said she'd meet me there at four."

"She won't be able to come."

"Is something wrong?"

"She's not feeling well. The doctor has already been, but he still doesn't know what the problem is," answered Mother.

"Oh, poor Klarie. What can I do to help?"

"There's nothing we can do. Lazar is with her all the time."

I got up just as the door opened, and Olga, Klarie's best friend, came in with her mane of black curls, captivating smile, and abundant energy. The smile disappeared from her face as soon as she saw Mother's worried expression.

"How's Klarie? She wasn't feeling well at the office today."

"Lazar called an hour ago to say she has a high fever and he's calling a doctor," Mother said.

"Oh, I'm really worried. She's got a very important debate the day after tomorrow."

"You worry about yourself first. You've done enough damage putting all those communist ideas in her head," Mother scolded her.

"You have nothing to worry about, Madame Louisa. Your daughter won't cross the line."

"I most certainly don't want anyone knocking at our door in the middle of the night and taking her away to be interrogated. Would you like to spend time in a jail cell?"

"Madame Louisa, I'd willingly sit in jail for such a noble cause," answered Olga, and her smile brought the two dimples back to her face.

"Nonetheless," Mother said crisply. "You two can be good friends and have fun together, but leave politics out of it. Agreed?"

"All right, Madame Louisa, don't worry. I'll try to go visit her in the city," said Olga turning to leave.

Olga is a real heroine. She's not afraid of the police or even of going to jail, and she's willing to fight for her beliefs. At our youth movement, they've been talking about being loyal to your beliefs. Our movement instructor, Itche, explains everything about Zionism and how we can fulfill its vision by emigrating to Israel and working on the land—a barren, dry land crying out for our love. But would I be willing to go to jail for the Zionist vision, like Olga?

I wish I'd asked to go with her to visit Klarie. I badly wanted to visit her, but Father says eleven-year-old children shouldn't wander the city by themselves. There are dangers in the city, especially gypsies who kidnap children. I wish I could be more independent, like Peter or Joachim from my class. Only today, they told me again that they took the tram downtown all by themselves, got off, and saw all the shops in Aleksandra and Mihailova streets. Father won't let me go downtown by myself until I'm fifteen, not even with Pauli.

***

Mother's friends sat out on the patio drinking their five o'clock tea from floral porcelain cups. Victoria was dressed like a queen in a long, blue velvet dress, a red kerchief embroidered with golden threads around her neck and shoulders, and a white parasol edged with lace in her hand. Victoria's husband is also called Emil, and he's a rich fabric merchant. He'd arrived from Istanbul ten years before the Great War and became the main fabric supplier for the army and the government. Victoria is very active in city social circles and arranges balls for the Serbian nobility at their luxurious house in the Dedinje neighborhood. Even though they've lived in the city for thirty years, she still prefers to speak French.

Unlike Victoria, Angela, wife of the Austrian consul, arrived in sports clothes, like the dress you'd wear for a Sunday family tennis tournament: a tennis dress with a short plaid jacket and a gray narrow-brimmed fedora hat. She'd brought a box of records with an elegant cover. "Highlights from *Die Fledermaus* conducted by the virtuoso Austrian conductor Erich Kleiber, a rare recording," she told Mother knowledgeably and gave her the box. I've noticed that Angela never comes empty-handed.

Vivian came with Adolph, her pinscher dog, who goes everywhere with her. She always carries him under one arm.

As soon as Mother noticed that Vivian was coming, she asked me to put Lord in the cellar, but Adolph's nervous temperament woke Lord the minute Vivian was at the door. Lord erupted into a loud fit of barking. Luckily, I was able to grab his collar at the last moment and prevent him from knocking down Vivian and Adolph. I signaled her to go around through the kitchen and out the door close to the pantry.

I was still holding the wildly panting Lord by his collar when I heard a knock at the door.

"Who is it?" I shouted.

"It's me, Peter."

"Come inside, quickly. I'm holding Lord."

The door opened and in came Peter, my good friend and neighbor. He was wearing white tennis clothes, his black hair carefully combed. Peter lives with his mother, two bodyguards, and several servants in a majestic palace bordering the western side of our garden. A tall wall separates our house from their palace. It was all to keep him safe, the crown prince who would inherit the throne when he turned eighteen.

I remember the day Father came back from work and told Mother even before taking off his coat that King Alexander, Peter's father, had been assassinated in Marseille.

"A Bulgarian assassin," he said with disgust, shocked by the outburst of joy flooding the country as the news spread. "He wasn't much liked," he summed up.

Meanwhile, Peter lives the life of a careless teenager, just like me. During the summer months, when he comes home on vacation from a military boarding school in England, he visits us to play tennis and swim in our pool. He told me he had a hard time at boarding school, with its strict British discipline and even stricter teachers. He'd be happy to move back here and go to school with me.

He once told me he preferred our cozy, noisy household to the cold, quiet air of their royal mansion. It's always fun here. There are noisy children and summer garden parties; we even have a swimming pool and a tennis court.

Peter had seen me waiting for Klarie next to the practice wall and offered to play with me instead. I went up to my room to fetch the racket and balls while he watched over Lord.

We passed the patio on our way to the court. The five women were drinking tea and talking loudly. I motioned to Peter to go on to the court and that I'd join him in a moment. I listened to the women's conversation, hoping to hear something about the events that so troubled Mother.

"You live in a bubble here in your beautiful mansion," declared Vivian loudly to Mother.

"What do you mean, 'a bubble'? Aren't we Jewish? Don't you think I've been following the news from Germany?"

"I'm afraid it could spread to other places, even here," said Vivian.

"You're right," Victoria interrupted. "My sister has lived in Germany for many years, and she says their hometown school has already fired two Jewish teachers."

"Well, for now, it's only happening in Germany," Mother tried to reassure everyone, handing Vivian the sugar-cube bowl. "No one here would dare fire a teacher just because he's Jewish."

"Edmond says that many of the most successful Austrian artists and architects working in Germany should move back to Austria and end their careers in Berlin or Munich," said Angela, adding that she'd heard of places where Jews are not allowed to teach in government schools and that the Jewish communities there have had to open their own high schools.

"Exactly," said Vivian. "And I tell you it'll end up here too. What's happening in Germany is madness. At first, they said it was only against the communists. Now, it's mainly against the Jews."

I tried to imagine this happening in my own class, that one day they might tell me not to come to school anymore.

"Hey, Hanne! Are you coming or not?" Peter called impatiently.

"Coming!"

I ran to the court. We played for an hour and a half. Peter won most of the matches, but I still felt pretty good, because I'd managed to beat him a few times and return some really difficult serves. Lord brought back all the lost balls. Toward the end of the game, Pauli showed up and asked to join us. We told him we were in the middle of a tournament and another player couldn't just butt in. Besides, he wasn't even properly dressed. In response, Pauli took all his new clothes for summer camp out of a large paper bag, just to annoy me and make me jealous.

When we'd finished our game, I invited Peter to come and play with me the next day, but he was leaving for end-of-year exams at boarding school and would only be back at the end of the summer.

We parted with a handshake. I went up to shower and change my clothes.

When I came down for dinner, I found Mother at the dining table with a worried expression on her face.

"Why so late?" she asked.

"Late? We always eat at seven thirty. Where's Father?"

"Your father stayed in town. He's with Klarie now," she said worriedly.

"Any news?"

"Yes. The doctor says he thinks she has pneumonia and needs to be treated in the hospital."

"Hospital? Can they cure it?"

"I don't know," she said impatiently. "We'll have to wait and see."

***

Alan had been sitting beside his father for four days now, there from morning till late afternoon. When his sister came to take his place, she made sure he went home to rest. In a conversation with the doctor the previous day, they'd been told their father's condition was no longer critical and that he'd be transferred to the neurosurgery ward the following day for further treatment.

The photos he'd stashed in his jacket pocket on the first evening continued to wait for a moment when he could actually communicate with his father.

Meanwhile, he'd been sitting next to him for hours, without the two of them exchanging a single word. He helped his father with small tasks, such as sitting up in bed or going to the toilet, which made him realize how hard nurses worked there. He found it difficult to help his own father. He had never seen him so dependent on others. It embarrassed him. Nurses needed to help complete strangers for at least eight hours every day. He'd have gone insane if he had to work as a nurse. Dr. Paritzker said they were now waiting for the moment his father's eyes were focused again and his speech became clearer. This could happen in days, weeks, or even months. They would need a lot of patience. Alan ran out of patience. This was no longer an emergency situation, and he could start thinking of flying back to New York. Not right away, of course. He needed to change the flight date. But could he leave his father like this? Could Bracha take care of him alone? Was it fair to expect it of her?

"You idler!" His father sat up in bed with a glare. "I asked you to see Inge. Was that too much to ask?"

Alan took the three photos he'd found from his jacket pocket.

His father tried hard to focus on the photos. He drew the photo of the two girls leaning against the swimming pool rail closer to his eyes, then, in a rage, tossed it to the floor.

"No, no. These are Klarie and Frenzie, can't you see? I asked to see Inge!"

Alan carefully picked up the photo his father had tossed away and heard him say, "Where did you find Frenzie? I don't like Frenzie."

Alan handed him the third photo. His father looked at it and began to wail.

"Oh, Olga, my poor Olga. What have they done to you?"

Bracha came into the room and immediately noticed the change they'd hoped for.

The next day, Alan was already busy making phone calls to get on an earlier flight and called New York as well. Rachel said she and the girls were doing fine and that he shouldn't worry. Charles calmed him down as well and said that the project was progressing nicely, and that it would be great if he could come back a little earlier so he could supervise the completion of the first phase. That would be great; he'd be able to get back in time to manage the project, which in the meantime was being handled by Charles's assistant. Satisfied with the discussions, Alan returned to the hospital in a good mood. But his father, who had shown encouraging signs of coming back to life the previous day, was again sunk in apathy, his eyes glued vacantly to the ceiling. Alan asked him if he wanted anything, but his father didn't answer, just lay there in complete silence.

Alan took another photo of an unidentified woman from his pocket; he'd found it while rummaging through the drawers and envelopes—an older woman, elegantly dressed, on her head a broad-brimmed floral hat with a feather, a parasol raised to shade her face in one hand, and a flat-nosed dog held in the other.

"Vivian!" His father returned to life. "Where did you find all these photos? Have you found the notebook too?"

"What notebook?" Alan straightened up.

"The diary I wrote as a child and translated into Hebrew. I haven't shown it to anyone yet."

"You kept it a secret? Why?" asked Alan, surprised by his father's sudden outburst of wakefulness and the new information.

"Because… Because I haven't yet decided if the time is ripe," he faltered.

"Ripe for what?"

"For exposing everything. For revealing what I've gone through."

"So, can I read it now?"

"Wise guy!" his father said angrily. "You've found it already, haven't you? What can I keep hidden now?"

"But I haven't found Inge yet."

"You won't find her there. My business with her is elsewhere. But you have to find her. Do you hear me?"

AKIBA 1937

My best friend at school is Isaac. Although we're very different and he lives downtown, I like him a lot. He's a real redhead with frizzy, rust-colored hair, and he's also very stubborn. Isaac's the kind of boy who always has adventures, just like the ones you read about in books. I don't know what he sees in me; I feel like such a coward next to him. Isaac needs me to help him with his homework, and I need him to help me learn to be brave like him. Isaac likes to tease me because I belong to the rich upper class, while he belongs to the oppressed working class. He sometimes calls me a spoiled rich brat.

They're very nice to me at Isaac's house. Whenever I go over there, his mother always brings us chocolate, fruit, and juice to his room.

Today, Isaac and I were walking home from school together when two older boys suddenly jumped out from a street corner and grabbed him. One held him from behind while the other took his soccer cards out of his pocket. I was paralyzed with fear and just stood there without even trying to stop them. After those thugs had gone off with their loot and Isaac finished looking in his pockets for cards they might have missed, he asked me angrily, "What's wrong with you? Why did you just stand there like an idiot?"

I felt so ashamed. If only I wasn't so weak and scrawny. I feel strong, but something keeps holding me back. Today, I decided this has to change.

It takes a good few minutes to walk from school to Isaac's house, and the road passes through narrow side streets filled with shabby, old houses. On warm summer days, people sit out in the street at their front doors, drinking black coffee and smoking cigarettes. The clattering of dice on wooden backgammon boards fills the air, along with curses and profanities I'd never heard grown-ups use before. At the end of the street, there's an Ashkenazi synagogue. In a few months, we'll celebrate my bar mitzvah there. Father took me to that synagogue to show me a Torah scroll before I actually read from it during the bar mitzvah ceremony. Father only goes to synagogue once a year, on Yom Kippur, to hear the Kol Nidre prayer. When he goes, he takes the prayer book, prayer shawl, and tefillin he received from his father for his bar mitzvah.

Isaac's house is not far from the Hashomer Hatzair youth movement meeting place, or *ken* as they call it, and he spends a lot of time there. I went with him a couple of times but didn't tell Mother and Father about it. Father wouldn't have let me go. He wants me to go to the Akiba[3] youth movement, like Pauli, who has become more mature and responsible since he started going there, and talks a lot about Israel and Zionism. He even offered to be a counselor for younger boys at the *ken*. Father thinks that Akiba is more traditional and Zionist than Hashomer Hatzair. But personally, I feel closer in spirit to Hashomer

---

3   Akiba (not to be confused with the Bnei Akiva youth movement) was the largest youth movement in Poland before the rise of Nazism. It was founded in Krakow, and then spread to various other cities in Europe.

Hatzair, because they discuss important issues like justice and equality. Father doesn't understand that. Maybe he really is an oppressive rich man. Sometimes I think he abuses his employees. I've heard him shout at them a couple of times.

The leader of the Hashomer Hatzair *ken* is a young man called Itzko. For him, revolution and manifestation are not only words, they're a call to action. I'm really starting to admire him for bringing a fresh new spirit from Israel. He makes us youngsters aware of the wrongs and injustices in daily life and talks a lot about the revolution necessary for us to create a better society. Thanks to him, I'm beginning to look at Father and his lifestyle in a more critical way; Mother, too, with her blind admiration of German culture. I understand now that the school curriculum is dictated by government authorities. We have a king, which means we have a dictatorship and not a democracy. That's why my parents don't like Hashomer Hatzair and their meetings. They don't like anything with an ideological background that's different from theirs. I'm afraid to tell Father I've already been there a couple of times, because he doesn't like "provocateurs," and that's what he thinks they are.

Today, I went to Hashomer Hatzair again. This time, it was all about camping. Itzko taught us how to build a fence, a ladder, and a bridge with ropes and poles. At the end of the activity, we talked about the civil war in Spain. The stories coming from over there are different from those published in our newspapers here. Isaac told me his uncle is in Spain, helping the fighters for the republic. No one in our house talks about the Spanish civil war, certainly not about idealists going off with nothing but a backpack to help the freedom fighters. I'm excited by the idea of young people fighting for really important things, like freedom and equality.

In addition to my private lessons in French and German, I'm also studying the section of the Torah I'll need to read for my bar mitzvah. Rabbi Menahem teaches me to read from the Torah like a parrot and explains what it means. Hebrew is such a strange and difficult language! It's not like any other language I know.

Father says it's very important I learn the section of the Torah and the blessings properly, otherwise I'll shame him. But he hardly observes any of the laws and rituals of Judaism, even though his grandfather was a renowned Jewish scholar in Zemun, a town near Belgrade. My mother's family also had a famous rabbi, Judah Chai Alkalai, a Zionist pioneer, who preached settling the land of Israel. At the beginning of the century, many Jews left the Ottoman Empire to resettle in Jaffa and Jerusalem. But our family doesn't follow in Rabbi Alkalai's footsteps. Father sometimes says we should emigrate to Israel, but I don't think he really means it. "Nonetheless," he says. "One mustn't abandon tradition. In the same way a baby enters Judaism through circumcision, a boy should at least be familiar with the world of tradition when he turns thirteen and has his bar mitzvah."

Today, like every Friday evening, the entire family gathered around the dining table, including Father, who was late from work, and Klarie, who came from the city with her husband.

Father said that if the situation in Europe continued to deteriorate, we'd have to think about emigrating to Israel. Mother, as usual, said the time wasn't right yet and that we needed to wait until it was less dangerous there before we could actually consider it.

Klarie, who is busy with her career from dawn till dusk, says there's no point in talking about emigrating to Israel. There's no work there, no culture, nothing but pogroms and disease.

Because everyone was talking about Israel, I took advantage of the opportunity and told them I'd been to a few Hashomer Hatzair meetings with Isaac. As expected, Father got very upset. He doesn't think Hashomer Hatzair is right for me; he thinks I should go to a youth movement closer in spirit to Jewish tradition. When I told him my opinions about the moral principles upheld by Hashomer Hatzair, he got even angrier and said that Ezra, Mr. Yosipovich's son, had participated in a few Hashomer Hatzair meetings and got some strange ideas into his head. In the end, Mr. Yosipovich actually had to request the aid of the police. The police had wanted to lay their hands on that youth movement for a long time because it incited youths to support irresponsible ideas. Mr. Yosipovich said the police had saved his child.

At these words, I could no longer contain myself.

"What ideas are you talking about, Father? What irresponsible ideas?"

"Ideas about rebelling against society," he said. "The war they've declared against the very society that nurtures them."

"You think bourgeois-capitalist society nurtures anyone but the rich?" I asked, suddenly realizing I was opposing him.

"You've forgotten where you come from. Many boys in the youth movement come from bourgeois families," Klarie intervened.

"Of course, because it burns more fiercely in the hearts of those who know bourgeois society from the inside."

"Really, Hanne? You're burning to destroy your own social class?" said Klarie incredulously.

"It just goes to show how different you grown-ups are. Even you've become a bourgeois."

"I was young once too. I also rebelled against my father," Father said angrily. "You think the generation struggle was invented by Hashomer Hatzair?"

"So you agree with me that it's legitimate to criticize grown-up society, if it is unable to criticize itself?"

"Young man, I advise you to choose your words carefully. You are my son, and you're a part of this society."

"You don't understand, Father. The revolution intends to correct things. On the ruins of the old, sick society, a new and better one will be founded."

"I suggest we stop all these arguments right now and finish our meal in peace," Mother ended the discussion and asked Sophie to serve the last course.

After our argument, I couldn't sleep.

The next morning, when playing tennis with Klarie, she spoke to me about what had happened.

"I think Father was really offended. You shouldn't have opposed him like that."

"Look who's talking. Three years ago, you thought exactly like me."

"That's right, but I've grown up since then. Perhaps because I got married. Perhaps because I wanted to be financially independent. But I ended up thinking my own personal interests are more important."

"More important than your ideals? Aren't you best friends with Olga, that communist?"

"Yes, but listen, Hanne, sooner or later you'll leave home to start an independent life. Till then, you need to compromise. Go to Akiba like Pauli and don't provoke Father."

"You think I'm saying this just to provoke Father? What's happened to you? You used to be so passionate about your beliefs."

"Just so you know, Hanne, and this must stay between the two of us, Father's financial situation is not as good as it used to be. I don't know if you've noticed, but his office no longer gets as many new clients. Perhaps this has to do with all the incitement against Jews. But it might be something else. And things may get even worse."

***

I'm spending a lot of time studying for my bar mitzvah. Hebrew is simply an impossible language! But today, I heard Rabbi Menahem tell Mother that I've made real progress and he thinks I'll be ready in time. I'm also going to Sunday school now, to improve my knowledge of Hebrew and Judaism.

During my Sunday afternoon walk with Pauli in Kalemegdan Park, we met Telbi and had a chat. I know Telbi from Sunday school. He's two years older than me. He's very talented and knowledgeable about a lot of subjects, but he's very modest and good-hearted. He was sitting drawing on the green, grassy hill overlooking the confluence of the rivers. He noticed us and invited us to see his drawing. Pauli, who also likes to draw, took a good look and said, "You're talented. Where did you learn how to draw?"

"Nowhere. It just comes from my heart," Telbi answered.

Pauli went off to meet some friends from his youth movement, and

I stayed to watch Telbi drawing. I admired his patience and serenity.

"Why don't you come with me to our Akiba *ken* this evening?" he said. "We dance the *hora* there every Sunday. Akiba probably won't change the world, but we do know how to have a good time."

I accepted his invitation and went along to see what was going on at the Akiba *ken*. The place looked like a gymnasium. Ropes with rings dangled from the ceiling. The mattresses and parallel bars had been placed against the wall next to the ladders to make room for the dancers. Telbi explained that it was all just camouflage. The law prohibited all gatherings with an ideological agenda, but having an afternoon sports class was acceptable. Even the name of the place, "youth," was also meant to disguise the fact that it was used for movement meetings. Almost immediately, I noticed the big difference between Akiba and Hashomer Hatzair. In the Akiba *ken*, there was a far livelier atmosphere, youthful enthusiasm, and dancing. Hashomer Hatzair meetings were much more serious in nature. Their ideology made them take themselves very seriously. Embarrassed, I stood to one side. The boys and girls danced passionately, their faces flushed. Branka was there as well, happy and laughing, very much unlike the quiet Branka I remembered from her tea-time visits to our house with her mother. She had once told me about the Akiba youth movement, but back then I was determined to go to Hashomer Hatzair. Now, there she was, dancing, her face full of joy. She invited me to join the circle of dancers, but I was afraid I wouldn't be able to do the dance steps and fit in.

Then I heard a familiar sound from a side room—the clatter of a ping pong ball.

There, in the side room, I finally found my place and earned some respect at the ping pong table. In our garden at home in Dedinje, everyone was afraid to play against me, even Father. The first time I beat him, he threw his bat on the table, ran over to hug me, and immediately asked for a rematch. Now, in that small room at the *ken*, I became a table-tennis champion for an evening. Everyone wanted to play against me, and word of the new champion quickly spread. I hadn't felt so happy in a very long time.

***

At the Akiba *ken*, we have Bible study and discussions about the weekly chapter of the Torah—the *parashah*. As I listened to Dr. Kaufman's lectures, I began to get a better understanding of what it means to be Jewish. He reads us a chapter from the Torah and then interprets it. After we read about Abraham and the covenant with God, he compared the story with events in our own time and said that God is now telling us, "Rise up! Go to the land that I will show you!" Of course, he's actually talking about Israel. No matter how difficult and dangerous it is over there, we must rise, leave our native land, and emigrate to our real homeland. We were enthralled by his words but actually acting on them seemed almost impossible. When we asked him why he didn't go to Israel, he said he had to complete his educational mission first.

When some of the boys confided their fear of an unfamiliar country, he told us the story of the spies in the Book of Numbers. He spoke of the contradiction between those who said the Promised Land flowed with milk and honey and those who spoke against it and chose to talk about the dreaded giants that ruled the land. He said the people in our own time are very much the same. There are those who are afraid to emigrate to Israel, think only of the dangers they would have to face there, while others think Israel is truly the land of milk and honey. They don't care if there are giants there, or what their current incarnation is—Arabs—which is what he called the nations populating Jaffa, Haifa, and Tel Aviv.

He knows a lot about many subjects. Sometimes he even teaches us physics and astronomy and takes us outside to show us the heavenly bodies.

***

Today, I went home with Isaac after school. He asked me rather offhandedly why I wasn't coming with him to the Hashomer Hatzair *ken* anymore. I looked for excuses and told him about Rabbi Menahem and my bar mitzvah studies. But Isaac said his friend had seen me at the Akiba *ken*. He asked me what I was doing there. I told him Telbi had persuaded me to come to a meeting to see what it was like. I knew that Isaac would be angry, but didn't realize how much; when I made excuses, referring to my father's objections, Isaac turned red all over. When his face goes red and he spits out his words with fury, it can be really scary to be near him. He said he had known all along that I was "like that." That my entire family was "like that," that we don't care about anyone except ourselves and our expensive house and that he would never set foot in our house again.

It was very hard to hear such words from him. He's my only friend in class, and now he's turned his back on me. I thought about the harsh things he'd said to me all the way home. He's my best friend, after all.

OCTOBER 1937

I've never seen Rabbi Menahem as upset as he was today.

"Your bar mitzvah is only two weeks away, and you're nowhere near ready for your reading!"

I didn't say anything, just lowered my head and accepted his scolding.

I arrived late at the Akiba *ken*, my head still spinning from the lesson and Rabbi Menahem's reproaches. Today's meeting was all about the coming August summer camp. We were going to spend three nights in Žirovnica in the Slovenian mountains. I've never gone camping without my parents, so I'm very excited about it. Telbi, who had already been there, told me about the special town situated next to a lake surrounded by forests. We'll build tents and dance the *hora* by the campfire till the small hours. Even though it was still a few weeks away, I could already picture the bus ride. Perhaps I'd sit next to Branka. She'd grown so beautiful and looks very mature for her age. She's no longer shy like she used to be when she and her mother came to our house for tea. Now she constantly smiles at me. I'd forgotten all about her embarrassing visits, when she'd play Schubert for my mother and I was forced to sit quietly and listen. Now I wanted to get closer to her but was afraid she wouldn't want me to, so I was waiting for an opportunity to present itself. Perhaps if I sat next to her on the bus we would get a little closer.

"Tomorrow is your big day," Mother whispered to me in the morning and gave me two wet kisses on my cheek.

Father's three aunts arrived from Budapest on the afternoon train. Soon, I'd be eating Aunt Emilia's delicious *gomboti*;[4] I'd been waiting all year for this! As soon as she'd freshened up in her room, Aunt Emilia put on Mother's special apron, tied her hair back, and began the wonderful ceremony of preparing *gomboti*. I thought Sabina, the cook, who stood by the sink and peeled one potato after another, looked a little insulted by the fact she'd been robbed of her control over the kitchen. Under the hands of Aunt Emilia, the sweet balls of dough came out like an army of marching soldiers, incredibly precise and similarly sized. Her face was flushed and red and her hands fluttered over the dough. I stole my way into the kitchen, tore off a little piece of dough, as small as an olive, and placed it in my mouth. Aunt Emilia said I was lucky it was my bar mitzvah, otherwise she'd have smacked me. I offered to help spreading breadcrumbs, sugar, and cinnamon, and Emilia, much to my surprise, agreed. She said I was a big boy now and needed to learn how to do practical things and not only how to read the Torah. I carefully placed them on the trays, which already contained piles of *gomboti*. When Emilia had finished, Mother and Sabina began to prepare Mother's famous homemade Viennese apple strudel. The fresh apples, picked that very day, were gently cut into thin slices, then spread like fans over the jam-coated dough. The

---

4   A Hungarian pastry made of cheese, eggs, and semolina.

apfelstrudel trays were carefully arranged in rows next to the *gomboti* trays. The whipped cream would simply have to wait for tomorrow…

***

The big day finally came. The brown suit specially tailored for the event made me sweat. I walked to the pulpit in front of the Holy Ark like a groom marching to the wedding canopy, Father on my right and Rabbi Menahem on my left. Father was just as excited as I was. My heart was pounding like a train engine. I didn't think I would ever be able to read the section of the Torah or the speech in front of such a large crowd of people. But as soon as I opened my mouth to say the *Barechu* call to prayer and everyone answered in unison, I gained confidence and felt relieved. After I finished, everyone came to hug and congratulate me, and I felt big and important.

I promised myself I'd put on tefillin every morning and observe the religious commandments. Well, perhaps not all of them. Even Rabbi Menahem said only the righteous of the righteous can uphold all the commandments, but from now on, I'd strive to be a better son to my parents and listen to them without arguing.

When the guests began to arrive at the house, I stood at the gate to welcome them. Father insisted I keep my jacket and tie on and shake the hand of every guest. Only after the last guests had arrived, including the chief city engineer and the deputy mayor, to whom father introduced me, was I allowed to leave the garden entrance and join the guests.

Mother and Father were first on the dance floor, to the sounds of

Strauss's "Blue Danube," Mother's favorite waltz. I hadn't seen them dancing together in a long time. After them, the dance floor filled with other dancers. Elegant waiters walked among the guests, carrying trays filled with little sandwiches, herring, and, of course, trays with glasses of Tokaji wine and *slivovitz*, Father's favorite alcoholic beverage. The *gomboti* would be served as dessert.

When a band of klezmers played the song "My Yiddishe Mama," Mother wiped away a tear; then it was my turn to go up there and read the speech I had worked so hard on. I put my hand inside my pants pocket to look for it, but all I found was a page of grammar exercises in German. My heart was pumping hard, and my face flushed scarlet. I couldn't even think. Mother noticed and asked me if everything was all right. She wasn't at all upset by the disappearance of my written speech and simply placed her hand on my shoulder, "Just thank all the guests for coming and you'll see everything will be just fine."

I hoped none of the guests had noticed my embarrassment. I stood on a stool beside the klezmer band and looked at everyone. I took a deep breath and began to thank the guests for coming to celebrate with me. I thanked Mother and Father for raising me so well. Then, suddenly, I remembered everything I'd written—that I intended to become a better son to my parents and a better companion to my friends; that I'd decided to try and uphold the commandments of Judaism, but not all of them, only the ones that really matter, the ones that are meaningful to the people around me. Finally, I spoke of my decision to try and uphold the values my parents had taught me throughout my adult life. I noticed everyone listening very quietly. Klarie hugged Father, who was standing next to her. When I finished, everyone clapped and came to shake Father's hand again and tell him what a talented boy he'd raised, the kind of boy who could make such a graceful and eloquent speech without reading it from the page.

***

The doctor told Alan his father's condition was sufficiently improved for him to move to a rehabilitation center. He was hospitalized in a spacious room, sharing it with another elderly person with a similar condition.

Alan came to visit him every day and take him out for a stroll in his wheelchair, skillfully navigating the narrow corridors, careful not to bump into walls and corners.

His father mentioned Inge each and every time they met. He told him about their first meeting on board the riverboat the *Tzar Nikolai* and how resourceful she'd been in all the chaos. He told him how attached she'd become to his mother, Louisa, who was like a mother to her.

"I loved her," he said suddenly. "I just never realized how much."

He held Alan's arm and drew him close.

"It's important to have love in your life," he said in a sudden, rare moment of candor. "I chose life, there on the Sabac railway platform."

"But wasn't choosing life the obvious choice to make?" asked Alan.

"Back then, at the railway station, we didn't realize we were choosing life. Who knew?"

"I'm here because you chose the life you've lived. Doesn't that mean anything to you?"

"She was a nurse, you know?" his father suddenly revealed another detail.

"Just like Mother," said Alan.

"That's right. Perhaps that was why I fell in love with your mother. Perhaps I was attracted only to women with a passion for helping others. Strong-willed women, maybe to compensate for my own weakness."

When he got home that evening, Alan continued to read the diary. He'd already realized he wouldn't find any information about Inge there. Still, he was spellbound by the diary. The situation in Europe continued to deteriorate, and with it the situation of the David family in Belgrade—Emil, Louisa, and their three children.

MAY 1938

I heard the sound of gravel under car wheels on the driveway leading to the house and realized that Father was home early from work again. I remembered how Lord and I used to wait for him in the doorway. Long before I could see or even hear Father's car, he'd bark and wag his tail in excitement and anticipation. Two years have passed since Lord died. For several months, his eyesight gradually dimmed and he simply faded away until, finally, he could barely support his own weight.

Father came inside and told me he'd like to have a word with me before dinner. I tried to guess why he was so serious and was nervous about it all afternoon.

Lately, Father seems constantly troubled and depressed. He hardly ever laughs now and doesn't clap my shoulder like he used to. When he walks, his shoulders are hunched and his back is bent as if he were carrying a heavy burden. Klarie told me a few months ago that Father's financial situation wasn't as good as it used to be. I hadn't noticed anything then, but lately, I've started to connect clues.

He no longer takes the early train to Budapest with his briefcase and morning paper. He used to go there very often. He'd designed houses in Budapest, he proudly told us. Sometimes, he would come home that very same day. Other times, he would go for two or three days and bring Pauli and me gifts from the big city. When I was eight, we went to visit Aunt Emilia in Budapest for the first time. I'd always thought Belgrade was the largest city in the world, until I saw the bustling traffic in the streets of Budapest, the large stone houses with their ornate marble pillars, the tram passing in the middle of the street, and the cafés in the Váci *utca* promenade. Mother was very impressed by the beautiful store windows and occasionally stopped to examine a dress or coat.

At six o'clock, I knocked on Father's study door. He opened it, holding a glass of *slivovitz*.

"Come on in, Hanne. Come inside and sit beside me," he said, motioning to me to close the door.

He sat down at his desk, sipped from the glass in his hand, and said, "You probably know things haven't been too good lately. Now that you've had your bar mitzvah, I can talk to you like a man."

"I've heard there's a world crisis. That's what our geography teacher told us. He said it could start here too."

"Well," said Father. "I don't know if the two things are related, but we have another problem."

He raised his glass and took a long look at it before taking a small sip.

"What problem?" I asked, immediately realizing that Father had been hiding things from us.

"How are things in school?" For a moment, he seemed to be trying to change the subject. "I see you're very good at languages. How's your Serbo-Croatian?"

"It's fine, Father. I got an A in my last test."

"Then I have a favor to ask of you."

He opened one of his drawers, took out a page bearing the symbol of the Serbian lion, and handed it to me. "Here, read this."

I felt like an adult, proud that Father was sharing some of life's real problems with me.

The letter went like this:

Serbian Ministry of Internal Affairs, 05.11.1938

Re: A final extension of your residence permit.

As you know, the residence permit allowing you to remain within the borders of Serbia is about to expire on 07.31.1938. This permit also includes your work and business licenses. This is the final extension granted you by order of the Minister of Internal Affairs. You are entitled to submit an official appeal at our office at 65 Dragoslava Srejovica Street, within thirty days of receiving this letter.

Signed: Victor Petrović, Assistant Office Manager.

As I read the letter, I realized that my father, this upright, proud man feared by so many, was himself afraid. Afraid he wouldn't get more work, afraid of losing his assets, even afraid of being deported with his entire family.

Father sat frozen in his seat while I read the letter, then he rose, started walking about the room, and said he knew he could count on me, because my Serbo-Croatian was excellent.

"I'll be happy to help, Father. Just tell me your answer and I'll write it down."

"Very well, son. There's a reason I'm asking for your help. I'm afraid that sending back a badly written letter in broken, badly spelled Serbo-Croatian might make the wrong impression on officials there; they might even decide I'm not a true Serbian."

"Can they really deport us?" I asked, unable to hide a sudden surge of fear.

Frightening thoughts raced through my mind. What would happen to me? Mother? Pauli? And what about school?

"This was my third extension. I haven't shared this with any of you yet, and I don't want this information to leave the room. I don't want to upset your mother. To answer your question, yes, they can."

"You can count on me, Father. I can keep a secret, just like I learned in Akiba."

I sat in the soft leather chair with its tall backrest and ornamental wood carving. On the table in front of me lay a sheet of paper on which Father had written all the reasons and justifications for extending our residence permit. Father strode about the room. Now and then he'd stop, saying, "The Ministry of Justice on Karlova Street, add that too. You've already mentioned the House of Commerce, right? They need to know how much I've done for this city. I may not have been born here, and it's true that I was an officer in the Hungarian army more than twenty years ago, but we've lived here long enough not to be treated like immigrants."

Having folded the paper and placed it in an envelope, I was about to leave the room, when Father stopped me and told me he'd sold our house. We'd be moving on June first to an apartment downtown, not far from the Ashkenazi synagogue.

I was shocked. Wholly unprepared for such news. I'd spent my entire childhood here on the hill. How could I ever get used to a new place?

And yet, I'd be closer to school and to Isaac, even though we've hardly spoken since our last argument.

I asked him what had happened and why he'd had to sell the house.

He said that maintaining such a large house with a garden and a swimming pool costs a fortune. It was a very difficult move for him as well, but there didn't seem to be any other choice. Office revenues had sharply declined, and we needed to cut down on our expenses.

THE APARTMENT ON KRALJA PETRA, NOVEMBER 1938

For the past five months now, we've been living in a downtown apartment at 47 Kralja Petra Street, on the fourth floor of an old building in front of the Ashkenazi synagogue. At first, I had a hard time with the move to that part of the city. I didn't feel I belonged in the new neighborhood, and I missed the open spaces. But I got used to everything pretty quickly. I can walk by myself to school and even to the Akiba *ken*. I'm more independent here, and I've made lots of new friends. Even Isaac is in touch with me again. He no longer thinks of me as a spoiled child in a lofty palace. He doesn't even care that I go to the Akiba *ken* while he goes to the Hashomer Hatzair *ken*. "We all do what we think is best for us," he said with sudden generosity.

At the Akiba *ken*, now closer to our home, I made more new friends, two brothers from the De Mayo family: Alfonso, one of the elder brothers, is a very well-educated young man, who went to work on a farm so he could get a Hechalutz immigration certificate, and Samito, who's about my age; he and I have become very close. I also meet Branka Garai there, the girl I used to dream about at night.

During the summer, we all went camping in Žirovnica. We spent a lot of time hiking, and one day we climbed all the way up to one of the summits of the Triglav, the highest mountain in Slovenia. From the top of the mountain we could see as far as the Austrian border. There was a fine view of mountains and forests, and in between, a green plain with several turquoise lakes like precious stones embedded in a piece of jewelry. Our camp was surrounded by a forest, and the lake was close by. We bathed in it, boys and girls together, which was thrilling, especially after studying at a boys' school for so many years.

Branka and I went walking together outside the camp while the boys were playing soccer. Once, we even went around the entire lake. Branka let me hold her hand as we walked alone down the hiking trails. At night, I dreamed she let me kiss her, but I was too afraid to try. Although she always accepted my invitation, I found her a bit distant, even condescending. I was afraid I wasn't good enough for her. Then Omer Bihali appeared and began to pursue her, and we grew apart. I felt the bitter taste of missed opportunity for many days after that.

Apart from Dr. Kaufman, who spoke to us about physics, history, and a bit of Judaism, there was a man called Hugo in our *ken*. He came from Israel and told us what was going on there, about the *kibbutzim*, about farming. Many of us dreamed of being farmers in Israel. He taught us Hebrew songs. At evenings around the campfire, we enthusiastically sang along with him, accompanied by Telbi's accordion, and we danced the *hora*.

So I easily forgot we'd once lived on Dedinje Hill, in a large house with a garden and a swimming pool. It simply all became a distant dream. I was able to create a new and less lonely life for myself.

At home, my parents increasingly talk of fulfilling the Zionist dream and emigrating to Israel, especially Father. It isn't only the economic situation that makes him want to leave. I think he is also disturbed by not having any national identity, not legally belonging to the place he'd lived in for dozens of years. The detailed letter we sent the authorities didn't help. They hold a grudge against Father for fighting with the Hungarian army against the Serbs in the Great War; this is why they won't give us Yugoslavian citizenship.

Father wants to emigrate to Israel, but Klarie won't hear of it, probably because she has such a successful career as a lawyer.

In conversations with Father, she vehemently objects to the idea. Once, she even said, "You go to Israel if you like; go live in tents and catch malaria. I'll stay here, hold onto my peaceful life, go on living in my beautiful house, and see a good movie or an opera once in a while."

She tries to convince Mother it would be a grave mistake to emigrate to Israel, that conditions there are no good for people their age.

One day, Father came home with sorrowful eyes. He'd tried to arrange immigration certificates for us all to go to Israel, but apparently, he wasn't eligible for a capitalist certificate because he'd gone bankrupt, and he wasn't eligible for a Hechalutz certificate because he'd never been a Hechalutz. A student certificate wasn't relevant, of course. The only option, and the most dangerous, was for them to illegally immigrate to Israel.

Mother saw it as an opportunity to dissuade Father from emigrating to Israel, saying that Klarie might be right after all. Perhaps it just wasn't for us.

"Look at the DeVecchio family, Albert, Leon's father," she said. "They're leaving for America. If we really need to leave, perhaps we should go and live in America?"

But Father thought Israel is where we belong and where we must go; it's where our roots are. Father reminded Mother about her relative, Rabbi Judah Alkalai, who is buried on the Mount of Olives near Jerusalem. So many Jews had taken his advice decades ago and emigrated. It's our turn now.

But Mother wasn't convinced.

"The boys are finally happy in school. They have friends here. Isn't that important enough?"

"Louisa, you aren't seeing things clearly enough; read the writing on the wall. I think the situation is getting worse by the day, and we've got to wake up. With Hitler in power, new decrees against Jews are being issued all the time."

"But that's taking place in Germany and Austria," said Mother. "We're in the Balkans. Why would it happen here?"

"It's gradually influencing things here as well. This is why I've been getting fewer and fewer projects at the office. I have every reason to suspect this is happening just because I'm Jewish."

"But if we can't get a certificate, how can we emigrate?"

"There is a way. It's called illegal immigration." Father lowered his voice, as if saying something forbidden.

Mother was very worried about getting into trouble with the law. Father tried to calm her down, telling her he'd met with Mr. Spitzer from the Federation of Jewish Communities, an influential man with a lot of connections. It might take some time, but Spitzer has been trying to arrange a way for us to leave Europe without immigration permits. They would organize group certificates for the transport.

"How can they organize certificates? Who exactly would be responsible for that? It just doesn't sound right. It's no way to move an entire family to another country," Mother voiced her concerns. Her arguments silenced Father; his confidence seemed to crumble before the solid wall of her objections.

The tenth of November. I will never forget that day. The day Mother was finally convinced we should leave.

The ringing telephone startled us from our sleep at seven in the morning. From outside my room, I heard Mother talking with Grandma.

Suddenly, she let out a great cry. I ran to her. From the bits of conversation I managed to hear between her fits of crying, I understood what had happened. The previous evening, hooligans armed with clubs and iron bars entered Grandma's town in Austria, looking for Jewish homes and businesses. They tore down doors and smashed windows. Mother's parents and her younger brother hid in the attic, trembling with fear and waiting for it all to be over, while the hooligans smashed the entire house, destroying all the furniture, expensive china, and glassware.

When the loud smashing sounds and curses gradually subsided and they thought it was over, Grandpa went outside and ran to his fur shop to see if his valuable merchandise was safe. On his way to the shop, thugs stopped him and beat him with sticks and clubs, breaking both his legs. This was how they found him in the morning, lying at the side of the road and weeping with pain.

Mother put down the receiver with a shuddering sigh.

"Grandpa is in the hospital. His entire lower body is in a cast. They burned down Jewish homes, smashed windows, even violently attacked people."

The door burst open and Father came in. He took off his coat and gloves and threw the morning edition of his Hungarian newspaper on the table.

"This is disastrous," he told Mother, unable to control his voice. He opened the newspaper and showed Mother a photo of smashed Jewish store windows in Berlin. Similar things happened during the night all over the Reich!

Mother told him about the terrible phone call she'd received from Grandma.

"That's it, Emil. I've made up my mind! I don't want to stay here anymore."

KLARIE GOES TO BUDAPEST, JUNE 1939

We've been on our own for a week now with Sophie and Aunt Vera from Budapest. Mother and Father are with Klarie at Brody Adel Hospital in Budapest. The doctor says it's pneumonia again, but more severe this time, and Klarie must go to a better hospital. Father remembered an old army friend of his who works at a hospital in Budapest, and his friend immediately made arrangements to admit Klarie.

Pauli and I went with Father to visit her while she was still at Alexander Hospital in Belgrade, just before she was taken by ambulance to Budapest. Mother remained at her side all the time and was very worried.

Klarie smiled weakly at us when we got there. We stood by the door with our hands in our pockets, not really knowing what to say.

"Come on in, boys. I'm not going to bite you," she said faintly.

We went in and approached her bed. A mass of bright curls surrounded Klarie's pale face on the large white pillow. Her smooth, freckled skin, which always looked fresh and healthy, now looked sickly pale, and her bright eyes were sad. I noticed she needed to make a real effort to straighten up and greet us, but a little spark returned to her eyes as we approached.

Mother said it was a good thing her fever had dropped, because they'd be taking her to the hospital in Budapest the next day.

The room had a strong smell of medicine and starched sheets. I hate the smell of hospitals. I'm afraid as I pass by the hospital rooms, hear the groans and cries, smell the medicine and disinfectants; I keep thinking that each of the people lying there in their hospital beds could die at any moment. But the saddest thing for me was seeing Klarie, normally so full of life and laughter, wearing a hospital gown, having to swallow medicine, and lying in bed beside a toothless old woman who was groaning and calling out in rural Croatian.

Klarie is beautiful, even in a floral hospital gown. Doctors in white gowns, holding clipboards, came in and out and wrote all sorts of things on the medical chart on her bed.

"Well, say something. How's school?" Klarie tried to encourage us to break the silence.

"Everything's fine, Klarie. Yesterday, I was chosen outstanding student of 1939," I told her with pride.

"Wonderful," she said. "I always knew you were a genius. You just don't try hard enough. What about you, Pauli?" asked Klarie.

"Nothing special. I want you to come home so we can play tennis again."

"Don't you think I do too? As soon as I'm better and out of the hospital, we'll have a big tournament."

A doctor entered the room and asked us to leave.

Mother left with us. Just as she was wondering where Father was when she needed him, he showed up. Looking very upset, he said he'd just found out that Karl, Caroline's husband, had been arrested in Vienna. Two months before, he'd been fired from the university, along with all the other Jewish faculty members.

Mother sighed deeply and said she didn't envy the Jews in Germany and Austria. Father took advantage of her momentary weakness and said we must start packing up to make *Aliyah* to Israel. I felt so confused at that moment. On one hand, I wanted to fulfill the dream of making *Aliyah* to the land of Israel, as Dr. Kaufman had taught us at Akiba, but on the other hand, I also felt very sad at the idea of leaving my school and friends. Mother again broached the idea of America. "Who said we have to emigrate to Israel, of all places?" she said. But Father insisted that as far as he was concerned, emigrating to America was out of the question.

Then they began to whisper, and I realized they were talking about Klarie. I pretended I wasn't listening, while trying to hear every word. Father spoke again about Budapest and his army friend, Professor Otto. Professor Otto was the Director of Brody Adel Hospital and was expecting Klarie the next day.

When Mother tried to object, Father told her in a low voice that they didn't have the means to treat Klarie properly in this hospital, and Mother was convinced.

The door opened and the doctor called Mother and Father. They disappeared to the end of the corridor, and we returned to sit at Klarie's bedside.

"Enough with the long faces. Say something happy," Klarie whispered.

Pauli put a hand in his jacket pocket and took out a folded piece of paper. Ceremoniously, he presented it to Klarie, humming a melodramatic Mickey Mouse cartoon tune. He unfolded the page and showed her a charcoal portrait he'd drawn of her, curly-headed and smiling.

"It's the spitting image of me," she said in admiration.

"I used a photo Father took of you. It looks just like you, doesn't it?"

Klarie thanked him with a tired little smile and said he had really improved.

"It's for you," said Pauli. "I wanted to frame it, but there wasn't time."

I was mad at him for not telling me he had a gift for Klarie. If he'd told me, I'd have brought her something as well. I can't draw as well as he does. He draws Walt Disney cartoon characters all the time. Father even framed and hung a few of them in our room. I felt so bad. He'd thought of her and brought her a gift, and I hadn't done anything. He probably didn't tell me on purpose. He's always doing that to me. I stood there, ashamed, my hands in my pockets.

Mother and Father returned, and Mother said it was time for us to go. We couldn't stay at the hospital any longer.

That night, I couldn't fall asleep. I tossed and turned in bed, thinking about Klarie, how the next morning, accompanied by a nurse, she'd leave for Budapest by train; she'd travel by a special ambulance carriage together with Mother, Father, and her husband, Lazar. In Budapest, an ambulance will be waiting to take her straight to the hospital. Again, I had bad thoughts, remembering how wretched I must have looked next to Pauli, coming to visit her empty-handed. What if the doctors in Budapest couldn't cure her either?

Early in the morning, I woke to the sound of slamming doors. Father had arranged for the ambulance from the hospital to take them to the station, and he'd ordered a special carriage for them.

"Don't worry," he told Mother. "Everything has been arranged.

We'll have a local ambulance waiting for us in Budapest to take us all to the hospital in the city center."

"Do you want something to eat?" Mother asked him. "Poor man. You've been running around all morning."

She was afraid we'd be late for school and sent me to wake Pauli.

Because Mother was so busy that morning, I'd made us both cheese sandwiches just the way we like them, wrapping them in paper like Mother does. I put two in my schoolbag and two in Pauli's. He always gets up late, even on a critical day like this, as if he didn't care.

I went to say goodbye to my parents with my schoolbag on my back. Mother hugged me close and started crying.

"I don't know what will become of us," she said tearfully. "I feel as if everything is suddenly falling apart."

"It's all going to be fine, Mother," I said confidently. "We're not little children anymore. We'll be here with Vera. There's no need to worry."

Father came over to me and hugged me man-to-man.

"I'm counting on you, Hanne. We'll send you postcards from Budapest."

"Goodbye," we waved to them from the doorway. "Bring Klarie home healthy and well again."

Then we were on our own with Vera. That very first day I began to hate her. She treated us as if we were little children and not almost fifteen. She kept following me around and gave me no peace.

Three days later, a postcard came from Budapest.

11/06/1939

Dear Children,

We've arrived safely at Brody Adel Hospital in Budapest. Everything here is bigger and more modern. The doctor who is treating Klarie is very nice and sounds optimistic. Klarie is feeling better this morning. She even smiled for the first time in ages. We were very happy.

I immediately sat down and wrote them a postcard.

Dear Mother and Father,

Everything is fine with us. Vera keeps too close an eye on us all the time. Yesterday, we all went to town to buy swimsuits and pants for summer camp.

We love you,

Pauli and Hanne.

P.S. Yesterday, a man came to the house and introduced himself as Sime Spitzer. He asked about Father.

Two days later, another postcard came.

13/06/1939

Hello Dear Children,

The skies outside are gray, and a spring rain is falling. Even the skies are weeping with us for Klarie. We are at her bedside all the time, and our mood is as dreary as the weather outside. We don't have any good news. Her fever went up again yesterday and isn't coming down. She has no appetite. The doctors took some blood this morning and said we need to wait.

No more postcards came. The fear that something was wrong began to rise from my stomach to my throat. I was mad at the whole world. At the lying doctors, at my parents who simply accepted everything the doctors told them. I thought about studying medicine when I grew up, or maybe I'd be a researcher and discover cures for diseases. That way I could save people.

At the Akiba *ken*, we are busy rehearsing a play we will perform on the coming Saturday evening. I've been going to rehearsals every day. We're putting on Shakespeare's *Twelfth Night*. I'm playing the role of Sebastian, Viola's twin brother. Branka Garai is playing Viola, and Pauli plays the duke who woos her. While my real sister is fighting for her life in Budapest, it's difficult for me to play one of the twins whose ship sank at sea; though they were saved, each was convinced the other had drowned. Luckily, Viola swears not to marry any of her suitors, because she is grieving for her brother. That way, I wasn't jealous of Duke Orsino, played by Pauli, and whose advances Viola rejects.

I was hoping Mother, Father, and Klarie would be back in time to see the play, but as time passed, I realized this would not happen.

On that ill-fated Saturday, while we were on stage, dressed in the costumes of Sebastian and the duke, waiting for intermission and the applause, Alice, the director, suddenly came over and asked us to come with her to the office.

Vera was waiting for us there; her face was sad. "Your father called this morning. He said the situation is very grave. Klarie hasn't woken up in two days."

I didn't know what to do. My heart went out to Klarie, who was fighting for her life, while here, the show wasn't over yet. Pauli angrily took off his duke costume and threw the cloak on the floor. I saw he was holding back his tears, unable to decide whether he should go on with the show. I sat in a chair and prayed with all my heart that a miracle would bring Klarie back to us. I imagined her playfully tossing back her curly hair and saying with a typical smile, "Hey, little one. What are you so upset about? I just wanted to see how sad you'd be if I'm not around." Suddenly, all the tears I'd been trying to hold back burst out.

"You don't have to continue if you don't want to, Hanne," Alice said and placed a comforting hand on my shoulder. "We'll let everyone know we've had to stop the play for personal reasons."

Her voice shook, and her eyes, too, were bright with tears. She knew Klarie well. They'd gone to the same school.

The show must go on, I reminded myself again and again. I got up and straightened my clothes.

"Come, Pauli," I tugged his hand. "We can't disappoint everyone."

Pauli reluctantly picked up the duke's cloak, placed it on his shoulders, and followed me back on stage.

After the play ended, each of the actors took a bow before the audience. Alice later explained to me why I had received the loudest ovation. "Your face showed real distress, which completely fit the part. That's what it's like when real life meets acting on stage."

At home, we realized we should expect the worst. We were right. On Tuesday evening, June 20, 1939, Father called and asked to speak first with Pauli and then with me.

"Be strong, my beloved son. The situation here is very bad. Vera will bring you to Budapest on the night train."

Klarie was buried on Wednesday afternoon, June 21, 1939, at the Jewish cemetery in Budapest.

***

Alan stood next to his father, who was sitting in a wheelchair on the large balcony of Fliman Geriatric Hospital in Haifa. His father had been transferred there three weeks before. Other patients sat in wheelchairs on the spacious porch overlooking the view. Haifa Bay was visible to the north, and even the Bay of Acre could be seen on the horizon. However, due to their medical condition, most patients were indifferent to the beautiful view.

"I'm going back to New York tomorrow," Alan said.

He waited for some sort of reaction—approval, protest, anger. All he got was silence.

"I have work to do, and my wife and the girls are waiting for me, you know…"

"Your wife, yes. What's her name again? My memory is going…"

"Rachel. She's fine."

"Do you love her?"

After a long, embarrassing silence, his father added, "Look, I've already lost Inge. But you, don't you give up on love."

"Why are you telling me this?" asked Alan.

"When I visited you in New York and met Rachel for the first time, I realized a few things, but was reluctant to say anything."

"We've been to counseling since then. Everything is fine now."

"I've often wondered what happened to Inge. But I've never had the time or the means to find out. She might even be living somewhere else. New York, maybe, or London. Have you started looking for her?"

"I have. So far, I've only found your Belgrade childhood diary, the one you translated."

"I met Inge later, on board the *Tzar Nikolai*."

"Why are you talking about Inge now? You've never mentioned her before."

"I've never been close to death before," said his father.

Another silence fell between them.

"I wrote about the *Tzar Nikolai*. I wrote about her as well."

"Are there more diaries I haven't seen?" asked Alan.

"Not diaries, a memoir I wrote a few years ago."

"Why didn't you tell us?"

"I planned to tell you about it once I'd finished, but then I got ill. Not even your mother knew. I used to write at the library. She thought I was studying Arabic."

"So where are the memoirs?"

"Under the tractor seat. The cover says something like 'Saul Czernichowski.' No one will find it there."

"But why did you keep it a secret?"

"Because I haven't finished writing. I wanted to publish it one day— the story of my life and the story of that wretched attempt to emigrate.

***

That very same day, Alan went to the tractor shed. He lifted the tractor seat, and beneath a gray blanket smelling of grease, he found a notebook with the words "Selected Poems of Saul Czernichowski" written on its cover.

With the memoir in his hand, Alan again wondered why it had been so important to his father to hide the story.

He opened the notebook and began to read.

> I have recently decided to write my memoirs. I've come to the realization that it is my duty to write our story, the story of the Kladovo group, for the sake of future generations. After what happened to Shmarya, I realized that my life could also be cut short and the story left untold. Two years ago, I met a man and sat talking to him about farming. He spoke of growing olive trees and improving them, and I told him about the orchard I had to uproot because of the expenses involved in its maintenance. That evening, he had no idea that I was one of the passengers on the Kladovo boats who was waiting for a ship to take us to the Black Sea, and I had no idea he was Shmarya Tsameret, the mysterious Mossad agent who had bought the ship the *Darien* from a Greek in Piraeus, and paid for it with money he'd got from the Joint. The *Darien* was supposed to wait for us at the port nearest the Danube outlet to the Black Sea and sail with us through the Black Sea to the Mediterranean and Israel.

Shmarya was killed in a terrible work accident at the olive grove he loved so much. About two years after our meeting, and after he'd passed away, I discovered that the very man who'd sat talking with me over coffee and cake at Kibbutz Beit Hashita was actually Shmarya Tsameret. He never said a word about his exemplary past in the Mossad L'Aliyah Bet. After his death, his wife published his memoirs in a book called *Eternal Morning*. When I read the book, I realized that unless I wrote about what happened in Kladovo, the story would die with me, untold.

I drove to Baruch's stationary shop in Acre. There, I bought a large notebook, just like the one Mother had given me for my birthday almost forty years before and that I'd used to write my first diary. I reread my childhood diaries, which brought about a powerful reawakening of the rest of my memories, memories that demanded to be written down on paper.

THE TZAR NIKOLAI, DECEMBER 1939

A thick blanket of fog covered the water when we reached Vukovar harbor on the banks of the Danube. The far bank was almost invisible, and we could only guess that it existed at all.

We enjoyed the two-hour train ride from Belgrade. Father had been told ahead of time that the boat would dock briefly in Vukovar at the Hungarian border, where we would board. Both he and Mother were in a cheerful mood, making plans for the future and talking about what they'd do once they reached Haifa.

The occasional horn of a passing boat could be heard in the distance. We stood there in the mid-December cold. Father wore his long winter coat, a blue wool scarf wrapped around his head, along with a brimmed hat that hid his growing bald spots. In his suitcase, he'd packed just a few clothes, toiletries, and a small photo album he'd put together at the last moment before we left. Mother also wore a long wool coat, light leather gloves, and a kerchief on her head. In one hand, she held a large handbag, while the other held tightly to Father.

Mother had told me and Pauli to pack warm clothes and extra underwear. We packed clothes for a week or so in the backpacks we'd used for summer camp. The voyage wasn't supposed to take long. Just two to three days down the Danube. Then, at a port in the town of

Sulina on the Black Sea coast, we'd board a real ship and sail all the way to Haifa.

This is our second move in just two years. The first move was from the house on the hill in the Dedinje neighborhood, on the outskirts of Belgrade, to Kralja Petra Street in the city. Our first move was from our large mansion to a small apartment in a house in front of the Ashkenazi synagogue. It had a dark stairwell that always smelled of cooking. This is our second move. We'd sold a lot of our heavy furniture before the first move because the apartment in the city was too small. The remaining furniture had been packed to be shipped to Haifa. Just as he'd done for the previous move, Father had arranged for a moving truck and a gypsy driver. We'd wrapped the furniture in brown packing paper; every armrest of each sofa and every table leg was carefully wrapped and tied.

Father packed his photos with great care. He placed the framed ones in a separate box. He wrapped them in paper and marked the box "fragile," both in Serbo-Croatian and English. He asked me and Pauli to put the rest of the photos and photo albums in cardboard boxes. There were photos I'd never seen before. There was one of Father in the uniform of an officer in the Austro-Hungarian army with Mother standing next to him looking young and beautiful. I guess she'd come to visit him at the front. In her arms, she held little Klarie, all curls and smiles.

At the end of August, a few days before the Germans invaded Poland, Father went to Budapest by train. He told Aunt Emilia he'd be coming for a short evening visit. Mother was very angry with him and said he should be concentrating on getting us immigration permits to

Palestine so we could get out of here, not going all the way to Budapest for a few photos.

"Emil," she'd said. "I'm frightened. The ground is burning under our feet."

Mother herself had packed the expensive tableware sets and crystal glasses. Each glass was wrapped in a thick layer of soft wrapping paper. Pauli and I were responsible for packing our own things. It was very difficult to decide what to take to Palestine, because each of us was allowed only one box. I left the tennis clothes behind, as well as the good racket Father had bought me two years before. Father said we probably wouldn't have time for tennis in Israel. There was no point in taking any of my books, certainly not the history books. After all, in Palestine, they teach everything in Hebrew. Besides, history is being written at this very moment. That's what Father said on the first day of school, when the German invasion of Poland was announced on the radio. Father was very upset and said history was repeating itself. Once again, the world was in confusion. It just didn't make any sense to me and Pauli; what exactly did this war have to do with us? Poland was so far away. But Father's agitation was contagious, and we realized something really big was taking place. I said that perhaps we shouldn't go to school, but Father wouldn't hear of it, stating that for now, we need to maintain our daily schedules as usual. Mother, who still hadn't recovered from the tragedy of Klarie's death, was mostly indifferent to the news. The next morning, Father cut out the large headline announcing the beginning of the war from the front page of the Hungarian newspaper *Ageinlusag*. He hasn't been the same man since.

He deliberated whether or not to take the camera with him in the suitcase as well. He used to take it everywhere with him. Finally, he gave up on the idea and said better it get to Israel in one piece, safe from the hardships of the transport. He carefully wrapped it and found a place for it in one of the boxes. I saw that at the last minute, Mother had decided to take the wooden box with the cherished memento of Klarie's beautiful curls.

After Father told us we'd be boarding a ship to Palestine within the week, I went to part from all my friends and teachers at school. Mr. Marimovich was the teacher I admired most. He was fond of me and often praised my hard work and accomplishments. When I went to say goodbye to him, I found him sitting as usual in the teachers' lounge, holding a glass of tea and absorbed in a history book. I thought he'd be happy for me that I was going to Palestine, so I came especially to tell him about it. But he just sat there silently, not even raising his eyes from his book, as if I didn't exist.

"Mr. Marimovich, I came to say goodbye before leaving for Palestine."

He raised angry eyes from the book and said, "Go then. Go to your Palestine, and take all the rest of the Jews with you."

Deeply hurt and insulted, I turned my back on him and left.

We waited at the docks for the arrival of the *Tzar Nikolai*. That was the name written on Father's papers, four members of the David family will board the *Tzar Nikolai*.

It wasn't our first time there. But this time was very different from our Sunday afternoon cruises during the summer holiday. Back then, it was a pleasure cruise. Who knows, maybe we'd even sailed on board the *Tzar Nikolai*. Father would sit with his friends, wearing white shorts and a fashionable straw hat, talking to them about soccer or politics and drinking *slivovitz*. They'd invite the gypsy sr to accompany us on the accordion, and he'd start singing louder and louder while everyone clapped their hands and stomped their feet. Mother, Mrs. Steindal, and a few of her friends would sit on the other side, chatting comfortably, drinking tea, and eating cake. Pauli used to stroll about the boat and try to befriend the captain or ask the helmsman to let him hold the wheel for a moment. I used to sit next to the large paddle wheel that rotated slowly, pushing the water, and watch the colorful spray splash into the air. I could sit like that for hours, until Mother called me to come and eat with everyone.

And so, we stood there with our suitcases and waited for two hours, but the boat didn't appear. Every now and then, Father asked me or Pauli to run ahead and see if we could see anything on the horizon. Mother started worrying that something wasn't right.

"Something's wrong, Emil," she hissed. I guess she thought I couldn't hear her. "Perhaps you've bought tickets for a trip that doesn't even exist," she voiced her doubts.

"That's impossible," Father said confidently. "Everything was arranged by envoys of the Mossad L'Aliyah Bet. They're very reliable people."

The mists began to clear, allowing us to see twinkling lights on the far bank. Two horn blasts were heard, and we saw the mast lights of an approaching boat. As it drew nearer, our excitement grew.

"I told you there was nothing to worry about." Father smiled in satisfaction.

The boat that arrived bore the name the *Kraljica Marija.*

"That's not our boat," said Father. "According to the papers, ours is the *Tzar Nikolai.*"

And indeed, the *Kraljica Marija* sailed on a bit and approached the dock. Crew members ran about the boat and loud shouts were heard. It appeared that they were waiting for two fish barrels, as well as coal for the remainder of their cruise.

Mother was just beginning to lose patience again when the lights of another boat appeared.

"Nothing to worry about," said Father. "I was told there are three boats, a total of eleven hundred passengers. It's either going to be this boat or the next. We just need to wait patiently."

The next boat was the *Tzar Dusan* and it, too, sailed on.

"Here's another one," Pauli called happily and pointed at the approaching lights. This boat was the largest of the three, the *Tzar Nikolai.*

"Just like two princes and a queen," Father said, trying to bring a little humor to our nerve-wracking wait.

After the gangway was lowered, two crew members wearing uniforms and black caps decorated with gold stripes disembarked from the boat.

Father handed them our paperwork, which they carefully examined before allowing us to board.

A sharp smell of salted fish mixed with the sour smell of sweat and vomit hung in the damp air. As I walked on board, I felt a growing sense of nausea and found it difficult to breathe. In that claustrophobic space, I heard an unfamiliar murmur, the jarring sound of different languages spoken at once. At first, I only heard German, which we spoke at home, then an Austrian dialect. Finally, I heard more voices speaking in Hungarian and Slovak. A cacophony of languages, like the Tower of Babel.

Shouts in Serbo-Croatian were also heard now and then from crew members running along the deck or rolling huge wooden barrels emitting a strong smell of fish. Others pushed trolleys filled to the brim with coal. A multitude of people were crowded on the small deck, like industrious, restless ants. Their unwashed clothes testified to several days of traveling. In our luxurious wool coats, scarves, and gloves, we immediately stood out.

Father held Mother's hand and tried to stay calm. He looked about him, as if wanting to ask where to turn or what to do. Mother's face expressed her anxiety, turning as white as a blank piece of paper, and her lips trembled. I wanted to support her. I tried to reach out my hand to her, when she suddenly fainted and fell to the floor. None of us was able to stop her fall in time. Father kneeled beside her. He seemed to have lost his confidence. I shouted in panic, "Mother, Mother!"

Her eyes were wide open, staring at a fixed point high above. Her face had turned even paler.

Father said, "Go quickly and get a doctor."

Before I could obey, someone in the crowd, which closed in on us like a hangman's noose, placed a hand on my shoulder to stop me and said, "Don't go running. The only doctor is on board the *Kraljica Marija*."

I felt the blood drain from my body.

A girl emerged from the curious crowd. She looked only slightly older than me, but still managed to act and sound both practical and adult. She instructed me and Father to raise Mother's feet a little and keep them raised. Meanwhile, she leaned next to Mother and massaged her temples with quick and agile movements. Someone handed the girl a metal cup with water, but she refused it and said, "Not now. She simply fainted because of the transition and the tension. That's quite natural. There's nothing to worry about."

And indeed, a minute or two later, Mother's eyes focused, and she looked at us and tried to raise her head.

"You can lower her feet now, but carefully, and have her lie down with her knees bent for a few more minutes until she recovers. My name is Inge," she introduced herself. "And I'm here with the Mizrahi[5] group."

She sat at Mother's head, gently stroking her forehead and continuing to soothe her. Father, now more himself, stood up and straightened his coat.

"I'm going to get the doctor anyway," he said and tried to make his way through the crowd that still surrounded us. When he saw how difficult it was, he turned on the curious onlookers, calling angrily, "Let her breathe, for pity's sake! Why must you stand here and watch us?"

"Here comes Dr. Bezalel. Good thing we haven't sailed yet," a voice sounded from the crowd.

A tall man wearing round glasses and holding a black, square

---

5   The Mizrahi religious Zionist organization in Germany included three main movements: the Mizrahi Youth, established in 1926, supported the values of agriculture and the Torah and founded the religious kibbutz.

leather bag briskly approached us.

"Anyone who isn't family should move along and go about their business. You're interfering with my work," he commanded as he approached.

He kneeled beside Mother and skillfully placed two fingers on the back of her wrist, his eyes fixed on his watch.

"Are you her daughter?" he asked Inge, who continued to place her hand on Mother's forehead.

"No, I'm here with the Mizrahi youths. I just came to help," she said gently.

"Very good. You've done a wonderful job."

He turned to Mother and started asking her a lot of questions. The word "panic" was repeated several times. Had she suffered similar attacks in the past? When? And how many times? Finally, he said, "Madame Louisa, I don't think this trip is for you. It would be better for you to get off this ship with your husband and send your children with the other youths. You and your husband should join another, perhaps more organized ship, at a later stage. I don't think your condition is going to improve later on."

Mother, who had meanwhile managed to straighten up a bit, glared at him.

"How dare you tell me to leave my children now? After we've sold the house and packed our boxes and suitcases, now you tell me this voyage is not for me?"

The doctor saw the determination in her eyes and said, "Excuse me, Madame Louisa. It was just a recommendation, not an order. I'm just not sure you'll be able to deal with the conditions here. I recognize a weakness in you. It might be because of the sudden move, but it might also be a real problem. I merely made a suggestion."

He rummaged in his black bag, placed a jar with valerian pills in front of Mother, opened it, and placed a few pills in a small packet.

"Take one a day. It will help you relax and regain your strength." He turned to Inge and me and said, "You two should remain by her side until she recovers."

Inge turned to speak with Mother. I didn't really listen to their conversation. I only heard Mother saying that thanks to her resourcefulness she was now recovering. Inge laughed and encouraged her by saying she would have recovered anyway, only a little slower. Inge told her she'd taken first-aid classes in school, and before the world had turned upside down, she'd planned to study nursing.

Then she asked Mother, "Tell me, what chased you out of Belgrade? Isn't it peaceful there now? I wish things were like that in Germany. I thought the restrictions against the Jews hadn't yet reached this country."

Her accent reminded me of Martha, my German teacher, and I realized she came from the Berlin area.

"If I were living here, I might not be in such a hurry to leave. I've left my sick mother at home."

I noticed her sharp features, her thin lips, stretching up into half a smile, and the freckles around her nose. Her auburn hair was tied back with a ribbon and swung from right to left as she spoke. It gave her face a light and playful appearance that completely contradicted the mature, responsible behavior she'd demonstrated just a few moments ago.

Supported by Father, Mother was able to stand. Inge volunteered to help us find a place on board that would serve as our sleeping quarters. A cabin of our own was out of the question. The boat was full and crowded. Inge told us it probably contained ten times more passengers than it was officially allowed to carry. She took us to the resting and sitting areas on deck. There, between the benches, or sprawled upon them, families gathered with their few belongings, each family trying to create its own small territory with bags or suitcases.

"Here, on board the *Tzar Nikolai*, you'll find many young religious and conservative people, among them youths from the Mizrahi Movement from Vienna and Germany, like me," Inge explained. "Emil Shechter is in charge of us here on the *Tzar Nikolai*. But the younger members, the children, are overseen by a young man called Teddy. You'll get to know him in time."

"What about the other boats? Who is in charge there?" I asked.

"Emil Shechter's brother. And the boat with the best organization and the most social activities is the *Kraljica Marija*. There, you'll find all the Hechalutz and Blau-Weiss[6] youth. Their ship is always neat and polished, and you can hear an interesting lecture every day. They are also the first to dance the *hora* whenever we get a bit of good news."

She fell briefly silent.

"I have an idea. Maybe you could stay next to the chimney? The nights are getting colder now..."

"Good thing it's only for a few days. The smoke and soot would

---

6   The Blau-Weiss (Blue and White) youth movement was established in 1912 and was very influential among the Jewish community in Germany.

probably kill us," said Father, trying to find comfort in something.

We carried our suitcases to the little corner we'd found. Suddenly, our suitcases seemed too large, or perhaps it was other people's suitcases that were too small. I really couldn't tell. We pushed the backpacks and suitcases under the bench and sat on it.

"About the chimney, don't worry, it's tall and the smoke rises high into the air."

We approached the chimney area and saw that it was indeed still vacant. Maybe people were really afraid of the rising soot. Father said it was better to breathe soot than die of cold.

"You'll need blankets. That's the most important thing now," said Inge. "I'll show Hanne where the storage room is. You look so different from all the others on board, as if you were going on a pleasure cruise rather than a Hechalutz immigration operation," she added laughingly.

"We weren't really told what to expect. Have you also paid a lot for this pleasure cruise?" asked Mother, who by now was somewhat restored.

"I didn't pay anything," said Inge. "We came here as a group. Perhaps the group paid as a whole, but no one has asked us to pay."

While Mother and Inge were talking, the frantic activity on deck continued. Sweaty dock hands pushed carts filled with coal and shouted at everyone to clear the way. Others, their clothes stained with coal, carried heavy sacks on their shoulders and shouted loud cries of encouragement as they heaved and tossed the sacks into an opening leading straight to the belly of the boat.

The hours passed, but the ship did not set sail. The sun emerged from among the clouds, and it became warm.

Mother suggested Pauli and I explore the boat while she and Father rested a bit on the bench.

Pauli disappeared before I could turn my head.

"Come, Hanne," Inge told me. "I'll take you to the storage room. Let's see if they have some warm blankets for the night. It's going to be awfully cold."

"It sounds as if you've been here a while. When did you come on board?" I asked.

I tried to keep up with her. She managed to walk very quickly, in spite of her long skirt, which I guessed was part of the Mizrahi girls' uniform. Her ponytail swung to and fro as she walked.

"It's a long story. We've been on the road for more than a month. I joined on November nineteenth in Berlin. Everything was done in a highly secretive way. They gathered us together in the community building and didn't even let us call home. I so badly wanted to say goodbye to my mother, but they wouldn't let me. They said we'd travel by train to Vienna early in the morning and warned us that we must not be recognized as a group while on the train." Suddenly, she stopped, covering her mouth with her hands.

"Oh, no! I completely forgot! I was on my way to the *Kraljica Marija* to bring Yokel some soap and cleaning utensils. You can come with me. I'm doomed…"

She pulled me down a long corridor that ended in a heavy iron door.

Inside the corridor, the sound of engines and machinery was so loud I could hardly hear her.

"Right here," Inge pointed at a sink containing large bars of soap and a brush, with a bucket and a mop next to them. "Yokel sent someone here, but he couldn't find anything, so he asked me to come and look, but then I saw people crowding around your mother and forgot all about it. Never mind. There's still time to bring it to them."

"Aren't you afraid the boats will start moving while you're still here?" I asked in shock.

"Don't worry. They sound a loud horn before they sail. It'll give me a few more minutes to run."

She handed me a bucket and a rag and took the broom and mop.

"Let's run. I'll show you something else on the way," she said, panting. "There's a place on the boat I love to sit when it's cold, especially when the sun goes down."

She continued to run along a maze of passageways filled with large pipes. The noise of heavy machinery became louder by the moment, and the heat was insufferable. By the time we reached the engine room, I couldn't hear her at all. I tried to tell her she wouldn't hear the horn blast from there, but she pointed at a door to her left and asked me to open it. I needed a lot of force to open it. Behind it, stairs were revealed, leading to a hidden corner with a wooden bench and a small table.

"This is the turbine engineers' rest room. They hardly come here, because they prefer to rest in their cabins," she said, sitting down on the bench for a moment.

"Isn't it nice? It's pretty quiet here," she said, immediately getting up and setting off at a run.

"So why didn't we make a corner for ourselves down there?" I asked, trying hard to keep up with her.

"Not many people know about this place. We're not actually supposed to be here."

"Pity. We could have been very comfortable there."

"Let's go back up now. I'm really afraid the horn will sound soon, and I still need to get to the other ship."

"In summer, almost every Sunday, our entire family used to sail down the Danube on a boat just like this one. Then, we were just a few families and a gypsy musician. No wonder Mother had a seizure when she saw how crowded the boat was."

We ran up a spiral staircase, Inge with the bucket and me with the broom and mop.

"What do you mean by 'seizure'? Has she ever had such seizures before?"

"No, but that's what the doctor said, a panic attack or a seizure."

"Yes, that's what it looked like to me."

"How do you know so much medical stuff? You acted just like a real hospital nurse."

"I'll tell you some other time."

"Can't you tell me now?" I pleaded with her.

"Last summer, I took a two-month first-aid seminar, in preparation for nursing school."

"Really? So you already know what you want to do when you grow up?"

"Do I look like a child to you?"

"No, I meant a real grown-up, with a profession and everything."

"I only have one year left in high school. I was thinking of studying at a nursing school in Berlin after that."

"I still have no idea what I want to study."

Meanwhile, we returned to the deck and heard a loud horn blast from the next boat. It was immediately followed by a loud horn blast on our boat. A large cloud of black smoke rose from the chimney.

Excited shouts rose everywhere on deck.

"We're sailing! It's about time!"

The enthusiasm proved to be contagious and spread to everyone on board.

"Oh, now I really must run. Yokel will be so angry. He's such a stickler for order. It wasn't for nothing that he asked for cleaning materials for his boat. Everything always has to be spick-and-span over there."

I wanted to go with her, but she'd already run off.

"Goodbye, Hanne. I'll see you this evening! We're on the same voyage, after all." She lifted the front of her long skirt so she could run faster.

A few minutes later, shamefaced, she returned with the broom and bucket. When she reached me, she placed them on the floor, stamped her foot angrily, and said, chokingly, "I was just about to set foot on the gangway, but they stopped me. The *Kraljica Marija* has already pulled away from our boat. What will I do now? You don't know what Yokel is like when he's angry."

"So the boat will be a little dirty. What harm is there in that? It's all so crowded and filthy here anyway," I tried to calm her down.

"It doesn't work like that," she said. "You don't know us German Jews. We're not like Viennese Germans. Viennese people are very disorganized, but with us everything has to be spick-and-span."

We stood side by side on the deck, looking into the water below. Inge finally settled down and continued, "At first, I also had a hard time with the crowded conditions and the filth on board. These are very small boats, and they aren't equipped to hold so many people."

"A real cataclysm," I used the word that seemed appropriate to describe this nightmare.

"What did you say? What's a cata…?"

"It's just a word describing something terrible that's about to happen, even worse than a catastrophe."

"Oh, I get it," she said and burst out laughing. "I've never heard it before. Where were we, then?"

"You started telling me how you got to these crowded boats," I tried to get the conversation back on track.

"In Bratislava, we boarded *Uranus*, which is a really large ship. Everything happened at night and in extreme secrecy. They let us know we'd be divided according to our youth movements, or something like that. We Mizrahi and Brit Chalutzim youth got Emil Shechter as our supervisor. He's a great guy. So we were ready to board ship when an urgent message was suddenly received, telling us we had to wait twenty-four hours at the Bratislava community center. People became restless and didn't understand what was going on or why we'd been delayed."

"And did you find out?" I asked.

"No. We didn't know anything. So of course, all sorts of rumors began…"

"What rumors?"

"You know—rumors. It doesn't matter. And so we spent another night and a day in Bratislava before we finally boarded."

"I guess people went wild with joy."

"Wild is the right word to describe it. Everyone joyously yelled that we'd finally managed to get out, that now we could finally scream without fear."

"And that was that? It's all been smooth sailing since then?"

"No, not really smooth sailing…"

"What happened?"

"We moved on pretty quickly. They told us we were already close to Hungary. Then, suddenly, we felt the boat slowing down, almost to a halt. Then, we actually saw the bow turn around. We couldn't believe we were going back. The singing and celebrations stopped. Everyone became nervous and restless again. We realized we were heading back to Bratislava, and there were more scary rumors. It was really frightening."

I turned my head aside and noticed a woman standing close to us, leaning over the rail, her head turned down toward the water and her hand clutching her stomach.

"It happens pretty often here," Inge told me. "No need to get excited. All this rocking doesn't suit everyone. I wish I could help each and every one of them, but Dr. Bezalel finished his metoclopramide right on the first night of the voyage."

"I'm not surprised. I feel sick to my stomach just from the smells here."

"And not only that. Poor Dr. Bezalel. You'll see what I mean soon enough."

"So you headed back. Then what happened?"

"After two more days nervously waiting at the community house, with rumors constantly flying and without anyone really knowing why we'd returned, only then, at night, of course, did we finally board *Uranus* and begin to sail down the Danube again."

"And was that the last time?" I asked, hoping it was indeed the end of her misadventures.

"I think so. When we crossed the border into Hungary, we realized that was that—it was final. We all danced the *hora* like we'd never danced before. Everyone sang and congratulated each other. I'll never forget the moment we arrived in Budapest and saw the great bridge over the Danube for the first time. It was a spectacular sight. We could see the green and yellow lights from a distance, twinkling like stars, and as we approached, we saw the arches between the high masts. Only when we were really close did we see the huge construction of the steel bridge towering above the Danube. Emil Shechter told us it's called the Liberty Bridge. Our ship sailed under that mighty bridge. There were more bridges after that, but none as impressive."

"So when did you transfer to these small 'luxury' boats?"

"In the middle of the river, in the middle of the night, again. Suddenly, they told us to separate into our original groups and move to the smaller boats."

"Weren't you afraid?"

"Of course I was afraid. My teeth were chattering with cold or fear or both. We walked along a short bridge that connected the ship to the smaller boat, and it swung from side to side. I thought I'd fall into the water."

"It sounds as though you've had quite an adventure so far," I said.

"Perhaps everything will go smoothly from now on and there won't be any more stops or turnarounds."

"Oh, no, Hanne. Now I really need to get going. Emil Shechter has some sort of social activity planned for us at nine o'clock in the morning."

"Perhaps we could meet later on?"

"Sorry, today I'm on cleaning duty. It was my turn yesterday, but…"

"This evening, then. I'll be waiting on the bridge."

"I'll see," said Inge and kept me guessing.

The sun had meanwhile climbed in the sky, sending golden rays into the water and transforming its surface into thousands of glittering, gold-tinted glass shards. We saw the gray buildings on the shore gradually disappear to the sound of the cheering crowd on deck. But the joy did not last long. Every time the boat slowed down, a wave of increasingly loud grunts and complaints was heard. Suddenly, the bow began to change direction, and it appeared the boat was turning back. "We're going back again. God in heaven!"

Numerous cries of resentment could be heard on deck. People began to lose their patience. Mother, Father, and Pauli sat on the benches, their downcast faces saying it all.

"We were worried about you, Hanne. Where have you been for so long?" Mother asked.

"There are rumors going around that we won't be continuing," said Pauli, and then added, "I didn't like the idea of this voyage in the first place."

"Patience, Pauli," said Father. "We've hardly even started out, and you've already got something to say."

"Just listen to what people around us are saying," answered Pauli. "Haven't you been listening at all?"

"Do you mean all those rumors? There are two dubious characters here who keep trying to frighten everyone and spread panic," answered Father.

People around us began to get up and walk in a particular direction.

"Lunch!" a woman wearing a headscarf and black clothes called to us. "You'd better come now, because in a few minutes, there won't be much left."

When we found the long line next to the staircase at the other end of the boat, we realized we'd come to the right place.

"I'm not even hungry," Mother said. "After what I've been through this morning, the last thing I need is food."

"I'm not hungry either," said Father. "But who knows when they'll be giving out food again."

"Some people are quick. They get there first and take more than everyone else. I bet the Fleishmans are there already, right next to the pots," said the woman in front of us angrily.

"You're talking nonsense," said her husband, a large man. "They give everyone exactly the same portions. Besides, who's stopping you from getting there first?" He turned to Father, "I see you're new here on the boat. Where are you from?"

"We're from Belgrade," Father answered. "We boarded this morning."

"I'm Abraham, but the young people here call me Mr. Goldman," he said. He pointed at his skinny little wife and added, "And this is my wife, Rebecca. We boarded in Bratislava about a week ago, on

December ninth. What's the date today? I've lost track of time with all this sailing back and forth."

"Today is the seventeenth. You mean to tell me you've been going back and forth for the past eight days?" asked Father.

"You thought this would be a picnic, did you? At first, we advanced very quickly and got all the way to the city of Győr in Hungary. Everyone was in a good mood and singing pioneer songs, but then we suddenly changed course and sailed back to Bratislava."

"Why did you sail back?"

"Well, as you can imagine, there were a lot of rumors, and rumor-mongers had the time of their lives. They said the German shipping company wouldn't continue, because there wasn't a ship to take us further into the Mediterranean. So Sime Spitzer, you'll hear a lot about him, he's the General Secretary of the Federation of Jewish Communities in Yugoslavia. Well, he contacted a Yugoslav shipping company that brought the queen and the two princes, that's what Naftali Bata Gedalja, Spitzer's deputy and all-powerful aide, calls the boats. He's the one looking out for us here."

"I know Sime Spitzer personally. He was the one who recommended this voyage to me," said Father, and then added, "So where did you board the boats?"

"It was the night… Wait a minute, let me think. I'm confused… Yes, the night before last. If today's the seventeenth, it must have been on the fifteenth or so."

"Did you dock at the Hungarian or the Yugoslav port?"

"That's the thing. We never even docked. We were in the middle of the river, next to Bazden, a town in Yugoslavia. Suddenly, three riverboats appeared. We couldn't believe they wanted us to move to such small boats. We're more than a thousand people here."

"You were divided into groups, weren't you?"

"They gathered everyone before we boarded the boats, and Naftali Bata Gedalja, who represented the Federation of Jewish Communities, explained that there were already about a thousand people altogether and that we'd be divided into groups, based on the organizations we belong to. This is how several groups were created, each with its own supervisor and deputy. All this happened even before the three boats arrived."

"And who decided on the groups?"

"The voyage management appointed in Vienna. It included the brothers Emil and Jozsi Shechter, and Arye Dorfman, the beloved leader of the Blau-Weiss and Netzah[7] youth movements. They divided us into three groups, based on our organization's origin; each group boarded a different boat. They must have known there'd be three ships even before we sailed. Yokel received the largest group, all members of Hechalutz and Blau-Weiss who boarded the *Kraljica Marija*. Emil received the Mizrahi youths from Vienna and Germany, as well as families with children. This is our group, here on board the *Tzar Nikolai*. The rest are members of the Youth Aliyah and young couples, about three hundred people, headed by Jozsi Shechter, on board the *Tzar Dusan*.

"That's such a disappointment! To sail off only to return."

---

7   Netzah, Zionist Pioneer Youth, was a youth movement established in 1930 and closely associated with Hashomer Hatzair.

"Why don't you tell him why," Rebecca, Abraham's wife, interrupted.

"There were all sorts of rumors and prophecies of doom: that there was no more money to pay for the voyage, that the German shipping company had gone bankrupt, and the scariest rumor of all—that Agami[8] hadn't managed to arrange a ship to transfer us from the Black Sea to the Mediterranean and that there was probably a long line of refugees waiting at Sulina without a boat to take them across. It all begins and ends with Sime Spitzer. He's the one who's supposed to arrange everything, but there is such chaos around here that no one really knows what's happening anymore," Abraham added.

"I hope that from now on we'll be able to sail through without any further interruptions," said Father.

Meanwhile, the line began to move forward. Mother looked tired and leaned on the stairway rail as if about to fall again.

When we reached the lower deck, we saw that the line continued all the way to the main passenger hall, where the buffet and bar had been located back in the good old days. Father and Abraham continued to talk.

"You look so smart, as if you were about to go on a pleasure cruise."

"Yes, we came as private passengers. We don't belong to any of the groups. They haven't really told us anything about this voyage. We paid well enough, so we expected a different service and different conditions," Father laughed.

"You must have been well-off in Belgrade. Why did you decide to

---

8   Moshe Averbach, called Agami, a prominent member of the Mossad L'Aliyah Bet, was in charge of foreign affairs, first in Italy and later in Romania.

leave, then?"

"We were very comfortable," said Father. "But you might say we've lost our assets in the course of the past year."

"I thought there weren't any problems in the Balkan area, only in Germany and Austria," Abraham was surprised.

"It's not as bad as your area. We'd heard about what is going on in Austria, but my office simply stopped getting new clients, and I felt something bad was fast approaching our neck of the woods."

"New clients? What's your profession?"

"I had a very successful architecture firm. I designed many buildings in the city. How about you? What's your profession?"

"Teacher. I used to teach Hebrew and Bible studies in a Jewish school in Vienna," Abraham answered, adding before saying goodbye, "You're welcome to come and visit. I'm downstairs in the cabins. I have a shortwave radio. We can listen to world news together."

I could smell sauerkraut and potatoes… I could also hear screams in Austrian German from people who were close to the distribution point. Someone cursed and another answered him, "Shame on you, punk."

I remembered a similar food line at my last summer camp in the mountains. Meanwhile, a spoonful of pale mashed potatoes landed on the plate I was holding.

"Move along, young man. You're blocking the line," scolded the man who was serving.

I moved on to the next pot. A boy not much older than me, wearing a gray beret, stirred the bottom of the pot and pulled out a lump of sauerkraut. Taking a colorless hot dog from another pot, he roughly placed both on my plate.

We couldn't find anywhere to sit. Pauli and I leaned against the wall, setting the plates between our legs. Two youths considerately rose from their seats next to the table and offered Mother and Father their places. They thanked them and willingly accepted. We ate in silence, each engrossed in his own plate.

"You're going to miss my home cooking," said Mother, trying to find something edible. "Maybe you and Pauli won't be so spoiled after this."

I kept thinking about our last days in Dedinje, about Klarie, who was still with us on our last pleasure cruise across the Danube. Everyone was so happy. Klarie, Lazar, and her friend Olga laughed and sang along with everyone. A few months later, Klarie got ill and everything changed. We didn't go on a cruise this last summer. It was a year of mourning. Mother stopped holding her garden parties. She said it wasn't just because of Klarie, but she really changed after Klarie died. I would see her eyes fill with tears during meals. Every time I secretly listened to her conversations with Father, I heard how determined she was about emigrating to Israel, despite her initial opposition. After Klarie died, there seemed to be nothing left for Mother in Belgrade. She was angry with Father for not obtaining immigration certificates for us. He would calm her, saying we'd obtain the certificates soon. Then we could sell the house and board a train or a boat to the Black Sea. But the certificates never came.

At school, I started to feel that the teachers didn't really know what to do with the Jewish students. They moved me, Simon, and Nissim, the other two Jewish students, to the back benches in class. They said it was because they wanted the weaker students to be closer to the teacher, but Mother interpreted it differently.

Father said we should probably go back up on deck, because our belongings were there and we shouldn't leave them unattended for too long. Upstairs, the atmosphere was becoming tense. Abraham said that the rumormongers were plying their stories again.

"People can't stand them," Abraham explained. "They go around spreading all sorts of imaginary stories. They just love getting everyone upset and nervous. Take everything they say with a grain of salt, as they say."

"But what is it this time? Did something actually happen?" asked Father.

"The boat changed direction and headed mid-river again, as if about to turn back at any moment, but there's nothing to get excited about, Mr....Emil, right?"

Good thing Mother wasn't listening. Father tried to remain calm when, suddenly, we saw the bow really was turning, and cries of despair were heard everywhere on deck. I saw that Abraham was also uneasy. Everyone raised their eyes in concern. One particularly vocal group was now certain it was the end of the transport, that we were about to return to Bratislava and it was all over.

Mother began to feel the pressure as well and used the expression she reserved for stressful situations. "Oh, my dear God, this is the last thing we need!"

Father tried to calm us down and remain optimistic, but with the general atmosphere on board, the bow changing direction, and the vocal group next to us constantly shouting, "It's the end; this is the end," he too began to show signs of doubt.

Someone headed up the stairs and called, "Friends, there's nothing to get excited about. I came on behalf of the captain to tell you we were considering returning to Vukovar to pick up something important, but we've decided to keep going."

He seemed very decisive, as if he knew what he was talking about. Sighs of relief were heard like a great sweeping wave from one end of the deck to the other.

The anxious atmosphere eased as the bow straightened and the boat continued to sail on down the river.

Mother and Father suggested we go for a little walk on deck to calm our nerves. We passed among the people, and everyone greeted us politely and asked if we'd found a decent place to sleep for the night. Father said we had, and Mother added, "Although, I don't know if you could really call it 'decent.'"

"It's not so bad here," said a young couple, sitting on a sack of flour or sugar.

The woman, in her last months of pregnancy, said she hoped to give birth after reaching a safe haven. Everyone continued to greet us and ask where we were from and if we recognized the views on the opposite bank.

"Yes, this is Belgrade," said Father, explaining that we were sailing south toward Belgrade and that the houses we would soon see were its northern suburbs.

Two Serbian crew members passed by, wearing peaked caps and gold stripes on the epaulets of their white shirts. They turned to Father in Serbo-Croatian, "We couldn't help but hear you're from Belgrade.

We're from Belgrade as well. Pleased to meet you." They introduced themselves as Ulrich and Kreinovich and shook hands.

They must have been impressed by Father's appearance; he stood out among the other passengers because of his height and elegant clothing.

"Pleased to meet you too," said Father. "Allow me to introduce my wife, Louisa, and these are my children," he pointed at me and Pauli.

They gently kissed the back of Mother's hand like two real gentlemen.

The conversation quickly turned to the subject of mutual acquaintances and finally to soccer and the fact they were all Red Star Belgrade fans. They invited Father to visit them on the bridge, parted from him with a pat on his shoulder, and promised to treat him to a drink and a bite of fine mackerel.

Father wasn't in any hurry to visit the two crew members on the first day. Perhaps he didn't want the others to think he was over privileged because he had connections with crew members. We returned to our spot next to the chimney, and Father tried to make the place ready for sleep.

"It's better if we organize everything before the sun goes down," he said and opened a suitcase to take out some warm clothes. "Let's see what we need for the night."

Mother suggested we each prepare a pillow out of our clothes to elevate our heads a little, and we followed her advice.

Meanwhile, the sun began to set, and purple-pink clouds hung above the river bank. I looked at the glittering lights, which suddenly seemed familiar.

"Hanne, Pauli," Father called with excitement. "See the lights up ahead? That's Kalemegdan."

Entranced, I looked at the lights. Kalemegdan is a beautiful park on a hill overlooking the junction of the Sava River and the Danube. We used to go there on weekends with our parents when we were children and roll on the grass and play war games among the high walls of the fortress while they walked hand in hand along the pathways. Later on, when we lived in the city, I used to go there with friends from school. I knew every pathway and each green hill. The park was also where I'd first met Eva, the year before; she was the most beautiful girl in our class. We walked together in the park. It was twilight time at the end of summer. Then I invited her to our house for a game of tennis, but she feared we were still too young for such an intimate friendship and that her mother wouldn't approve. Eva wasn't particularly excited when I told her I was leaving for Palestine. She just asked where it was and said she'd see me next year.

I stood in the stern, staring at the glittering lights and felt the spray splashing up from the white water, rising to mix with the tears flowing from my eyes. I knew I wasn't going to be in Belgrade next year, or the year after that.

***

I waited impatiently for evening to fall. I hoped Inge would come. After all, she'd told me she might come. I simply had to see her again. Oh, how I wished she'd show up. She simply had to.

It was a dark, starless night. I told my parents I was going out for a walk and they shouldn't worry. I took my good pair of pants from the small suitcase and made sure they were smooth and wrinkle-free. I put them on, together with my wool jacket. I took the steps leading to the upper deck two at a time. Perhaps she was already there, waiting for me.

The command bridge is the tallest point on the ship. It's where the ship's navigator sits, and no one is allowed to go in. But there was a roped-off balcony from which one could enter the command cabin.

The chill crept through my wool jacket and seeped into my bones. My thin pants couldn't stop the cold, either. My cheekbones ached, but I still stood there expectantly, thinking perhaps she'd come up in a moment or two. I heard someone running up the stairs and thought it must be her. I was overcome with joy and my heart began to race, but then I heard the sound of a man's voice humming a familiar Serbian song. It was only the ship's navigator returning from the dining room in a good mood. I looked at my watch. I'd been waiting for twenty minutes. I realized that Inge probably wasn't coming. Alert to every rustle, I decided to wait five more minutes. The only sound I could clearly distinguish was the creaking of the ship's paddle wheel. I counted the rotations of the wheel. I decided to wait twenty more rotations, and if Inge didn't appear, I'd leave the bridge. But every time I reached twenty, I'd count again, until finally, I gave up and descended, filled with disappointment.

Father had spread the brown wool blankets I'd brought up from the storage room on the deck. Inge said that all the blankets, equipment, and supplies had been sent by the Federation of Jewish Communities in Belgrade. Each of us received one blanket to spread on the floor and two blankets with which to keep warm. The cold penetrated the thin wool blankets. I tried to fold my jacket into an improvised pillow and closed my eyes, attempting to digest the events of that fateful day. The rocking of the boat and irritating sound of the engine coming from below drove sleep away. My thoughts kept drifting back to our boarding, Mother fainting, Inge's beautiful face, and how she'd suddenly appeared out of the crowd like an angel. She was so practical and vigorous, and I thought to myself, *I wish I had these qualities.* She always knew exactly what to do, how to calm situations. She even managed to calm Father down, and I'd never seen him so stressed.

Time passed and I couldn't sleep. The chill gradually worsened. The sound of Father's regular snoring reached my ears. Mother was lying next to him, but seemed very uncomfortable and kept tossing and turning.

"Why aren't you sleeping, Hanne?" She suddenly sat up, the blanket covering her knees.

"I'm cold, and I keep having lots of thoughts."

"Try to think a little less. We need to save our strength for the morning."

I must have fallen asleep for a little while, because I woke up with icy-cold feet and a full bladder. I remembered Mr. Goldman showing us where the restrooms were that morning. I was afraid to go there by myself in the dark. I thought about waiting for morning, but the pressure worsened and I couldn't hold it in anymore. I felt my body grow rigid from lying on the cold wooden floor without a mattress. The mere thought of going downstairs in the dark to search for the toilets was enough to send chills down my spine. But I tried to get up and discovered I had to gently step over the sleepers, carefully directing my feet like a tightrope walker. When I finally reached the restrooms, I saw a long line of nervous people. So I finally decided to try and hold it. Perhaps I could wait till morning; perhaps it'd pass. I tried to ignore the pressure and closed my eyes. I guess it helped; I was so tired, I wasn't even aware of falling asleep. But not for long. I woke with a start on the cold hard deck, a wet warmth spreading beneath me.

Oh, no. What was wrong with me? What a baby! How could I ever face the embarrassment? How would I hide it? How would my clothes dry? How would I get rid of the smell? And what would Inge say if she found out what had happened? She'd probably think me a child, that I may look like a nice boy, but one who still wets his pants…

I considered my options, rummaging deep in my backpack. Luckily, everyone was still asleep, and I managed to find a change of clothes. Rolling up the wet clothes, I placed them next to the backpack. I decided I'd go and wash them early in the morning, before everyone else was awake. But what would I tell Mother and Father? Pauli would laugh at me for sure. What could I do? I simply had to hide the shameful evidence.

In the morning, as the first light of dawn rose above the east bank of the river, I took the rolled-up bundle and hurried to the engine room; I remembered the sink with the bar of soap and the coarse brush.

Luckily, no one was there. I washed the pants and wet underpants with water and soap, and then hung them to dry on one of the hot pipes carrying steam from the engine. I sat huddled below the pipe, warming up my frozen bones. I was afraid to leave the clothes unattended, but when I saw that no one came near the engine room, I decided to go back to our spot, thinking that perhaps Mother and Father were awake and worried about me.

When I returned upstairs, everyone was awake, and Mother worriedly asked where I'd been. I told her I'd gone to warm myself under the steam pipes because I'd felt cold during the night. An elderly man wrapped in a tallit prayer shawl walked among the passengers, looking for a minyan of ten men to hold the *Shacharit* morning prayer. Father told him he only prayed *Shacharit* on religious holidays and festive days.

After breakfast, which consisted of a cup of lukewarm coffee and two slices of bread spread with jam, I hurried downstairs. The clothes were there, but still a bit damp. I remained by the steam pipe and waited for them to dry.

When I returned upstairs, I invited Pauli to join me for a walk around the boat. Pauli said we might as well stay with Mother and Father instead of wandering about. They might need us. Mother was very upset by the crowded conditions and the sight of so many people just lying on the floor with their belongings. I said that perhaps they would feel less stressed without us. "We don't need to spend all our time with them, you know."

Finally, he relented and we set off. I tried to recall the way to the secret place Inge had shown me. We went down the stairs next to our sleeping area, all the way to the lowest level. There, we turned right along a corridor lined with wide pipes and full of deafening noise, but I couldn't recall which door led upstairs to the resting area. I tried one door, but immediately realized it wasn't the right one. We went on, and I tried another door, which led to another corridor without any stairs. The third door barely opened, just like the previous morning,

SHMUEL DAVID | 129

and I was pretty sure it was the right place, but wasn't entirely sure, because I could hear laughter and obscenities in Serbo-Croatian. I began to hesitate, and Pauli, who had paled slightly, said we should probably get back to Mother and Father because they might be worried. I tried to convince him that these were the right stairs and that we could always hide if we felt threatened. Pauli said I should go up and check if the place was empty. After climbing three stairs, I saw four burly sailors in sleeveless undershirts with cards in their muscular hands. I was just beginning to quietly retrace my steps when a voice suddenly rasped, "Hey, kid, what are you doing here?"

I at once started to run, screaming for Pauli to follow me, and that's how we reached the deck again, pale and frightened.

Mother was lying on the bench, her face as white as a sheet. Father rolled one of the blankets into a pillow and placed it under her head.

"Perhaps you should drink more water. It will refresh you," he urged her.

"No, Emil. Please. I know you're worried about me, but this nausea is simply killing me. I can't put anything in my mouth, not even water. The water might be bad here."

"Perhaps I should call Dr. Bezalel again…"

"But he's on board the *Kraljica Marija*," answered Pauli.

"I've never heard of anything like it! One doctor for three boats."

"Maybe we really shouldn't have taken this foolish trip…" said Mother, desperation apparent in her voice.

"Don't forget this was our only opportunity. Sime said the Danube is the only way to move between the various countries without being arrested. It's a neutral water route."

"Yes, but there might have been other, more normal means of transport. You can't just cram hundreds of people into one riverboat."

"Perhaps lying down is not good for you," said Father. "Try sitting."

He tried to help Mother into a sitting position, and her face immediately turned from white to green. She gasped, and her entire breakfast burst out of her mouth, staining Father's coat and collecting in a puddle on the blankets spread out on the floor.

Mother placed a hand on her chest and turned her face aside so as not to dirty the place. She began to take deep breaths, and then said, "Children, I'm so sorry you have to see me in such a state. This is terrible."

"It isn't terrible, Loui. These things happen," Father stroked her back gently. "There's no need to feel uncomfortable. Everything will be all right. A few more days and this nightmare will be over," he tried to comfort her.

A few minutes later, she sighed deeply. "Thank God. I finally feel a little better. I don't understand. This isn't my first time on such a boat, and I've never been seasick before."

"But Loui, this isn't the same. Back then, we sailed for three hours at the most. Now we've been sailing for two days. And the conditions… It's just not the same."

"Mother's right. We shouldn't have come on this trip in the first place," said Pauli. "We should have gotten off as soon as we saw the conditions on the boat. There will be other boats. This isn't the only one."

"Instead of talking so much, why don't you think of a way to clean this up?"

"I know where there are buckets and mops," I volunteered, immediately thinking of Inge. Now I had a real excuse to go looking for her. "Wait here. I'll be back soon."

I hurried to the stairs that led to the belly of the ship and ran toward the cabins. Two thirteen-year-old girls were sitting at the entrance to a cabin playing knucklebones. Two other girls were running shouting and screaming along the corridor. Someone opened a door and yelled at them to stop making such a racket and disturbing the peace. I asked them where their parents were, but they just shrugged. I descended another level, and everything became very quiet. I was wondering why it was so quiet when I suddenly heard the sound of a muffled voice.

Someone, probably the leader or instructor of a group of youngsters, was lecturing them while they sat in a semi-circle next to him. My eyes examined the group of youngsters, hoping to find Inge among them, but I couldn't see her. I looked and looked, but couldn't recognize her as they were all wearing the same uniform. The instructor was speaking about the pilgrimage to Jerusalem during biblical times. I listened a little, but didn't understand much. Finally, I recognized Inge, wearing a red wool hat that covered her ears. She flashed a big smile at me and looked even prettier than she had yesterday. I suddenly thought that after only one night in this hell, I had already forgotten the warm bed I used to sleep in, and that it was only yesterday I was propelled into these crowded and foul-smelling conditions. I signaled to her, and she asked the instructor for permission to get up. She approached me.

"I waited for you on the bridge…"

"I was tired and fell asleep on my blankets. By the time I got up, it was already too late."

"I need your help. Mother's not feeling well again. She threw up, and I need a bucket and a mop. I also need two clean blankets."

"Hold on. I'll tell Emil. Be right back!"

She came back a minute later.

"Come on," she said. "Let's start with the bucket. Then we'll see what we can do about the blankets."

She walked quickly, and it was all I could do to keep up. We went up and down stairs, entered narrow corridors, crossed rooms, and finally arrived.

"Here, let me hold it," I told her.

When I returned, Father wasn't there. Mother said he'd gone to visit the two crew members he'd met yesterday. He wanted to relax a bit, perhaps have a drink with them. Inge helped me clean up our sleeping area. We replaced one blanket. Mother warmly thanked her for her help. After everything was neat and tidy again, I accompanied Inge back to her group.

"Perhaps I'll make it tonight. Wait for me on the bridge, but no more than ten minutes," she said when we parted.

Father returned with a broad smile I hadn't seen on his face for quite a while.

"Come, Loui, Hanne. Where's Pauli?"

"Pauli met a boy who knows one of his classmates. He's with him now," said Mother.

"All right. I have a surprise for you," said Father. "Let's take all our belongings and move."

"Emil, I trust you've arranged a much better place for us," said Mother.

"You're about to be pleasantly surprised."

Father showed us the way and we followed. We got away from the chimney area, descended to the dining hall, crossed it, and climbed to an elevated balcony surrounded by ropes.

"We're not there yet," said Father.

We descended half a flight more, close to the bow, and entered a medium-sized hexagonal room with four of its six windows facing the water. The other two faced the rear side and were covered by blue curtains. There was a wooden table surrounded by four upholstered chairs.

"This is it. The officers' dining room," Father said with satisfaction. "They're letting us sleep in here. They have an arrangement some-where else inside the boat, next to the engine room."

"How come they agreed to give you this place?" Mother asked suspiciously.

"They told me they felt very uncomfortable yesterday, when they first met us."

"Why should they feel uncomfortable?" asked Mother.

"They immediately realized we're a distinguished Serbian family. When we were talking, we discovered we have several mutual ac-quaintances, such as the soccer team's trainer and Ivanovich, the per-son in charge of players' uniforms. We drank and talked a little. They asked me what it was like to sleep next to the chimney, and I told them the truth. What's there to hide? We've all suffered, haven't we?"

Pauli suddenly showed up.

"Where did you all disappear to? I've been looking for you all over the boat for the past half hour. Good thing Mr. Felix, that man who spreads all the rumors, saw you heading in this direction."

"He always knows everything, that Felix," said Mother.

"And you know where he sleeps?" said Pauli. "He and that little fellow, David Tauber, sleep on the net in the engine room. He bragged this was the best possible arrangement on the boat."

"I think there's room for a few more people here," said Father.

"That's right, there's room for more here," said Mother. "I also feel uncomfortable about only the four of us being in such a place."

"So let's invite another family. Perhaps even two..."

"But who?" asked Mother, and Father began to move toward the exit.

"I thought about the Reiss family. They seemed very stressed, and the father once worked with me," said Father, and descended to the great hall.

***

Winter. The surrounding landscape was drab, dreary, and monotonous. Now and then, a few chunks of ice floated downstream, remnants of the previous night's frosty temperatures. At least during the day, the water was still unfrozen and the boat could sail on.

When I raised my eyes, I could see steep cliffs at one end and bare cliffs at the other. Father explained that the cliffs to the right were in Yugoslavian territory, and the ones on the left belonged to Romania. Both sides were a brown-gray color. If there are any forests there, the trees must be bare by now. Father said we were sailing east and would soon see the Djerdap Gorge.[9] The taller of the two cliffs was suddenly fully revealed, rising to the height of a tall building. On one side, it was steep, while the other gradually descended into the water, some of it hidden below. Father had once said that the true test of every marine navigator was to successfully maneuver a boat between the two straits. All the passengers gathered on the upper deck and fearfully looked at the two approaching massive rocks that seemed about to fall into the water with a deafening roar and crush the boat like a tiny toy.

The moments of tension finally passed, and the cliffs gradually disappeared behind us. But joy at the navigator's successful navigation of the passage between the cliffs quickly transformed into a new dread, when the bow changed direction and the boat appeared to be turning back. Cries of anger and panic were heard among the passengers. Everyone expected an update that would explain this sudden change. Perhaps it was only temporary; perhaps chunks of ice were blocking the passage and hindering the boat's progress. Suddenly, the engines switched off. We wanted someone in charge to tell us what was going on.

Felix and Rudy, that pair of rumormongers, took advantage of this dramatic moment to cause even more anxiety. They said the harsh winter conditions would not allow us to move forward. According to them, the captain had said we shouldn't continue and must find

9　The Iron Gates (in Serbo-Croatian, Đerdap Gorge, the last part known as Đerdapska klisura) are two mighty cliffs that form a narrow gorge on the Danube River, which is part of the boundary between Serbia and Romania and hampers the passage of ships along the river.

a proper docking bay, just as many other boats were now doing. The dread and tension intensified when the engines growled and we began moving again, not southeast, but back toward the Djerdap Gorge. There were rumors that the ice wasn't the real reason for the sudden stop but that that there might not be a boat waiting for us at Sulina, on the coast of the Black Sea.

Naftali Bata painstakingly explained to everyone that, according to the agreement between the Federation of Jewish Communities in charge of the trip and the state river shipping line, we were not allowed to leave the borders of Yugoslavia until a passenger ship was waiting for the group at Sulina.

"This is exactly what is written in the agreement," I heard Naftali Bata telling Father in Serbo-Croatian, as he himself came from Belgrade.

"Why can't we wait in Sulina until the ship arrives to take us to Israel?"

"You don't understand," said Naftali. "Sulina isn't in Yugoslavian territory. You have no idea of the effort I've made to warn the river shipping line that if the river freezes over, we won't be able to sail on."

On our way, we passed a large town, much bigger than the one from which we'd embarked. I heard Father telling everyone the town was called Prahovo. He said the train from Belgrade to Bulgaria stops there and that it serves as an important transportation center between Yugoslavia and Bulgaria. Meanwhile, another rumor began to spread; people said Sime Spitzer himself was on his way to Prahovo to provide explanations for everything that was happening, and that we might need to wait at Prahovo Bay for another day or two, until we had official notice of a ship waiting for us at Sulina. The great turbine wheel began to slow down, and as it slowed, it dawned on us that our journey was coming to a halt. Finally, with a loud grating sound, the wheel stopped moving and complete silence fell on the boat. Then, sounds of protest and misgivings from people on deck intensified as we watched with expectant, uneasy eyes.

We all stood on the dock at Prahovo to hear what the man in charge of our trip had to tell us. It was an especially cold, sunny day at the end of December, and the remains of heavy snow that had fallen two days earlier had frozen in curious, transparent shapes on the branches of the trees. We all stood expectantly in a semi-circle, huddled up in the wool blankets we'd been given. Only Father stood erect, towering above everyone else, wearing his eternal brimmed hat, expensive, now oil-stained wool coat, and his fine leather gloves that were already worn out. The minutes passed and expectations grew, gradually mixed with impatience.

A cold wind blew, stinging our exposed cheekbones. Men and women pulled up the edges of their blankets to protect their faces. A wave of whispers passed through the crowd. Many tried to hazard a guess as to the nature of the message, a message so important that Spitzer himself had to deliver it.

It grew so cold that people started to jump up and down to keep warm. A few had even given up and returned to the boats when, suddenly, the sound of an engine was heard and a long, black car appeared around a bend in the road. It slowly drove closer, and we all waited to hear what the man in charge of this trip had to say. He emerged from the car, an elderly man with gentle, yet tormented features, dressed in a long wool coat and a gray broad-brimmed hat similar to Father's. A cigarette was stuck in the corner of his mouth, and he walked with stern, assured steps to where his deputy, Naftali Bata, was waiting for him. Everyone called Naftali Bata Gedalja "the almighty," because there was nothing he couldn't organize in his quiet and pleasant way.

They shook hands. Mr. Spitzer threw away his cigarette stub and began by thanking everyone who had helped to arrange this trip, such as Avriel and Braginsky, whose names I'd heard before. He went on with a detailed and tiring description of his efforts to enable us to continue our journey. He had sent letters with pleas for help to everyone. But so far, he'd encountered only inertia and apathy. He was trying to arrange a large ship to carry us all from Sulina Bay to the Mediterranean. He detailed the letters he'd sent, the ones he'd received, and even took them out of his pocket and waved them at us. And yet, in spite of all his efforts, the ship that was supposed to reach Sulina had not yet arrived. The moment he received a telegram with news of the waiting ship, he'd give the order for the boats to continue their journey.

"It's very close. Closer than you imagine. But so far, a week has gone by and the telegram is yet to come."

A wave of booing and catcalls passed through the crowd of listeners. Sime tried to shush everyone, claiming he had some more important news for us, but people simply wouldn't let him speak. Finally, "the almighty" Bata asked for permission to speak and managed to silence the crowd, though not for long.

"Ladies and gentlemen, I'm sorry I can't bring you good news, but we must be patient. We've decided to wait in Prahovo Bay until the telegram arrives."

The booing and insults hurled by the crowd at Sime Spitzer became louder and louder, until two young men leaped forward with raised fists, and shouted, "Liar, liar! Do something, and do it right now!"

Father, who was standing close by, rushed toward them, grabbed one of them by his shoulder, and prevented him from getting any closer to Sime.

"Shame on you, hooligans," he shouted angrily. "He's come to help, and this is how you treat him? Who do you think is feeding you here?"

Sime appeared to feel threatened, because the two burly men who accompanied him shielded him with their bodies as they made their way back to the black car.

The large, yellow December sun was about to set and the bitter huddle of people began to disperse and return to the boats.

Unlike everybody else, I was more concerned with my approaching meeting with Inge that evening and less with the fact we had to wait here for another day or two. This time, she'd promised to come. I thought about how lucky I was to meet such a bewitching person on this trip, and I actually didn't mind if it lasted a few days longer.

That night was even colder than the previous one. Clear skies hung above, embedded with a multitude of twinkling stars. I wore my elegant pants and a short wool coat, and my teeth were chattering with cold. I stood on the bridge leading to the command cabin and looked around. My ears were peeled to hear each footstep from below or from the deck. The river was tranquil, and only ripples of water occasionally brushed against the sides of the boat.

Something in my heart told me that tonight she would come. I waited patiently. Now and then, I walked back and forth on the bridge to relieve the tension and warm myself. And there it was. I heard the sound of footsteps coming up the stairs and saw a shadow approaching. Surely, it must be her.

"Good evening, Hanne," she came up to me. "Have you been waiting long?"

"Not so long this time. I'm so happy you came."

"It's awfully cold," she said. "I should have arranged to meet you somewhere else. I had no idea it was so cold up here."

"Look up. See how beautiful the sky is. 'The hoar-frost fell on a night in Spring… It fell on the young and tender blossoms…'"

"I didn't know you had such a poetic soul."

"The poem? It isn't mine. It's Heine's."

"You know Heine? They didn't teach us about him at all."

"That's because he's Jewish. My mother has all his books. Goethe's too."

"Your mother looks like such a gentle woman. I had no idea she was so well-educated."

"She used to hold literary evenings in our house. People would read poetry while she played the piano."

"Your mother looked very special to me right from the start. I'm not like that. I'm more practical. And I consider myself a believer. It's how I was brought up."

"What do you mean, 'a believer'?" I asked, surprised.

"A believer in Almighty God and the commandments of Judaism. You don't observe the religious commandments, do you?"

"No. Father only goes to synagogue on Yom Kippur. But so what? That doesn't make us any less Jewish. We're simply more liberal-minded."

"You don't understand," she said, and I felt her drawing closer. "I meant to say that when you are closer to religion, you are also closer to God, and being closer to God means upholding his commandments."

"Yes, but you can be both Jewish and liberal. You don't need to observe all the *taryag mitzvoth*, the 613 religious commandments of the Torah," I answered.

"Enough, Hanne. Stop philosophizing and come closer. Can't you see I'm freezing?"

I drew closer to her, until our bodies rubbed against each other through the layers of coats separating them.

"That's better," she said. "Now give me your hand."

I offered her a hesitant hand, and she held it in her own ungloved hand.

"Well, that's so much better," she said and rubbed her hand against mine.

"I didn't mean to philosophize." I felt the need to apologize. "We may not be so close to God or observe the laws of the religion, but I think God isn't about the spirit, or divine spirit, or the existence of God as a spiritual entity, but a matter of the heart, between one person and another. That is what they taught us in Akiba."

"What's Akiba?" she asked.

"Akiba is a Zionist youth movement, but they follow the principles of Judaism in a much more liberal way," I tried to explain.

"What about us? Does that mean we aren't liberal?" she asked, offended.

"No. We have a Shabbat meal on Friday evening, for example, but we don't need to actually observe the Shabbat."

"That's odd. It's the first time I've ever heard of anything like it. My mother always says that you can't be half-pregnant."

"What does that have to do with it?"

"You'll see…"

"Why can't we observe some of the commandments and ignore those that aren't suitable to our day and age?"

"But that's the whole point. Either you're a believer or you're not. We are believers."

"Well, we also have the Hashomer Hatzair here. What do you think about them?"

"They're even worse…"

"I prefer the way things are done in Akiba. It seems much better to me."

"Just you wait. I'll teach you things about Judaism you never knew or even imagined. For example, what is this week's *parashat hashavua*?"[10]

"How should I know?"

"See? '*Vayeira*. And the LORD appeared unto him…' I'll be happy to help you become really Jewish."

"Don't worry. I already feel very Jewish or I wouldn't be here. We had a great life on Dedinje Hill. We had a car, a swimming pool, a tennis court…"

"So what happened?"

"It has to do with the Serbs. They don't like people who served in the Hungarian army. My father served as an officer in the Hungarian

---

10 The weekly portion of the Torah read in Jewish synagogues. Vayeira, for example, is the fourth weekly parashah, or Torah portion.

army during the war, and that's why they have a score to settle with him."

"So that's the reason you're here?"

"That's why they boycotted him, denied him citizenship, and stopped giving him work."

"You have no idea what's going on in Germany. This isn't about work anymore. This is about life and death."

"My Mother heard everything. She has parents and a brother in Vienna. She's the one who finally pressured father to emigrate. But let's forget about all that. It's not why I asked you up here. Look up. What a beautiful starry night! You can't see anything like this in the city."

We looked up at the night sky with its myriad glittering stars.

"Can you see the Big Dipper? There, see? Isn't it beautiful? No, not there. Over there." I turned her in the direction of the north. "There's the North Star, right at the end of its shaft, see?" I felt the warmth of her breath on my cheek.

"I never knew their names. I've heard about the North Star, but never knew you could actually see it."

"There you are. You might learn a thing or two from me as well…"

"Do you see? You and I look at the sky in different ways… You give the stars names and recognize them, while I learned to look at them and say, 'When I consider thy heavens, the work of thy fingers, the moon and the stars, which thou hast ordained.'"

I felt so close to her at that moment. The warmth of her body seemed to flow into mine through all the layers of our clothes. We were both looking up at the star-strewn sky, when suddenly, she quoted in a voice full of yearning:

"All truly wise thoughts have been thought already thousands of times; but to make them truly ours, we must think them over again honestly, till they take root in our personal experience."

"Goethe..." I answered and immediately realized she also knew something of the great poets. "But what does that have to do with what we were talking about?"

"Can't you see? I'm trying to tell you about the greatness of God, and you're trying to tell me about the greatness of God in a different way, through the stars in heaven. Wise thoughts that we simply try to think about for ourselves."

She looked at her watch. "It's getting late. I need to go. Just tell me how your mother is doing. Is she better now?"

"Since the last crisis, she's been fine. But she was really miserable. She told Father that perhaps we should leave the boat, but he convinced her that everything would turn out all right."

"Your mother is a very special woman. I really feel close to her. She reminds me a bit of my own mother. I'm sorry, but I need to go back now. I have a long day tomorrow."

We parted with a handshake, and she hurried off the bridge.

The longed-for telegram did not arrive in the next few days, and we continued to dock at Prahovo until the last day of December, when the officials of the state river shipping line instructed the captains of the boats to return to the winter bay at the Kladovo fishing village, not far from the Djerdap Gorge, opposite the Romanian town of Drobeta-Turnu Severin.

THE ICE HARBOR, JANUARY–MARCH 1940

For the past two weeks, the boats have been stranded in the icy Klado-vo harbor, waiting for the ice to thaw. Other boats, apart from our three, are docked in the harbor, but most of them are empty. On our boats, the crowded conditions as well as the cold and tension are un-bearable; a terrible uncertainty hovers over us all, and rumors are rife.

Everyone here hates the rumormongers, but we are all preoccupied with rumors; when will we sail on, why are we stuck here in the first place? There's so much confusion. Some people don't believe the ice is the real reason for our stop.

Today, Father was angry with me again for eavesdropping like a spy.

"When will you stop this annoying habit?" he grumbled. "It's not an attractive quality in a young man. Find something better to do with your time."

Actually, there were better things to do on the boat, like getting water, for example. We needed water for drinking, cooking, and wash-ing. I took turns drawing water with a few other boys my age on the boat, including Efraim and Jacob.

Jacob, who suffered from the cold temperatures on the boat more than anyone, was the son of a wealthy family from Berlin. His parents had wanted to send their children away from Germany at all costs, but their daughter, Eva, and their youngest son, David, were too young to travel on their own, and Jacob was the only one who could join the cruise. His parents took comfort in the fact that at least one of their children was already safe.

Water duty consisted of drawing water from the well or the river and carrying it in containers to the boat. We took turns going to the well behind the post office, lowering the bucket to the bottom, and raising it back up with a handle. Once that task was completed, we had to be careful not to slip with the bucket on the frozen ice on our way back to the boat. The easier water duty was pulling up cold river water in a bucket from the wooden bridge next to the boat. We used the river water for washing.

One morning, after drawing water from the river, I saw Efraim running toward me from the direction of the well, looking very upset and confused.

"It's because of the damned frost. The rope was so slippery that the bucket slid from my hands into the well."

The rope tied to the bucket was covered in a thin layer of frost, and Efraim could hardly pull it up with the full bucket. He was afraid the bucket would slip and fall. When the bucket was already close, he tried to pull it to him, but the rope, almost fully stretched, suddenly slid from his hands and fell back into the well along with the bucket. Efraim got scared, left everything, and ran back to the harbor.

"Don't tell anyone," he urgently pleaded with me. "I feel bad for dropping the bucket."

"But you could have tried to bring it up again," I told him reproachfully.

"I was afraid it would just happen again and everyone would find out. Promise you won't tell anyone."

Of course I promised, and no one ever discovered the incident. Only now, while writing my memoirs, am I allowing myself to reveal it. Who knows if anyone will ever read them?

Jacob frequently asked me to replace him on water duty. He suffered greatly from the cold. His feet were frozen, and some days he could barely walk. One day, I accompanied him to the grocery store, not far from the harbor. He bought a bottle of *slivovitz*, which he said would warm him more than all the blankets they'd given us. He tried to convince me to drink with him and said many of the adults, and even some of the younger people on the boat, drank alcohol to keep warm. He pleaded with me to try and promised it would help me bear the chilling temperatures during the nights.

One evening, when I came to visit him on board the *Kraljica Marija*, I found him sprawled on a wooden bench, an almost empty *slivovitz* bottle next to him, and Inge leaning over him and bandaging his leg. Shlomit, his girlfriend, placed rags soaked with hot water on his other ankle.

Jacob urged me to drink with him. I took a large sip, just like Father does, then another one, and felt a fireball descending from my gullet all the way down to my stomach, spreading warmth and a pleasant stirring sensation throughout my body.

At this time, our stay in the officers' dining room came to an end, and we had to go back up on deck and huddle with everyone else. When Officer Ivanović returned from his vacation, he politely asked Father to clear the small room. He was a very strict officer who showed no favoritism, even though he really liked Father and invited him to drink and play cards with him in the small room. It was Mr. Reiss and Sylvie, his large, loud-mouthed wife, who were offended by the evacuation. Father had invited them to share the officers' dining room with us so he wouldn't be seen to be self-centered. Even though Father had always socialized with people of his status, he didn't want to appear over privileged here.

Mr. Reiss was on the verge of hysteria when he found out we had to clear out of our little "royal suite."

"What do you mean, 'clear the room'?" he cried out. "Please tell them we have two small daughters. One of them is only four years old."

"No. We're not leaving, Emil," his wife was even angrier.

Father had to make it clear to them that we didn't have much of a choice.

We went back to sleeping next to the chimney. Father on the floor, almost touching the chimney, Mother on a wide bench with a backrest next to him, and Pauli and me on the floor next to the bench. The next day, I heard them whispering before going to sleep.

"You reap what you sow. I told you not to invite them. They seemed like a pair of ingrates to me right from the start. I know their kind well."

"They have a lot of nerve. They make it sound as if I signed an agreement with them," said Father angrily.

"You probably invited them thinking you'd have someone to play cards with. I know you."

"Loui, I already explained to you it wouldn't have looked good if we were the only family in that room."

"At least you get along with him. I can't stand his wife," said Mother, lowering her voice. "She talks as if she were the only one suffering here. As if I'm here on a pleasure cruise…"

"Oh, Loui, let's just forget this episode. It will pass. After all, a week or two from now we'll be in Israel and can forget about the whole thing."

"You know what I think now, Emil? Maybe the doctor was right. Maybe this trip just doesn't do my nerves any good."

"But why, Loui? You know everything will turn out all right in the end. We just need a little patience."

"Look at what's going on all around us. It looks like utter chaos. No one really knows what's going on."

"So what do you suggest? That we get off now?"

"No. Of course not. I'm just thinking aloud, just between the two of us."

"Are you having second thoughts?"

"Not yet. I won't be the one to ruin our chances. You know me. When I decide to do something, I stick it out to the end."

"True. Even when you agreed to come with me to Yugoslavia, 'that backward country' as your mother called it, you made a brave decision and acted upon it."

"That's right, darling. Because I knew I had someone I could trust and I was right. Mother even apologized. Now come closer and hug me. Tell me that everything will be all right this time as well."

"Trust me. I'm only concerned about the fact our furniture might get to Haifa before we do."

"Never mind. The furniture can wait. Let it suffer a little too." I finally heard the sound of her laughter.

I fell asleep, waking in the middle of the night to the sound of Mother's sighs.

Father woke up as well, went to the toilet, and came back. I still can't get used to this nightmare they call toilets here. I was afraid to go there last night, the obstacles in the form of sleeping men, women, and children on the way. But my stomach was pounding and aching for the third night in a row, and I simply couldn't go on like this.

The way to the toilets seems like a never-ending nightmare, and once there, I realize I'm not the only one. The stench and filth are disgusting, and I have to force myself to enter the overflowing toilet cabin instead of getting off the boat to disappear among the buildings in the harbor under cover of darkness.

***

"What's wrong, Hanne?" asked Mother after she saw me running to the toilet during the night and that morning.

I told her I wouldn't be coming for breakfast because I had no appetite, and then I curled up and lay on the bench. I felt all the strength drain from my body.

"You look very pale. I think I'll call Dr. Bezalel."

Dr. Bezalel felt my stomach with skillful fingers, pressed here, released there, and determined, "Dysentery. Four other children on the lower level have caught it."

"What do we do?" asked Mother with concern.

"Maintain hygiene so you won't get it as well. Take care to wash your hands before eating and after visiting the toilet cabin. Wash them with soap! I'll ask for more soap to be brought from the storage room and see that it's placed on all the sinks. And drink water. Lots of water!" Dr. Bezalel finished his instructions.

"This is bad. Hanne is so skinny as it is," Mother voiced her concern.

"Normally, I'd isolate him, but we haven't got an isolation room on the boat as yet. You'll need to take care of him by yourselves for now," he said and turned to go.

Mother immediately began to follow Dr. Bezalel's instructions.

"Come, Pauli. Let's go to the kitchen and ask for a pitcher of drinking water."

Mimi, the wife of Fredl, the composer, was on duty in the kitchen and would only agree to give them two cups.

"I'm sorry, but I was instructed not to give anyone more than two cups. There's a shortage of drinking water."

Mother silently took the two cups. I couldn't bring myself to drink more than one anyway. I tried forcing myself to drink more, but simply couldn't.

Mother and Father urged me to follow the doctor's instructions.

"Are you sure that's what they told you? A shortage of drinking water?" Father sounded angry.

"Yes," said Mother. "It was Mimi, Fredl's wife, who was on kitchen duty. It's not her fault." Mother tried to defend Mimi, a thin and fragile-looking young woman who arrived pregnant for the journey.

"She's lucky to have Fredl. He takes care of her really well."

Mr. Fredl, whom everyone said was an excellent composer, was constantly busy with his sheet music and his trumpet, which he guarded like diamond treasure.

Mother had immediately noticed that Mimi needed help.

"Setting out on such a journey while pregnant is very irresponsible," she said.

Mother had forgotten she herself had objected to the doctor's advice to leave the boat in her condition. But her health had improved since then. Now she works in the storage room, sorting out clothes, blankets, and food rations for the kitchen. Inge had taught her how to mend socks and woolen hats. At first, Inge worked in the storage room and suggested that Mother help there, that it would help pass the time and she could forget her troubles. But then Dr. Bezalel had taken Inge to help him care for the sick.

That very same day, after the doctor examined me, Inge handed out notices with strict instructions from the doctor—six important rules that would help the passengers avoid catching dysentery. She gave a written notice to every few families and added verbal explanations.

"Drink lots of water," she told me. "I'll see you once you get better."

After barely eating a thing for twenty-four hours, I was weaker and could barely stand on my feet. Mother kept going to the kitchen to get water for me, until she said they wouldn't give her any more. They were saving water for cooking dinner. Father exploded when he heard that.

"No water? What is the meaning of this? Do they want our son to die from dehydration?" His face turned red. I had never seen his eyes blaze with such anger, not even when I was seven years old and we'd gone to one of the large buildings he'd built in the city where he'd screamed at the contractor. I was so afraid of him back then that I hid behind a nearby tree and waited for him to calm down.

"I'm going to the kitchen right now," he said angrily. "I'll show them."

"Calm down, Emil. I'll go again soon and talk to Carl; he's in charge of the kitchen. I know him because I bring him food supplies from the storage room. It's just that he wasn't there now," Mother tried to calm him down.

"Don't tell me to calm down! This is our son!" he was very upset. Mother ran after him and tried to stop him.

"Father, it's all right. I'm fine," I tried to call with what little strength I had, but he didn't hear me. He shrugged off the coat Mother grabbed in the hope of stopping him and went on his way.

I couldn't see the rest. I heard people running and shouting and kitchen pots crashing on the floor or against a wall. Two days later, Inge told me what had happened. I was already hospitalized in the floating isolation ward Dr. Bezalel had managed to arrange with the aid of the Federation of Jewish Communities. Inge took care of me and the other patients.

Mother was worried about my condition and called Dr. Bezalel again. He arrived with a grim expression on his face and told us there were eight more patients. One of them was Jacob, who was severely ill. There were also two adults among the patients, but Jacob's condition continued to deteriorate daily. The doctor was concerned about the possibility of mass infection and asked the Federation to provide him with one of the unused ferries docking at the winter bay and equip it with hospital cots. It would serve as an isolation room for all the patients. He said that if we followed the rules, the disease could be contained within three or four days.

The following morning, a small ferry docked next to our three boats. It looked more like a large raft than a ferry. By then, we were over twenty patients. We were transferred to hospital cots on the ferry, and we each received several woolen blankets. Dr. Bezalel put Inge in charge of the isolation room. He gave her a white nurse's cap, so everyone would recognize her. The cap made her look even more beautiful. She walked among us, poured water into cups, took our temperatures, and kept meticulous charts, just like the nurses I'd seen in the city, when Klarie was hospitalized.

"Now I know exactly what I'll do in Israel. I'll go to nursing school and help sick people. I heard there's a nursing school in Jerusalem, on Mount Scopus," she said, while sitting on my bed and pouring water into my cup. "Just so you know, your father can be really scary sometimes," she suddenly added.

"Why is that? Because of what happened with the water two days ago?"

"Yes. He seems like such a quiet and noble man, but when he loses his temper, God help us all…"

"What happened? I only know it helped get this ferry here."

"I was there, and all I can say is that something terrible could have happened. Your mother and I tried to stop him, but it was impossible. He screamed at everyone there, claiming that some people are getting more water than others on the boat."

"But it's true. He was right. I've seen the Zukerman sisters showering with buckets of water every morning."

"But they're not using drinking water, Hanne. You're not making any sense!"

"I'll admit they're using river water, but I've also seen people getting buckets of water from the well."

"Nonsense! Who told you that?"

"Efraim. One day, the father of those two sisters took the bucket Efraim had struggled to bring from the well, and after Efraim walked off, he used the drinking water from the bucket to wash his two girls."

"All right, but it has nothing to do with this. Do you want to hear what happened in the kitchen, or don't you?"

"Of course… You know I'm dying of curiosity."

"It was scary. He screamed at Carl that he'd kill him unless he gave him some water for his sick son right away."

"I can't believe it. He's never acted that way. He's always so restrained. I don't understand."

"It's because of all the pressure here. Everyone reacts differently. You can actually see people's true faces, instead of the masks they wear most of the time."

"Are you trying to tell me this is my father's true face?"

"Maybe…"

Dr. Bezalel arrived.

"I see you're having an interesting conversation," he said smilingly. "Just don't forget the other patients. Do you have this morning's report?"

"I'm just finishing it."

"Bring it to me when you're done. I think I'll transfer two more patients here," he said and turned toward the bridge connecting the isolation room with the *Kraljica Marija*.

"You've become very busy," I told her.

"Yes, I must go now. I don't want to upset Dr. Bezalel. He's been working so hard these last few days."

"So have you. Isn't that true?"

"Yes, but all the responsibility is on his shoulders. Everyone expects him to solve their problems because he's a doctor. What could they possibly expect from me? I have to go now."

All that time, Jacob lay burning with fever next to me.

Once he started to feel better, he told me about his family in Berlin. About his sister, Eva, who was one year his junior, his little brother, David, and his father, a successful fur trader, a stern and serious man.

"He says I'm reckless and confused," Jacob complained. He told me the money his father had given him had almost run out. "If he knew what I'd spent the money on, he'd go crazy," he said, on the verge of tears. "And it's not that he's against drinking, but he'd tell me, 'Why didn't you buy smaller bottles? Why did you buy the most expensive ones?' You saw what I've been buying, didn't you? So tell me, Hanne, what do you think I should do? Do you think I should tell him the truth? That I ran out of money?"

I didn't know what to say.

"I don't know. My situation is very different from yours," I answered him.

He persisted.

"I have an uncle named Max. He really likes me and always said that I could turn to him if I ever needed anything. What do you say?"

But I had no answer for him.

Inge had taken good care of Jacob, and so did Shlomit, his girl-friend, who often came from the *Kraljica Marija* to visit him. She sat beside him, even though the doctor had warned her of infection. But she was a brave and practical girl and occasionally helped Inge with the other patients.

***

Toward the end of the week, the isolation room had become intolerably crowded. Luckily, I already felt well enough to give up my bed to another patient.

"I'm going ashore," I told Mother, putting on some warm clothes. "I could do with some fresh air."

"Don't stay outside for too long," said Mother. "I have enough to worry about."

I walked off the boat along the slippery gangway and walked along the river, toward the edge of the village.

Cold air filled my nostrils. Everyone sat in the crowded boats all day long. Maybe if they'd get out for some fresh air more often, there'd be less illness on the boats. I suddenly felt pretty much on my own. Pauli, thanks to his charisma and leadership skills, had befriended the Hechalutz and Blau-Weiss youths from Vienna, and they were always busy with social activities and lectures. I couldn't find a place for myself among them. Inge was the only one my age I could actually speak to, but she was busy with her new duties now.

I reached a small dock where fishing boats were tied to docking poles on the platform. There were several buildings next to the dock.

They looked abandoned, but emitted a strong smell of fish and had tall towers of crates next to them, probably intended for storing fish.

An old man sat at the entrance to one of the buildings; next to him were large piles of fishing nets. He held the end of a net in one hand and a large needle in the other and was preoccupied with his work. A packet of cigarettes and a small glass with the remains of coffee were on the chair beside him.

"Hey, boy, what are you doing here?" he called to me.

"I'm just out for a walk," I told him. "I come from the boats in the ice harbor."

"Oh, you're one of the Jews."

"Yes," I answered. "What are you doing?"

"Can't you see for yourself?"

"Is that your work?"

"Look how many nets I have here. Doesn't it look like work to you?"

His work looked endlessly repetitive. There were countless holes in the net, and I couldn't tell which ones he'd already mended.

"It looks like hard work," I watched his fingers running back and forth between the loops of the net, tying, stretching, and moving on. I couldn't tell which parts needed mending.

"It's all a matter of understanding the method. To the onlooker, the holes appear to be endless."

His lips remained pursed around a cigarette butt as he spoke, and its long trail of ash threatened to drop to the ground at any moment. He took one final drag from the short stub, blew out blue smoke rings, and dropped it on the snow, painting it yellow and black.

"The way I see the net is different from the way you see it. I can see exactly what has already been mended and what still needs mending."

He became immersed in his work again. His fingers fluttered nimbly along the net. I felt a mixture of pity and compassion.

"When will you be finished with the nets?" I asked.

"At about two o'clock. Then I'll eat the sandwiches I've brought in my lunch box. What's your name?" he asked. "You haven't introduced yourself. My name is Dragisa Petrović. You can call me Dragisa."

"I'm Hanne. It's short for Johann. My mother is a great admirer of Goethe."

"So how come you're Jewish? That's a German name."

"Right. My mother speaks German."

"So you're not really Jewish?"

"We're a Jewish family, but we used to live in Belgrade because of Father's job."

"My family has lived in the same house in Kladovo for nine generations."

"And what do they all do here?"

"As you can see," he said, pointing at the fishing nets. "Most of them are fishermen. Some are farmers and raise cows and pigs next to the house."

"And there's enough for everyone to make a living?"

"Not really. The river is not what it used to be. There are fewer fish and too many fishermen. I don't go out on the river with the boat anymore. I'm too old for that. So they pay me to mend nets."

"And don't you get bored mending nets all the time?" I asked.

"I learned to get over it," he answered with a smile. "Do you know how to solve crossword puzzles?"

"Of course I do," I answered. "Do you solve crossword puzzles?"

I never would have thought a simple man like him, who spent his days mending fishing nets, would know how to solve crossword puzzles.

"Not only do I solve them, I also invent them," he said proudly.

"Can you give me an example?" I wanted to make sure he wasn't simply making up stories about himself.

"Sure," he answered, flashing a toothless smile. "A Jewish-Austrian author, five letters."

"Well, that's easy," I said. "Stefan Zweig."

"Easy indeed," he answered and took the cigarette box from his pocket again, along with a bundle of papers. "German composer, five letters," he fired at me.

"There's lots," I said and counted the ones that came into my mind. "Handel, Wagner, Bruch, which one did you mean?"

"Wait," he said, picking up a page full of empty squares. He flicked the cigarette from between his fingers and took a pencil from his pocket. "Let's write a list of words and then create questions for them."

"That's a great idea. We could memorize the words we're studying like that. We'll choose a subject. Geography or history, for example. We'll put in words such as names of mountains, countries, major and lesser known cities: Drina, Danube, Yangtze, Yellow River, Seine, Rhine."

He wrote the words into the empty squares with large letters, some vertically and others horizontally. Then we added the names of mountains, crossing the words.

And so we sat and created our first crossword puzzle, and I didn't notice how time flew by. Only when I glanced at my watch and saw that it was almost two o'clock did I realize I needed to run back to the boat.

"I have to hurry back to the boat now," I said. "Can I have the crossword puzzle?"

"Sure. It's yours," he answered.

"I'll come again tomorrow, and we'll make another one."

"Sure. I'll have coffee waiting for you."

"I don't drink coffee yet," I told him.

"Then I'll teach you."

***

As expected, Mother was furious.

"Where have you been? I told Father we should go looking for you."

"I'm not a child anymore, Mother. You don't need to look for me. I met someone interesting. A toothless old man who mends fishing nets and knows everything about crossword puzzles. Where's Pauli?"

"I haven't seen him since this morning. He's probably on the *Kraljica Marija*. He's found some friends there."

I knew that Inge was busy and went across the connecting bridge to the *Kraljica Marija* with the crossword puzzle in my pocket.

Pauli was sitting with a group of Viennese youths. They were singing "Capitan, Capitan" in Viennese German, accompanied by Fredl on the accordion. "Capitan, Ho, Capitan, Capitan the only one. He feared neither cannon nor gun."

They invited me to join them, but I didn't feel comfortable about it and went to look for Efraim. I found him with Jacob. They were playing checkers on an improvised cardboard board Jacob had drawn. The wooden pieces had been carved by Joseph the carpenter. After Jacob's second victory, Efraim's face reddened with anger, and I suggested they try to solve the puzzle I'd prepared with Petrović. At first, they refused and said that crossword puzzles were boring, but once I managed to convince them and saw how enthusiastically they competed, looking for the right word for each question, I realized the puzzle would be even more popular if I could create a competition.

After a while, Efraim had to leave, and Jacob took his father's last letter out of his pocket.

"Do you remember I talked to you about whether or not I should tell my father? Just listen to what he wrote me.

Why didn't you listen to my advice about saving money? If you'd have listened, you wouldn't be in this miserable state, without a penny in your pocket. If you buy yourself alcohol, buy smaller bottles. Don't buy the most expensive ones. Who on earth would come up with such a stupid idea? Of course you need to keep warm with a little drink during the winter. But not when the weather is warm. I'm told that you keep buying things without thinking twice about the cost. I'm very disappointed in you. You've bought so many things—you need suitcases and backpacks to store them in. Why don't you consult with Reiss's brother? How many times have I told you to do that? And most importantly: when you need money, write to me and not to Uncle Max.

This is simply unbelievable. How do your friends manage?

Many of them probably have nothing…

I calmed him down and said it's good that he'd told the truth about asking for money from Uncle Max. Then he got upset with me as well. "You don't get it. Uncle Max told on me. That's much worse!"

**

When evening fell, I went to look for Inge in the floating isolation ward. She didn't have much work left to do there, as most of the patients had already been discharged and had returned to the boat.

"We finally got rid of that disease. Just know that Dr. Bezalel deserves a lot of credit for insisting on maintaining hygiene."

"You deserve a lot of credit too."

"You don't know how hard he worked—he kept running around the boat, reminding all the passengers to wash their hands with soap, and making sure there was enough soap at all the sinks."

I told her about Petrović, the old man on shore, and how he hadn't believed I was Jewish with a name like Hanne.

"I also have a German name. But everyone always knows I'm Jewish. Perhaps because of the way I dress…the skirt and all the rest. And I also light Shabbat candles and try to observe all the religious commandments."

"I'm not so sure it's all that important to observe all the religious commandments."

"Back home, when my father was still alive, the Friday night Shabbat meal was truly magical."

"You haven't told me anything about your father. I didn't even know he'd died."

"It was a long time ago, and I don't really feel like talking about it. But he was a very special man. He had a great voice, and when we sang Friday night Shabbat songs, like '*Bo'i Kala*,' he always had tears in his eyes."

"In our house, there was nothing special about Friday night, other than a festive meal."

"That's exactly your problem. You need to rediscover your roots. Wait a minute."

She got up, straightened her skirt, and went to the far end of the ferry, where Dr. Bezalel had instructed her to sleep. She came back two minutes later, holding a small volume that looked like a prayer book.

"Have you ever seen this?" She handed me the book. "I carry it with me wherever I go. *Tseno Ureno*.[11] It was especially written for daughters of Israel who want to understand Torah."

"No, I'm not familiar with it. I never saw my mother or sister reading it."

"I heard about your sister. Klarie, right?" she said sadly. "That was one of the first things your mother told me. She loved her very much. She simply can't get over her death."

Inge took my hand between her palms. I felt heat passing from

---

11 *Tseno Ureno* (צאינה וראינה, *Tze'nah u-Re'nah*), also spelled *Tsene-rene*, was sometimes called the Women's Bible. A Yiddish-language prose work of circa 1590s parallel to the weekly Torah portions of the Pentateuch and Haftorahs used in Jewish worship services.

her body to mine. But then Dr. Bezalel came in and said he needed to examine a patient. He asked Inge to accompany him. Inge hastily dropped my hand and got up.

On my way back to the *Tzar Nikolai*, I passed an empty bed in the floating isolation ward. Suddenly, I heard a woman groaning from one of the beds. I thought there might be a patient there, suffering from stomachaches, but when I looked, I couldn't see anything. I just heard quiet moaning sounds coming from one of the beds that gradually increased. I carefully approached that bed and saw a huge pile of blankets moving up and down. I went even closer, and in the darkness, I saw a woman's head, slightly tilted back. The head belonged to Anita, the woman everyone called "Romantic Anita." There was a strange expression on her face. I wasn't sure if it was pain or pleasure. Her eyes were closed, her mouth slightly open, and she was breathing hard.

"Do you need the doctor?" I asked. I tried to pull down the blanket and, to my amazement, discovered the body of a large man lying on top of her. Both of them were completely naked. I recognized the bald head and broad white back of Shishko, the boat's cook. To my great shame, I only then realized what was happening there. I threw the blanket back over them and fled.

I returned to our corner. Father told me Mother was with Mimi, Fredl's pregnant wife. A few days ago, Mother had told him that Mimi was weak and there was no one to guide her through the stages of pregnancy and birth.

That night, I couldn't fall asleep. I was haunted by the strange sight of Romantic Anita lying naked in bed in the floating isolation ward, with the cook's large body on top of her. I thought of Inge and the way she adhered to the commandments of the book she always kept with her. Her piety seemed a little strange to me, but perhaps it suited her. After all, she wanted to become a nurse and take care of sick people, which was also a *mitzvah*, a good deed in the eyes of God. Then came thoughts of old Petrović, and I kept imagining torn nets and crossword puzzles. Then I remembered Anita's smooth, naked body and her moaning. I wondered if Inge would also lie naked like that one day, sighing in pleasure.

Just as I was on the verge of sleep, loud shouts came from the dining room. I tried to ignore them and go to sleep but saw Father getting dressed to go there. I dressed as well and followed him.

Dozens of men and women were standing in the dining room. They were all screaming and cursing. At first, I couldn't understand who they were screaming at, but then I saw their victim. Little Anita stood there, her hair disheveled, a humiliated and tortured expression on her face. Two large, strong women held her arms. I recognized one of them—the self-righteous Mrs. Zonshein, the only one who could afford to prepare fresh omelets for herself and her daughter every morning. A cardboard sign hung from Anita's shoulders, with words in German saying "I'm a promiscuous whore."

The people standing next to her spat in her face, then moved back to make space for others who wanted to participate in that terrible, humiliating scene.

Mother, who stood next to me, tried to urge Father to do something to stop that shameful act. Then, she couldn't contain her anger anymore and lunged forward toward the women who were holding Anita.

"Shame on you! Animals, all of you! Leave the girl alone!"

But the people in the crowd simply screamed at Mother not to interfere. Mother got closer to Anita and tried to take the sign off her neck, but the two large women pushed her away and cursed her, then held Anita even tighter.

Father began moving toward Mother to try and help her when suddenly, a huge, bald-headed man burst into the screaming crowd. He quickly made his way toward the helpless Anita, pushing aside anyone who stood in his way. Once he reached Anita, he punched the surprised faces of the two women holding her. They were both hurled to the floor, screaming with pain. Shishko took advantage of the element of surprise, wrapped Anita in his big arms, lifted her up, and carried her outside, quickly disappearing from the eyes of the crowd.

Before falling asleep, I kept thinking about Anita and Shishko, about how he'd saved her at such a difficult moment. I heard Mother telling Father, "She's not such a poor soul. I'll go on calling her 'Romantic Anita.' She really is a romantic soul and not a whore at all."

"I'm sorry I couldn't do anything, Loui. By the time I arrived, they were already…"

"At least you tried, Emil. I feel terrible about her. She followed her heart without fear."

"I know someone else who followed her heart…" Father said.

I wondered what he meant. I felt my eyes closing.

***

The sound of the engine turbines woke me early in the morning. They occasionally turn on the engines so the water won't freeze in the pipes. When I looked up, I saw the outside rail coated by a layer of frozen snow. I could hear the snow crunching under the feet of the people walking on the deck above. Suddenly, I heard screaming.

"Help! Help! Someone has fallen into the water! Help! Quickly!"

I pulled on my shoes, grabbed my coat, and ran up on deck. Beneath the bridge stretching from the *Tzar Nikolai* to the *Kraljica Marija*, I saw a man with flailing arms shouting for help. It was Sender, a young Hungarian man. It looked as if he was about to drown. The bridge connecting the boats was made of narrow wooden boards and ropes covered with morning frost—a thin layer of slippery ice stretched to both ends. The bridge itself was also slippery with ice.

The cries for help intensified. Sender was not only about to drown, he was also being swept toward the huge paddle wheel that was still slowly turning. I couldn't understand why no one had stopped the wheel. While we all stood watching helplessly, a splashing sound was heard. Someone had jumped into the freezing water and was quickly swimming toward the hapless Sender. Something about the man's swimming movements looked familiar. I remembered the broad shoulders and the long arm movements from our garden swimming pool. It was Father! How was he able to control his fear and swim in that freezing water toward the spinning paddle wheel? People on the bridge shouted, "Stop the wheel! Quickly! Somebody run and tell them!"

Everyone was astonished by the sight of Father approaching the drowning Sender while the large wheel gradually slowed its rotation. Father was now very close to the now motionless paddle wheel. He grabbed Sender by the scruff of his neck and began to swim with him back to our boat.

Someone threw him a rope from above. Father wrapped the rope around Sender's arms and shoulders; he appeared exhausted. They pulled him up to the height of the bridge, but he was unable to hold on to the slippery planks and slid back down. A young man offered him a hand and helped him hold onto the pole around which the rope was tied. Father managed to pull himself up with the rope.

There was a lot of excitement on deck. Father almost fell when everyone patted him on the back and congratulated him on his daring rescue mission. They all complimented him on his bravery and swimming skills. Mother, who was extremely worried while Father was in the water, welcomed him back with a hug and a kiss.

Life went back to normal, but that morning, people were afraid to stand on the bridge and draw washing water as they normally would. Many simply gave up on their regular morning bath. Even Pauli and I, who would normally bring three buckets each, brought only a single bucket for washing the dishes. Mother was very strict about washing and saw to it that we washed our faces and armpits every morning, in spite of the freezing temperatures, and insisted that we wash our entire bodies once every few days.

The Zukerman family did not give up their morning washing ritual. The father had brought a bucket into the corridor, and the two girls, ten-year-old Rivka'le and her sister, Haya, who was two years older, stood half-naked beside the bucket, and he scrubbed their bodies with a hard bath brush. Their father had tied a blanket to the rail of the boat and held the other end to hide his daughters' nakedness. When I passed by on my way to get another bucket for the kitchen, the blanket slid down for a brief moment. For a single second, the sisters' white bodies were exposed. A deafening scream made all heads turn toward them. Their embarrassed father hurried to raise the blanket and hide them once more.

That morning, rumors started flying about Sender's personal life and the reason for his fall. Sender, married to Hilda, who was about his age, had apparently not joined the transport for ideological reasons. Both he and his wife did not belong to any of the movements. I heard Father telling Mother that there were rumors of Sender having a lover on the *Kraljica Marija*, and that he was hurrying back to his wife from a night with her when he slipped into the water.

"I just cannot believe the sort of people there are here on this voyage," said Mother. "Tell me, Emil, what kind of a man is he? I feel sorry for his poor wife."

Father had become the hero of the day and was surrounded by people who wanted to get close and talk to him. Perhaps now they'll stop thinking his Serbo-Croatian had paved his way to the officers' dining room.

Mother bore her suffering silently and rarely complained aloud. But at night, I would hear her moaning and tossing from side to side. At one point, she simply accepted the harsh conditions of our journey. She realized we would have to spend the harsh winter there, but hoped the future held better things for us. This is why she quietly bore the stale food, the gray, tasteless porridge we received for breakfast, and settled for a slice of bread spread with jam and a cup of lukewarm coffee. She'd also gotten used to the freezing temperatures and cold water, washing our clothes in the water we brought in the bucket. I was in charge of drying them on the hot steam pipe on the engine deck. Mother, who had been so spoiled in Belgrade, always surrounded by maids and servants and who never had to work for her living, suddenly became very active and involved here on the boat. She asked to be allowed to help in the dining room and the storage room; she was willing to do any job. One day, when Inge told her she needed someone to help her in the room where food and clothes from the Federation of Jewish Communities were stored, Mother offered to help without hesitation. Since then, she's there every day from morning till noon, mending and patching torn clothes, distributing clothes, and she also took over the receiving and arranging of food products.

Most people on the boat settled for what little supplies were received from the Federation of Jewish Communities. Even those who had sold their property and joined the voyage with enough money in their pockets weren't eager to flaunt their wealth—apart for a few, like Mrs. Zonshein and her daughter, Rosie. Mrs. Zonshein didn't settle for the meager kitchen meals like the rest of us. The daily ceremony in which she prepared a two-egg omelet for her daughter and herself enraged many members of the group. Teddy, our guide, was especially sensitive about the subject. He talked to us a lot about things like sharing a destiny and mutual responsibility. This morning, when he saw Mrs. Zonshein breaking two eggs into a frying pan resting on an oven, he could no longer contain himself and said to her, "Mrs. Zonshein, you are preparing a feast fit for a king…"

"You are more than welcome to join us," answered Mrs. Zonshein.

"No, thank you, Mrs. Zonshein. I eat the same meals as my group members, and we all receive our rations from the Federation of Jewish Communities."

Teddy, whose full name was Theodor, was a twenty-three-year-old Viennese, with a highly developed sense of responsibility. He saw us teenagers as his protégés. When I was sick and hospitalized in the floating isolation ward, he visited me at least once a day, brought me tea, and sat there talking to me. At the Hanukkah party, over a month ago, he took all the party preparations upon himself and assigned roles to everyone. I really wanted the role of Judas Maccabeus, but as usual, Pauli ended up getting that part, and everyone burst out laughing when he went on stage and recited the lines from Handel's oratorio. It was funny to see a child with such a European face performing the part of a hero in the ancient land of Israel. Teddy hosted the entire event. He also wrote new and contemporary lyrics to the song "Mi Y'malel."[12] Martha, who had been a singing teacher in Vienna, conducted the children's choir she'd cultivated on board the boat. Mr. Fredl accompanied the singing with his accordion, and for a short time, we all forgot about our troubles and rejoiced with some genuine Hanukkah potato latkes.

After his confrontation with Mrs. Zonshein, Teddy came to us very upset.

"She has some nerve. And in front of everyone, no less. If there is an equal ration per person, everyone should share equally." Then he

---

12   "Mi Y'malel" (or "Mi Yimalel") (Hebrew: מי ימלל "Who can retell?") is a very well-known Hebrew Hanukkah song. The opening line—which literally means "Who can retell the mighty feats of Israel?"—is a secular rewording of Psalms 106:2, which reads "Who can retell the mighty feats of God?"

turned to me, "Hanne, I want you to be in charge of telling all the youth on board that there will be a talk with Zeev Dvoriansky this morning. At ten o'clock on board the *Tzar Dusan*, all right?" Then he added, half-jokingly, hinting at this morning's incident, "Just be careful while crossing the bridge."

I had to finish washing the dishes first. Pauli and I were on duty that day. My hands were red from the cold water and mounting piles of soaped dishes next to me. They hadn't prepared us for such duties at summer camp in the mountains. Just a year ago, we were at the forest camp in Slovenia, sleeping in our pajamas in wooden huts in the forest. No one there had ever thought of anything like preparing food or washing dishes, especially in the cold February temperatures. The kitchen staff had been in charge of such duties, and our job was to have fun. The food was great, there were tennis and volleyball courts, and the lake with its pleasant turquoise waters invited us in for a dip.

Pauli brought me another pile of dishes. He looked like a ragged, homeless refugee. Only a year ago, he was crowned as the summer camp's tennis champion, towering above everyone else, with his winning smile and green eyes that attracted all the girls.

I remembered an event that had taken place in a forest in Ljubljana, at which Pauli had been awarded a medal for beating the Croatian champion. He wore his white tennis clothes, and his golden forelock was carefully combed to the right. He held the tennis racket Father had bought him the year before for the annual tournament, the new medal dangling from his neck.

We used to go out on field activities. We thought of ourselves as very mature, and our instructors taught us how to survive in the wild, but no one back then had any idea of what real survival meant—survival as taught here by that eternal boy scout Zeev Dvoriansky. After seven motionless weeks on the Danube, he'd managed to infect us all with his enthusiasm for history, and no one would dream of missing one of his classes. Zeev first taught on board the *Tzar Dusan*, and then moved to the floating school, where the isolation ward used to be.

While I was busy washing the soap from the plates, Inge suddenly came up behind me, a broad smile on her face.

"You'll only be done tonight at that pace," she said. "Let me help you."

"No need, you have enough work with your group as it is."

"I also wanted to tell you we probably shouldn't meet this evening," she said in a low voice.

"Why not?"

"I heard some people talking about us this morning."

"What could they possibly say about us?" I asked. "We meet on the bridge in the evening, take a stroll outside, or visit the net-storage shed. What's wrong with that?"

"No, Hanne, you don't understand where this is coming from…"

"I don't know what you mean."

"With us, the Mizrahi Movement people, chastity is a way of life. I don't want people to talk about me as if I'm…"

"You shouldn't worry about what people say. We feel good together, don't we?"

"Yes, Hanne. But you know what? Your father, he's… He's not really…"

"What about my father?" I was surprised.

"I see the way he looks at me, the way he ignores me, as if he were angry…"

"My father? Angry?" I placed the semi-washed plate beside the pile and wiped my hands on my wet pants. "I don't know what you're talking about!"

"Hanne, come on. I've already told you this before. In a different way, perhaps…"

"I don't remember you ever telling me something like that about my father. He's a wonderful man."

"Yes, wonderful. A hero as well. We all saw how he jumped into the cold water this morning to save Sender," she said, fixing the kerchief on her head. "Maybe he doesn't like me because I'm too religious for his taste. He probably thinks I'm not a suitable match for his son."

"No way! My father's a very liberal man."

"Yes, I've noticed just how liberal he is," she said angrily. "You should have heard the contempt in his voice when he answered friends from my group who invited him to pray the *Shacharit* morning prayer with them. I'm not even talking about his not putting on tefillin in the morning, but why does he look down on anything to do with religion?"

"It's not like that," again I tried to protect him. "He just wants to be left alone to live life his own way. He doesn't want other people to dictate to him." I motioned with my finger for emphasis, "And he especially doesn't like all the external, ceremonial aspects of religion."

"It doesn't matter. Let's not get into it now, because it's not what I wanted to talk to you about."

"What did you want to talk to me about?"

"About the fact that people are talking about us, pointing a finger at me when I go past."

"So what? It's probably just a few bored chatterers."

"What's that? Did you just invent a new word again?"

"I can't believe you're influenced by the fact that people are talking about you and want to change your behavior because of it. You of all people. I always thought you were strong-willed and independent. Now you tell me you're influenced by gossip?"

"When it comes to such matters, maybe I'm not as strong as you think I am, Hanne. Please try to understand where I'm coming from."

"Look, Inge, about my father. I can talk to him; find out what he really thinks."

"No, no! Don't talk to him. Maybe we just shouldn't be seen so much in public together."

"I think you're just imagining things."

"I'm not imagining anything, Hanne."

"What are you saying? That we won't be meeting on the bridge this evening?"

"No. And I don't think we'll be meeting tomorrow evening either. Let's just try and give each other some space for a while," she said and turned to leave.

I stood there, rooted to the spot for a few seconds. I hadn't expected anything like that. I understand the people in Mizrahi. I'm not angry at them. It's just their way of life. But my father? Why was he letting Inge feel unwanted? I joylessly turned back to the freezing water in the bucket. The pile I'd already cleared had returned to its original height with new plates Pauli had brought.

The dining room at the *Tzar Dusan* was already full when I got there. The youth sat on the floor and the adults on the surrounding benches. I sought Inge among them in vain. She didn't come. I was afraid she was already trying to avoid me.

We all deeply admired Zeev, the eternal boy scout. We called him that because he was a member of the boy scouts in Germany, then he was in charge of Hechalutz training and the Aliyat Hano'ar organization in Austria. Dizzy, his girlfriend, a short, smiley woman, was on the boat with him, and they spent a lot of time together.

This was our third meeting with him, and each one was more fascinating than the last. He spoke about topics related to our lives on the boats, as well as news from the war. Today, he spoke about day and night navigation and navigation systems on sea and land. He promised we'd go up on deck on a bright night, and he'd teach us to recognize the stars and constellations, especially the North Star.

At the end of the meeting, Zeev suggested that we try and solve a geographical quiz he'd prepared on the subject. I raised my hand and told him I had a crossword puzzle we could all solve together about the same subject—rivers, mountains, cities, and towns all over the world.

"Only if you'll draw it on the blackboard for us," said Zeev. "Next lesson, come a few minutes early and draw the crossword puzzle on the blackboard."

I agreed, and meanwhile, Zeev began with his quiz. Even though I knew the answers to most of the questions, the winner, as usual, was Haim'ke, a fifteen-year-old boy from the Blau-Weiss group for whom everyone predicted a great future.

Zeev prepared us for the following day's lesson, after Mr. Goldman's Hebrew lesson.

"Tomorrow, we'll talk about survival and learn to make knots. Those who can should bring a short rope. Just don't cut ropes off the boat..."

After the lesson, I went back to the *Tzar Nikolai* and joined my parents for lunch. We stood quietly in line, when raised voices were heard from the distribution area.

"This is already the second time I've seen you do that!" someone shouted.

"Get your hand off me! You rude idiot!" yelled another voice, thicker and louder.

"You took more than your share yesterday as well!" the first one shouted.

The line dispersed, and everyone hurried to see what was going on.

"I'm stopping the distribution," said Mrs. Deutsch, who stood next to the pots with a ladle in one hand and a large serving spoon in the other.

It turned out that Mr. Gaetzer, the rumormonger, had asked for a larger portion of rice, and Mr. Goldman was trying to stop him from taking it.

"You're not alone here! There are people who haven't received anything yet."

"It's none of your business!" screamed Gaetzer, Goldman still holding his arm.

He yanked his arm free of Mr. Goldman's grip, and the latter just couldn't contain his anger and slapped his face. Gaetzer immediately retaliated by punching Goldman's shoulder.

"You miserable parasite!" Mr. Goldman raged and tried to punch him back, but Father was already behind him and grabbed both his arms.

"Take it easy, Abraham, take it easy," Father tried to calm things down.

"Don't tell me to take it easy. That bastard is eating at our expense. I've seen it with my own eyes!"

Meanwhile, Teddy arrived, grabbed Gaetzer's arm, and twisted it back, just like the self-defense grip they'd taught us in Akiba.

Things gradually settled down and Mrs. Deutsch continued to distribute food.

Mr. Goldman whispered to Father, "If I were you, I would have given up long ago and escaped from this cursed trap with my family."

"What have we gained by being here?" asked Mr. Goldman. "Absolutely nothing! They promise you the world and give you absolutely nothing."

Father answered that he too could simply leave and seek his fortune elsewhere.

"But that's the difference between us," said Mr. Goldman. "You are in your own country here, surrounded by people who speak your language. You could simply take a train from Prahovo and be back in Belgrade in two hours. You yourself have said that."

"It's not that simple," Father explained to him. "What exactly would I go back to?"

"Don't you have a house? Relatives? Someone who would welcome you?" asked Mr. Goldman, surprised.

"I sold most of my property before boarding the ship. Closed my office as well. I hardly had any work anyway in the last few months before we left," Father answered resentfully.

Mr. Goldman walked away and Father, Mother, and I sat in a remote corner, silently eating. Everyone was lost in their own thoughts, thinking of the unpleasant scene they'd just witnessed. Mother hissed, "Emil, we simply cannot go on like this."

In the afternoon, I went down for my daily walk along the riverbank. The snow had frozen into a slippery layer of ice and was too dangerous to walk on. I went along the platform and looked at all the boats docking there. Many boats were completely empty, while ours were overcrowded to bursting. I wondered why they couldn't arrange another boat for us, to ease the crowded conditions a little. I took the same path I had taken many times before, to the net-storage shed. On my way, I saw three guys from Hechalutz trying to skate on the ice using improvised wooden skates. They laughed loudly every time one of them fell down.

I found old Petrović slowly sipping from his small glass. The pleasant smell of black coffee hung in the air.

"You're just in time. Come on, I'll make you a cup."

"No, there's no need," I tried, but he was already kneeling next to the red-hot coals. In one hand, he held the coffee pot, and in the other, he held a cigarette stub. He beckoned me closer.

"Promise you won't tell anyone?" he whispered secretively.

"Of course I won't. Just tell me."

"Your cook won't be coming back anymore," he said.

"Who? Shishko?"

"Yes. He and his girlfriend Anita slept here in the net-storage shed last night. She cried all night."

"Yes, what happened the day before yesterday in the evening was terrible," I recalled the degrading scene. "Everyone was shocked, especially Mother, who tried to protect her from all the 'righteous people,' as she called those who humiliated Anita and spat in her face."

"She was a wreck. I couldn't refuse them and gave them permission to sleep in the shed. I just can't understand you people. This is how animals behave," he said and placed his coffee glass on the large stone beside him.

"We think the same," I told him. "My mother couldn't sleep that night. She thinks these women feel jealous or threatened."

"You should know, Hanne, there isn't much love in this terrible world. There's a lot of jealousy and bad blood." He took a long sip from his coffee. "And when there's love, you need to protect it, honor it. Especially on your boat, where it's so cold and crowded."

"Some people on our boat thought just like you and called her 'Romantic Anita.' But there were a lot of others, especially women, who called her 'Anita the whore.'"

"Why call a girl who has found someone to love her a whore? She told me a little bit about herself last night," he said, and his eyes filled with tears. "She told me about her childhood in Bratislava. Her father never loved her, and her mother was a sickly woman and couldn't help her much. She had nothing going for her in life. And now, fortune smiled on her at last and sent her Shishko, the cook. He gave her love. He warmed her with his hugs during the cold nights on the boat, made her feel she was special, and then…"

A tear dropped down his wrinkle-furrowed cheek.

"I haven't slept either. I felt very bad about what they did to her," I answered.

"It's a shame that you're exposed to these ugly sides of love at your age. I saw you here two days ago with that beautiful girl. Is it serious between the two of you?"

"We met here, on the boat. I really like her, but I can't tell you if it's love or not. I think about her a lot."

"You're still young. One day you'll understand. Sometimes people fall in love without even realizing it."

"So how can you know for sure?"

"I'll tell you," he took a crumpled packet of cigarettes from his inner coat pocket, toyed with it, and replaced it. "My wife died many years ago. She came down with an illness none of the doctors in the area knew how to cure."

"Did you love her?" I asked.

"I wasn't sure either, back then. I was a young fisherman and spent many nights in my boat, away from home. I did a lot of the foolish things young men do. Always wanted more. And she, Tanya, was always with the children. When I came back with a boatful of fresh fish, I'd give them to her and she would sell them at the market."

"You still haven't told me if you loved her."

"Most of the time, I was looking for women to excite me and saw her as no more than the mother of my children, not as a woman one would desire every night. But then one night, about four years ago, she got ill; there was a terrible storm, and I had to return early from my fishing. I reached the dock, tied my boat, and ran home. From afar, I could see a faint light from the kitchen window. Normally, the houses were completely dark at night. I got closer and saw a bicycle leaning against the plane tree in the yard, and my heart pounded insanely." He stopped his story for a moment and lightly patted his coat pocket, "I don't even know why I'm telling you all this…"

He took the packet of cigarettes from his pocket again, lightly tapped the bottom, and took out another cigarette with two fingers.

"I flung open the door. I was sure I was going to kill someone. I only managed to see his back. The bedroom window opened with a loud noise, and he was gone. She sat by the kitchen table, her long hair flowing about her shoulders, and a look I'd never seen before on her face. A kind of longing or desire I'd only seen on other women's faces. I saw her as a mother, always badly dressed."

He took another long drag from his cigarette.

"At first, I couldn't understand the terrible emotion that overwhelmed me. Only after I calmed down did I realize it was jealousy. But not just jealously. I banged my fist on the table and was raising my hand to slap her, but only then, when I noticed that special look on her face, did I realize something else," he said, flicking away the cigarette stub. "It took some time, but I finally understood I was living like a fool. I realized I'd been stupid not to love her enough, that she was a treasure. I realized that for all those years…" he choked for a moment, his shoulders trembled, and he fell silent. A moment later, he regained his composure and was back with me.

"What about, what's her name, your girl? Does she love you?"

"Her name is Inge. I don't know. We don't talk about it. We are simply in this…experience…"

"I'm sorry for getting so emotional. It's been years since I've opened my heart to anyone like that, even to those who are close to me. Now with you, it just simply…"

"No, I think it's wonderful. I see you really trust me," I said and looked into his tear-drenched eyes. "Maybe we could make another crossword puzzle?" I suggested, trying to change his emotional mood.

He agreed and started rummaging through his pockets again to look for the papers. I suggested we make another crossword puzzle about geography and history, one that would be more challenging, so I could bring it to Zeev's class and make everyone sweat a little.

Petrović surprised me with his knowledge of areas in the world I had never even heard of—ruined cities, submerged ports from King Herod's era, and the kingdoms of the crusaders. I ended up asking him to make the crossword puzzle less difficult, so the children wouldn't just give up. When we finished the crossword puzzle, I parted from him with a handshake.

"See you tomorrow," I said.

"Goodbye, comrade," he said laughingly.

I ran quickly along the icy path across the Danube until I reached the ship's gangway.

"You look pale, Hanne," Mother said worriedly. "Are you feeling all right?"

"I'm fine, Mother. I have to go and meet Inge now."

I found her in the floating isolation ward, cleaning the infirmary with typical nimbleness, her hands fluttering with a rag that emitted the sharp smell of alcohol. At first, she didn't even turn her head to look at me.

"I've no time now, Hanne," she said when she finally noticed my presence.

"Just for a minute," I tried. "I want us to sit down and talk."

"But we've already agreed on something, haven't we?" she said decisively, as if the subject was closed.

"Perhaps you did. I never agreed to the idea of surrendering to the chattering of a few gossips," I said, realizing that pleading with her would get me nowhere. "If you decide you want to see me after all, you know where to find me," I said and left her.

At night, I listened to the whispers exchanged by my parents again. I learned how to distinguish their words, even when they spoke in low voices. Father spoke of Mr. Gaetzer, that troublesome man who keeps spreading rumors.

"He's convinced we're not stuck here because of the ice."

"Why then?"

"He's talking about some conspiracy, as if someone is deliberately trying to sabotage our transport for some obscure reason."

"And he says that…based on what information exactly?"

"He's in correspondence with someone from Vienna, who says he knows for a fact there isn't a ship waiting for us at the confluence of the Danube."

"This simply can't go on, Emil." Mother sighed.

"We need to be patient. Things will work out eventually," said Father, but I could hear he wasn't very certain of that himself.

"How will it work out? How? Have you seen how skinny the boys are? And not only them. Look at the other children. At their age, they need proper nutrition for their growth," she continued in a whisper.

"What would you like me to do?" Father grumbled. "Do you want me to start a local black market for eggs and butter, like Mr. Gaetzer?"

"I wish we hadn't embarked on this adventure in the first place. I'd go back to Belgrade right now, if I could."

"You know that's impossible," Father whispered.

"I feel so bad for taking the children out of school. We've ruined their entire future," she said.

"You think it's not hard for me to see everything that's going on here? At least you have something to keep you busy…"

"So what! Just a few hours in the storage room, that's all. It's not that I gain something from it, not even an egg for the children or a piece of sausage," said Mother and then was silent.

"Maybe I'll go to the Kladovo market tomorrow. Although we don't have much cash left."

"I told you not to give all the money to your sister, Lela, but you are so stubborn."

"We'll need that money in Israel yet. Carrying it with us just seemed impractical."

"Do you want me to go to the market tomorrow? You were always better at haggling with the peddlers."

"I'll go tomorrow morning. I promise, all right?"

"At least you know the language better than Gaetzer."

"You know he's asked me to teach him Serbo-Croatian? I thought of sending him to Hanne…"

"Everyone knows he goes to the market every Wednesday to buy food from the villagers. God knows where the money comes from. He doesn't look like someone with assets in Vienna."

"That's easy enough to understand," said Father. "Simple arithmetic. He buys stuff cheaply from the market peddlers, and then sells it at inflated prices to anyone with money on the boat. I didn't like the man from the moment I laid eyes on him…"

"I never meant to say you should behave like him. You were the one who mentioned him. I meant to tell you something entirely different."

"What did you mean to tell me?"

"That you're the only one here who can contact Mr. Sime Spitzer. Talk to him."

"Don't you think he wants to give us more?" said Father. "I'm sure he'd give us more if he could."

"Emil, forty dinars a week is nothing. It's not even enough for two days."

"I'm willing to try and check in with him. I'm sure he'll come to update us about the situation soon."

"Please promise me. If you won't do something, I will. Now I'll try to go to sleep again. I've hardly slept at all the last few nights."

I think Father promised just to make Mother feel better, but he didn't really mean it.

The next day, I got to the classroom early, before Zeev's lesson, to draw the crossword puzzle I'd prepared with Petrović on the blackboard. Efraim volunteered to help me, and together, we drew the outline of the crossword puzzle and filled the black squares with *X*'s. When Zeev came in, he was very pleased with what he saw and tried to solve some of the questions.

"I can see it's not going to be easy," he said.

During the lesson, he divided us into three groups, according to boats. The *Kraljica Marija* group with representatives from the *Kraljica Marija*, and so forth. I didn't participate, of course, but nonetheless, the *Tzar Nikolai* group was winning, thanks to the knowledgeable

Haim'ke. Still, there was a lot of tension, and it seemed as though an experienced judge was needed to determine which group should get the points. Each group received two minutes to solve a question. If the group didn't know the answer, the next one got the chance to answer. Everyone thought the crossword puzzle was a great idea, both for memorizing the subjects we had discussed in class and for creating an interesting competitive atmosphere. I was asked to bring another crossword puzzle for the next lesson.

***

Saturday morning. I was lying down wrapped in three wool blankets and still felt the cold. I suddenly felt a blow of yearning for Saturday mornings back home in Belgrade. I remembered how I used to spoil myself in bed on Saturday mornings and stay under the covers, even though the house was heated and warm. Lord would nap too, sprawled comfortably beside my bed. Soon, Mother would come to knock on our doors, Pauli's first, then mine, and tell us to come down for breakfast.

I lay on the hard floor, and my thoughts wandered back to Inge.

I really felt bad about her asking me to stop seeing her. Except for Mother, perhaps, she's the one I feel closest to in this living hell. I can talk to her for hours and hours. We have so much in common—except for our disagreement over matters of faith and religion. I just can't understand how an intelligent girl like her could blindly believe everything written in those books, and I don't like the fact she's always trying to draw me into her faith. I just can't accept that. But then

I remembered how we'd embraced two days ago and looked at the moon together. We felt so close to each other then that I was willing to forgive her.

I was lying down, in no hurry to get up to another breakfast of luke-warm tea, bread, and butter. People were saying we'd run out of butter soon and started rationing the jam as well.

Some people had already written to their relatives, asking for food. I stayed there, snuggled up and thinking of the good life in Belgrade, a life I'd never appreciated enough. Here on the boat, Mother doesn't come knocking on our doors like she did back home. It had all hap-pened just three months ago, but the apartment in Kralja Petra now seemed like ancient history, and the large house on Dedinje Hill, a lifetime ago.

Mother was also curled up in thin wool blankets. She'd set off on a short trip of a few days with a small suitcase, leaving her warm, com-fortable house behind, and now here she is, stuck with three hundred people, struggling to survive the cold nights on her narrow bench. She's no longer the fragile woman who boarded the boat. Now, she seems more confident, maybe because of the appreciation she's been getting for her work in the storage room. I'm proud of her ability to cope with everything that's happened on the boat. But from the conversation I heard last night, I realized everything could crumble in a moment. Her face had become gaunt, and black circles had ap-peared under her eyes. Even Father, who used to put his arm around her when they walked together on the deck, now seems distant and self-absorbed.

He'd also lost a lot of weight in the past few weeks. The heavy coat his body had always filled so nicely now hangs on his shoulders like a sack.

Eventually, all four of us went to eat breakfast together. Pauli was self-absorbed, angry at the whole world. I think he sometimes forgets he has a younger brother on board, because he spends most of his time with youths from the Hechalutz movement.

"Nice of you to finally remember we exist," I said, deliberately, so he'd know how I feel about being abandoned.

"Why do you have to go on at me all the time?" he said angrily. "You're not a child who needs a babysitter anymore."

The Pomeranz couple stood before us in line, Max and Elisheva, with their little son, Yost. Yost was a quiet, dreamy boy. Elisheva, or Ellie, as we called her, was a handsome woman with a trim figure. In the mornings, she used to sit on deck, next to the boat helm, and draw. She draws the views from the deck and, lately, portraits of people in our group. Mother sat for her one morning, on the bench next to the boat helm, and received a flattering portrait. Max was a bald, grim-faced man, who wasn't seen much around the deck, except once a day, when the three of them would stretch their legs. According to Ellie, it was the crowded conditions below and lack of fresh air that caused all the illnesses on the boat. I heard Ellie telling Mother how much she enjoys drawing, how it improves her mood and makes her feel better about herself, especially now that she's allowed to draw next to the boat helm.

By the time we reached the distribution point, there wasn't much jam left, and they'd almost run out of butter as well. The pot with the boiling tea had cooled and there was only a little left. The tea poured into the enamel cups couldn't warm my freezing hands.

Each of us received a single slice of bread and just a little butter. Sometimes, something small can suddenly break your spirit, and that's exactly what happened to Mother. She really loved jam. Back home, she and Sophie, the cook, used to make jam out of almost every fruit in season. We sipped the lukewarm, tasteless tea. It was the first time I'd seen her on the verge of breaking down. She turned her head aside and stifled a sob.

***

Bible lessons with Mr. Goldman are a very special experience. When he speaks, there is complete silence in the classroom; the tension is so thick, you could almost cut it with a knife. We all sit there quietly, focused and attentive. Even though his explanations are in German, he repeatedly reads from the Bible, and excitedly spices up his speech with Hebrew literary phrases. When he tries to explain a difficult verse, he raises his hands and waves them in the air, his small face shrinking even more, and his little mustache quivering with excitement.

Mr. Goldman is up-to-date with everything going on in Israel. He has a small shortwave transistor radio he brought with him from Vienna. At nights, when I can't fall asleep for thinking of Inge and possible ways of winning her back, I can hear Jerusalem Calling broadcasting from his radio.

A few days ago, in a discussion about the prophet Jeremiah and his political doctrine, he tried to draw an analogy with our times and spoke movingly about the prophet at the city gates, a heavy burden on his shoulders, shouting at his own people, the Judeans in Jerusalem absorbed in their vanity, trying to warn them of the impending danger that might destroy the land and its people.

"And what does this remind us of?" he asked, as if waiting for an answer, but immediately replying to his own question. "It's just like our own great exile in Europe. But nowadays, we have no one to warn us of impending disaster." He waved his hands. "Just like the people of Judea in Jeremiah's time, we were all too busy getting rich and worrying about material possessions to care about our spiritual assets."

One of the boys asked where the prophet had come from and who authorized him to speak in the name of God. It's not like God has a mouth and can speak. A great commotion erupted in the classroom. Mr. Goldman hushed everyone and explained that a prophet is a person who speaks in the name of God and serves as his living mouth.

Someone else jumped and said, "But anyone can wake up one morning and decide he's a prophet and that God has been revealed to him."

"That's true," said Mr. Goldman. "Anyone can say God has been revealed to him in a dream, but just look at the life Jeremiah led, how he was thrown into a cistern and nearly died there, how Hananiah Ben Azzur desired his death. But in the face of all these threats, he persisted. He kept on standing at the gates of the city to warn the nation that a war against Babylon was hopeless and would bring about disaster. Not just any man can become a prophet. Only a man with great personal strength, an influential, charismatic man who can mesmerize the crowd with the power of his words. Not a man who babbles like the Jerusalem Calling announcer, who sounds as if he hasn't eaten in two days."

Mr. Goldman was so angry with the unimpressive announcer that everyone in the classroom immediately shared his dislike of him. Then he added, full of pathos, "Because that Hebrew voice, the only one in the entire world, should be imbued with great strength, and not sound like a meaningless babbler. Now, the lady announcer who speaks at the end of the broadcast sounds as if her voice could electrocute the air and carve pathways through thunderstorms. That was probably how Jeremiah spoke when he appeared in front of King Zedekiah and tried to convince him that destruction was approaching."

Mr. Goldman is also in charge of teaching us Hebrew and Hebrew grammar. In the first few lessons with him, I couldn't understand anything and had to ask for Inge's help, but after a few lessons, my talent for languages helped me become one of the leading students in class. Pretty soon, I was the one helping Inge with conjugations and roots.

Classes took place in an improvised classroom on board the *Tzar Dusan*. In order for us to have a better learning environment, the Federation of Jewish Communities had bought us all notebooks. Each child received one math notebook and one writing notebook. Physical education classes were taught by Yokel; at first it was only for the youths of the Hechalutz and Netzah, but later on, he accepted others who realized just how important it was to maintain body fitness in such conditions of inactivity and physical deterioration. Yokel was himself an athlete. Back in Vienna, he'd participated in professional gymnastics classes. He divided us into small groups and taught us various exercises to improve our strength and agility. Every lesson began with a warm-up, in which we would run and jump on the spot; the crowded conditions did not allow us a lot of room for movement.

***

One night, while preparing to go to sleep, spreading blankets on the hard, wooden floor, the terrible screams of a woman calling for help could be heard from the boat's lower level.

"Doctor, doctor!"

The sound of quick footsteps came from the staircase, and people on the boat were alarmed. I quickly folded my blanket, placed it in its usual corner, and went down as well. Mother called after me, "Why go, Hanne. I'm sure there are already more than enough curious people down there to disturb the doctor."

But I couldn't help my natural curiosity, and by the time I got down, Dr. Bezalel and Inge were already there. Old Mr. Weiss lay sprawled on the floor. I recognized his face but had never spoken to him. He once tried to convince Father to put on tefillin, without much success. He lay on his back, his face pale and shrunken, sweat covering his forehead. Inge kneeled beside Dr. Bezalel and helped him roll up Mr. Weiss's shirt. I could see his ribs sticking out through the white skin.

Dr. Bezalel placed both his hands on the man's chest and pressed down hard. It was hard for me to look at that horrifying sight, and I began to walk away. From the corner of my eye, I saw the doctor pressing hard a few more times. All that time, Mrs. Weiss stood next to them, weeping with fear. When the doctor rose and raised both his hands, as if to say, "I've done the best I could," she broke into terrible cries.

"I'm sorry. He's suffered a severe heart attack."

The sound of sobbing was heard from the deck.

The following day, as the sun began to set beyond the barren western hills, painting the heavens with shades of pink tinged with purple, a sad funeral procession emerged from the boat. It began in the corridor in the belly of the boat and continued all the way to the white-gray fields of Kladovo village. There, in the hardened soil, a proper burial place was found. Equipped with shovels and pickaxes loaned to them from the village's agricultural toolshed, three strong men dug the grave for the first of our dead. There was no one to say *Kaddish* for him, but someone in the crowd said the *El Male Rachamim*[13] prayer, and we went back to the boat to continue our seemingly never-ending wait. Two days later, a smooth slab of stone was placed on the fresh grave. On it was engraved the following words: Yehuda Weiss, Born in Vienna—1890. Died in Kladovo—1940.

***

Tonight, I again eavesdropped on my parents' conversation. They were sitting on the bench not far from me, speaking in hushed voices. But I'd learned by now to hear Mother's whispering voice, even when lying in my usual spot on the floor, pretending to be asleep.

"I had another interesting conversation with Emil Shechter today. He always has reliable sources of information," said Father.

"And what did you find out?" she asked.

---

13 *El Male Rachamim* is a funeral prayer used by the Ashkenazi Jewish community that the *chazzan* recites for the ascension of the souls of the dead. It is recited during the funeral, when visiting the grave of the departed on memorial days, and on any other occasions commemorating the dead.

"Good news…and you know how hard it is to get good news out of him."

"Don't tease me. What good news?" There was excitement in her voice.

"There's a rumor we'll be out of here in a few weeks."

"Where? What did he say?"

"We'll sail part of the way on boats down the Danube, then board trains that will take us to the shores of the Adriatic Sea. From there, we'll take a ship to Israel."

"Emil, that's wonderful. Why didn't you tell me right away?"

"I didn't want you to get too excited, Loui. Not until we're told to pack our things and leave. I still have my doubts."

I also felt excited and spent the night thinking about what it would be like. After all, we're used to each other here, and even the villagers are kind to us. I couldn't fall asleep for excitement. I simply must meet Inge and tell her. She's the only one I'll tell. Then, perhaps we could go together to say goodbye to old Petrović, who will still be here mending nets when we are under the bright blue skies of Israel. That's what Mr. Dvoriansky told us, that there are blue skies in Israel, even on most winter days, and we'd all stared at him in disbelief.

This morning, after the lesson with Mr. Goldman, I stayed in the classroom to speak to Shlomit. She told me about her brother who lives on a *kibbutz* in the Jezreel Valley and is waiting for her to join him, and how she yearns to see him and wants to live on the *kibbutz* just like him. I told her what I'd heard from Father the night before, and she jumped for joy. Suddenly, Jacob came running toward us, holding a small parcel in his hand.

"This just came in the mail," he exclaimed joyfully. "For Inge and Shlomit, who took care of me so well." He took two bottles of *eau de cologne* and handed one of them to Shlomit.

"This is for you, from my sister, Eva." He gave her the bottle with a little bow. Then he took out the attached letter and read.

> We're sending you original *eau de cologne* bottles from Cologne for the girls who took care of you, but only two bottles. We'll send the third one later today. You can tell them I really appreciate how well they're treating my older brother.

He folded the letter, placed it back in the envelope, took out the second bottle from the parcel, and handed it to me.

"Please give this one to Inge. She deserves it too, after taking care of me so well."

"Don't you know we don't see each other anymore?" I asked, overwhelmed by a sharp pang of yearning.

At noon, Fredl's trumpet sounded, signaling us to gather on deck for an important announcement. The music Fredl had chosen as the signal for a general gathering was "The Blue Danube."

"A happy tune," he said, explaining his choice. "Why should I depress everyone with a military march?"

Half an hour later, we were all standing in the cold, huddled in our coats and blankets.

"This won't take long," Naftali Bata prepared us. He stood on a large rock so we could all see him. "I owe you an explanation, because I know there are a lot of rumors."

A murmur passed through the crowd. Bata raised his voice and said, "I'm happy to announce that things are beginning to clear up, and there's a chance we'll be leaving in about three weeks, even before the anticipated date. The Federation of Jewish Communities has decided to change the plan. The ship will wait for us on the Adriatic Sea. We'll sail down the Danube some of the way, the rest by train. But nothing is finalized yet. We'll give you a week's notice, so you'll have enough time to get organized and pack your belongings."

Cheers rose from the crowd. People shouted for joy and clapped their hands. Some even began to sing, "For Bata is a jolly good fellow," while he meanwhile got down from the rock and disappeared.

It was three o'clock and I hurried to the *Tzar Dusan* so as not to miss the geometry lesson with Mr. Kommer, the engineer. Everyone sat in front of the long classroom tables. Mr. Kommer, whom we nicknamed "the dandy," stood in front of the improvised blackboard in his beautiful clothes and showed us how to solve various problems he'd prepared for us. Rosie Zonshein stood shyly beside him, with her back to us and a piece of chalk in her hand, not daring to approach the blackboard for fear of betraying her ignorance.

About fifteen minutes before the end of the lesson, we all started yelling, "Sto-ry time, sto-ry time." Then Mr. Kommer put his bag on the table and took out the book that had fascinated us all for the past week. He'd decided to add interest to our geometry lessons by reading us chapters from *Treasure Island* in a German translation. We were all enthralled by Mr. Kommer's voice. After all, every one of us could identify with Jim Hawkins, sailing off into unknown adventures with the aid of a map and in the company of dangerous men. The hair-raising adventures he endured with the cruel pirates reminded us a little of our own great adventure, here on the Danube. But in our case, the map was leading us not to Treasure Island, but to Israel, and we'd learned to survive in this cruel world with ropes and rods from Dvoriansky, that eternal boy scout.

***

It's been two weeks since I'd last met with Inge in private. She didn't come to meet me on the bridge or on our regular bench in the floating isolation ward. During classes we took together, I would sneak glances at her, but she never looked back. Maybe she was trying to show me there was nothing between us. But today, she finally looked at me and I saw that something had changed in her eyes.

That very same evening, in spite of the fierce cold, I went up to the bridge as usual. I looked up at the sky. The moon was bright, and I thought of the way Inge had looked at me that morning. A few minutes later, footsteps came from the steep staircase leading to the bridge. And while I was still trying to guess who it could possibly be, she appeared beside me.

"Good evening, Hanne," she said, still keeping a distance, as if unsure whether to approach.

"Inge. What a surprise. I've missed you so much."

"Me too. I suddenly felt tortured by the thought that I'm forcing myself to stay away from you, my closest kindred spirit here," she said.

"I never really understood why you chose to do so in the first place."

"Never mind," Inge drew closer to me. "The main thing is that we're together now," she said and took my cold hand in her warm one. "It's warm, isn't it? I kept it deep in the pocket of my coat. Would you like to?" And she placed my hand inside the pocket of her warm coat.

"Look at the huge moon hanging in the sky. Only the moon can see us now," I said.

"Right. And I already know a few stars," she said, pointing at the Big Dipper.

Then, putting her head on my shoulder, she sang a well-known German ballad about a hunter who mistakenly shoots an arrow at his beloved. We stayed close to each other for a long time, and I could feel the warmth of her body through our coats.

The next day, we sat together on our usual bench in the isolation ward. My head was still spinning from all the verses we had learned in Mr. Goldman's Bible lesson yesterday.

"What seest thou? And I said, I see a seething pot; and the face thereof is toward the north. Then the LORD said unto me, Out of the north an evil shall break forth upon all the inhabitants of the land."

I read and the strange alien words jostled in my head, refusing to come together in meaningful sentences, just like those far-off days, a lifetime away, when Menahem, the teacher, had taught me to read the *parashah* for my bar mitzvah.

Now Inge decided she could explain the final chapter we'd learned with Mr. Goldman, especially the part about the "seething pot."

"Look at my face," she said, and suddenly made an angry face, straining her neck until her cheeks turned all red. "I'm seething." Then she puffed up both her cheeks and whistled like a boiling kettle.

The atmosphere on board the three boats was very depressing. Not much excitement from the day Naftali had "dropped the bomb" as Father jokingly called it. At first people's moods really improved. They smiled at each other, and some laughter was finally heard on the boats. But later on, when the anticipated message didn't arrive, the laughter died. Mr. Goldman, who went out of his way, at first, to compare Bata with the prophet standing at the city gates, went back to being irritable and angry. Even Mr. Dvoriansky, who was always so optimistic and taught us some of the folk songs of Israel, had lost his enthusiasm.

The turnaround came during the last days of February. We were informed that the plan would be implemented in four weeks' time and we should begin our preparations. Mother told us a lot of canned food had been ordered for the long voyage, as well as warm clothes for the long stay on the river. People began to get busy with preparations. Many sat on deck, writing their families in Israel to expect them sometime at the beginning of April.

But one day, I heard Father whispering to Mother again.

"Something strange is going on here. Shechter spoke to me again today."

"What's happened, Emil?" Mother asked with concern.

"They've changed the plans again. This doesn't feel right."

"Are they postponing the trip?"

"No, they're not postponing it, but there's no train involved now. They want us to sail all the way to Sulina in the Danube Delta."

"What's wrong with that? You had me scared for a minute."

"You don't understand. All it means is that there isn't any real plan," he raised his voice now. "It's all just *bobe-mayse*—stories and lies."

"I don't care," she said quietly. "So long as we finally get out of here, I don't care how."

***

The days go by. With each passing day, we see more and more chunks of ice floating on the thawing river. At night, I'm no longer freezing when wrapping myself up in three blankets. The road by the river is more slippery now with a mixture of snow and mud.

Inge and I walked hand in hand on our way to part from old Petrović. We haven't visited him as much in the last few days, because we've been busy preparing for imminent departure, but after Father told me we'd be leaving in just a few days, I decided to take Inge for one last visit with the net mender. The trees had long shed their coats of snow but were still barren, not a single bud blooming on their branches.

We approached the buildings that served as areas for repairing fishing boats and saw boats set on concrete blocks and fishermen busy repairing or painting them. Next to the netting-shed wall lay the never-ending pile of nets, and next to that, we saw Petrović's hunched figure. He sat there as usual, the small glass of black coffee, with its unique aroma, beside him. When we got closer, he leaned over his little primus stove.

"Oh, welcome, my young couple," he greeted us warmly. "I've just finished making a fresh pot of coffee. Will you drink with me?"

"Gladly," I answered. "I can't drink coffee anywhere else. I don't think what they serve in the boat kitchen could actually be called coffee."

"So how are you, my friends?" he asked while stirring the water. "They tell me you'll be leaving soon."

"That's what they told us, and that's why we're here. We've come to say goodbye," I said. "This might be our last coffee together."

"Whoa, not so fast!" he held the handle of the coffee pot and, with a quick and skillful movement, drew it out of the fire.

"A minute more, and the coffee would have boiled over and clogged my primus. I've had it ever since my fishing days. That'll be forty-four years now."

"I've learned quite a few good things from you. The first—how to drink coffee," I sat down and placed the small glass under the coffee pot's spout.

"Hold on, what about the lady? Ladies are always first," he said, pouring a glass for Inge.

"What else have you learned from me?" he asked with curiosity, while slowly pouring boiling coffee into my glass.

"I learned how to mend holes in nets and how to write crossword puzzles," I said, slowly sipping the coffee, just as he'd taught me. "And you still haven't told me where you learned all the things you know…"

"You think all the knowledge in the world comes from schools or universities, and that only the right sort of people can learn, those who live in luxury houses and get a higher education, but that's not exactly how it works."

"I don't think that at all," I was a little insulted. "And don't forget, I'm young and still haven't seen much in my short life."

"So maybe in a few years' time, when you're a professor at some university and live in a fine, large house, you'll remember old Petrović and his stories and how he taught himself everything he knew."

"First off, I'm not going to be a professor. I'm going to be a farmer and work the fields of the Jezreel Valley."

That was the name of the valley I'd heard about from Mr. Goldman a few days before, when he'd read a letter from his son who lives in Israel.

"Good, good! Just don't regret not making the right choice many years from now," he said and turned his eyes to Inge. "Even though you've already made one right choice. I'll give you credit for that."

"I'm going to be a hospital nurse, perhaps even work in the operating theater," said Inge.

"That'll suit you just fine," he said. "You love helping people and have the hands of an angel. I saw how quickly you learned to mend nets."

"And what about me?" I asked, insulted. "Don't I have good hands?"

"Hanne, you have a bright future ahead of you. I can see that you have a unique way of thinking. We all have our different qualities. Here's another example of something you won't learn at university. It's called intuition," he said, and added, "Just promise me you'll forget about farming. It's definitely not for you."

"A few days from now, we won't be here, and we wanted to come and thank you," Inge tried to change the course of the conversation and return to our reason for coming.

"You see? A practical girl. You philosophize and she goes straight to the point," he said, collecting the empty coffee glasses from us.

"Listen, Petrović, we don't take your kindness to us for granted. I don't have as many heart-to-hearts with my own father."

"Well, when I was younger, I never used to speak with my children like that. I certainly didn't have heart-to-hearts with them." He sighed from the bottom of his heart. "Now my daughter is in Sarajevo, married to a Muslim and the mother of six children. I hardly ever see her. My son was killed in the Great War. He was an artillery officer."

"It's our gain, then, that we've met you now, when you have so much life experience and can see things differently," I said.

"That's one of life's tragedies. When we're young, we don't see life as we ought to. We're too busy living it. Perhaps it's best that way. A time to live life and a time to speak about it," he summed up, lighting a cigarette. "You've told me what you're going to do over there, but I don't really understand why there, of all the places in the world. After all, the Jews don't have their own country there," he said while blowing smoke rings into the cold air separating us.

"There's a danger that this whole war will reach us here too. And there, in the land of our forefathers, that's where we belong," Inge shared her enthusiasm with him. "In the covenant, God promised Abraham that his descendants would inherit the land of Israel, and just like the kingdom of the kings, David and Saul, it may still be established in our own time. This is the return of a people to their own country."

I felt a bit embarrassed by her decisive words, as if the covenant was a contract signed just a few years ago. Even old Petrović looked at her with incomprehension and took a long drag from his cigarette.

"The problem is, we don't have visas to immigrate to Israel. Even though it's the only place in the world where Jews can actually feel safe," I said. "The British won't let us in."

Meanwhile, it was growing late, and beyond the hills, the winter sun began to set.

"We need to get back to the boat before it gets dark," said Inge. She rose and offered him her hand in parting. Petrović took her hand in his and said, "I wish you all the best there in the land of Israel. You deserve a place where you can live peacefully, without persecution. I say the same to the gypsies, but they don't have a country of their own waiting for them."

"You're a wonderful man…" I tried to find more words, but couldn't and felt my throat tightening till I was speechless. I just stood there and shook his hand in parting.

We quietly made our way back down the snowy, muddy trail, careful not to slip.

Just before we said goodbye, Inge said, "Petrović is a wise man. It's a shame he has to stay here."

"If everything could have stayed as it was before Hitler, we would also have stayed here. We had a good life here before all this evil."

"Don't start with that again, Hanne!" she scolded me. "I've already told you we Jews belong in the Promised Land, no matter what happens here."

Just before dark, Mr. Fredl's trumpet was heard. "An important message," murmured the voices in the gathering crowd. We all went down to the pier, and Mr. Bata told us excitedly that we all had to be ready to sail as soon as tonight. He still couldn't tell us the exact time, but the plan was for us to sail to Prahovo, and from there, take a train to a port on the Adriatic shore, where our ship was waiting.

It was a long and feverish night. At first, everyone was in a great mood. Nobody even thought of going to sleep. From the deck of the *Kraljica Marija* came the sound of people singing "Hatikvah," and they were quickly joined by the passengers of the *Tzar Nikolai*. Others simply walked about idly, busy only with packing and rechecking their belongings. Mother checked the contents of our backpacks and suitcases. She took out my torn sweater, turned it this way and that and said, "Is this how you want to arrive in Israel—with a torn sweater?"

She opened her suitcase and took out her sewing kit. She sat in the light of the flashlight fixed to the chimney, spread the sweater on her knees, and began to mend the torn sleeve. Father sat on the bench playing solitaire with a deck of cards on his knees. He always does that when he needs to pass the time while waiting for something. The hours passed, and people began to move about restlessly, waiting for something to happen, for the engines to start, for a message, or the visit of an important personality. This time, we were all waiting for the Geneva emissary, Mr. Averbuch.

"Nothing will come of it again, just you wait and see," said Pauli, trying to ruin what little hope remained.

Father, who was still a little optimistic, answered him angrily. "It's hard enough for us as it is. Do you think it's so easy to get the money for a ship? I trust Mr. Averbuch in Geneva knows exactly what he's doing."

***

Around midnight, we heard a woman screaming in the lower cabins, "Dear God, I can't take it anymore!"

Mother immediately recognized Mimi, Mr. Fredl's wife.

Yesterday, before they fell asleep, Mother had whispered to father, "Mimi will give birth in a day or two. I'm really worried. She has no idea what to do. She has no one to guide her. I at least had my mother to guide me through my first birth."

"Judging by the amount of time you spend with her, you're like a mother to her," Father remarked.

"My heart goes out to her. I know how hard it is, and here, of all places."

Mother ran toward the cries of pain that gradually intensified. I tried to follow her, because we were all awake anyway, but Father grabbed my arm and stopped me.

"We should let the women handle this, Hanne."

We stayed there in anticipation, hoping everything would turn out all right. For a while, we even forgot about the fact that we were waiting for the boats to start moving, but the engines remained silent. Suddenly, the air was torn with a long scream, replaced by the wail of a baby, then silence. Cries of happiness were heard from below. "*Mazel tov! Mazel tov!*" After that, it was quiet again and we returned to waiting. Sometime later, Mother appeared, blood stains on her sleeves and a happy smile on her face, as if she herself had just given birth.

"You'll never know what it feels like," said Mother, beaming with happiness. "Mimi cried for joy when I placed the baby in her arms."

"Well, and what will they call her?" I asked.

"They haven't decided yet. But some clown has already suggested they call her Karlitza Maria."

***

Hesitant sunbeams broke through the soft blanket of clouds hanging above the river. People began to realize the great hopes we had all shared at the beginning of the evening were once more about to prove false. Some completely lost patience and began to speak out against Mr. Averbuch, who still hadn't arrived.

It was around eight in the morning when Mr. Averbuch's car finally arrived, and he was immediately taken to Naftali Bata. When the new father, Mr. Fredl, sounded the trumpet, it sounded more like a sad tune than a fanfare, almost a wail admitting defeat. They told us an announcement would be made at noon.

Warm sunbeams accompanied people who began to descend from the three boats around one that afternoon, in the direction of our usual gathering spot on the pier. Their heads were lowered, and disappointment was written all over their faces. Mr. Averbuch got up on the large rock; he was accompanied by Naftali Bata, who tried to silence the agitated crowd. He raised his hands, and then lowered them with a sharp motion requesting silence.

"Shame on you!" someone suddenly called out.

"Let him speak now!" came another voice.

"I do not come bearing good tidings today," Mr. Averbuch began. "I know this isn't easy, after all the hopes you've nurtured over the past few weeks."

"We've nurtured hopes? You're the ones who keep giving us false hope!" someone else raged.

"No one has deliberately tried to give you false hope. All of us have the best intentions. If only you knew how hard people are working to help you reach Israel. And not just here in Yugoslavia, but also in Geneva, Istanbul, and Rome. Even in far-off New York," he added with pathos. "People are working to solve problems that keep coming up. The situation is complex, as you probably all realize."

"You're useless, the lot of you! All you do is travel all over Europe without doing anything!" another shout was heard from the crowd and immediately silenced.

"I have come here straight from Geneva. I did everything in my power to raise the missing sum. It was agreed that even if I don't get the entire amount, a ship would be given to us in return for a commitment to pay the remaining amount. But tonight, this agreement was withdrawn."

Angry voices and boos came from the crowd; some even spat on the ground and cursed. Naftali raised his hands in the air to calm everyone, and then shouted, "Let the man finish!"

"Dear friends, with the utmost regret, I must tell you we have to be patient and see what happens. I promise you everything will turn out for the best in the end," he said.

Boos sounded again, and Mr. Averbuch added, "One more important thing, if I may, please." He sounded as though he was pleading with the crowd. "In order to ease your stay here in the meanwhile, and please don't see this as the harbinger of a longer delay, I have managed to get a large Greek tugboat to join our three boats and ease the crowded conditions. Management will know how to distribute the passengers among the boats and the tugboat. It will arrive here in two or three days."

Penelope was the name of the tugboat.

KLADOVO, MAY 1940

It's been two weeks now since we disembarked from the *Tzar Niko-lai* and moved into temporary lodgings in Kladovo. Even though this meant our journey was again delayed, at least we could stretch our legs a bit and feel more comfortable in the fresh air and open expanses of the village after so many long months in terrible, crowded conditions on the boats.

Morning. It's still cold and dark outside, and the smell of damp hay and pig manure pierces my nostrils. I put on the old boots given me by Mikhailo, the gypsy-like farmer in whose house we were staying. Every morning, Mikhailo goes out on the river with his fishing boat. His two sons, who once shared all the chores and duties with him, had been drafted into the army, and he needs help with the pigs, so I agreed to help him.

Mikhailo took me to the pigsty, where we were greeted by about twenty mainly small pigs running around the yard. When they noticed us, they hurried over to sniff our boots and rub their noses against them. Mikhailo said I had nothing to fear from them, not even from the larger ones that looked plump, slow, and heavy.

At dawn, the morning chill still lingering over the yards and houses, I open the pigsty and fill the wheelbarrow with vegetable waste mixed with grass that Mikhailo had mown the day before. At first, the smell bothered me a little, but after a few days, I got used to it.

Mikhailo and his gypsy wife, Militza, live in a dilapidated-looking house in the western part of the village.

"This place is barely fit for pigs to live in," said Father when we saw the house for the first time.

Militza and Mikhailo live in the house in a small spare room.

"Don't worry about them," said Father, when he noticed my discomfort about the couple's great generosity. "They get a generous rent from the Federation of Jewish Communities for the hovel they're renting us."

One morning, while I was in the yard, Mikhailo came back from fishing. He was wearing tall boots that went all the way up to his knees. As I'd already fed the pigs, I asked to help him mow grass for them. He taught me how to hold a scythe, and corrected me when I flung it too high above the tall grass.

"Hold it like this, right hand on the handle in the middle and left hand on the upper one. Like this, see?"

With steady hands, he raised the scythe high and swung it down at the bottom of the green stems that toppled with a whistle. Then he stood behind me and had me repeat the correct movements.

"Excellent," he said. "You'll make a fine farmer."

I was happy to receive some encouragement for my farming dreams, especially after what old Petrović had said when we'd gone to say goodbye to him just before the last journey that never took place.

Father was happy to see me doing well at manual labor. When we sat down to eat the dinner Militza had prepared, he said it showed independence, and pretty soon, I'd be able to provide for myself.

Every morning and evening, we ate Militza's corn bread sitting around the small kitchen table, covered with a checkered tablecloth Mother had bought at the local market.

"When I was your age, I was already working for my father in the winery," Father told me. "During the summers, I'd work harvesting grapes, and then help with repairs around the winery. A winery is like a factory. Every so often, a pipe needs to be replaced here; a leaky faucet needs to be fixed there. Father saw that I had good hands and told Mother, 'he simply must study engineering.' That was how they decided to send me to Budapest Polytechnich University. That's the story of how I became an architect."

I didn't say anything. I wanted to tell him about my plan to be a farmer and work the land in the Jezreel Valley, but I knew he had great things in store for me and thought I should continue my studies.

"What hurts me the most is the fact you and Pauli have had to stop going to school. I had a pretty clear picture of your future. I'm sure after graduating from high school, you two would have continued to study at the Polytechnich University, just like me, and learn a profession."

The pigs pounced on me, squealing joyously as I upturned the contents of the wheelbarrow, scattering the food with gentle kicks, so they wouldn't need to crowd and fight for the food. I like the touch of their snouts on my tall boots. Once I'm finished, I carefully wash the boots so as not to bring the smell into the house.

Mother looks much better now since we left the boat. She is busy arranging the two small rooms and the kitchen, cleaning and polishing everything as if we were going to spend many more days here. She managed to get some fabric remnants at the market and sewed pillows and a blue drape for the room I share with Pauli. Father, on the other hand, walked sulking and idle between the people on *Penelope* and our small house. Now and then, he wrote letters to the authorities in an effort to obtain immigration permits for us.

***

Going ashore had left Father very worried about the immigration certificates. It was another blow after Mr. Averbuch's announcement that the money he'd tried to raise in Geneva would not, after all, be forthcoming. Father had taken that announcement very badly and told us that, from now on, he would try and take care of us himself, without any favors from such an amateurish organization.

Everything seemed to be working against us. Even *Penelope*, which was supposed to join us, had been stranded about fifteen hundred feet away from us. Its steam engine died with several long sighs, emitted a final cough, and that was that. All efforts to repair it were in vain. An announcement was issued over the *Kraljica Marija*'s radio that someone with knowledge of steam engines was required. The rumor spread throughout the three boats, but no one with such knowledge was to be found.

"You're an engineer, aren't you?" Mr. Goldman asked Father.

"Not exactly. I'm an architect. I plan buildings, offices, and residential houses. But you know what? I don't mind trying. We have nothing to lose either way."

After the *Penelope* crew had been alerted that someone had been found, they radioed him to take one of the fishermen's boats and come immediately. Everything was done with the utmost speed.

Mother couldn't understand why Father volunteered to help fix a ship engine. But when Father decides on something, nothing in the world can stop him. He took a fishing boat that set out from the harbor in the direction of the stranded tugboat. Tension among the people of the group was high. Everyone was waiting for *Penelope* to ease crowded conditions on the boats.

We were twice as nervous, hoping both for the rescue of *Penelope* and for Father's mood to improve, as he'd seemed like someone whose whole world had fallen apart in the past few days. From Mother's worried looks, I realized just how much she wanted him to succeed.

After two hours of nervous anticipation, a cloud of smoke began to rise from *Penelope*, and the happy announcement was heard on the radio.

"The engine has been fixed! We'll be arriving in just a few minutes."

Mother's happiness knew no bounds. The tears in her eyes proved just how nervous she'd been. People standing on the decks reacted to the news with an outburst of happiness and applause, as if they'd heard we were actually about to set sail. Father returned on the deck of *Penelope* and was welcomed with applause, just like the day he'd rescued Sender, who had almost drowned about two months before. Now, too, everyone surrounded him, asking eagerly, "How did you manage to do it? What exactly did you do?"

Father spoke in his usual deep, slow voice, trying to play down his accomplishment. To those who insisted on details, he explained that the engine was choked because the coal burner's air vent had clogged and needed cleaning.

"That's the whole story," said Father. "Just like any combustion process, you need air. It's not so complicated."

It was Father's day, and nothing in the world could ruin it, not even worrying about our immigration certificates.

Penelope joined the three boats and helped ease conditions, but with the arrival of spring, trees turning green and gray fields in the west transforming into green and inviting meadows, the Yugoslav shipping companies demanded the return of the three boats. A group of about five hundred youths remained on board *Penelope*, and the rest of the passengers were lodged with local Kladovo villagers, after an agreement of generous rental fees was reached with the Federation of Jewish Communities.

***

One morning, the fragments of dreams still lingering in my mind and the first sunbeams peering through the morning mists, I was pushing the wheelbarrow full of vegetable leftovers and grass for the pigs when, suddenly, I heard the noise of feet hurriedly shuffling down the road leading to the river. I raised my head and noticed a few of our people, among them Mr. Globerman with Gaetzer, the swindler, in his eternal cap, the long-bearded Mr. Schneider, and Malik the *shohet*,[14] who was dragging a large calf with a sack over its head and a rope around its neck. I realized this was intended to be the calf's last journey. Leaving the wheelbarrow, I quickly ran outside and tried to catch up with them, intending to rescue the poor calf. What sin had that poor animal committed to be led like that, head covered, to the slaughter? If the people on board *Penelope* were hungry, let them eat canned food, it's not so bad. It wasn't any different from Militza's corn bread that I was forced to eat each morning.

I hid behind the nearby fence. I have to stop them, I thought. But they're stronger than me and would probably make fun of me. "You're a wimpy, stupid kid," they'd say. "You need to grow up. Would you rather our people starved?" They'd hurl angry accusations at me and say to Mother and Father, "What kind of a son have you raised?" I heard Gaetzer and Globerman chatting about some other matter, completely ignoring what was about to happen. I could almost hear the heartbeats of the calf. Gaetzer smiled at Globerman. He wasn't at all concerned that the calf was about to lose its life. I wanted to scream at them to leave the poor animal alone. They stopped by a water faucet. Mr. Schneider turned on the faucet and filled the pitcher he was holding, and Globerman removed the sack from the calf's head, probably to give it water. Schneider tilted the calf's head up a little and forced water down its throat. The calf shook its head as if to resist, and water poured from the sides of its mouth.

Meanwhile, Mr. Globerman began to release the rope that was

---

14 A person certified by a rabbi or Jewish court of law to slaughter animals for food in the manner prescribed by Jewish law.

rolled in his hands and tie the calf's legs at the hooves. I wanted to leave my hiding place and scream in protest at this impending disaster, but instead, I covered my eyes with my hands and was unable to overcome my weakness. I heard the sounds of a struggle, of something dragged on the ground, then the sound of thudding. It must have been Globerman beating the body of the beast. But I remained glued to my spot, as helpless as that bound calf.

When I opened my eyes a crack, I saw the calf had already been pinned to the ground, and Malik the butcher had taken a large knife from his bag while muttering a prayer. I rose from my hiding place and ran as far as my feet could carry me away from that terrible place and didn't look back.

At breakfast, I couldn't touch a thing. Mother asked if I had a stomachache, and I shook my head.

"Perhaps we should go to Dr. Bezalel? You look pale."

All that day, my heart tormented me for being weak and not standing up and resisting the terrible act taking place before my eyes.

That evening, I heard Mother and Father talking. Mother expressed concern that Pauli and I weren't in school, and Father tried to calm her down.

"It won't hurt them to learn about life, about surviving difficult situations. That's just as important."

But Mother just wouldn't calm down.

"How can they learn about surviving if they don't have enough food to survive? Hanne hasn't eaten anything all day. Did you see how skinny they both are?"

"I heard they were handing out meat on *Penelope* today. We haven't seen any of it, though," said Father.

"My heart contracts," said Mother. "When I see the local children going to school as usual, while our children just wander about aimlessly. Sometimes I think we should go back to Belgrade until the children finish school. At least they studied a little while we were on the boats. Why did they stop teaching them? Just because we're on shore now? Is it because some of us are spread out in different houses?" Mother wondered.

"Perhaps we can establish a school for them right here and run it just like a real school…" Father came up with an idea.

Father's idea quickly came to fruition. Goldman and Dvoriansky were thrilled about it. Max Pomeranz, Yost's father, also liked the idea and said he was willing to be in charge of vocational studies. Father volunteered to design the school building and started to draft plans. A few days later, a pickup truck arrived, with timber for building the shed that would be our school. Benches and tables were built from the same timber. Joseph the carpenter became very busy and was assisted by four men from Gordonia[15] and two from Hashomer Hatzair. Pauli and I also helped with the construction. We carried the beams and handed them to the men who were building the walls and the roof. Father supervised construction, making sure everything was built exactly according to his plans.

It's been a week since I last saw Inge. It all started with a heated

---

15 Gordonia (Hebrew: גורדוניה) was a Zionist youth movement. The movement's doctrines were based on the beliefs of Aaron David Gordon; i.e., the salvation of *Eretz* Israel and the Jewish people through manual labor, and the revival of the Hebrew language.

argument we had on board the *Tzar Dusan* after one of Mr. Goldman's lessons dealing with the weekly *parashah*.

"Sometimes it seems so ridiculous," I said.

"What's ridiculous?" she asked naively, and I, not yet realizing just how sensitive she was about the Torah, said, "Well, you know, all the commentaries and interpretations for each verse in the Torah."

"What's so ridiculous about that?" she asked again, her tone now scolding. "Maybe you're the one who's ridiculous?"

"Don't you understand? Anyone can interpret the Torah any way he wants to—even make what's written to fit his own agenda."

"It shows that you've never received a proper Jewish education at home," she answered defiantly.

"True. My education was intended to make me a better person, a citizen of the world first of all, and only then a member of the Jewish community."

"So…" she stamped her foot, as she often did when she was angry. "Now you're finally admitting that you don't think the commandments of Judaism are important."

"In Akiba, they taught us differently, to listen to the words of the prophets. Amos, Hosea, and Isaiah spoke of morality and justice, not of ritual and commandments." I could see that she was deeply offended. Perhaps she thought my words were directed at her.

"Hanne, but everything is written. Who are we to decide what's true and what isn't?"

"So what if it's written?" I tried to rebuke her. "For example, the *parashah* we talked about today, *Emor*. 'And if a man cause a blemish in his neighbor; as he hath done, so shall it be done to him.' You really think the Torah commands us, a tooth for a tooth?"

I was surprised I'd managed to remember the verse we'd learned that morning.

"I see that there isn't anything to keep us together. Sometimes I don't even understand what I'm doing with you," she said and turned away.

"Why are you getting so upset?" I felt angry as well. "There's nothing personal here. Can't we speak like two adults, without you taking everything personally and getting upset every time?"

But there was no one there to talk to.

I thought she'd settle down after a while. That she'd realize she'd been irrational and come to apologize, or at least come to meet me without saying anything. I waited. I thought I'd see her in Mr. Goldman's classes, but she stopped attending. I came to class every morning. Right after feeding the pigs, I ran there, my heart beating in anticipation of a possible meeting—would she be waiting there by the door? But she didn't come. During the lessons, I eagerly waited to see the door handle turning and the door opening, revealing Inge's beautiful freckled face. She'd say she was sorry for being late, then come and sit beside me as if nothing had ever happened. When she didn't show up, I became distracted by thoughts of her, trying to understand what in my words or behavior had pushed her away from me. Mr. Goldman noticed I was daydreaming during his classes and even rebuked me once in front of the whole group.

"Young Mr. David, I've noticed something is bothering you of late. Perhaps you would be kind enough to share your thoughts with us?"

After the lesson, I went to help with the building of the new school that was taking form according to Father's plans. It helped ease the heartache I felt about not meeting Inge. After a few days, I gave up and decided she was too important to me and I didn't want to lose her because of my ego. I went to the infirmary to look for her.

"She's busy with the doctor now," an elderly woman in the waiting room told me in a local Serbo-Croatian dialect. "My daughter's inside. She's been suffering from stomachaches for quite some time."

I sat impatiently waiting for the door to open. It took an eternity. What could be taking them so long? Why weren't they finished already? Then the door opened. A young woman, her face and eyes shrunken and emaciated, came outside with Inge's hand placed warmly and gently on her shoulder. Inge saw me and smiled. She actually seemed pleased that I'd come, and even asked me to translate the doctor's instructions for the local patient. The three of us sat on the bench. Inge gave me the instructions, and I translated them for the sick young woman and her mother.

When they left the infirmary, we sat on the bench together.

"I'm sorry if I insulted you the other day. I didn't mean to." I gently placed her hand on my knee and softly stroked it.

"I've thought about it a lot as well," she said, and I saw the sorrow in her eyes. "I was wrong to be so angry with you; after all, it really wasn't personal. I'm sorry too." She placed her warm hand on mine.

That moment, a great weight lifted from my heart. The moment I'd longed for so much those past few days had finally come, and I was filled with happiness. I told her I was in a hurry, because I'd promised Mikhailo I'd help him with the harvest. Today, I would cut the grass by myself for the first time and take it in a horse-drawn wagon to the pigsty.

We parted with my promise to come and visit her at the infirmary that afternoon, and I ran lightly back toward the house.

***

The construction of the school was finally completed, and Wednesday afternoon was declared the date for the festive opening ceremony. Sime Spitzer, chairman of the Federation of Jewish Communities, had also been invited to the ceremony.

"Even in such times of waiting and uncertainty, it is our duty to maintain hope and go on with our lives," said Mr. Sime Spitzer at the humble ceremony.

Dvoriansky spoke next and said that it was important to have a school for children and youths who had to discontinue their studies for a noble cause.

"We are building a school that will serve as an example for all other schools in the area, also because of our fine teachers." He mentioned their names, and the large crowd responded with enthusiastic applause. "We've received a supply of school uniforms, khaki clothes with a black beret bearing a golden star. This will be a school in the full sense of the word!" added Dvoriansky enthusiastically. "At the end of the ceremony, we will distribute the uniforms in the supply room. There are three sizes."

Martha's children's choir sang three songs in honor of the event, and Fredl accompanied them on his accordion.

Then came the first day of school and I was very excited. It had taken me longer than usual to feed the pigs that morning, and as I wanted to get there early and save a seat for Inge, I planned on skipping breakfast.

"Sit down, Hanne, and eat some breakfast like a decent human being," Mother scolded me when she saw me wearing my school uniform, about to leave for my first lesson. "Sit down this very moment and eat something," she said, cutting a few slices of Militza's corn bread.

I just couldn't stand that bread, and the cheese leftovers were moldy.

The Mayer family from Vienna, whose daughter Stella was six years younger than me, had moved into the house next to ours. Mother was very angry about the smell of meat patties constantly issuing from their kitchen. She saved every penny so she could buy food for us at the Kladovo market on the weekend, but the smell of meat coming from the neighbor's house had made her feel she was neglecting us.

Unwillingly, I finished my breakfast then ran to the southern end of the village, where the new school was located.

The first lesson was with Mr. Dvoriansky. I really like his lessons. He always manages to include something about survival. In the previous lessons, we'd learned about the First Jewish–Roman War, about Elazar Ben Yair and the ploys that helped the rebels survive the siege. In my imagination, I pictured myself as one of the rebels in Ben Yair's army, a skillful sniper, able to shoot an arrow straight into the forehead of a Roman soldier while the walls were being breached. I planned on going to the forest after school, to find some branches suitable for a bow. For my bowstring, I planned on using a fishing line I'd found not far from Petrović's fishing-net shed.

In literature class, we read another chapter from Franz Werfel's book *The Forty Days of Musa Dagh*[16]—dealing with the Armenian community that had managed to resist the Ottomans on "Mount Moses"—Musa Dagh. Five thousand members of the community went up the mountain and fortified themselves under harsh conditions to protest the deportation and exile decrees handed down by the authorities. The book's lead character, Gabriel Bagradian, is a wealthy man living in Paris, who returns to his homeland for ideological, patriotic reasons—in order to lead a rebellion.

Bagradian had become a sort of idol to us, as if he was one of ours. After reading another chapter in the classroom, I was certain that one day, I'd be just like Gabriel Bagradian.

There is only one copy of the book in the Hechalutz group, and I haven't been able to get it yet. There's a whole list of readers waiting to read it, and we'd already asked Naftali Bata to get us more copies.

Mr. Goldman asked if such a terrible disaster could happen to another nation. Everyone said that nothing in the world could compare with the cruelty of the Turks, and that it seems that only the uncivilized nations of the orient could act in such a cruel way.

Mr. Goldman tried again.

"Could the persecution of the Jews in Europe today lead to a similar catastrophe?"

He listened to our silence, then added, "Think of Bagradian, living in Europe with European manners and etiquette, language and

16 The book was published in Germany in November 1933 and immediately became an international success. It helped raise worldwide awareness of the persecution of the Armenian community and predicted the way the Germans would treat the Jews.

culture, almost forgetting that he was Armenian, until the Turks came along and reminded him. Doesn't it remind you of anything?"

"It definitely reminds me of something," I said. "My father never imagined we'd have to leave all the luxury and comfort of our lives there to join this expedition, but then a time came when the writing was on the wall. We didn't fear for our lives like the Armenians, but there was less and less work. My father couldn't get new contracts, and we were treated poorly by the authorities. It was easier to make up our minds about leaving after we heard about what was happening in Germany and Austria."

"Thank you, Hanne," said Mr. Goldman. "That's exactly what I wanted to hear. We are now in the midst of a historical process, and while it's still too early to draw comparisons, things appear to be headed in a similar direction."

After the lesson, I allowed my imagination to run wild again; this time, my thoughts wandered to the land of Palestine.

I thought about the fact that when we finally reached our land, we'd build a Jewish nation that would serve as a model for the whole world. We'd be strong, but we'd treat the meek and the persecuted with compassion.

On Mr. Goldman's shortwave radio, we keep hearing about the horrific riots in Palestine, about what the Arabs are doing to the Jews and the British. I'm willing to be drafted into the fighting units. I'll join the fighters who are trying to protect the land from Arab rioters and help get rid of the British, who are preventing the Jews from emigrating to Israel. We will show the whole world that the Jews are no longer a persecuted foreign minority, but transformed into courageous fighters in their own country.

Meanwhile, I want to prepare, so I can join the fighting forces the moment we get there. I don't have any way of practicing with firearms, but I can practice shooting with a bow and arrow, or wrestling and judo, just like the people of the Bosnian resistance who fought the Austrian Empire before the Great War.

In the afternoon, I wanted to walk with Inge along the riverbank. I was hoping she'd finally accept my invitation today. She refused, of course. She's always in a hurry after school to get back to Dr. Bezalel's infirmary. He has a cabin that serves as an infirmary on board *Penelope*, and she cleans and organizes it every day.

I decided to go on my own, make a bow and arrows, and do some target practice, perhaps even use my arrows for hunting and self-defense. I headed toward the well. Behind the remains of an ancient wall, a narrow pathway winds its way into the forest. I'd been walking down that path for the past few days, curious to learn where it led. Tall trees tower on both sides, vines cover the bark of the trees like a green wall strewn with flowers, like the robe of a king from one of my childhood picture books. I decided to pick a flower for Mr. Schuster, the science teacher, who kept telling us how excited he was about the coming of spring. I was looking for the point I'd reached the previous day when I heard the soft sound of trickling water. I looked around for a supple branch suitable for a bow. The trickling sound became louder and my feet got wet. A short walk later, I found myself on a wooden bridge crossing the stream. I stopped and sat down to look at the clear water. Plump fish swam lazily, and two crabs rested on the bank, enjoying the springtime sun. If I had a fishing rod, I'd try to catch some trout for Mother. I knew how hard the food shortage was for her.

But the fishing line in my pocket wasn't long enough to serve as a rod. Two weeks ago, old Petrović had showed me how to make a fishing rod from a long pole and a thin nylon fishing line with a hook on the end: He made a slit with the edge of his pocketknife at the end of a flexible wooden rod. Then he threaded the end of a fishing line he'd pulled from the bottom of a pile of nets into the slit, winding it around the rod several times. Finally, he grabbed the line and pulled it tight.

"You see, that's how you tie the line to the rod so it doesn't get loose."

He took a metal box of various-sized hooks from his pocket. Choosing a medium-sized hook, he tied it to the other end of the fishing line and said, "Simple, huh? Now we can go fishing."

I decided to ask him for a fishing line and a hook so I could go fishing in the forest. Perhaps Inge would join me. She'd probably love to go out for some fresh air in the woods. These past few days, I'd been thinking a lot about Inge. I felt that she was drifting away from me again. Perhaps this was because I was with my parents in Mikhailo's hut, while she's with all the youths on board *Penelope*. I was afraid this might draw us apart. I had also noticed a tall fellow called Menachem hanging around her. I don't know if she has feelings for him, but I really miss her during my lonely nights in the hut.

I wonder what she'd say about the fishing rod I'm planning to make. Perhaps she'd take some fish back for her group. But first we'd both eat, collect firewood, and light a fire, just like the children in *Treasure Island* when they learned to survive on their own.

I took out the pocketknife Father gave me for my bar mitzvah. I always keep it in the pocket of my trousers. I opened it and gently started to shave both sides of the branch until the edge was bright and smooth. I cut away all the bulges on the sides, as Petrović had taught me. I cut slits in both ends of the branch. I took the fishing line from my pocket to wrap it around the end of the bow. Then, looking up, I saw that the sky had filled with black clouds, and a wide, colorful rainbow stretched across the western horizon. I finished wrapping the string and ran toward the village.

The sky was black and the sun had completely vanished. The wind grew stronger, bending the treetops. The rain, which started as a light drizzle, gradually intensified, forcing me to take cover under the branches of a vine-covered tree, which formed a thick protective roof. The rain fell like a curtain of water. A blinding flash of lightning was followed by a loud clap of thunder rolling across the sky. I sat hunched up, waiting for the rain to slacken so I could run back to the village. Time seemed to stand still, and I prepared myself for the possibility that I might not be able to get home. I was afraid Mother and Father would be worried.

Luckily, the rain subsided after a while. The powerful downpour became a light drizzle. Shivering with cold but fairly dry, I left my hiding place and ran toward the village. I could already see the pointed spire of the church from a distance, when I suddenly heard the sound of crying coming from the bushes next to the pathway.

As I got closer, I heard wailing.

"They're going to kill me. Help, they're going to kill me…"

He lay on the ground, his pants pulled down and his torn coat thrown next to him. His face was covered with blood, his lip torn open, and his left eye swollen. Despite this painful sight, I was able to recognize Gaetzer, the swindler, who had brought the calf for the *Penelope* groups on that unforgettable morning. Wherever there was money to be made, Gaetzer was there. Everyone had taken pleasure in hating him as early as the *Tzar Nikolai* days. Even back then, everyone complained that he was exploiting the misery of people on the boats for personal profit. They also said he'd received a generous sum for that calf. When we disembarked from the boats, he opened a store and everyone started calling him "Gaetzer the profiteer." He would always show up elegantly dressed, wearing gold chains and expensive watches.

"I hope he turns green with envy," said Mother.

Now, I bent over him and tried to encourage him to speak, but he was too badly hurt to say anything intelligible. I didn't know how to help him or dress his wounds. I didn't have the necessary means either. I had to go for help. We were close to the harbor. I told him to hang on and ran toward Dr. Bezalel's infirmary.

"What's wrong, Hanne? Why are you so wet and out of breath?" asked Inge with concern.

"Come quickly. We need the doctor urgently," I answered while trying to regain my breath. "Bring the first-aid bag, and tell the doctor to bring one too."

She took the first-aid bag from the corner next to the stretcher.

"The doctor went out to examine a patient on *Penelope*," she said. "But tell me, what happened?"

"It's Gaetzer. He's hurt and needs urgent help." I beckoned her to follow me.

On the way, we met Efraim at the well and took him along to help.

"Come with me," I said, taking the first-aid bag from Inge.

"What's happened?" asked Efraim with concern.

"Someone has beaten Gaetzer half to death. He's bleeding all over. It's terrible."

"I knew this was coming," said Efraim. "He's been asking for it."

"But not this. You won't believe what those barbarians have done to him."

"Don't be naive. The man was getting on everyone's nerves with his greed," Efraim said, trying to keep up with me.

"It doesn't matter how much they hated him," Inge interfered. "You can't act like that. A Jew must never hit his brother."

"Oh, come on," said Efraim. "Everyone knows he's a thief and a profiteer. He had it coming."

We reached the place where I'd found him. Gaetzer was still mumbling.

"Kill me… They're going to kill me."

Inge bent over him and examined his wounds. She tried to make him tell her where it hurt. With the skill of a physician, she felt his limbs from head to toe and checked for fractures or hemorrhages.

"You're very lucky, Mr. Gaetzer," she said with a broad smile, the one I thought was reserved just for me. "Let's check your back and stomach as well."

He had a few blue bruises on his back, probably from a club or a metal rod. Gaetzer didn't speak, and Inge took out an antiseptic and started to clean his bleeding face.

"Hanne, hand me the bandages and help me cut," she gave me the scissors. Efraim just stood and watched. "Don't worry, Efraim," she turned to him. "You and Hanne will take him to the sickroom once I'm done."

After Inge had finished dressing the wounds, we picked him up carefully. Efraim grabbed his feet and I supported his shoulders. With slow, measured steps, we made our way down to the harbor. When we finally reached the infirmary, Dr. Bezalel was already waiting for us there.

"Lay him down on the second bed on the right," he said. "I'll be with him in a moment."

"I never imagined they'd punish him so harshly," said Efraim once we were outside.

"Yesterday, my father told me he'd approached him a few days ago as a representative of the committee and asked him to contribute some money to the common fund, just like everyone else does, but he refused," he just added fuel to the fire.

"But who would hurt him like that. One of our own people? Maybe he was robbed by gypsies?" said Efraim.

"Do you remember what they did to Milos?" I asked. "Inge told me it was terrible."

"Yes, I remember," said Efraim. "But you can't compare the two cases. Milos was just beaten up a little. No one's ever died from some pushing and shoving."

"It was because of the walnuts from his uncle in Belgrade."

"Right. Everyone asked him for some, because that's what a friend should do. But he acted like a spoiled little brat," Efraim said scornfully.

"Yes. And that wasn't the first time. Remember when he got the parcel of *halva*? He ate it right in front of everyone, out of spite."

"Are you coming to *Penelope* with me?" he asked. "The *schiffsre-view*[17] are going to perform after dinner."

"I'd love to. I heard there were a lot of funny gags last time, and a lot of dirty language. They made fun of Mr. Globerman. Wasn't he insulted?"

"At least all the weird people around here give us something to laugh about. I laughed until I cried, and the songs… That guy whose wife had a baby, Fredl, played on three instruments simultaneously. I've never seen anything like it in my life," Efraim was excited.

"I hope my parents will go tonight. They could do with a good laugh."

"So tell them to come to *Penelope* at eight. Everyone's coming."

"Now that I think of it, I don't know if there's even going to be a show tonight," I answered him. "Not after this incident. They've almost killed one of our own," I told him.

"I don't think they'd cancel," answered Efraim, a hint of condescension in his voice.

∗∗∗

I couldn't fall asleep that night either. The sight of Gaetzer's torn lips and swollen eye preyed on my mind. I must have fallen asleep eventually, because I dreamed of Inge, dressed in white like a bride, a wreath of flowers on her head. No one accompanied her, as Mother had held Klarie's arm to lead her to the wedding canopy. But where was the

---

17 The Ship's Review.

groom? I was in the audience and wanted to tell her I was willing to be her groom, but couldn't utter the words. I wanted to hug her and whisper it in her pink, almost transparent ear, which was now very close to me. I could also feel the gentle scent of her skin, the smell of good soap, not the cheap one we use here. I wanted to tell her something when she suddenly began to walk toward me, taking off her white dress. She wasn't wearing anything under her wedding dress. Not even underwear. Nothing but a soft, white body. I saw her breasts, and she held out her hands in invitation. I embraced her and whispered that I'd never leave her. I could feel her nipples against my skin. I cupped her breasts with my hands…and woke up with a warm wetness spreading from my loins.

***

It's been a couple of weeks since we'd moved in with Mikhailo and Militza. All that time, Mother continued to work in the storage room. She was now managing it and in charge of the distribution of all food products and clothing. Everyone loved the pleasant way she did her work and treated her with respect. Father, on the other hand, was dwindling from day to day. His face was drawn, as if his entire world had crumbled. When Inge told me he scowled when he saw her, I explained that it wasn't just her, but the entire world. He'd lost his authority and was hurting, which was why he'd been hurting others, including Mother and occasionally me too.

One morning, when I returned home from Mr. Dvoriansky's lesson, I went by the storage room adjacent to the kitchen to greet Mother. I went in quietly, walking on tiptoes to surprise her, when suddenly I saw her standing between two shelves, taking down a roll of sausage, tearing it in half, hastily wrapping it in newspaper, and shoving it into the large pocket of her coat. I was shocked to see her do something like that. I retraced my steps silently, not wanting her to see me and realize I'd caught her in the act.

Come to think of it, our breakfasts and dinners had been richer lately. We ate sausage, cheese, and even *halva* for breakfast. I didn't think much about it; I thought everyone was finally getting better rations from the storage room. When I asked Efraim, he said he hadn't noticed any change. The same unsavory food, tasteless porridge for breakfast and dry bread for dinner. Sometimes the cook would make meat patties for lunch, but only when there was meat.

"What about sausage?"

"Rarely. It's been days since I've eaten sausage," said Efraim.

When we were eating dinner, Father asked, "Where are all these delicacies coming from, Louisa?"

He pointed at a plate with slices of sausage on it, very much like the one we used to have back home, as if he'd just discovered something was wrong. Pauli said he didn't even like sausage, and as far as he was concerned, we could just go on eating corn bread every day. I don't really like sausage either, but didn't want to say so at the table after Mother had taken such a personal risk for our sakes. Just so we wouldn't become "all skin and bones," as I'd heard her say to Father more than once, begging him to do something so we'd have something to eat.

"Uncle Nissimov sent us a package from Belgrade," she said. "He sent it with the Federation of Jewish Communities straight to the storage room. Maybe that's why I hadn't told you?"

I saw Father's face fill with surprise and realized it was very difficult for Mother to hide the truth from him.

"I'd no idea. How come you didn't say anything?" he asked in surprise. "Don't you think we should write and thank him?"

"I'll write him a letter, Emil. Don't worry about it. I just haven't had the chance yet…" Mother said, shifting uncomfortably in her chair.

"But he's my uncle, nonetheless. It's important that I be the one to write him. Leave it to me."

"Perhaps you don't need to. I saw a lot of people getting packages from families in Vienna or Belgrade. It's not…" Mother continued to wriggle in her chair.

"I don't understand why you'd object to a simple demonstration of gratitude. This isn't like you at all."

"Yes, yes, you're probably right. I'll sit down and write him," answered Mother. "And I don't think I deserve such treatment after making sure there's always food on the table. When was the last time you went to the market?" She banged her hand on the table. "You're always busy with those letters of yours. The devil knows what good they'll do us."

"My letters? I'm trying to arrange papers for all of us," he responded angrily. "You think I enjoy humiliating myself before the authorities? Do you have any idea what they're asking now?"

"No," she answered. "You never share anything with me."

I felt Mother relaxing because the subject of the package from our uncle was finally dropped and she didn't need to lie anymore. I was

afraid Father would find out about Mother stealing food from everyone just so Pauli and I could eat better. I didn't want to think about
what Father would do if he ever found out.

***

Today, Inge came with me to fish for trout in the stream. Last time, I
brought Mother two trout, and she prepared them for dinner. Everyone enjoyed it and Father complimented me.

"Next time, you should sell some fish at the Kladovo market," he
said with a smile.

We sat on the small bridge, our feet dangling above the water,
and looked at the flowing stream. Suddenly, I felt Inge's leg rubbing
against mine, and the next moment, she even crossed them together
and raised them both. I was surprised but let her do what she wanted.
Then she turned her body toward me, and I felt the heat of her face
close to mine. She brought her cheek closer and pulled me to her. I
hadn't kissed a girl yet, but thought this time it was going to happen.
I'd once seen Mother and Father kissing when they returned from the
opera and were in their room. I'd been waiting for this moment ever
since I'd met Inge, but I was still surprised. Only when I felt her head
close to mine did I feel certain the time was right. Holding her head,
I turned it toward me and drew her closer. For a moment, I looked
into her blue eyes and saw them shining, then I pressed my lips to
hers. They were smooth and pleasant, intoxicating. I pressed her lips
to mine, and she yielded to the touch. I'd never felt such a pleasant
sensation and wanted it to go on forever, but Inge quickly drew her

lips away with a hesitant laugh.

"That was your first kiss, wasn't it?" she asked.

"Yes," I answered shamefully. "Could you tell?"

"But it was wonderful. You kiss like an experienced man. You're in love with me, Hanne, aren't you?"

I remained speechless.

"I could tell from the very beginning," she said, lightly patting her skirt, as if trying to smooth wrinkles that weren't there. Then she asked, with blazing eyes, "Do you think I'm too forward?"

For a girl from the Mizrahi group, I thought she was a little forward, but I didn't want her to think I was a child. I wanted her to continue to be forward, and mumbled, "No... Not really..." And to try and correct the impression, I said, "It's just that you surprised me a little."

She looked at me with her blazing eyes and said, "I had someone serious once. A fiancé. We almost got married..."

I looked at her with surprise, and she said, "I loved him very much."

"Why didn't you get married, then?" I asked naively.

"It's hard for me to explain. Something terrible happened. Something that still bothers me."

"What happened?"

"I think about him a lot, but I know there wasn't any other choice. He was no longer himself."

"What do you mean?"

"Alfred was his name. Freddie. We were very close, you know... serious. We spoke of marriage. I was deliberating whether I should go and study before getting married, and Freddie said he didn't mind, that he'd even help me. He told me he loved me and that we should get married. I was still very young, and he was already well-off. He was working for his father in a large clothing store in Berlin."

Inge slowly swung her feet back over the stream. She spoke quickly, almost breathlessly, finally telling the story she'd withheld from me all the months of our friendship.

"One day, we'd scheduled to meet next to the fountain in Alexanderplatz, and he didn't show up. I continued to wait, an hour, then another. I tried to think of good reasons for him to be late. He was always very punctual. There were already rumors back then about Dachau, but I didn't even want to think about it. Only when I got back home did my mother tell me. 'Haven't you heard? They came early this morning and took a lot of people to Dachau.'

"Freddie wasn't very politically aware. He was also an optimist. He never thought about stirring up any political unrest. He and his father weren't taken because of a political issue. They took them away just because they hadn't registered as Jews. Would you believe it?" her voice began to choke with tears. "And so I waited for him, for weeks and months, a year, but he never came back. Letters came, but they were difficult to read. They worked in an ammunitions factory, hard manual labor. His father was sickly, unused to that type of work. Whoever didn't meet his daily quota was beaten. At night, when they returned exhausted to the barracks, they took them to do maintenance work around the camp, although they suffered from sub-zero temperatures and malnutrition. He didn't write me all that, of course, because their letters were censored. He told me all that later. I've asked myself so many times, how is it possible? How could people be taken away from their homes and families and sent to a living hell? It was in every way a living hell."

Now she could no longer control her tears. She cried, her entire body shaking with sobs. I gently wrapped her in my arms.

"We'll be together forever, always. No one will ever separate us," I whispered to her.

"I'll never forget the day he returned. July 22, 1938. I didn't even recognize him. He was emaciated. His cheeks were sunken, his head shaved. He'd always had a plump, smiling face. His eyes were dull, and he kept looking down. He came back alone, after three years. Like many others, his father died there from cold and starvation. And he… he…"

Unable to finish the sentence, she placed her head on my chest and wept.

"He didn't even recognize me when he came back. He wasn't the same Freddie. His mother later told me that he couldn't sleep nights and hardly ate. They had to amputate one of his feet because of frost-bite from walking in the snow without proper shoes. Two months after he'd returned, when his nightmares became unbearable, she was forced to commit him to a mental institution."

I pressed her trembling body to mine. I held her for long moments, and she silently cried with her face in my neck. It was hard not to cry as well. I felt my throat tighten, but forced myself not to get carried away. I wasn't sure what excited me more, the first kiss I'd just experienced, its sweet taste still in my mouth, or Inge's sad story, mixed with my happiness.

When I got home that evening, I was surprised to find Dr. Bezalel there. He'd come to examine Mother, who'd complained of a stomach-ache. In the morning, she'd told Father the pain was bearable. But it had grown worse since then.

When I saw the doctor's serious expression, so unlike his usual cheerful manner, with his jokes about Mother getting better in time to dance at our wedding, I immediately realized something was seriously wrong. There weren't any jokes this time. He and Father looked very concerned. They spoke in hushed voices in the kitchen. I could hear the words "hospital," "appendicitis," and "urgent." Father asked how dangerous it was, and the doctor answered that every moment was crucial.

"The infection might cause a rupture and lead to a general infection of the intestinal membranes. It's dangerous. Very dangerous."

I listened, my heart beating fast. Mother once told me every person has a star to keep him safe. *Where was her star?* I found myself asking.

Late at night, Pauli and I stood with Father on the pier. Mother lay on a stretcher beside us. The doctor had given her some pills to relieve the pain, and we were waiting for the boat to come and take her to Prahovo.

Father simply wouldn't hear of Mother going by herself for the operation. From Prahovo, they'd take the train to Belgrade. Father, who'd recently been busy writing letters to various offices to speed up the process of arranging our immigration papers, was hoping he'd have time to go to the Ministry of the Interior and take care of our paperwork. As we saw the lights of the approaching boat, Inge came running to say goodbye to Mother.

"I'd have gone with you. It would have been good for someone from the medical staff to come with you to the hospital, but Dr. Bezalel needs me here," she said and gave her a tight hug. "Feel better and come back quickly. I don't want to sail to Israel without you," she said, handing her a box of pills. "Here, for relieving pain. But only if it gets really bad," she continued. "Because it also subdues the symptoms."

Mother promised everything would be just fine and hugged her back.

Meanwhile, the boat to Prahovo had arrived and docked next to us. Father held Mother's hand and they boarded the boat. Pauli and I went inside too, so we could say goodbye. I hugged Mother as hard as I could and tried to tell her I'd find her star and we'd keep her safe together, but I wasn't able to say a word and felt tears coming.

"Take care of Hanne. See that he doesn't do anything foolish while we're not here," I managed to hear Father whispering in Pauli's ear.

We stood on the pier until the lights of the boat had disappeared into the night.

***

As the days passed, my concern for Mother grew. I would get up every morning and wonder what was happening to her. Was she out of danger? Had she had the operation? Father had promised to update us, but we hadn't received any letters. Mrs. Mayer, Stella's mother, invited Pauli and me to eat dinner with them a couple of times. She asked a lot of questions about Mother, but we had nothing to tell her. It was only on the fourth day that we received a brief postcard.

Dear Pauli and Hanne,

Mother had the operation on Sunday. Right after we arrived with Dr. Bezalel's letter, she was examined and immediately admitted to the operating theater. The operation was successful, and she now needs to rest for a few days.

We will be back on Monday.

Kisses and love,
Mother and Father

P.S.

Belgrade hasn't changed since we left. Everything is still beautiful. I went past your school and saw happy boys playing soccer during recess. My heart ached when I thought about how you've had to leave everything behind and are now stuck in an idle routine of waiting that could drive even the sanest of men crazy. I hope that one day we'll be able to settle in Haifa or Tel Aviv and lead a good, normal life together.

I read the postcard to Mrs. Mayer and saw that her eyes were tearful.

"Good. I'm so happy she's all right. I was so worried about her."

***

One day, during the first week of June, I'd just come back from a walk along the stream with Inge. We saw Teddy, head of the Mizrahi group, gathering all the group members next to the infirmary and explaining something to them about setting sail soon. We joined them and listened.

"For the benefit of the couple who've just joined us," he said. "I'll repeat the main points. A week from now, we should receive instructions to set sail at very short notice." He looked around to check that everyone was present and said, "Efraim, you're in charge of updating everyone who isn't here."

Efraim immediately said, "But how could I know who isn't here if they aren't here?"

Everyone burst out laughing, then started talking among themselves. They all wanted to ask questions and understand when, where, and how we'd reach the ships. They also wanted to know if we could already send letters to families waiting in Israel. Teddy raised a hand to silence everyone and added, "We'll board the ship they send us as a single group. The larger groups, those from Hechalutz and Netzah, will be divided into two groups."

"What about us, the families?" I asked. "Do you already know where we're supposed to board?"

"I still don't have answers to such questions," said Teddy. "We only received the message this morning. Within two days, everything should be settled at a meeting in Budapest between the representatives of the Joint and Sime Spitzer."

"Can I let my aunt in Hadera know we'll be leaving soon?" someone asked.

"It's better not to write before the meeting is over and we receive final and definite approval," Teddy answered. "But in the meantime, it's important that we get ready. There'll be another meeting tomorrow, and it's important that everyone attend. I need to prepare a list of names to send to the Federation of Jewish Communities as early as tomorrow."

There was great joy. Everyone hugged. I took Inge in my arms and lifted her into the air. We heard the Austrians from the Netzah group singing *hora* as loud as they could, probably erupting into wild dancing.

But I was suddenly consumed with fear. *What if we need to leave before my parents come back?* That fear made it difficult for me to join in the general jubilation. They'd written that they'd be back on Monday, but if I've learned anything, it's that you can never rely on promises.

The next day, when I came back from harvesting clover and finished feeding the pigs, I saw a group of people gathering at our house with the evening paper in their hands. As they often did, they asked me to translate the news from Serbo-Croatian to German. I realized that this time, something important must have happened. Since the invasion of Belgium the week before, everyone was very tense, wanting to be updated about what was happening at the Franco-Belgian front. Three days ago, I'd read them some encouraging news from the front; the breach created by the German army at the northwestern border of France was almost sealed. I'd also read them further updates from the front about French tanks in action, and all the optimistic forecasts about the French Ardennes, which were steep and therefore considered impassable for armored vehicles.

Today's headlines screamed "The Miracle of Dunkirk"[18] and the photo showed a boatful of armed soldiers with more soldiers boarding, expressions of urgency on their faces. The caption read, "British boat rescues expeditionary forces from France." And below, "Evacuation of hundreds of thousands of French and British soldiers from the beaches of Dunkirk now complete."

I read the news and sensed that my listeners were finding it hard to accept.

I continued, "Over nine hundred boats participated in the rescue of hundreds of thousands of British soldiers and a hundred thousand French soldiers from the expeditionary force. The operation, begun on May 26, was completed today, June 4."

An outburst of shocked and fearful cries rose from the listeners, as they realized the Germans had managed to invade France and that the British expeditionary force was about to be defeated as well.

The next day, Dvoriansky came to me at the end of the lesson and thanked me.

"It's not only the translation. Anyone could do that," he said. "You have the ability to sort out the most important facts and relay crucial information. I think you will be a great teacher one day."

Then he shared his own love of teaching with me. In Vienna, he'd studied history and dreamed of becoming a historian. But when war broke out, he decided his life's mission was to teach the lessons of the past, as this could help shape the minds of youth and so influence the future.

---

18 The Miracle of Dunkirk refers to the evacuation of Allied soldiers from the beaches and harbor of Dunkirk, France, between May 26 and June 4, 1940.

He asked me what I was planning to do when the war ended. I told him of my longing to become a farmer in the land of Israel, to help make the desert bloom and build the country.

"You're right," he said. "A man needs to follow his heart." He added, "But making the desert bloom is an expression that may hide other meanings." And he pointed at himself, "Many people foretold a great academic future for me; they wanted me to get university degrees and become a lecturer and researcher, but my heart yearned for other things. The ideals were more important to me, and you can see what I've accomplished. But not everyone is cut out for it. Perhaps the university would be a more suitable environment for you. Although, now that the cannons are roaring, the academic halls are as silent as the muses."

Tomorrow, Mother and Father are supposed to return from Belgrade. I waited for them impatiently, despite my busy schedule. Today, Mikhailo took me out in his fishing boat to improve my fishing skills. On the way, he explained to me about the *stiuca* fish—very common in the river here—and, of course, about trout. We left very early in the morning. Efraim did all my morning chores with the pigs instead of me. He came to sleep over at our place so he could get up early in the morning and tend to them. Fishing in Mikhailo's boat was pretty boring, even though we did manage to catch a few large *stiuca* fish. Most of the time, we just sat and stared at the unmoving water. Mikhailo can sit for hours without saying a word. We returned at ten that morning, and Mikhailo rode off to the market on his tricycle cart, carrying a sack of fish.

***

The following day, toward evening, Pauli, Inge, and I waited for the ferry from Prahovo to arrive at Kladovo harbor. We saw the ferry approaching and could already see Mother from where we stood, leaning feebly against Father's shoulder. They came down the gangplank, and Pauli and I ran to her and hugged her.

"Everything is all right, my precious ones," she soothed us. "I'm a little weak, but I'll regain my strength here in time for the coming trip."

Back in our hut, I volunteered to make tea for everyone. Mrs. Mayer from the neighboring apartment had come in, and everyone sat down to hear about what had happened to my parents, how the outside world looked, and, of course, to hear more about the operation. Mother said the doctors had treated her so kindly that she'd started to have doubts again; doubts about leaving everything in the first place. After all, we weren't in any immediate danger, like the Jews of Austria and Germany.

"Inge, do you remember asking me why we were in such a hurry to leave everything behind? Well, now I don't know if the answer I gave you was true. After seeing life going on there as if nothing had happened, I asked myself why we'd interrupted Hanne's and Pauli's studies. We could at least have waited for them to finish high school and get their diplomas."

Father placed his cup of tea on the table and said firmly, "You can't look at the situation like that. Just look at what happened in France just a week ago, for example. Who would have imagined the French and English allowing the Germans to invade?"

Instead of making us feel better, his words simply fueled our tension and fear. He tried to soften the effect of his words.

"All signs show that we'll get instructions to leave Kladovo any day now. That's what I understood from Sime when I met with him in Belgrade. He told me about a very important meeting in Budapest and sounded very optimistic," said Father soothingly. "We just need a little more patience."

Inge rose and said she had to go back to the infirmary. I offered to walk her back, because it was already dark. When we arrived, we saw people crowding around, looking at a special edition of the evening paper.

"Oh, here comes Hanne, just when we need him," someone called and shoved the paper into my hands. A large photo showed a multitude of people standing in a main square while someone wearing a fez hat was standing on a balcony and giving a speech.

"Translation, translation! German, please," everyone asked me.

I started reading and translating. "Italy Joins the War!" I read the main headline that took up almost a quarter of a page. Underneath, in smaller print, "Mussolini sends his army against the weak French front." I continued to translate the caption beneath the photo. "From the balcony of the Palazzo di Venezia, Mussolini announces: Italy is joining the war."

There were mingled cries of incredulous anger. No one could believe it. A mixture of cries and insults against the fascist tyrant rose in the air. Just a few days ago, Mussolini had announced that Italy had no interest in joining the war. Now he was claiming Italy had done everything humanly possible to avoid war, but to no avail. At the bottom of the same front page, I read, "French government forced to leave Paris. Relocates to Bordeaux."

The first thought that passed through my mind was that Father had been right when, just fifteen minutes ago, he'd said, "Just look at what happened in France only a week ago." The world could turn upside down in a second. My listeners wouldn't let go and clamored for me to keep reading. Shechter, who enjoyed spreading rumors and dark prophecies, shouted, "Now we're really stuck here. The Italians will close the sea to us and we won't be able to set sail."

***

Three days had passed since Italy entered the war and still no new announcements. Everyone was hoping there'd be no change of plans and that we'd still be leaving in a few days.

We were all encouraged by the meeting that was supposed to take place in Budapest, the meeting Father had told us about so happily and optimistically, following his conversation with Sime Spitzer in Belgrade.

At noon the following day, on the fifteenth of June, Fredl's trumpet call summoned us to the pier again. It was said that Sime Spitzer himself would be arriving to give us the message. There was a great commotion. People huddled in little groups and spoke excitedly about the news Spitzer would bring us regarding our imminent departure.

After waiting for over an hour, just as voices predicting the postponement of the meeting were beginning to be heard, the sound of an engine came from the road to the pier. Usually, vehicles coming from the main road had something to do with voyage management: trucks carrying equipment, or vans bringing food supplies. Not everything came via the river from Prahovo.

Mr. Spitzer got out of the car. He was wearing casual clothes this time. His head was uncovered, without his trademark hat. Hesitantly and heavily, he walked toward the center of the gathering, as if carrying a heavy burden on his shoulders. There was great tension in the air. He clearly couldn't bring himself to open his mouth and speak. He placed a hand on his mouth and cleared his throat a few times.

"Friends," he said, somehow regaining his confidence. "It is no easy task to be speaking before you today."

A wave of anger, shock, and protest rose from the crowd.

"Yes, I have no good news for you today."

The angry screams grew louder. Sime cleared his throat again.

"As you all know, four days ago, Italy joined the war. And now, our worst fears have been realized," he coughed nervously again. "Today, we found out that Italy won't allow any naval movement in the waters of the Mediterranean."

Someone in the crowd started to curse angrily, but stopped himself at the last minute, and Sime tried to continue with his explanations.

"This means that we will no longer be able to try and reach Israel through illegal immigration by sea. The only way forward now is by legal immigration."

The wave of angry protests now turned into an outburst of loud and desperate cries. An elderly man standing beside me said that Sime and the voyage management should be held accountable.

"You can't just keep us here. We've been stuck in this rotten place for six months!" he yelled.

Others shouted, "Liars! You're all liars! First, it was the ice on the Danube. Now, it's Italy. Why in hell's name did you wait so long? What have you been waiting for? For Italy to enter the war?"

"Crook, swindler. Haven't you filled your pockets with enough of our money?"

"He's been living the good life at our expense. Let's show him we're not the cowards he thinks we are."

It just went on and on; they didn't even let Spitzer try and explain what would happen next. He continued to try and pacify the crowd.

"Patience, friends. We mustn't lose hope!"

But the outraged crowd would not let him speak, and he was forced to retreat to his car and leave the place in shame, chased off by raging voices and raised, angry fists.

JULY 1940

One evening, when we gathered in the square in front of the infirmary, a round, yellow moon above our heads, Bata told us that *Penelope* would have to be evacuated soon, because the Yugoslavs wanted it back. We'd barely had time to recover from Mr. Spitzer's message that we were doomed to wait indefinitely for legal immigration permits. Now, another terrible decree had been handed down. Everyone had to go ashore and settle there permanently. Our departure seemed to be drifting further and further away from us.

"But there's nothing to worry about," Bata added. "Tomorrow, small tents will be delivered as a temporary solution for all the Netzah, Mizrahi, and Hashomer Hatzair youths. Later on, we'll get larger tents for permanent accommodation."

At least I have something to keep me busy, I thought, raising a hammer above the small pegs of another tent. Dozens of tents had been erected in three rows for the Mizrahi and Hashomer Hatzair youths. They were all busy setting up camp on the hill overlooking Kladovo harbor with a wonderful view of the river. We erected low, small tents, two youths in each, with separate areas for boys and girls. We padded them with mats and small rugs, and then built a fence around the camp.

Our crowning achievement was a timber entrance with the Star of David and the words "Youth Aliyah Community."

When I came to visit Inge at the camp on the hill, I saw many young people strolling along pathways or sitting and talking under the trees or next to the tents. I couldn't help but feel jealous, even though Mother was making a real effort to make the little place we shared with Mikhailo and Militza cozy. From the outside, our hut looked dilapidated, but inside, there was a warm comfortable atmosphere thanks to curtains, rugs, and a decorative tablecloth. Since there wasn't much food, the only thing missing was the smell of home cooking. Still, I envied those teenagers.

During that time, I'd grown closer to Yost, who must have been four years younger than me, but I'd come to like him. I used to visit the small, cultivated house he lived in with his parents, and we'd play his favorite game—chess.

Despite our age difference, we were evenly matched.

Yost was always neat, tidy, and as carefully combed as if he were going to a garden party with his classmates in his German hometown. He reminded me a bit of myself, the way I used to be in Belgrade, when Father would call me "softy" and "Mummy's boy."

Yost's mother, Ellie, was constantly busy cleaning or sewing in the little kitchen that was always full of pleasant cooking smells. In her spare time, she'd draw. After they'd settled into the small house, she received an easel, a palette, and charcoal pencils. Her paintings and drawings filled the walls of their small house and were also proudly hung on the walls of other houses.

One day, Yost told me about his brother, Grad, and sister, Erna, who were already in Israel. They'd managed to get immigration certificates while still in Germany. Erna got to Israel first, Grad just a year ago, and he was living on a *kibbutz*. His parents constantly worried about him and kept sending him letters. In his last letter, he told them he was riding horses and working in the fields. Yost said he'd really wanted to go with Grad, but his parents wouldn't let him because he was too young and there was no one to take care of him there. Soon, they'd all be together on the *kibbutz* in Israel. He also told me that Grad and friends of his parents in Jerusalem were working hard to arrange immigration certificates for him and his parents.

Yost had a deep craving for chocolate and sweetmeats. He told me about the big chocolate store in his hometown in Germany. They lived there with his grandma Johanna, Elisheva's mother, on a bustling street where the sound of trams would rattle the walls of the house. So when Yost first heard the *halva* vendor calling out his wares as he cycled to Kladovo harbor, he simply couldn't help himself.

"Nuts and chocolate-flavored *halva*, just one dinar a packet!" the vendor called at the top of his voice, and Yost, who loved *halva*, told me how much it reminded him of the home he'd left behind in Germany.

One afternoon, when I came to Yost's house to play chess, I found him in a happier mood than usual.

"Mother said I can go down to the harbor to buy *halva*. She's given me a dinar," he said with a smile. "Do you want to come with me to buy it?"

I gladly agreed. We could hear the shouts of the *halva* vendor even before we actually got to the harbor.

"*Halva*! Nuts and chocolate-flavored *halva*! Just one dinar a packet!"

The local children were already standing in line, and so was Bertie. That annoying boy, who always bought whatever he wanted and never shared anything with anyone, was standing just in front of us. People said that his aunt in Belgrade sent his mother letters with money in them. Everyone hates Bertie, because he doesn't like to help or share with others, because he doesn't uphold the important values Teddy taught us. That's why he doesn't have any friends.

We were waiting in line when two older boys came up and asked Yost if he could loan them two dinars till tomorrow because their parents had no money for food. They looked like gypsies, even though they weren't dressed like gypsies. Yost felt threatened and said he didn't have any money to loan them. One of the boys caressed his shoulder while the other grabbed his hand, trying to force him to give up the dinar bill. Yost resisted and I jumped the thief from behind. I almost managed to bring him down, when a fist landed right in my face. It was the other boy, coming to his friend's aid. Blood trickled down my nose, through my upper lip, and into my mouth. But I didn't give up. Everyone around us started shouting, "Thief! Thief!", and I hung on to the thief's neck in spite of all the blood and pain. But he twisted loose, and in the middle of all the shouts and screams, the two boys ran off, disappearing between the harbor buildings. Someone lent me a hand and helped me to my feet. I felt a sharp, stinging pain in my upper lip. Someone else shouted, "Get him some ice!" But meanwhile, I managed to get up, brush the dirt off my clothes, and look for Yost. He was standing mortified beside me, his fist still tightly clenched around the dinar bill.

"Come on," I said. "Let's go buy some *halva*." I was in so much pain that the words sounded slurry.

Everyone made way for us to go to the front of the line.

"Hanne, maybe we should go to the infirmary first?" said Yost. "We'll get *halva* some other day."

"No, we'll get it today," I said, pressing my lips with my fingers to stop the bleeding. "Come on, I'll buy it for you."

The vendor gave the *halva* packet to Yost, clapped my shoulder, and said, "Well done! We mustn't give in to them."

At the infirmary, Inge cleaned the cut on my lip.

"Bertie told me what happened. Hanne, you're a real hero."

The cut on my lip was very painful. I didn't answer because the words came out so slurred and also because I felt so proud that I actually had nothing to say.

***

The small camp we were all so fond of remained on the hill for an entire month. We were then instructed to dismantle it because the larger, permanent tents had arrived. On July 9, the Hashomer Hatzair youth, along with the members of Hechalutz and Mizrahi, were transferred to another camp on the outskirts of the village. Huts were built for the older youths, and huge tents were erected for the younger children, one for each movement. We built a large wood foundation with tall, horizontal wooden posts and supporting beams on top. We stretched tarpaulin sheets over the wooden skeleton. At the entrance, we built a door with a nice curtain and even hung up a bell. There were wooden sleeping bunks on both side of the tent and straw mattresses covered with blankets. The Federation of Jewish Communities had sent all this equipment.

Yokel ceremoniously announced "the most beautiful and original tent competition," in two weeks' time. He set up a committee to choose the winning tent. The competition brought a wave of feverish activity to the camp. Everyone tried to make special constructions and decorations. The girls were all busy decorating the inside of their tents, cleaning and arranging the furniture.

Hashomer Hatzair ended up winning the competition, and everyone was invited to the winning tent after the ceremony. The tent included an organized changing room at the rear, separated from the main area by a colorful curtain. A bulletin board hung on the front pole of the tent. Planters were placed outside, on each side of the colorful curtain at the entrance. At the entrance to the camp, visitors were welcomed by the youth movement's symbol made of gravel stones and grass, and the entire complex was surrounded by a low wooden fence. At the center of the yard, they'd made an area for a campfire out of two large stones with a grate over them for brewing coffee. They undoubtedly deserved the prize. Inge and I would often join their sing-alongs on evenings around the campfire, and we all sang pioneer songs about making the desert bloom.

Inge and I have been spending a lot of time together. Sometimes we sit at the campfire into the late hours of the night, enjoying the warmth, or we take walks along the paths around the camp. We're not the only couple to go out hand in hand for some fresh air. There are couples who even walk about with their arms around each other, simply ignoring the fact that everyone is staring at them. When we want to be alone, we take a walk to the trout bridge where we'd first kissed. We often sit talking about all kinds of subjects. Mainly about us, of course, and about the future waiting for us in Israel, but also about the situation in the camp and Europe in general, about poetry and literature. I told her my mother dreamed I'd become a writer someday.

"Not only did she teach me to read and write German like a native, she also made sure I was familiar with Schiller, Goethe, and, of course, Heine."

"I remember that from our first meeting; you quoted a line from one of his poems."

"When I started writing poems of my own, she read some at the literary evenings she used to hold in our living room."

"And what was your dream?"

"Back then, I did want to be a writer or a poet one day."

"And now?" she asked.

"When I started going to Akiba, I realized there are more important things in life, like ideals and pioneering. Building something you strongly believe in."

I told her about my good friend's brother in Belgrade, the one who joined the rebels in Spain and was killed while preparing explosives. I told her how much I'd idolized him. His death had seemed glorious to me, because he'd died fighting for an ideal he believed in. I told her I wanted to join the fighters struggling to liberate Israel we'd heard about in summer camp.

"And what about me? It sounds as if you don't have any room for me in your plans for the future."

"Of course there's room for you in my future!" I protested.

Inge was disappointed and said it didn't fit in at all with what we'd promised each other before, about setting up a house of our own, raising children, and dealing with farming in Israel, not wars.

"Right," I answered. "But one thing doesn't contradict the other. You'll go to nursing school and become a certified nurse."

"But I also said we'd get married and have four children and a large house in the village where we could raise them according to the values of Judaism and love of Israel."

"We're stuck here right now, and I haven't even finished school yet… How could I possibly promise you something like that?" I told her.

"I've already chosen you, Hanne," she said. "And you say that you love me. So let's have our own secret engagement ceremony, just for the two of us. Would you like that?"

"This is a lot for me to consider, Inge. I'm still young, only sixteen."

"Promise me, Hanne. I'm not saying it has to be now or a week from now. But promise me, all right?"

It's late at night and I can't fall asleep. I listen to the night sounds, hear the pigs snorting just beyond the wall. In the distance, I can hear the sad howls of a dog. Thoughts of Inge and our recent conversation are all-absorbing. I think about her a lot and want to be with her all the time. I think I love her. But I don't know what to do with her demand for commitment. It seems strange to me. It's hard. She's almost eighteen already. She was engaged once, to the man from Germany who went mad in Dachau. She can really picture the two of us living in some rural settlement with four children, but I'm still so young. I still have so much to experience. She's my first girlfriend. Yes, I used to be infatuated with Branka Garai in Belgrade, but we were children so it doesn't count. I'm not ready for this. I have my whole life ahead of me, and there's a good chance we'll all go our separate ways after the war and forget about everything that's happened.

I remembered Bruno, my tent mate on my last summer camp in the mountains. He told me then that he already had a girlfriend and that they were doing it. She didn't agree at first, but he persisted until she gave him what he wanted. He said it was the only thing worth living for in this complicated life.

I suppose Inge would have agreed long ago, if it wasn't for that religious *negiah*[19] thing. She explained to me about Maimonides's interpretation of this religious rule. But when we're alone together, I find it almost impossible to stop myself. Every time I'm overwhelmed with desire and think it's time, she quotes more Bible verses at me. Sometimes, I think I'll explode. Kisses are allowed, she tells me, and I feel myself getting hard down below every time our lips meet. She doesn't say anything, but I'm sure she feels it. I want to do something before I explode. Perhaps I'll take her to the new creek I found. We'd never be disturbed there. I imagine her naked body on the soft grass and the two of us swimming naked. I see us lying on the grass while I cover her body with kisses, all the way from her soft white neck down to her...

In the silence of the night, after the pigs had stopped snorting, I

---

19 The term *negiah* (Hebrew: נגיעה), literally "touch," is the concept in Jewish law (*halacha*) that forbids or restricts physical contact with a member of the opposite sex (except for one's spouse, children, siblings, grandchildren, parents, and grandparents). A person who abides by this *halacha* is colloquially described as a *shomer negiah* (observer of *negiah*).

suddenly heard a monotonous sound coming from my parents' room. I listened to the soft sounds like muffled groans, but the thought that they were actually doing it, at that very moment, in the room next to mine, seemed far-fetched. Could they really be doing it, now, right next door to me? I couldn't imagine Father doing it; lately, he'd been spending his days in a brooding silence, walking downcast, his shoulders bowed and unsure. But the sound of moaning intensified, and I recalled the day I'd mistakenly pulled the blanket from Anita and Shishko's naked bodies. I kept listening until I heard another long, deep groan, and then silence.

After feeding the pigs that morning, I went to look for old Petrović. I hadn't seen him for two weeks and found him mending nets in his usual spot.

He was happy to see me.

"Want some coffee? Where have you been?"

"I'd love some coffee," I said. "I haven't had any breakfast yet."

He filled the coffee pot with water and lit the fire, protecting it from the wind with a wooden board.

"What's going on with you, young man? You haven't been here in ages. You must be very busy with your friends over there. Any news? When are you leaving?"

"No news, really. Not since they let us know we can no longer immigrate illegally. We're just waiting for the paperwork to arrive."

"What about your girlfriend, Inge?"

"Busy at the infirmary. There's a lot of work there."

"So…" he said while pouring coffee into two small glasses. "You two aren't together anymore?" he asked, crossing two fingers.

"Actually, we are," I answered. "And that's the real reason I came to see you…" I added hesitantly, "Maybe you could give me some advice."

"Well, now… That calls for a cigarette," he said, fumbling in his trouser pocket for his eternal cigarette packet.

"Want one?" he asked.

"No… You know what? Maybe I will," I answered, extending two fingers to take the cigarette he'd popped out of the packet. "It's my first one," I said. "I just want to try it once."

I placed the end of the cigarette between my lips and bent to the match flame dancing between Petrović's fingers.

"Welcome to the world of smoking men," he said and clapped my shoulder hard enough to make me cough. "Not so bad," he said, giving me a piercing look. "It always stings the throat a little the first time."

"Not bad at all," I coughed again and felt my head spinning a little. "I actually came to talk to you a little, you know…"

"I could tell something was troubling you as soon as I saw you coming down here. I read you like an open book, Hanne."

I took another drag from the cigarette and erupted in a fresh spate of coughing.

"Excuse me for putting it out and wasting one of your cigarettes, but it's my first time." I threw away the half-smoked cigarette, putting it out with the tip of my shoe in what I hoped looked like a practiced movement.

"That's all right," he said. "Now what did you want to talk to me about?"

"Well, suppose you were my age, and suppose you had a girlfriend…"

"Oh, dear God, what I wouldn't give to go back forty years. You know what? Twenty years… Even ten!"

"Hold on, you haven't heard my question yet."

"You think I don't already know?" he asked with a cheerful look in his eyes.

"Yesterday, I remembered the story you told me, about the woman you once loved and ended up almost losing."

I told him what was going on with Inge and me, how she wants us to get married once we get to Israel and have children in the village, and how much that scares me. He listened attentively, blowing smoke rings from time to time.

"Don't let her go," he declared, puffing smoke.

"But I'm so young, I'm afraid I might ruin my life."

"You won't be ruining anything. For now, your life is on hold because of this never-ending transport of yours. It's wartime and the world has gone crazy. You need some sort of stability in your life. You love her, don't you? So what have you got to lose?"

"Maybe you're right… Maybe I'm just being selfish…thinking about other opportunities, instead of…"

"At least tell her you promise to be faithful to her. You know what? I have something to give you. Something you might…" he took a small ring from his pocket. "Just think about it for now. But if the right moment ever presents itself, give her this ring and tell her something that will make her happy." He held the ring between his fingers. "It's silver and very dear to me," he ceremoniously handed me the ring.

"Then why are you giving it to me?"

"It can't help me anymore. Maybe it can still help you."

"Where is it from?"

"That's the ring I gave my wife when I married her. She loved it very much... After I buried her, I took all her jewelry. She didn't have much."

With the ring in my pocket, I parted from old Petrović in a pensive mood.

Over the next few days, Inge was very busy. There was a fresh outbreak of dysentery in the camp. A few days ago, Peretz Frenkel from Hashomer Hatzair came to the infirmary suffering from severe diarrhea, fever, and exhaustion. Dr. Bezalel immediately put him in an isolation ward, suspecting it was typhus. Inge took it upon herself to remind everyone in the camp to follow Dr. Bezalel's hygiene instructions. She hung up her handwritten instruction leaflets about cleanliness—washing hands and dishes—on all the bulletin boards. Even so, the number of patients coming to the isolation ward continued to rise. Inge was constantly busy and didn't have time for anything else.

Dr. Bezalel demanded that the Federation of Jewish Communities send typhus medication urgently, but by the time it arrived, Peretz's condition had gradually deteriorated.

One morning, when I came as usual to take Inge to Mr. Goldman's Hebrew lesson, she opened the infirmary door with red, swollen eyes and told me Peretz's weak body had succumbed to the disease. He was buried in a field not far from camp, next to the grave of Yehuda Weiss, who had died on board the *Tzar Nikolai* in February.

***

Again, Father is walking restlessly about the house and camp. Ever since he returned from Mother's operation, he just can't seem to find a place for himself. He spends a lot of time sitting under the huge plane tree next to our hut. Sometimes Yehuda, who used to live with us in the officers' room, sits and plays cards with him. They're often joined by Carl Gottlieb and Zvi Epstein, also from the *Tzar Nikolai*. Much to Mother's dismay, they can sit around playing cards for hours; she's scolded Father more than once for this.

"When I see you playing like that for hours on end, it drives me out of my mind," she told him one evening, after a meager meal of corn-bread with a little hard cheese.

Father got upset and said that she at least had her work in the stor-age room to keep her busy, while he had nothing to do but play cards. Mother tried to hush him so we wouldn't hear them arguing and sug-gested in a whisper that he find himself an occupation.

"How about carpentry? You used to love carpentry. You have such good hands," she told him.

I felt sorry for Father. Pushed into a corner, he brought up the sub-ject of the certificates and the time he spent writing letters to all sorts of indifferent officials and lofty relatives in Belgrade or Budapest. Once he realized he wasn't going to appease her and that people were beginning to think him lazy, when he was used to being seen as a respectable, independent man in Belgrade, he suddenly said, "Well, I may surprise you in a day or two… Maybe I'll do something that will gain us some respect."

"This is not about respect," said Mother. "I just don't want to see you depressed and melancholy all the time. Perhaps this new mood has something to do with the fact that you're not doing anything."

"Well, there is something that might improve my mood. I've been asked to act as referee for a soccer game two days from now," Father said with satisfaction.

Mother was genuinely surprised and wanted to know why they'd approached him in the first place. He said that Otto Miller, the famous soccer player, had approached him after hearing he knew a lot about soccer and even knew the Red Star Belgrade players.

I heard contempt in Mother's voice, and Father said art and poetry weren't the only forms of culture in the world—sports, even soccer, were also a form of cultural activity. Mother fell silent, then told Father she'd seen Otto Miller at our house yesterday and didn't understand what he was doing here.

"I don't like him. He's too arrogant for my taste."

"He came here to give me his referee whistle," said Father. "They chose me because I speak Serbo-Croatian, and we'll be playing against the locals."

Father tried to explain to Mother who Otto Miller was and how important it was to have someone like him visiting us, a soccer player who, until a year ago, had played for Hakoah Vienna and who had even seen Otto Schiffling score a goal against Sweden in the World Cup five years ago.

"That's quite an achievement," Father summed up Otto's professional soccer accomplishments, and Mother finally gave up. She must have realized it was better for her to support him, now that something exciting was finally happening in his life.

The day of the game we'd all been waiting for finally arrived. A warm sun welcomed us, just the right weather for a soccer game. The

Kladovo youth team arrived carrying the flag of Serbia and the flag of Kladovo, and our team had a flag with the Star of David on it. Fredl, the trumpeter, had closed the betting list that morning and promised a winning prize sponsored by the Federation of Jewish Communities.

Fredl's daughter was already six months old, and he would take her for walks along the riverbank.

"We need to let little Mimi rest from time to time, don't we?" he said, rubbing his forehead against the baby's.

I stood in the middle of the large crowd of spectators, Inge by my side, her hand on my arm. I was concerned about what was coming. Inge noticed my concern and tried to calm me down.

"It's only a soccer game; don't be so anxious."

But I wasn't worried about the outcome of the game. I was worried about Father. I just couldn't understand why he'd agreed to act as referee.

There weren't enough benches for all the spectators milling about on the green grass. To the sound of loud applause, the players of both teams came running onto the field. Then, to our surprise, Otto Miller came onto the field wearing a shirt on which appeared the number nine, a shirt he used to take pride in wearing during his first days on the boat, before he started wearing a gray overall like everyone else. Now he bowed to the sound of the crowd's cheers, proud of his lucky shirt.

Right after that, the Kladovo youth team came on, and the local crowd rose to its feet and began to whistle and shout encouragement. Father came up with the whistle around his neck and raised both his arms. Inge and I held hands and watched. Tense and embarrassed, I tried to read Father's face, to see if he felt confident and wasn't intimidated by the boos and curses of the crowd, which sounded much like the ones I'd heard at the games in Belgrade that Father used to take me to. Mother refused to come to the game after their argument the previous night, saying she thought it was an uncivilized, even barbaric event.

Father blew his whistle and the game began. Miller's Viennese group dominated most of the game, the locals mainly defending their goalpost.

The atmosphere was fairly relaxed at first. About fifteen minutes into the game, after Otto Miller had scored the first goal to the sound of loud applause and happy cheers from our audience, I worriedly followed the Kladovo players' rising frustration. I heard a few curses in Serbo-Croatian. I felt very uncomfortable watching Father arguing with two players after calling an offside in a situation that could have led to an equalizer for the locals. Gregorovich, a big player from the Kladovo team, seemed to be threatening Father with his large, strong hands. I noticed Father's distress and was afraid he might get hurt.

"They're a bunch of savages," said Inge. "It's just a game. Look what they're doing to him, Hanne," she shook my shoulder when she saw Gregorovich raise his hand.

Outwardly, Father appeared confident and in control, but I could read the distress in his face. The situation worsened during the second half, when the local team managed to defend itself against our team's constant offense.

When the score remained the same, and our players realized they wouldn't be able to beat the locals, rage and frustration began to rise to the surface. The Kladovo youths initiated an offensive, but the Jewish defense player, Yehuda Stein, tripped up the Serbian player close to our goalpost, and the latter fell flat on his face.

That moment, I prayed Father would call for a penalty kick for the locals. It seemed that the rising anger would only be appeased by a compromise. I heaved a sigh of relief when Father blew his whistle and called for a penalty kick, but then our own team players crowded around him, cursing, "He didn't even touch him!"

Someone standing next to me screamed as loud as he could, "What kind of a referee are you?" He whistled loudly and started to curse. "The referee's a son of a bitch!"

I felt the blood rush to my head and turned to him.

"Who are you calling a son of a bitch?" I yelled at him.

He wore a peaked cap, and an unlit cigarette dangled at the corner of his mouth. He looked a little older than me, but I didn't care.

"What do you care if I call him a son of a bitch? He's not your father, is he?"

I could no longer contain myself, felt as if I were losing control. I approached him, puffed out my chest, and looked him straight in the eye. "As a matter of fact, he is my father."

Inge must have sensed the risk, and she hurried in between us, spreading out her hands as if to say, why don't you two stop acting like a couple of roosters.

The guy took off his peaked cap with one hand and removed the unlit cigarette from his mouth with his other, tossing it on the ground. He put out his hand. "Sorry, I didn't know the referee was your father."

"It's all right," I said, placated. "It's only a game."

A whistle was heard, and the Kladovo youth team gathered behind the penalty area. Tall, broad Gregorovich was chosen to kick the penalty. He stretched and faked a kick to one corner, but everyone knew he'd actually kick to the other one. In order to increase the tension, he even ran to the ball, leaping over it at the last second without kicking. Then he resolutely stepped back, took a deep breath, looked at Ziso, our short and agile goalkeeper, and quickly ran toward the ball. He gave a mighty kick, but the ball, as if pulled by the devil's hand, flew over the goalpost.

Gregorovich clutched his face in both hands and ran around the field, refusing to believe that the ball had betrayed him. That miserable kick saved Father from a fresh bout of curses. Ziso, who hadn't even touched the ball, became the hero of the day.

The final score was 1–0 in our favor.

Everyone spoke favorably of Father, who had bravely stood his ground while facing the raging crowd, and wasn't intimidated by the rival team either. But Father refused to continue to serve as referee, a decision that made Mother very happy.

***

This was one of my happiest days in Kladovo. As part of sports day, there was also a swimming competition, in which I represented Mizrahi as they didn't have a suitable swimmer. I made them proud, winning second place in the two-hundred-meter-crawl race. Twenty-five swimmers participated in the race, and the whole of Mizrahi supported me, Inge as well. She received me with a huge hug when I emerged from the cold Danube water. But it was Pauli who was the star of the day, excelling in almost every field of sport.

At the end of sports day, Teddy let us know that we'd be meeting with Mr. Kreis that afternoon. This was Kreis's third lecture; charismatic and broad-minded, he'd been sent by the pioneering movement in Israel to tell us about the country and prepare the youth for life on a *kibbutz*. At his last lecture, he'd spoken about ideals and self-fulfillment. Captivated by him, I responded enthusiastically to his words.

That evening, Inge and I went to the *schiffsreview*, now the talk of the camp. Since we'd come ashore, these variety shows had moved to the parade ground in front of the camp. The performances, which began as simple skits with two actors and an accordion on the *Kraljica Marija*, had turned into actual operettas. They kept the name *schiffsreview* to illustrate the performance's original location, while the performance itself became more sophisticated and an impromptu stage was even found.

We came early to get seats. My parents also came, because everyone was talking about the previous show, which was highly successful. Misha, from the Gordonia group, proved to be no less talented an accordionist than Fredl; he enthusiastically played the Kladovo anthem and we all joined in, singing a new song, "Raisele" (little trip). They tried to teach us the words.

"It's simple," said Misha. "It's a chorus, and we'll learn the words together, with 'one, two, three' at the end of each verse:

So we took a little trip, zilch
they promised us a few days on the river

and now we're all stuck here

And what do they tell us—zilch

That maybe we'll sail off tomorrow

Up the Donau, down the Donau

When will we ever get to Palestine?

One, two, three

We took a little trip, zilch

With a little backpack and some hope

We've been to Prahovo

and now we're in Kladovo

and we're crammed in here schlepper[20]

Up the Donau, down the Donau

When will we walk the streets of Tel Aviv?

One, two, three."

At the end of the show, after applause for Richart and Yossy, who as usual made everyone laugh, Inge suggested we take a walk along the camp paths. The moon was full, and many couples were walking among the tents, some hand in hand like us, some with their arms around each other, while others just walked aimlessly here and there, enjoying the soft moonlight. Inge suggested we visit the Greek boat that had arrived in port the day before. Long chains of colorful lights hung between the masts. Three layers of lights hung around the funnel, reminding me of the summer cruises we'd gone on with our parents two or three years before. When we went on board, Inge pulled

---

20 Drag.

me in the direction of the bridge; she remembered our first night on the *Tzar Nikolai*.

"I remember how you warmed my hands," I said. "It was so cold."

And she said, in her grave, sad voice, which I can't resist, "I wanted to talk to you about something… Look, from the day I first saw you…I knew you were the one for me. I saw your sensitivity. Your great heart, and…"

"And what?" I asked.

"I knew right from the beginning that we were meant for each other, and you felt the same. And at first, you promised me we'd study Torah together and the weekly *parashah*, remember?"

"Yes, I do."

"Ever since that *shaliach* Kreis arrived from Israel, the one you're all following about," she said reproachfully. "You've stepped back from the faith and started talking about self-fulfillment and liberalism and that kind of thing."

"But what does that have to do with us? Why should it interfere with our relationship?"

"Because I feel that Kreis and his ideas are coming between us," she said.

"He might be coming between me and the Mishnah and all that wordplay, but not between us," I tried to explain.

"Look, Hanne, I'm a girl who believes, and we said we'd build our home on faith, on learning. I won't insist on your going to synagogue, but there can't be such differences between us, the kind of chasm Kreis is trying to create."

I tried to explain Kreis's worldview, similar to Dr. Kaufman's belief, which he'd often discussed with us at the movement *ken* in Belgrade, subjects like the prophets' ethics, social justice, and upholding humanistic *mitzvoth*, and how much more important these are than the prayers and supplications to God, as the High Priests see it.

"Rabbi Akiba is turning in his grave from the attitude to the *mitzvoth* in the movement that bears his name," she responded.

I told her the story Dr. Kaufman had told us, one usually told on the Shavuot holiday, about Rabbi Rahumi, who spent so much time studying Torah he spent less and less time at home with his wife and children. And, on the eve of Yom Kippur, he was late and his wife waited for him all day. She was so upset she wept. A tear rolled onto the roof of *beit hamidrash*, where Rabbi Rahumi was studying; the tear was so heavy the roof collapsed, and Rabbi Rahumi was killed on the spot.

"A nice story," she said. "But does that mean you don't respect me or my faith?"

The ornamental lights on the boat tinted her beautiful face red and green.

"God forbid!" I hurriedly tried to appease her. "It's just an example of the absurdity of extreme study and faith at the expense of loving others."

"And here I was thinking we'd build us a home with four children and we'd have a farm and…"

"I still think so. But I don't see myself as an observant Jew."

"For a few moments there, I thought I'd managed to convince you… but I'm not giving up!"

I looked into her lovely face.

"You look so beautiful tonight. I love you, Inge. Look at the bright sky and shining stars. Why don't we enjoy this beauty instead of bothering with such heavy issues?" I drew her to me, felt her warm body against mine. Holding her face in my hands, my lips sought hers in a long kiss.

"I want to run away from here. Just the two of us. Would you like that?" I asked when our lips parted.

"How?" she asked wonderingly. "You mean leave Yokel and the group?"

"Don't worry, I have a plan. We'll get on a train at Prahovo and…"

"Hanne, have you lost your mind?" She cut me off. "Would you leave your parents, your brother Pauli, just like that?"

"They'll come later on, with everyone else. We can take care of ourselves."

"Remember the sixth commandment: Honor your father and mother."

"I was joking. But now I have something serious to say to you," I said and took Petrović's ring from my pocket, where I'd been keeping it for the right moment.

"What's in that pretty box?" asked Inge in surprise.

She gasped when I opened the box and with trembling fingers took out the ring. Although simple and smooth, its silver plating reflected the sparkling starlight, as if set with diamonds. She held out a slender finger, and the ring slid on as if it had always been meant for her.

"With this ring, I am betrothed to thee," I said almost in a whisper. I couldn't believe I was actually saying these words.

"Now we really are a couple," she said with a shy smile.

"Yes. But it's between us. We won't tell anyone," I said.

"I don't care about anyone else. Now nothing can part us. I love you, Hanne. I love you so much," she said, kissing my cheek.

I couldn't help myself. I wrapped my arms about her, our lips met, and I felt her kiss flame on my lips. We stood there, clinging to each other for several minutes. When our lips parted, I saw bright tears in her eyes, falling to her cheeks and wetting them. Placing a finger on a stray tear, I traced it along her cheek, down to her chin, and, holding it between two fingers, I tilted her head upward to the star-strewn sky.

"Maybe we'll find our star," I whispered to her.

"There, there it is!" She pointed at a falling star. "Did you see it?"

"Yes!" I said joyfully. "I managed to make a wish."

"What did you wish?" She cuddled coaxingly into me.

"For a family in Israel and to grow corn for humans and cows for milk."

"And that things will always, always go well for us," she added. "And that we'll be able to bridge anything that separates us. I'll light candles and make the blessing every Friday night, and we'll sing together, 'Peace be upon you, ministering angels.'"

I linked my fingers in hers, and together, we left the bridge of the *Kraljica Marija* and turned back toward the camp.

The summer of 1940 was an excited one on the banks of the Danube. A random stranger would think that the neat tents were a movement summer camp, and not the transit camp of a group of despairing, almost hopeless refugees on its way to *Eretz* Israel. The adults were preoccupied by one subject: how to obtain legal immigration papers. After Sime Spitzer's announcement that the original plan of illegal immigration was no longer possible, he insisted there was no reason for concern; all the *Ma'apilim* (illegal immigrants) would, in the end, receive immigration permits for Israel and immigrate legally through the Balkan countries. The group, outraged by this announcement, no longer believed his promises. To relieve our fears, Mr. Spitzer assured us that he was working hard on the order of the immigration permits: youths up to the age of eighteen were the first eligible for Youth Aliyah. Then came young girls who could be included in the Wizo Hakshara groups, and then the families, including married couples without children. Finally, Hechalutz members and veterans would receive priority over newcomers.

This hierarchical allocation caused tension among people. Everyone feared being pushed to the end of the line.

Father again sank into depression. The evening after Spitzer's dramatic announcement, I heard him and Mother talking. He was very angry with Spitzer. Although he knew him personally, he said, he'd lost all belief in the man. He reminded Mother how much this transport had cost him, how they'd been promised that papers were not a concern because this was an illegal immigration.

"It suited me; the Serbs would never have given me citizenship, and it would have complicated things for us."

I heard him say this to Mother when we were still in Belgrade, when he came to tell her that we'd be joining the immigration group from Vienna in a few weeks' time. They were both glad, even Mother, who wasn't always in favor of leaving our homeland. But now Father was upset, suspecting them of using the money people had paid for the transport for *foile-shtick*.

When Mother told him that not everyone had paid, he was even angrier and said that it was an outrage that some groups were privileged, and, all in all, something corrupt seemed to be going on there. Mother mentioned that Mr. Goldman was waiting for a letter from his son in Israel, who promised to act on his behalf in the context of their being emigrating relatives, and she suggested that Father write to Uncle Simon, who had connections in high places. Father flatly refused, saying he'd be ashamed to send such a letter, that it would make him look like an irresponsible fool.

"I don't want him to know what a bad situation I'm in," he said.

Mother again spoke of how worried she was that we'd stopped studying. She was mainly worried about me.

"I hardly see him. God knows where he's off to all day long."

"I'll tell you where," said Father, a slight tone of contempt in his voice. "He's always with that Inge girl. She's completely unsuitable for him. Do you think that at their age they're already…?"

"I don't know what they're doing. I think they're together a lot because they're in love. Unlike you, I really like her. She's a little older than him, but that's not bad. She's a delightful girl."

I must have fallen asleep, because in the morning, when I got up to feed the pigs, it was the only sentence I remembered.

In the late afternoon, the sun still high up in the sky, its rays warming the dense air, I took Inge to the creek, a small stream of water flowing from the river bank in among the tall trees, and creating a quiet hidden spot where we could even swim, far from the group's watchful eyes.

On our way there, I picked some small, beautiful white flowers, wisteria flowers, we were told in a nature class, and gathered them into a bunch. When we got to the grass next to the water, Inge cried out in joy and wonder.

"Oh, Hanne, what a Garden of Eden! Why haven't you told me about this wonderful place before?"

We sat down next to a tree to take off our shoes. Kneeling beside her, I tucked two flowers in her hair, one on either side of her head. Then we ran barefoot across the grass, enjoying the fresh feel of it on the soles of our feet. Inge teased me into catching her, and when I came close, she quickly evaded me, running toward the water, where she stopped, panting and pink-faced with exertion and excitement. Finally, I caught her in my arms, covering her neck with kisses, slowly approaching her mouth. Then we lay back on the grass and looked upward at the tall treetops. Softly, she sang a song in German. We lay there enjoying the birdsong, when suddenly Inge heard odd sounds.

"Do you hear that? It's coming from over there, the direction we came from."

The approaching voices came from among the trees. We had no trouble identifying the language. German.

"Listen," she said urgently. "Those are not our people. And they aren't locals."

I also got up in alarm.

"Come on, let's go. Maybe we'll manage to avoid them."

We didn't know in which direction to go. We didn't want to go back, but if we went forward, we'd probably meet them. We walked swiftly. I thought we'd try and go around them, and with a bit of luck, we'd miss them. But I quickly realized my mistake. The voices materialized into two adults and a child before us.

"Who are you?" asked the woman, who was quite old.

I was about to tell the truth, that we were from the *Ma'apilim* at the camp in Kladovo, but Inge tugged at my hand and answered first.

"I'm visiting with his family here in Kladovo. We wanted to fish in the river."

"What, can you fish here?" asked the man with interest. "I didn't know you could fish here." He turned to his wife, "Do you hear that, Paulina? Tomorrow, I'll come back and do some fishing."

"And who are you?" asked Inge without turning a hair.

"We're here with a group from Bukovina. We're on our way back to our homeland, Germany," responded the woman.

The man added, "Our family is originally from Germany, but they escaped into Bessarabia and Bukovina during the Great War. Now that Russia has occupied the area, we're returning to our homeland." He ended by standing sharply to attention. "Heil Hitler!" he uttered, raising one straight arm in the air.

Inge told them we were in a hurry to get home, and we parted from them. Horrified and afraid, we made our way back. On the way, Inge told me she'd once heard the term *Volksdeutsche*, explaining that these were Germans who had left the land of Germany before the Great War and were now living in Romania and Bessarabia.

"It didn't occur to me that just as we are running away from the Nazis, we would come face-to-face with their representatives, here of all places. They even salute like those animals in Germany."

When we reached the camp, we went our separate ways. I hurried home, not wanting to worry my parents after almost a whole day's absence. I arrived in the middle of a stormy argument on a subject Pauli raised daily with our parents: the Akiba summer camp. Now that he'd heard the camp was to start in two days' time at a lake not far from Kladovo, he felt he just had to join them.

"You will remain here with us, is that clear?" Although we were there for an indeterminate period, Father nonetheless tried to maintain an authoritative tone.

Pauli, who felt mature and sure of himself, retorted angrily, "But nothing is happening. What is there to do here except listen to all the adults grumbling and getting angry?"

Father and Mother couldn't take his pressure, and he managed to talk them into letting him go to camp for a week. He tried to persuade me to join him, but I refused. Firstly, I wouldn't leave Inge for even one day, and secondly, I was entranced by Hebrew language studies. I'd begun studying Hebrew with the young Mr. Bachi from Budapest, who'd been on the *Kraljica Marija* with the Hashomer Hatzair people. He taught a less archaic Hebrew than Mr. Goldman, and I was excited about the wonders of this language. In addition, I didn't want to give up Kreis's Judaism and Jewish history lessons.

Pauli left in a horse-drawn wagon early the next morning. Father refused to part properly from him, but Mother hugged him and wished him a good time after all the suffering he'd endured. But she didn't really think of herself as suffering in the camp after she'd left her entire life behind, her city and the cultural environment she'd fostered.

To our surprise, Pauli returned after only four nights. At first, he didn't want to explain why. He was enthusiastic about the camp, the open atmosphere there, how the world outside continued as if there wasn't a war in Europe; he told us about the Jewish youth from Belgrade who always show up for the summer activities. But in the end, he also told us about the controversy that broke out with the arrival of Nahum—a young counselor from Israel who fascinated all the youngsters.

Nahum came to the camp to explain how crucial it was to emigrate to Israel; how important it was to persuade their parents to pack up and leave before it was too late.

"I felt I was already fulfilling what he was telling us to do. But when I tried to tell him that we were on our way but have been stuck here in Kladovo for almost a year, he didn't know what to say. I was frustrated."

"You should have invited him here to see what's happening, to talk to Naftali Bata, who is doing all he can with the Federation of Jewish Communities to enable us to survive here despite the difficulties," said Father.

"In the end, he started quarreling with the counselors too," continued Pauli. At first, he talked about the *kibbutz* as if it were a sort of Garden of Eden, but when he got into politics, we realized that there's a huge controversy among the *kibbutzim* in Israel. It turns out that there are various movements, each one pulling in a different direction."

"I'm sorry to hear that there are already differences of opinion and quarrels," said Mother.

"The counselors tried to shut him up, told him not to slander Israel, but it didn't help. A split then formed. Quite a few youngsters followed him and left the camp," said Pauli. "I stayed with our counselors, but the atmosphere wasn't as nice anymore. Then a few more youngsters left, and I decided to come back here."

***

A few days after the strange meeting Inge and I had with the Germans, the driver of our supply truck encountered a group of people who were living in tents at the roadside. They asked him for the supplies in the truck, and when he refused, they attacked him and tried to take them by force.

"I noticed one of them climbing up onto the back of the truck; I hooted and put my foot on the accelerator. I didn't even look back to see what happened to them," he agitatedly told Naftali Bata and the people who gathered around to hear him.

Fritz Felks, Lucy's father from the Hechalutz group, was injured in a similar incident. Lucy also studies with Bachi, and yesterday, in the middle of class, Inge came to call her to the infirmary because her father had been injured.

The story of Fritz's injury spread around the camp like wildfire, and everyone had his own version of events. That evening, Inge told me that Erica, Lucy's mother, had arrived breathless and upset, calling for the doctor to help her husband who'd been injured. She was too upset to explain what had happened, able to gasp out only a few words, like "hooligans" and "Germans." Inge called two young men from the group, Hanoch and Erwin, to bring a stretcher and join the doctor who had gone to take care of Fritz. They found him groaning in pain, bleeding, with bruises on his arms and legs. The doctor found that his left arm was broken. They carefully put him on the stretcher, and the doctor set his arm, placing it alongside his body. Erica finally calmed down sufficiently to tell them what had happened. She and Fritz had gone for a walk along a path behind the camp. They often went walking there, although this time, they'd gone further than usual. They were suddenly stopped by a group of German thugs, *Volksdeutsche* apparently, who forbade them to continue, claiming that the area belonged to their camp. Fritz responded that they always walked there and asked to go past and return to camp.

"They started asking us questions about our camp and what we were doing there," said Erica. "When they heard it was a Jewish camp, they cursed us and very quickly started hitting and punching us. Fritz tried to protect himself, but they were stronger. When he fell, I escaped and ran to call for help."

The last attack was the talk of all *Ma'apilim* in the tents and huts. Fritz, who'd begun to heal, again took walks along the camp pathways. His injured arm was supported by a sling tied around his neck. At the time, rumors went around that we were leaving Kladovo. At first, we heard we'd be sailing, as long expected, along the Danube toward the Black Sea. But it very quickly turned out to be a move from Kladovo to another transit camp, as groups of German *Volksdeutsche* were getting closer to us and the incidents with them were increasing.

One day, Bata Gedalja called us together to clarify the new situation. He told us the administrators were looking for a safer place, because the proximity to the *Volksdeutsche* community, who supported the Nazi Party, was creating undesirable tension in our midst.

Father continued his independent efforts to obtain immigration permits. Every day, he went to the local post office to see if there was a letter from our uncle in Belgrade, but none came.

On these hot days toward the end of summer, Mr. Goldman was

a constant visitor. He'd sit talking with Father at the entrance to the house, in the shade of the plane tree whose leaves were white with road dust. Mr. Goldman was organizing a political group of General Zionists who could act as one group to obtain immigration permits. This happened once he realized that whoever belonged to an organized movement would receive preferential treatment.

"You know, Emil, the situation will only get worse. Now all the Hechalutz and Hashomer Hatzair activists, as well as other movements, are really only taking care of themselves. Whereas we families and single people are left out. You have to understand that."

Father tried to explain that any political organization repelled him, but Mr. Goldman went on regardless.

"Look, as an individual, your power is limited when confronting institutions. You need power, and power is found in an organized group of many people."

"I am not interested in a group," said Father stubbornly. "And do you know why?" He lowered his voice, as if afraid of being overheard, "Sime told me that the administration of this transport does not approve of such organizations; he even hinted that they would do everything in their power to thwart such things."

"But it has nothing to do with the administration; we would be confronting institutions. Confronting the *Eretz* Israel office in Zagreb," protested Mr. Goldman.

Father told him that Lucy Felks received an immigration permit two days ago, and it didn't come from the group but through her fiancé in Israel.

"I heard that the immigration permits come blank, without names.

The organizers give them to whom they please. Maybe they're even selling them," fumed Father. "Absolute *foile-shtick*."

"Selling them? Don't you worry, Emil. I will see to it that we get personal immigration permits. Almost a hundred and fifty have already signed up with me, and any additional person will only strengthen us. Think about what I've said, but I need an answer. I am preparing a letter to Oscar Greenbaum. He works for the General Zionist Aliyah Institution in Israel. I will describe our situation and request his help in the name of a large group of Zionists who have worked in various ways for the settlement of Israel."

"If I change my mind, I'll let you know," Father ended the conversation.

I couldn't understand why Father was so against Goldman's suggestion. I was afraid that his group would all get immigration permits, and we'd be left without.

When I went to see Inge at the infirmary that evening, we were surprised to learn from Lucy Felks that she'd decided to decline her immigration permit so that she wouldn't have to leave her aging parents behind, particularly her father, who was still recovering from the *Volksdeutsche* attack.

I found it hard to understand Lucy's choice, though if I'd been in her place, I didn't know what I'd have done. Let's say that Pauli and I and the rest of the youngsters get immigration permits, but Inge doesn't. Would I leave her? Would I leave my parents? On the other hand, they'd probably get immigration permits a month or two later. Would it be right to give up the opportunity for freedom, no matter the price? After all, this has been our heart's desire for almost a year now. Inge said she'd do exactly as Lucy had done. To this day, she's tormented by having left her mother in Berlin to join the transport.

There were days I thought of running away and even suggested to Inge that we run away together. Today, I see this as stupid and irresponsible. After all, we'd be checked for papers everywhere we went, which is why there is such a panic about these vital immigration permits.

I'd always believed we were traveling to Palestine as a family, Father and Mother, me and Pauli. But lately, there've been rumors that youth between the ages of twelve and sixteen will be sent to Israel under the auspices of Youth Aliyah, so Pauli and I might leave with them, and Father and Mother would remain here until their immigration permits arrive. Parting from my parents, and arriving alone in a new country and having to cope with another language and customs, seemed strange to me. Even if it's temporary, as everyone assures me, and my parents come a month or two later.

That evening, we heard two new reports. The first was that we'd be leaving the village soon, and the second—Lucy's immigration permit was the first of many more immigration permits about to arrive for the youth. Yokel and Shechter went from one Hechalutz youth to another, measuring each one from top to toe and filling out special forms with all the details. They noted name, height, shoulder width, and date and country of birth.

I anxiously followed the registration process, and as it progressed, I began to understand that they had no intention of including me and Pauli in the list. Maybe because we came with our parents and so we belonged to the family list and not to the youth list. And no one actually approached us with the list until evening. Father was annoyed and said he'd go and talk to Sime the next day; it was unthinkable that we'd be left out.

Night. I tried to fall asleep, but was constantly preoccupied with the questionnaires Teddy had filled out that day for each of the girls and boys in the Mizrahi group, with the exception of me and Pauli. When Father saw Teddy passing by and starting to fill out forms for our neighbors, the Mayer family, he almost snatched the forms from his hand. Their daughter, Stella, had been born in Austria and was almost four years younger than us. From the other room, I heard Father and Mother conferring.

"They've already registered all the Mizrahi youth, whether they're over the age limit or not," said Mother. "Inge's on the list, and she's already over eighteen."

"A lot of things to do with the immigration permits aren't clear," said Father. "Mr. Goldman set up the General Zionist group so we'd get papers more easily, and what happened? Three weeks have gone by, and apart from some vague excuse that the subject is under advisement, he hasn't achieved a single thing."

"They say that the British are delaying the immigration permits of anyone born in an enemy country or who is a citizen there," said Mother. "Which means that natives of Germany and Austria will certainly not be getting immigration permits in the near future."

"We don't come from an enemy country, so why aren't Pauli and Hanne on the list?" asked Father.

"That has nothing to do with it," said Mother. "It isn't about Youth Aliyah. They're only delaying immigration permits for adults from Germany and Austria."

The following day, fears were dispelled when all youth were instructed to register. Whoever had not already been registered was asked to go to Naftali Bata's office, provide details, and fill in questionnaires, including youth from family frameworks. There was an exhilarated atmosphere in the camp, and smiles were seen everywhere. It was clear to everyone that we'd be getting out of there within a few days. People started daring to hope that the promised immigration permits for the *Aliyah* youth were the first sign of their imminent immigration to Israel. There was particular joy when Yehuda Wolff and Yaakov Landberg arrived at the camp. They were two young men from the group near the river, and they announced that two boats with hundreds of Jewish *Ma'apilim* were sailing down the Danube, apparently on course for Sulina and the Bulgarian-Romanian border.

Yaakov was especially excited. His twin brother Shimon hadn't managed to join our transport but remained in Berlin with their parents. In the long months of waiting, they had written to each other, and in the last letter, Shimon had told him he was joining another transport on the Danube, just before the gates were closed, and he was apparently on one of these boats.

When Inge and I heard about the two boats, we dropped everything and ran down to the river, even managing to see the two boats with hundreds of *Ma'apilim* on their decks. They passed so close that we could even read their names. One was called *Pacific*, and the other, *Atlantic*. Those standing on deck waved to us, and we, standing enraptured on the river bank, waved back to them. Some of our group shouted greetings to *Eretz* Israel, among them Yaakov, who, waving energetically, shouted again and again, "Shimon, Shimon!"

Many years later, when he came to *Eretz* Israel, Shimon Landberg learned that the people waving to them from the banks of the Danube that cold and rainy September were indeed from the group, among them his twin brother Yaakov, who never made it to Israel.

But the joyousness of that afternoon was mingled with grief when that very evening, Mr. Bata called us to our usual meeting place for an announcement. We were all certain that this was a happy announcement about the approaching voyage, that we, too, could expect a similar destiny to that of the *Ma'apilim* we'd seen on *Pacific* and *Atlantic*, the two German boats on the river, making their way to Sulina. What could be more promising than what we'd seen with our very own eyes, two boats on their way to freedom? But that evening, our anticipation was to be as great as our astonishment and disappointment.

At seven o'clock that evening, Fredl stood with his trumpet at the entrance to the Hashomer Hatzair camp, which was as clean and tidy as it had been on the very first day. The petunias in the planters on each side of the path bloomed in purple, white, and crimson. Young people streamed from the tents and huts and filled the paths. People were also coming from the road leading to the village, adults with small children at their sides, or on their shoulders. Everyone was coming to hear the news from Mr. Naftali Bata Gedalja. Instead of telling us when we'd be boarding the boats for *Eretz* Israel, he began talking about the problematic friction with the *Volksdeutsche* population, how dangerous it was for us here in the camp, and what dangers the future held as a result of this intolerable proximity. Because the situation was getting worse, the Yugoslavian authorities were taking responsibility and had decided to move our camp further inside the country. He mentioned Sabac, a town we didn't know, which was located a few dozen kilometers from Belgrade.

Naturally, a wave of protest began to swell among the people. Faint voices very quickly grew louder, turning into yelling and turmoil.

An older man near me shouted at Naftali Bata, "Shame on you. Devils, all of you!"

Naftali Bata stood there, shamed and deeply distressed.

"Just today we saw the German riverboats sailing to Sulina, so please don't tell us stories!" someone else shouted, shaking his fists.

Bata shrank, as if wanting to disappear. He clearly felt the pain of every member of the group, but things were beyond his control, he was only the messenger.

"No. You are not going to take us in the opposite direction. After almost a year of waiting in cold and snow, heat and hunger, you want to take us back? Better you abandon this disgrace! Abandon this foolish, lame transport!" one woman shouted, and everyone clapped at her trenchant comments about the administrators.

Within the chaos, some adults tried to get close enough to Bata to threaten him, but three young men standing beside him protected him from the crowd. The commotion died down. The angry crowd began to disperse, angrily and bitterly going their separate ways.

On Sunday, Militza invited me and Stella Mayer, our neighbor, to go with her to the church square for the last time before we left. I'd gone with Militza several times on a Sunday to watch the gypsies dancing in their traditional clothes. There were magicians and jugglers, too, which added to the happiness there. Inge refused to go to the church square, because Jews were not supposed to attend non-Jewish ceremonies. She refused although it was just dancing and not a religious ceremony. But yesterday, she accompanied me on a last visit to Petrović, whom we hadn't seen for a long time.

The last time we came to part from him, it was just after the melting of the snow. We were sure we'd be sailing the next day, and he just looked at us with his wise eyes, as if he knew in his heart that it would not be happening. Things seemed different now. He seemed to know that this time we really were finally going to leave Kladovo. At our last meeting, three weeks previously, just after he'd heard about Inge's and my encounter with the *Volksdeutsche*, he said, "Better you go, all of you. Better you move somewhere else. I sense trouble ahead." Before we left, he called me aside confidentially. "Don't let her get away. Take care of her, Hanne."

Heads of groups prepared people for the move. Mother did one last laundry in the river, hanging everything up to dry on a rope stretched between the door post and the enormous plane tree in the yard, and again took out the suitcases from under the beds and started packing. Inside the open suitcase on the bed, I saw the tiny, pale blue wooden box with gold corners in which she kept Klarie's golden curl.

That evening, Mr. Haimbach from the Transport Administration came to tell us that the following morning, we'd all board the huge tug sent by the Yugoslavian Boat Company. Predictably, a commotion broke out again and people exploded in anger.

"We will not board the tug!" shouted Yechiel, a large man who was always the first to start a commotion.

He was followed by two older women, who shouted, "Isn't it enough we're being sent back, and yet you have the nerve to force us to travel jam-packed together on a tug?"

Everyone joined in the ruckus, taking out their anger on Mr. Haimbach and the other administrators, who tried to defend themselves from the agitated crowd. Movement youth took no part in the tumult. When Yokel saw Yechiel actually punching Mr. Haimbach, he jumped in between them. Teddy joined Yokel, and they caught him by the arms, twisting them behind his back until he calmed down. That evening, we were told the journey had been postponed for two days.

The atmosphere in the camp was very tense. The tents remained in place because no final leaving date had been received, and they might need to sleep there one more night. Our suitcases were packed, and Father was sitting outside under the tree as usual when Mr. Goldman came to visit. I thought he'd come to complain again about the Transport Administration and the Party in Israel that wasn't doing enough for the group he'd organized, but this time, he came to tell us that a spacious passenger boat was on its way that would take only the elderly and the sick. All the young people would sail on the tug. He said that an accurate list of the people who would board the passenger boat was in preparation.

"I've already registered my wife Rivka. You know she isn't in the best of health."

Father picked up a small branch, pulled off its leaves, and after a long pause, said, "I'll see to it that Louisa also sails on it. I won't permit her to board a crowded tug."

"You're right, Mr. David. She also deserves to sail in comfort. You should go and talk to Naftali Bata about it at once, before he leaves. He has a sympathetic heart; it's a pity he's returning to Belgrade and isn't coming with us."

"And where is Sime? Traveling back and forth again, I suppose. Always traveling and doing nothing," fumed Father.

"I keep hearing about someone else who's received a permit, and I haven't even received a letter in response!" said Mr. Goldman angrily. "It's a pity I didn't act independently. For myself and Rivka. I'd have gotten the immigration permits a long time ago. Mr. David, Sabac, this town they're talking about, do you know where it is?"

"It's on the banks of the Sava River, about seventy kilometers south of Belgrade," said Father, adding, "It's a large town with tens of thousands of residents. But with all due respect, I cannot understand why we're traveling back upstream, instead of advancing downstream."

"They say it's because of the *Volksdeutsche*, but apparently, the administration wants us to be closer to Belgrade so they can run things more efficiently," said Goldman, despair in his voice too.

"You'd think they had something to run," said Father angrily. "I'm going to talk to Bata."

That evening, the passenger boat arrived all lit up with colored lights. Father managed to get Mother a place on the boat, while he himself would sail with us on the tug. He told us that many people wanted a place on the boat, but Naftali Bata managed the list with a firm hand, and if it hadn't been for the Belgrade brotherhood, he wouldn't even have made a place for her.

That evening, counselors went from tent to tent, telling everyone that at dawn the following day the tents had to be packed up and stored in the hold of the tug. We were sailing to Sabac.

SABAC, SEPTEMBER 1940

The wagon jolted along the cobbled road leading from the dock to the town. Father, Pauli, and I walked alongside the wagon piled high with suitcases tied with ropes; blankets and pillows were wrapped in colorful winter coats, and there were a number of other bundles. Stella Mayer and her sister were perched on top of the pile, their father holding Stella's arm to prevent her from falling off the jolting wagon.

The driver urged on the horse that could barely pull the wagon. Before us was a long line of wagons, and our people, young and old, walked alongside. The older people's hunched backs and faltering steps revealed the hardship of the journey, particularly the feeling of despair and failure.

Townspeople, who looked like Serbs or Slovenians, lined the road. They gathered at the fences, women with scarves on their heads and men in peaked caps, gazing at us with curiosity. Barefooted children ran after the wagons, while the adults looked on in wonder. Someone called out to the driver in Serbo-Croatian, "Where are you taking them?"

He called back, "To Draga Toshkowich's granaries," adding, "At the end of Pop Luca Street."

Going up the road, we passed beautiful buildings and saw signs for a café with home-baked cakes, a bank, and a women's clothing store, before entering a broad street. Someone pointed out a tall building in the distance, and shouted, "*Der mühle*" (the mill). A few moments later, one after another, the wagons came to a stop. Someone called out, "Those getting off at the mill, take your things."

It was rumored that the mill would take as many people from the group that could fit in. Everyone else would go to the granaries at the end of Pop Luca Street.

"What about us?" I asked Father. "Are we also going to the mill?"

"No," said Father impatiently. "Spitzer said we'd be in the granaries. The mill is for the youth, single people, and couples without children."

The convoy remained until all the mill people had removed their possessions from the wagons and carried them into the yard. Our wagon stood waiting next to the mill.

"Don't get off," called the wagon driver. "You're going to the granaries!"

All the young people will be here. It'll be fun here, like the tents in Kladovo, and again I was envious. I'm sure Inge will be here. We'll be apart from each other again. Who knows how far away they'll house us.

The mill house is a long, three-story building that looks abandoned and neglected. Summer weeds grow out of the stone walls. The iron windows are rusty and dangling. The roof is also rusty and collapsing, and if we have to spend the winter here, the situation will be a grave one. The building is in a yard surrounded by a low stone wall, which also seems abandoned and full of dry thistles. A large iron gate leads to a square where a crowd of youngsters have gathered.

Yokel stood in his usual shorts and suspenders at the entrance to the mill. He directed everyone to the right floor, assigned beds, and top or bottom bunk. Yokel and the other counselors were thoroughly prepared, and people knew exactly where to put their things.

We stood out in the strong, late-afternoon sun for a long time, waiting for the last of the youths to take their belongings off the wagons in front of us. We continued, entering Pop Luca Street with its small, well-tended houses and gardens and planters full of flowers. At the end of the street, we saw two long, low buildings with large iron windows.

"Those really are granaries. You can tell from the style of building that they were built even before the Great War," said Father knowledgeably. "The side windows were designed to enable the grain to dry quickly."

We settled into a corner at the end of the short building near the road. Mother's face showed her dissatisfaction. Again, we found ourselves sharing a large space with other families, as we had on board the boat.

"I can't do this again, Emil. I don't have the strength," said Mother, despair and anger in her voice. "Please see if there is any possibility we could have a place of our own. I can't live here like this."

"Sime has misled me again. He said he would house old people and families in a storage granary," said Father. "And I didn't understand that it was one granary for a hundred families."

"Emil, see what you can do. I thought they were moving us somewhere better than Kladovo," her voice broke. "How much longer will they keep us here like refugees? I'm sick of this life. I've had enough! I'm afraid I'll break down."

"At least you have something to keep you busy... All I've done for the past year is play cards and feel bitter. If only we had a bit of *slivovitz* to raise morale."

"You'll probably be able to find work in a big city like this. It'll be good for you. Keep you busy, and two or three extra dinars a week will come in handy."

"The only problem with that is we could move at any moment. Finding work isn't easy in a situation like that. Anyway, first I'll find us somewhere normal to live. Then I'll find work. Most of the group work for the organization and are paid by the Federation of Jewish Communities."

"Just as well we have something to put on the table for lunch," grumbled Mother. As in the past, Father took this personally.

"For heaven's sake, Louie, I've had enough of your righteousness. You have nothing to worry about. I'll be fine."

As if regretting her rebuke, Mother tried to soothe Father.

***

Within two days, our living arrangements were settled. We rented a small apartment that suited our needs from Mrs. Olga Chaliti on Pop Luca Street, and Mother immediately had a fit of cleaning and arranging. The apartment seemed to have been vacant for some time. Spiderwebs hung above the kitchen counter and in the dim opening of the rusty wood stove. Inge offered to help, and the two of them scrubbed the floors with soap and water until they shone. Pauli and I cleaned the windows, and by evening, the entire apartment was bright and clean. Our landlady was an energetic and attractive woman, as befits a dance teacher. She lived alone in an upstairs apartment, and downstairs, next to the apartment we rented from her, she had a dance studio for girls from eight to ten years of age, as well as older girls. I would watch them through a glass window in the door. Long-legged, in tights and muslin skirts, they floated to the sounds of Tchaikovsky, stretching long legs on a wooden barre fixed to the wall. Olga, who had left the studio for a moment, saw me watching and said, "It's not nice to peep like that. If you ask me nicely, I'll let you come in and watch."

Pauli and I shared a room next door to our parents' room. He drew a picture of two gunmen against the background of a cowboy town and hung it above his bed. He also drew caricatures of Mr. Goldman, several of our school teachers in Kladovo, as well as Mr. Spitzer's apple-like face and cheeks against the background of the *Tzar Nikolai's* chimney. Father couldn't stop laughing when he saw the drawing, and forbade us to hang it up.

The days are growing longer now, and the sun sinks early behind the treetops along the Sava River. End-of-October coolness is in the air and smoke rises from the Sabac house chimneys. The pleasant aroma of burning logs fills the air.

I envied residents who could heat their apartments. Our wood stove stood unused. At night, we covered ourselves with three wool blankets Mother got from the supply warehouse, but every morning, I'd wake with frozen feet. I didn't understand why; Father was already working and earning, but we still didn't buy firewood. That morning, after Mother went off to work at the supply warehouse and Father went to work at Mr. Merimovich's carpentry workshop, where he'd been working for three weeks now, I decided to clean the stove and get it ready for use. For this purpose, I missed Mr. Goldman's first lesson. I wasn't worried. I'm good at ancient Greek history.

The school was in a long-abandoned house not far from the mill that housed the movement youth. After two days of cleaning and fixing it up, new lintels and doors were installed, which is how Father found a job at the carpentry workshop. He went to talk to Mr. Merimovich, the owner of the workshop, about lintels and doors for the school next to the mill. He responded that he had no one to do the work, and Father himself volunteered to do it. When Mr. Merimovich saw how Father sketched, measured, and cut the wood, he offered him a job. Father also made each tenant at the mill a small locker to put next to their beds. The Federation of Jewish Communities paid the carpentry workshop for the lockers, so our coming to Sabac brought in a great deal of work for Mr. Merimovich.

At the end of the school day, I went to the city library as usual. I asked Irina, the librarian, for something by Goethe, and she brought me *The Sorrows of Young Werther*. I was enthralled and read until she closed the library. When she saw the beseeching look in my eyes, she allowed me to borrow the book—until the next day. From the moment I discovered the library, it became my second home, and Irina learned to like me and even let me take out books that were not supposed to be lent out.

When I left the library with the book under my arm, the sun was already setting. I went by the infirmary to see Inge. Dr. Bezalel makes sure to see patients only during reception hours, except for emergencies. After reception hours, she cleans and organizes the medication table. The infirmary was sparkling clean, every instrument in place.

It's hard to believe the previous use of this building. When we arrived in Sabac, it was used as a stable adjacent to the granary and the mill that housed most of the youth. Our apartment may be small, but it is near the granary and the mill where most of the activities take place, and where Inge is. To see her, I'd be willing to go to the other side of town. She called me in.

"What are you reading today?"

I heard a note of criticism in her voice, as if I was wasting my time on books while she was doing important work in the infirmary. I felt a bit uncomfortable about walking around with this book instead of reading it in secret in the library or at home, but I was attached to the fate of Werther and his sorrowful love, as if I were the young writer who'd had enough of his comfortable bourgeois life. Except that while young Werther had escaped that life, I'd been cruelly cast out. Nonetheless, I have my own Lotte. Here she is, with a white head covering and coat. She put out a hand to the book under my arm.

"Are you afraid to show it to me?" she asked, lightly pulling at the book. "I see you have something to hide."

"No, no," I said, embarrassed. "You probably know *The Sorrows of Young Werther*," as if defending myself. "I was reading it in the library and got so involved that I couldn't leave it, and Irina allowed me to borrow it, for one day only."

"I just remember it being a romantic sort of book. I think it's Goethe's first book, isn't it?"

"It's the book that made him famous, and just about every German knows it."

"Strange you put it like that, as if a German is something good."

"I'm only saying it's important to distinguish. The Germans of Goethe's time were different, although Heine, for instance, predicted the events that particular nation would precipitate. And today they really are different. Ever since Hitler, they've become animals."

"True. Better you read this and not that book Kreis gave you."

"That book" was one Kreis gave me two weeks ago. It was written by A.D. Gordon, and from the very first moment, Inge had viewed it as an act of defiance.

"Narrow-minded and very dogmatic," she'd said decisively.

"It's a futile argument, Inge," I tried to tell her. "You speak from belief, and for Gordon, it's more a matter of philosophy. His confession is to himself, to the 'self.' But for that, we need a 'self' we respect."

"That's exactly what I said. It is the Lord whom we respect, and He expects a lot from us," she said immediately and triumphantly.

"Let's stop fighting about things like this, Inge. I've missed you and you're quarreling with me. I'm sorry I came with a book at all."

"You're right, Hanne. I'll finish washing the sterile instruments, and we'll go for a walk. Wait a few moments."

We walked hand in hand toward the bank of the Sava. The air was misty and chilly with an edge of fine rain. Through the mist, we saw a long line of wagons standing the length of Yanko Wieslinovich Street. The wagons were harnessed to bulls and loaded with firewood, and the smell of wood mingled with the fresh drops of rain.

"Who's all that wood for?" I asked one of the drivers in Serbo-Croatian.

"We brought it from the Drazih Forest for the Jews at the mill," answered the driver.

"All these wagons of wood are for the mill?" I asked, astonished. "How much firewood do they need there?"

"Yes, that's what the man with spectacles said, too," answered the driver. He must have meant Yokel, who was in charge of mill business.

Two people suddenly came running up. Speedy Misha, who was always in the right place at the right time, and the "noble" Mr. Komo. They lived with four other youths at Farmer Ivanowich's farm. When they heard about the wagons of firewood, they rushed over to buy some before everything went to the mill.

"Pity I don't have any money. I'd also buy a wagonload, or at least half a load."

I went over to one of the peasants, a tall, red-faced fellow with a thick upturned mustache. He introduced himself as Serajan Radoyevich. I asked him the price of one wagonload. After all, I'd just cleaned the stove, and it was ready for use.

"Three dinars per wagon," he said. "Including transport to the house."

The thought of further freezing nights made me want to buy the wood in any way possible. I tried to think of a way to get the sum, which seemed fantastic to me. I decided to suggest working for him to cover the debt. Unhesitatingly, I asked him if he needed help on his farm.

"What can you do?" he asked.

"Feed the animals, harvest vegetables," I mentioned everything I'd learned from Mikhailo.

"Are you willing to come at six every morning for one dinar a day?"

"No problem," I answered, calculating the number of days I'd have to work for him. "If you're willing to sell me a wagonload of wood, I'll work to cover the cost."

That evening, we didn't freeze in our little home. The popping sound of wood in the stove, the pleasant warmth spreading through the apartment, which Mother had carefully cultivated into the semblance of a home, made a pleasant atmosphere. I was uneasy about my parents' reaction, but they complimented me on my initiative and independence. I went back to a routine that was similar to what I had at Mikhailo's place. The days grew shorter and the mornings colder. The last days of October were behind us, and the first cold of November indicated the threshold of a tough winter.

It was hard for me to get up and go out into the cold that morning after a long talk with Inge. It was still hard for her to see me engrossed in Gordon's writings instead of the Torah and weekly *parashah*. The sun would only rise in two hours' time, and the street was still drowsy, apart from Anji's bakery. The fragrance of fresh morning rolls in the air reminds me of bygone days at home on the Dedinje Hill and the morning rolls that Sabina baked; Mother had never managed to replicate their intoxicating crispiness.

Anji was Moosa's mother, a girl who came every two days to the infirmary so that Inge could change the bandage on a sore on her leg. Yesterday, as I was waiting for Inge outside the infirmary, Anji was talking to a girl in Serbo-Croatian. She seemed about my age. Anji didn't stop praising Dr. Bezalel for his devoted treatment of her daughter and the clean and polished infirmary the Austrian Jews had established in a building that used to be a stable. I introduced myself and told them that not all the Jews in the group came from Austria; there was also a family from Belgrade. They were glad to hear it, and the girl introduced herself as Mara; she was the daughter of the Sabac school principal. Anji particularly marveled at Dr. Bezalel taking no money for the treatment.

Mara was very friendly and invited me to join her and her friends sometime. One of them was the gypsy musician I'd seen playing occasionally at Café Roma. I said that if she invited me, I'd bring my girlfriend who works at the infirmary, and we parted company.

I remembered this encounter as I passed the bakery with its tantalizing smell of rolls. I hurried toward Radoyevich's farm so as not to be late for work. On the way, I met Speedy Misha, who was hurrying to the bakery to buy fresh rolls for his group at the farm near the one I was off to. Despite how hard it was to get up in the cold mornings, I was happy that I, too, had my tasks; that Inge would see me as an equal, although her dedicated work with Dr. Bezalel every day was far more important than mine. Before then, I'd felt bad at spending my time reading and studying and not much more.

It was impossible to go walking here, unlike Kladovo next to the Danube, because the Sava landscape was less forested and mostly consisted of monotonous agricultural fields. I also missed the presence of old Petrović, the net mender at Kladovo, and our intimate talks.

Not far from Radoyevich's farm, on a hill near the road leading into the town of Waranska, is a large farm belonging to Farmer Ivanowich, which housed seven members of our group. I see the lights twinkling in the morning darkness every day on my way to work. Luckily, it isn't raining yet, and I can get to the farm on foot, but what about stormy days? I'd committed to coming every morning. I might have to sleep over at the farm. As I opened the gate, Dingo ran over to me. He was a large, hairy dog who was now used to my presence and happy to see me.

Farmer Radoyevich, dressed in blue work clothes and high boots, asked if I could stay longer today. He wanted us to bring the bundles of hay under cover and arrange them so that they'd be sheltered from the rain. We heaped the rest of the bundles outside under large plastic sheets. My pay doubled that morning. I didn't go to school, and on my way back, I passed the mill. The smell of cooking wafted out, and I decided to go in and see the kitchen they'd set up where the machine room used to be. Where once flywheels and rusty engine parts covered in spiderwebs stood silent, now everything was bright and clean. The engines had been replaced by a gas cooker. Mr. Mayer, Stella's father, was hard at work among the pots, supervising the work. At the large chopping table, I found several Mizrahi Movement friends busy peeling potatoes and carrots.

"Join us for a meal," said Efraim, washing mud off sweet potatoes.

"We'll see," I answered. "I've had a long morning at the farm, only just finished." I sat down beside him on the bench.

"Have you heard the latest news?" he asked with a smile.

"No. What now? Another empty promise?"

"Wait, wait a minute," he said, as if about to drop a bomb. "It's fresh from this morning, and it's no rumor this time. It's the truth."

"How do you know? We've been sure so often before."

"But they've never told us to hurry and fill out forms. This morning, a messenger came from the Federation of Jewish Communities with forms."

"*Nu!* Tell me what happened," I urged him.

"The messenger who came this morning said there's a chance that about seven hundred people could immigrate through *Aliyah Bet*, and quite soon, too."

"That does sound serious. So, can anyone immigrate, or will they select people?" I asked.

"Anyone willing to sign a form declaring that they're aware of the risks on the way. Here…" Efraim turned to a pile of forms next to Zeev, our observer, and took one out. "Here, take it. See for yourself."

I read with interest. It was a sort of contract. At the top of the form were all the usual personal details, followed by a brief description of the journey, which included sailing along the Sava and the Danube to Sulina on the Black Sea on a tug like the one that brought us to Sabac. And from there, on the Black Sea by boat through the Straits and into the Mediterranean. At the bottom of the page was a declaration whereby the passenger declared he was willing to take the risk of sailing the Black Sea, and that he would not blame anyone from the administration if it failed.

"It does sound serious this time," I responded, handing the form back to him.

"We'll see what happens. Will you stay? Help me peel these."

I took two carrots out of the pot.

What an uproar that evening! Everyone gathered in the mill square to hear all the details. The proposal changed the mood in a flash. From a situation of waiting for immigration permits, a window of possibility suddenly opened up in the form of illegal immigration. Within the great excitement that prevailed, Mr. Goldman's voice was suddenly heard.

"They're misleading us again. Irresponsible so-and-sos!" He meant the journey administration, and he even attacked Spitzer.

Someone shouted out, "We don't want monkey business. We want legal immigration."

Everyone clapped, calling out, "He's right, he's right."

Amid all the voices, it was difficult to grasp what everyone wanted. Mrs. Weinberg, who was standing beside me, tried to persuade Hanna Weinstock to join.

"In spite of all the risks, my husband and I have decided to take Kurt and board the ship. We have nothing to lose."

"Nothing to lose? Oho! Have you read what's written on the form? God help us, such risks! Would I put my Chaimkeh in danger? I'm not crazy yet," answered Mrs. Weinstock.

"It's better to do something. I don't believe we'll ever get out of here. If we don't try this, well, I don't know…"

That night, I heard my parents arguing. They were also agitated by the news.

"You are not going to sign, Emil. Please, I'm begging you," I heard Mother pleading.

"What do we have to lose?" Father said. "Is this the Garden of Eden?"

"At least we're safe here. And when the immigration permits arrive…"

"This quiet is coming to an end, Louie. You heard as well as I did that the Yugoslavian authorities have decided to pass laws against the Jews."

"I can't believe it could happen here. This isn't Austria, thank God."

"What are you talking about? I heard they've closed the border and are refusing to take in Jewish refugees."

"I'm not willing to risk our lives on that boat. They say this is a stormy season on the Danube."

"I don't understand you, Louie. It's more dangerous to remain here," he tried to end the argument. "And I'm returning signed documents tomorrow."

"Not mine or the children's," she responded decisively. "If you want to take the risk, do it alone. Not with us."

"I've already filled them in. We have until two thirty tomorrow to return them."

"I've talked with others as well. Mrs. Weinstock thinks as I do. She won't put her Chaimkeh at risk."

"Remember my words," Father raised his voice. "It will end badly here too."

"Keep your voice down. You'll wake everyone up."

"You're being unreasonable."

Despite all the excitement, I had to go to the farm early the next morning and needed some sleep. Finally, I dozed off.

This morning, when I returned from the farm, there was no school because everyone was either busy preparing for the voyage or arguing about whether to go or not. In the mill yard, a table had been set up for Mrs. Stern. Ever since Naftali Bata's departure, she'd served as secretary and was in charge of registration. She sat there, a stack of forms and files before her, making notes in a large notebook. Beside her stood a group of people arguing at the tops of their voices.

Mother suddenly appeared, ran up to the table, and demanded to see the forms. I've never seen her so upset. Mrs. Stern tried to hang onto the forms and spoke forcefully to Mother.

"Mrs. David, you cannot take them! Leave the forms alone, please!"

Mother snatched the forms from her, screaming, "Don't tell me what to do! I have to see if he signed! I must know! I also have a say here."

I was so ashamed, I didn't know where to put myself. Something was wrong with her. This wasn't the woman I knew. I was deliberating whether to approach and try to calm her down, or get as far away as I could so she wouldn't know I'd witnessed the scene, when Father appeared in his blue work clothes. He tried to stop her and held her firmly by the arm.

"Calm down, Louie, calm down. What are you doing, for God's sake?"

"You will not make decisions behind my back! I also have rights! I will not join this insane transport! Over my dead body!" She screamed furiously.

"Not now, Louie. We'll discuss it at home, darling. Please, calm down. I'll take care of it. Come, come with me." He put his large arms around her. She hid her head in his shoulder, and her body shook with sobs. "Enough, enough," he whispered in her ear. "Let's go home." They walked toward the exit from the mill, Father tall and erect in his work clothes, Mother held in his embrace, hiding her face from the staring eyes of people who stood aside to let them pass.

Ever since the first meeting about the voyage, steps had been taken to facilitate it. At Father's carpentry workshop, they were working hard on bunks for the tug. But five days later, people were already talking about a passenger boat and not a tug.

Two days after this, on the seventeenth of November, I was in the library as usual, when Yokel and Teddy approached me with the local paper. They asked me to translate an item of news in Serbo-Croatian underneath the photograph of a passenger boat.

"A passenger boat hired to carry hundreds of Austrian and Czech Jews currently in Sabac, down the Danube to Sulina on the Black Sea, where a sea liner is waiting to take them to Palestine."

Yokel and Teddy were very satisfied with this information and rubbed their hands together.

"There you are, another sign that the plan really is going ahead," said Teddy. "You see? Nothing to worry about. Yokel, go and calm everyone down," he said, clapping Yokel on the back. "And something else, tell them that the 'fairy godfather' will be here tomorrow."

This was the nickname the Aliyat Hano'ar youngsters gave Spitzer because of his wild appearance whenever there was trouble on one hand, and on the other because of his stories about secret operations and boats that sounded like fairy stories no one believed. Again, we heard that Spitzer himself was coming from Belgrade to finish up the final details.

"This will help more than anything else," said Yokel.

"You see?" added Teddy. "Some fairy stories seem to be true. Mr. Spitzer is one of them," he said, laughing.

And then another item caught my eye.

"There's something else here that might affect us," I said worriedly.

"What, what?" The two, who were about to go, were alarmed.

"The Yugoslavian authorities have published a decision taken several days ago to prevent Jewish emigrants from Austria, Germany, and Hungary from entering state borders. The prohibition will take effect in the coming days, constituting an additional step by Yugoslavia, like other European countries that have already undertaken similar prohibitions."

Teddy took Yokel's hand and ordered him to sit down again.

"Why are you so upset about this, Teddy? We knew it would happen sooner or later."

"Yes, but just think about what it means. What about the Jews on their way? What about us? They can prevent our sailing!"

"Yes, but we're leaving, not entering," said Yokel.

"It doesn't matter," answered Teddy. "You have to understand how urgent it is that we leave now!"

"I don't understand those who refused to sign," said Yokel.

I remembered Mother's stubborn refusal and again felt very ashamed.

Late that afternoon, I met Inge after she'd finished her shift, possibly her last. That's how everyone was talking about everything they did, because the voyage seemed closer than ever. I thought of inviting her to a movie, but in the meantime, we sat in the empty doctor's room. It was cold outside, and I told her about the meeting at the library.

"It's lucky I managed to get on the list," said Inge. "Did you see what a scramble it was? But there won't be room for everyone."

"I'll be left here alone. Without you. Didn't you think about that?"

"You aren't alone, Hanne," she said, putting her hand on my shoulder. "And anyway, we'll meet soon in Israel. It's only a matter of time."

"I don't know anymore," I said reflectively. "After reading that item in the newspaper today, nothing is clear."

She was silent for a long time, then said, "Hanne, you know I adore your mother, but I didn't understand her behavior that day."

"Don't remind me. You know how uncomfortable I feel about it."

"Yes, but to you I can say it. Because I love you, and because I admire your mother. That loss of control…"

"Maybe she understands something we can't see, some risk no one has considered," I tried to protect my mother's dignity.

"It reminds me of the first day, when I met you on the boat. Remember? The way she fainted and everyone was looking for a doctor."

"Of course I remember. I will never forget that day. And then you appeared like a ministering angel."

"Yes. Well let's not talk about the past. Let's talk about the future. Our future in *Eretz* Israel."

"You're finally leaving. But what about the fate of those who remain here?"

"But you do agree that I should take this opportunity, don't you? The problem is that I am older by one year and not considered youth. After all, they're preparing certificates for all the Aliyat Hano'ar youngsters."

"I agree to one thing," I said, amused. "And that is going to the movies on Thursday evening. They're showing *The Blue Angel* at the Olympia."

"Aha! With Marlene Dietrich. I love her!" She was suddenly carried away with enthusiasm. "A month before the journey, I wanted to go and see that movie at our cinema in town, but then preparations for the transport began and there wasn't time," she said sadly.

"So we're set for Thursday, then?" I said, trying to appear decisive.

"I'll come and get you at seven o'clock in the evening."

That night, I couldn't sleep. I imagined the emptiness, the void here after half the group left on the transport, the rest of us stuck here for a long time to come. Luckily, Dr. Bezalel was staying with us. He'd encouraged Inge to go. I'll probably never see her again. She'll join a *kibbutz* in Israel, and by the time I get there, and who knows when that will be, she'll have married someone else.

I am also excited about Thursday. It will be the first time I take a girl to the cinema, and I can even invite her. Since I finished my commitment to Farmer Radoyevich, he pays me once a week. I give some to my parents, and the rest I keep for myself.

Everyone said "fairy godfather" Spitzer would be coming on Thursday to present the transport plan in a hall at Hotel Paris, where all our Tuesday and Friday cultural performances were now held. Everyone was certain he'd also talk about the plans for those who were staying. But I had no intention of changing my plans in his honor. I had a date with Inge that night.

Tension rose that afternoon when Elli Haimbach announced that Spitzer would not be coming this time, although he hadn't come on previous occasions either. But he'd called to say that the final sailing date was set for the following Tuesday or Wednesday.

When I arrived to pick up Inge on Thursday evening, she received me in a flattering and elegant dress, looking very glamorous. Her hair was tied back, which emphasized her lovely neck and deep dimples in her cheeks. Though I felt that going out with Inge was a privilege, I wasn't happy. We sat down in the hall, my arm around her shoulders. I drew her closer to me, feeling the warmth of her body.

We empathized with Professor Rath's sorrow, suffered with him through his humiliation and abuse as a result of his great love for Lola Lola. We wept when his beloved students abused him. And toward the end, when he returned to his classroom, Inge held my arm tightly and blew her nose.

After the movie, we strolled arm in arm along the broad, illuminated Alexander Street, and from there into a small, darker street, the song "Lola Lola" playing incessantly in my mind.

***

Preparations for the journey were under way. Everyone had already finished packing. The youngsters at the mill and the granary had emptied their wooden lockers, and their eternal suitcases, previously hidden under their beds, were now out in the open, waiting beside their beds. Things looked exactly as they had a few months previously, when we'd waited with our suitcases for a transport that never happened. Everyone spoke enthusiastically about the coming voyage. Father was already resigned to the fact that we were staying, and once he finished making bunks for the tug, he began making wooden clogs for those who were staying. I thought I'd give Inge a pair as a parting gift.

There was a large headline in the evening newspaper about an uprising in several Romanian towns near the Danube. In Turnu Severin, there were demonstrations against Ion Antonescu's new regime; stores and market stalls were burned, and the police had to disperse people by force. Clearly, these incidents might affect any possibility of sailing along the Danube in the area close to the Romanian border.

And indeed, the following day, they announced that the final date had been postponed for two days, to the thirtieth of November, and Mr. Spitzer would come with a new date. On the evening of the proposed parting, in the hall of Hotel Paris, it was postponed indefinitely.

On the thirtieth of November, people were in an uproar once again. They began to fear the voyage would be completely canceled as a result of the situation in Romania. Zvi, who always understood and knew everything better than anyone else, came to visit Father and spoke to him for a long time. Mother served them tea because there was nothing to eat. I sat drinking tea with them. Lately, they related to Pauli and me as adults. Father no longer tried to prevent me from intervening in adult affairs, and I no longer had to listen in secret, unless they really didn't want me to hear. Mother also related to me as a man among men, even serving me tea.

Zvi analyzed the situation with the skill of a surgeon.

"One," he counted on his fingers. "They aren't going to cancel the transport just because of a few riots in Romania. They haven't even closed the Danube crossing. Two, I'm telling you, the problem is that they haven't made sure there's a boat at Sulina; it's nonsense. There's nothing there."

Father, who was originally in favor of joining, sat quietly while Zvi counted the dangers of leaving.

"And three—and listen to what I'm telling you—even if there was a boat, they wouldn't allow it to sail on the Black Sea. There are fierce storms now." Father tried to respond, but he was so immersed in what he was saying that he wouldn't allow interruption. "And four, if they don't leave within two or three days, they won't be leaving at all for a very simple reason: the Yugoslavian Company boats have to return to Belgrade for the winter. The river will freeze over again."

Now Father could no longer contain himself, asking impatiently and cynically, "Tell me, Mr. Zvi, how come you know everything there is to know about the Yugoslavian ships? Where do you get all your information about the weather and how the Yugoslavian Boat Company works?"

Zvi fell silent in the face of Father's aggressive contempt.

"I'm not the only one who says so," he faltered. "That's what they say. What do I know?"

"And you've come up with a whole theory based on these rumors?"

"Enough, stop quarreling," came Mother's calming voice from the kitchen. "Who wants more tea?"

"No, thank you," said Zvi. "I must go."

As he was leaving, Inge came to say goodbye to Mother.

"I came to say goodbye before we leave," she said shyly, standing in the doorway.

"Come on in, my dear," said Mother. "I also wanted to come and say goodbye. And thank you, as well."

Inge came inside. Mr. Zvi went on his way. Mother pulled up a chair, gesturing to her to take a seat.

"Thank me for what, Madame Louisa? I'm the one who should be thanking you."

"Everything comes so naturally to you. You saved me that first day on the boat, and you helped me clean the apartment. You know that's not my strong suit. In Belgrade, everything was always done for me."

"Well, I didn't actually save you. No need to exaggerate. But from the moment we met, I felt a kinship with you. You know how to listen and to advise. You're a special woman."

"I'll make you some tea. I don't have much to offer, you know. Actually, there are still some cookies left from a package we received."

"No need, thank you. Tea is enough."

When Mother returned with two cups of tea, she suddenly realized that she hadn't offered any to Father or me.

"I'll make you some in a second," she apologized.

I was embarrassed by all the affection Mother and Inge showed each other and was silent.

"*Nu*, say something," said Mother. "You're sitting there as silent as a mummy. We all know you're a couple. Everyone calls you a couple made in heaven."

I looked at a black spot on the floor and didn't know how to respond. Fortunately, Inge broke the silence.

"It's true. We love each other and have a great deal in common."

"Yes," said Mother. "And I am overjoyed for Hanne that he's found a girl like you. A girl with a good heart and a practical side too."

"Yes," I added. "It's just a pity she doesn't have enough time for me. She's busy all the time."

"That's just how it is when you choose the nursing profession," said Mother. "There is always someone who needs your care."

"But I have no complaints," said Inge. "There's a final date for our departure, the second of December," she said, changing the subject and raising the cup to her lips.

"I hope so, I hope so," said Father with a sigh.

"Why I hope so?" asked Inge. "I understand that this time it's certain."

"We've all had enough of these postponements," said Mother. "Packing and unpacking, packing and unpacking all the time. Just like that song 'Filth.'"

"Did you go to their last performance?" asked Mother.

"The last one? No. But I went with Hanne the week before. I don't go very often now that they take money."

"They shouldn't really take money. Emil and I don't go very often either."

"If it wasn't so sad, we could laugh at this situation, and they're really good at that."

"As long as you leave the day after tomorrow! They can't put it off any longer," said Father.

"It'll be all right," said Inge. "I'm sure we'll meet in Israel once you get your papers. It's just a matter of time."

"Apparently, storms are no longer a danger," I said. "I also heard that Spitzer called to confirm the departure date."

"I also heard that," said Father. "I was there when they got the call. Something doesn't seem right to me, but I wish you all good luck."

"Thank you. I have to go now," said Inge, getting up from her chair. "I am really very happy to have met your lovely family. I'm sure we'll be in touch, Hanne, and I have already planned our future together in Israel."

She went over to Mother and embraced her. Mother returned the embrace with fervor, and I saw two large tears trickling from her eyes. She parted from Father with a courageous handshake.

"I'll accompany her," I said, getting up and going toward the door.

"Goodbye Inge. Good luck and a safe journey. Keep us a place there!" Mother called after her. "Hanne, take something warm. It's cold outside."

We went out into the darkness and the cold. Inge held out her hand to me and so we trudged in silence toward the dark *Tzar Nikolai* Street on our way to the mill.

Inge was the first to speak. "Say something, Hanne. Your silence is hard for me."

"You know I get embarrassed in situations like that. What can I say?"

"Tell me we'll get engaged when we meet in Israel. It wouldn't kill you to say so."

"It's not that, Inge. You forget I'm only sixteen. Who announces an engagement at that age?"

"All right. We only have one more day together, and I don't know if there'll be time to meet, you know." She stood before me expectantly. I put my arms around her waist and drew her to me. Then I stroked her face and touched her lips with mine in a long, warm kiss. We stood embracing for some time.

"Promise me you'll let me know as soon as you get to Israel. I might not hear about your arrival."

"I'll try and let you know by all means possible, although I may not know where to look."

"You know what? I'll send you a postcard here."

We parted with heavy hearts. Something told me we'd not meet again. That bad things would happen to us here. Yugoslavia had already begun to adopt the racial laws in place in Germany, Austria, and Poland. Although there was no order as yet to wear the yellow star like other countries, it would probably come soon enough.

***

Mr. Spitzer indeed arrived. Not on the first of December, as planned, but only on the sixth of December. The second of December was the worst day in the annals of our transport. The tug stood ready, loaded with bunks and kitchen equipment. The travelers were ready and packed down to the last item. Some had even sold things they no longer needed to friends who were staying. The sellers regarded the buyers with compassion. Some tried to be encouraging and say things like, "We'll be together again soon."

On the morning of the second of December, everyone made their farewells. People who'd lived together for over a year were saying goodbye, for a short time, or an unknown time, or perhaps, forever.

But then, Elli Haimbach appeared, walking swiftly and holding a telegram in his hand from the Yugoslavian Boat Company. He didn't know how to begin to explain the enormity of the blow. He knew that this time, the disappointment would be infinitely greater than that of Kladovo two months before.

When Sime Spitzer arrived, four days later, in order to explain the reason for the cancellation, people simply lost control. The terrible blow of disappointment was mixed with depression, despair, and utter rage that they projected onto everyone: the Germans, the Yugoslavians, the Transport Administration, the Jewish leadership, everyone.

The rage had died down somewhat by December 6, but only a few came to the hall at Hotel Paris to hear the "fairy godfather" attempt to explain what had happened—how from a situation of complete confidence in the departure, everything suddenly fell apart again. Unlike other times, when the audience had booed, this time there was a thundering silence. People had lost hope. They were indifferent to what Mr. Spitzer had to say. Father, Pauli, and I went to the meeting. Spitzer appeared. He was simply dressed, without his eternal, cylindrical hat. This time, he didn't speak with his customary brisk confidence. He referred to the storms on the Black Sea as a danger not taken into account, about the riots in Romania, which caused the shore patrol to stop and examine any passing ship or tug. He said he didn't want complications and that the safety of the passengers was more important than almost certain danger.

"But do not give up hope," he said with pathos. "The most important thing is that we are safe here. I swear I will make every effort to get you all out of here."

There were no interruptions. Everyone sat quietly and let him speak.

"If not tomorrow then in a week, or a month," he said before leaving the stage. "Just don't lose hope, my friends. You will get to *Eretz* Israel."

After Spitzer left, people stayed behind in groups, sharing their concerns.

"It all sounds like a bunch of lies and excuses to cover up incompetency," said Mr. Weinberg. The veins in his forehead looked as if they were about to burst. He'd been so sure that this time he'd finally be on his way to *Eretz* Israel.

"I've already told our son, Kurt, in Palestine, that we'll be there in about two weeks. What will happen now? They'll probably be so worried," said his wife Marta, wringing her hands in anxiety.

Inge didn't want to come and hear him. Ever since the announcement, she'd tried to cover up the pain of disappointment by working long hours in the infirmary. I wanted to sit with her and comfort her, but she didn't even want to see me during the few hours at the mill. After a few days, she was back to herself and tried with all her heart to forget what had happened, as she said later, "Forget that foolish idea of trying to sail the Black Sea in a passenger boat."

Others meant to set out on that transport tried to get back into routine. The youth went back to playing football on the Matchva field that belonged to the local group. Others visited the local library, leaving with books under their arms.

***

A few days later, on the twelfth of December, a new rumor started: a ship called the *Dorian Gray* or the *Darien*, something like that, a huge luxury ship, was waiting at the Port of Sulina. We were told there'd be an important announcement in the Hotel Paris hall that evening. Again, excitement gripped the group of illegal immigrants. They were impatient to hear the representative of the committee make a formal statement about the plan.

Two groups had now formed: the group of illegal immigrants, more than seven hundred mainly young pioneers, and the group remaining behind in Sabac, who were waiting for immigration permits for legal immigration. They weren't interested in the story about the *Darien* or the *Dorian*.[21]

We were among the group that was staying. When Mother heard I was going to listen to what the administration had to say about the new arrangement, she was outraged.

"Don't go! Better to read something good than to listen to their drivel all over again."

"I'm just interested in their plans," I responded. "And in any case, Inge is in that group, and I'm going with her."

"Oh, I thought she'd given up this time," said Mother. "I heard her talking about it when everything was canceled."

"Yes. She was in despair. She said she didn't want any more disappointments and that she was staying here."

"So what happened?"

"You know, excitement's catching. Everyone has travel fever again."

The hall was completely full, and some of those present were even smiling. Mr. Haimbach went up on stage to speak. Yokel stood beside him, holding a list of names. Quiet prevailed.

"Friends, we are happy to announce that at long last, with the help of donations from American Jews, and the welcome initiative of the

---

21 The *Darien 2* was a commercial boat acquired for the *Ma'apilim* in May 1940, at Port Piraeus, by Shmarya Tsameret, a Mossad man with American citizenship. It was a ship that went through many transformations. At the time of the acquisition, she was flying the flag of Panama and bore the name of a ridge of mountains in that country. Shmarya bought her as an American citizen to avoid involving the Mossad in the acquisition. He handed her over to David Hacohen and Yechiel Arzi for the purpose of collaborating with the British, which was unsuccessful. Ultimately, she was returned in November 1940 in favor of the *Ma'apilim*, as narrated here. The *Darien* primarily symbolizes the "packing-unpacking" process endured by the *Ma'apilim*.

Aliyah Bet Institute in Istanbul, we've managed to organize a Turkish boat, the *Darien*. Not the *Dorian*, and not the *Dorian Gray*, as I've heard people saying.

"It was by no means easy and required a great deal of work by all parties involved. *Darien* is large enough for all those who registered and more. According to our count, there are about sixty more places, and anyone who is still interested can register afterward with Yokel. On the other hand, I will not hide the fact that the sea is still dangerous, and whoever does not want to immigrate in this way can remain here until legal papers are organized."

A wave of whisperings and arguments went through the audience. People were deliberating whether to immigrate now, or to wait.

"I give you my word that everyone will get there in the end. Whoever doesn't board the *Darien* will arrive legally, at a later date. But I have to tell you that there are risks involved. Even if everything goes as planned, the British will stop the boat near Israel's shores and will attempt to send you back to Cyprus or to one of the temporary internment camps. Whoever wants to join and has not yet registered can see Yokel now. He has the necessary papers."

He paused briefly; someone handed him a glass of water; he took a hurried sip and continued, "And now to the plan itself. On the nineteenth of the month, you will travel by train to Prahovo. You already know the place; it's not far from Kladovo. From Prahovo, a Romanian tug will take you to Sulina where you will board the *Darien*. Since there are a lot of people, one train won't be enough. You will leave on several trains leaving between the eighteenth and the twentieth. The Romanian tug, I've forgotten its name, will wait for you at the Port of

Prahovo. You will be met at the train station by one of our contacts, who will be waiting for you there and who will lead you on foot to the port. Board the tug quietly, and wait there until your departure on the twentieth of the month at eight o'clock in the evening, once the six-thirty train arrives in Prahovo."

He took another sip of water before continuing.

"Whoever wants to send packages or large suitcases before that date, instead of hauling them onto the train, can bring them to a small tug meant only for packages and suitcases. It will leave Sabac dock tomorrow, and the luggage will be waiting for you at the Port of Prahovo."

I'd arranged with Inge to take her suitcase to the tug. I ran to the infirmary, but Inge and the doctor were busy with a local woman's baby who'd almost choked on a bead. I waited outside with the mother, who was wringing her hands and pulling her hair in despair. When I opened the door a crack, I saw Inge sitting with the baby in her lap. She gestured to me to stay out. The doctor, who was standing next to her, lightly tapped the baby on its back, and the bead shot out of his mouth like a bullet from a rifle, and he immediately began to scream. I closed the door. The mother, still wringing her hands and pulling her hair, heard her baby's screams and burst into the room. A joyous smile I hadn't seen since the cancellation of the transport spread over Inge's face. She met the agitated mother with the crying baby on her shoulder, lightly patting his back, and said to me, "Hanne, tell her in Serbo-Croatian that everything is all right now. Her baby is safe. Tell her that he will cough and cry for a while but that she has nothing to worry about now."

Once the mother and baby had left, she called me to see her

enormous green suitcase in the corner of the treatment room.

"Look how big it is. I can't drag that thing onto the train."

"No problem," I responded, though I still didn't see how I was going to pick up the suitcase by myself.

"And that's nothing compared to what's waiting for me in the warehouse in Trieste." She sighed helplessly.

"My parents sent our big things to Haifa," I said. "They'll be waiting for us there. When do you want to transfer it? Now?" I asked, as if there wasn't a problem.

I tried to pick up the suitcase and immediately put it down again. I realized that taking it on foot to the port would be problematic, but I wasn't going to give up. And then I had an idea. I remembered that my father used a small cart on two wheels at the carpentry workshop whenever he had to lift heavy planks.

I suggested to Inge that we postpone the transfer of the suitcase till the next day, and I would bring the cart. That evening, I asked my father to find out if I could borrow the cart the next day.

So, the following evening, I loaded the huge suitcase onto the cart and took it almost effortlessly to the tug. The people we met on the way were in a good mood and laughed. Many of them liked the idea of a cart and called to us, "What a great idea!" Or, "Pity we didn't think of it." On the way, we met the Weinberg couple. Mr. Weinberg was my father's age and could barely manage their large suitcase. He asked us where we'd gotten the cart.

"Do you think we could use it?" Mrs. Weinberg asked politely, while her husband sat on the suitcase, wiping large beads of sweat from his forehead. Although I'd promised to return the cart to the carpentry workshop immediately, I had to help this old couple. I told them to wait there and I'd be back to fetch the suitcase.

The days swiftly passed, and the date set to board the train was approaching. On the first night of Hanukkah, candles were lit in the great hall of the mill. Many came wrapped in wool blankets or heavy coats. Some crowded together outside in the cold where the temperature was twelve degrees.

The food shortage was felt in the minimal number of latkes prepared in the makeshift kitchen. There were only a few potatoes and very little oil. Complaints were heard about the warehouse administration, and it seemed to me that some were directed at my mother.

The children's choir conducted by Martha sang Hanukkah songs, and Freddie played festive tunes on his clarinet. It was a farewell party for the group of pioneers leaving the next day for Prahovo and the anticipated voyage, but the atmosphere was sad and heavy. Mr. Goldman made a parting speech in the name of those staying behind. He mentioned the setbacks we'd had together and prayed for the success of this dangerous journey. He also spoke about the bravery of the travelers, and the hope of those remaining that legal immigration permits would arrive soon so they could all be united in Israel. He concluded that though no Hanukkah miracle had as yet occurred on this journey, they were, this Hanukkah, finally beginning to see the light.

But no light materialized. The following day, just as the first group was making final preparations before walking together to the train station, they again received bitter news. The voyage was postponed indefinitely.

JANUARY 1941

The cold hurts my cheeks and ear lobes as if they were about to break off. Father says its years since they had such a cold January. I was on my way as usual to Mr. Radoyevich's farm, wrapped up in a coat and hat I'd recently bought at the Sabac market. Despite the cold and hard work, I was content, for it brought us relief many others did not have. The people who were having a really hard time now were those who'd lived with the stress of packing and unpacking for over a month and who, ultimately, suffered a bitter disappointment as well as being left without their belongings. Some suffered from enormous anxiety about the future.

We who intended to remain in Sabac managed to use the time to prepare for a long, cold winter.

We were even able to heat our apartments with coal stoves. There were those who no longer believed that the transport would leave any time soon and requested that some of their belongings be sent back from the warehouses in Trieste. This is what Zvi and his wife did, and now, on cold nights, she wears her expensive fur coat that was returned from the warehouse with the rest of their belongings.

I was deep in thought that morning. Playing and replaying the details of a brief love interlude with Inge the previous night, which was abruptly cut short.

We were on our way back from a performance by the Fenit[22] theater. We'd laughed so much, in a way we hadn't for a long time. I accompanied Inge to the mill where she slept in a dormitory with twenty other girls. In one of the alleys on the way, I felt a warmth in my loins that spread to the rest of my body. I stopped, drew her to me, and embraced her passionately. After so many times of stopping myself, this time I allowed myself the freedom to let go. My hand touched the outline of her body through her long skirt. In the dim lamplight, I felt her giving in to her passion, although I was afraid something would stop her. I opened her thick coat, caressed her breasts under her blouse, and they rose and fell with her quickening breath as she whispered, "Hanne, oh Hanne."

For a moment, she seemed to relax her vigilance, but then she suddenly shook herself free, saying decisively, "Stop! No touching, Hanne!"

Everything stood still. I felt as if the sky had suddenly fallen.

***

That morning, when I got to the farm, Serajan Radoyevich was impatiently waiting for me at the gate. He called to me to hurry over to the large cow barn. I hastily changed my clothes, putting on high boots, my work overalls, and an old sheepskin coat he'd given me. I followed

---

22 From the Yiddish word *tinef*, meaning "soil" or "blemish," and written back to front as the name of the theater.

him between the high walls of hay. At the end of the path lay the red cow. She was motionless, her tail was brushed aside, and two tiny legs peeped out from under it. They were covered in blood and placental fluid.

"We have to help her," he said tensely. "Or it'll die."

Radoyevich was apparently very skilled in the ways of calving.

"Why? Can't it come out naturally by itself?" I asked, revealing my ignorance.

"It's the wrong way around, can't you see that?" he barked at me, as if I should have known the answer, known it should have been out by now but that she wasn't pushing enough.

I stood there, afraid to look at the cow as she weakly lowed every now and then in her suffering.

"Run to the storeroom and fetch two or three ropes. If you can't find any, cut some off from one of the bales of hay. And bring a pole or a stout stick."

I was glad to leave the scene, glad not to see the suffering of the red cow, or the two damp, bloody legs peeping from under her tail. I ran to the storeroom but couldn't find the rope. I took out my penknife and, cutting off rope from a bale of hay with two strong strokes, I ran back so as not to waste time. When I returned, Radoyevich was angry because I'd forgotten to bring a stick. I'd never seen him so stressed. I came back with the handle from a hoe.

"Do you know how to make a good knot? The knot must be tight so it won't come loose, but it mustn't press either."

I remembered our field lessons with Zeev, the "eternal boy scout," and the special knot he'd taught us.

"No problem, I'll tie it," I said confidently.

I made the knot and tied it securely, but was concerned it was too tight around the fragile legs of the calf and loosened it slightly. In the meantime, Radoyevich was preparing loops for the stick so that we'd have something to hold onto when pulling.

Our pulling was of no use. The calf didn't move. Radoyevich instructed me to continue pulling all the time, like the Kladovo tournament on sports day.

"Either we aren't pulling hard enough, or something is blocking the passage," he said. "Tugs like that should have gotten him out long ago."

Despite the cold, sweat poured down his face.

"This isn't going to work," he said finally.

"Let's not give up," I said. "Maybe call the vet?"

"No, it's not our turn today," he said in despair.

"So let's call a neighbor then."

To my surprise, the man who came was none other than Speedy Misha, as he was called. He rubbed his hands together as if getting ready for action.

"What's the problem, Hanne? Here, give that to me."

He kneeled down beside me and held the stick firmly. We pulled hard, and suddenly, I saw a damp pink nose peeping out, each tug revealing more of his head. By the third tug, his neck was out. With the last tug, all resistance disappeared as if it had never existed. On the hay lay a dead calf.

Radoyevich tried to resuscitate it, but its chest was still and it wasn't breathing.

"That's it." Radoyevich stamped his foot. "The calf's finished. Dead."

I felt a burden of guilt settle on my narrow shoulders.

There's not much work at the carpentry workshop at the moment, and Father only works there twice a week. On other days, he sits in the kitchen, the largest space in our small apartment, and plays cards with his usual group of friends. On Tuesdays, they sit playing at Café Roma, on the corner of Dushana and Kralitza Alexandra, a broad street not far from Hotel Paris; there, they drink and discuss the situation. Everyone talks about the situation at Café Roma, but they mainly come in to shelter from the piercing cold outside. The cold sends them scurrying back to the houses, the mill, or any other protected place.

The mill is an open space and impossible to heat. The youngsters tried to get the stove working, but the chimney was blocked by dry mud and they couldn't open it up. The most pleasant place to meet was Café Roma. It was owned by Mrs. Chalkeiwich, whom everyone calls Miroshka, a broad, large-bosomed woman. Her black apron was designed to hide her size but actually emphasized it even more. Her generous laughter was full of kindness and love for people as she made her way among the tables, asking if they needed anything. Although she employed a young waitress, Miroshka worked both in the kitchen and as a waitress. Her manners were cheerful and brisk. The aroma of coffee and fresh pastries from Anji's bakery filled the café.

I went there twice with Inge. Mara praised her friend Nicola, a musician who plays all kinds of tunes on the accordion and the harmonica, mainly gypsy songs, which he sings with Milka, his beautiful friend.

Inge asked them to sing "My Yiddishe Mama," and everyone was moved to tears. Inge was seized with loneliness and longing for her mother. I held her close to me and stroked her wet cheeks.

The prevailing language at Café Roma was Viennese German. Everyone talked at the tops of their voices about the transport, when we'd leave, if ever. Who was responsible for this farce, as the café gossips called it?

The noisiest table was Shesta's; he was known as "the loafer," because he spent most hours of the day there. Mother wondered how he got the money to sit there all day long. Mr. Gottesmann, "the hedonist," spent a lot of time there. He had endless stories to tell about rich meals in Vienna, going out to the opera in fine, fashionable clothes, and so on. Even in the conditions of our transport, his elegant clothes stood out, his hair brushed sideways to hide his balding head. Mr. Gottesman always has insights about the course of the war. He believes we have to get out as soon as possible, that we are living on borrowed time. He thinks the Germans will be in Sabac within two or three months, and then God help us all.

And there was Rudi Lempel, also known as "the Führer" because of his leadership qualities; he'd sit there at his usual table, always knowing about secret events taking place behind the scenes, which were known only to his close friends. But he trusted his friends not to tell. A month after the last cancellation, I was sitting with Inge, not far from him, and his authoritative voice filled the space.

"And what do you think this story about the *Darien* is really about? You were told that Sime Spitzer is looking after us and taking care not to send us off in a storm, but have you thought about what's really going on?" he asked, and of course nobody answered. "It has to do with the situation in Romania! Everyone knows that whenever there's unrest, the police close off roads, put up roadblocks, and make arrests. And you believe these clowns?" Rudi laughed ironically. "Oh, God help us, we are such miserable wretches." He suddenly lowered his voice as if telling a secret, " The *Darien* wasn't ever intended for us, I'm telling you."

"What do you mean, 'not intended for us'?" Shesta the loafer was roused from his apathy. "So who was she for?"

"They say she was brought to Sulina for refugees, but the real story is entirely different."

"Well? So what's the story?" asked Mr. Gottesmann.

"There was a secret agreement between the British and the Jewish Agency. The British wanted the ship to prevent supplies from reaching Germany via the Danube."

When he heard this, Mr. Gottesmann was furious.

"Nonsense!" he said. "Firstly, the *Darien* isn't built for sailing the Danube, and secondly, since when has the Jewish Agency collaborated with the British? Haven't they made enough trouble for us, these British, not giving us immigration permits to enter *Eretz* Israel? And now they're making deals with them? Are you mad?"

"I'm not forcing you to believe it, Mr. Gottesmann," said Rudi peaceably. "On one hand, you could say I'm talking nonsense. Time will tell."

"If what you say is true, we should get up and protest, do something! It's intolerable that Spitzer is always coming here just to throw sand in our eyes."

"Ach, you are all so naive!" said Mr. Rudi Lempel. "We should do something, not just sit here like idiots. Let's give them an ultimatum."

"Better to order a really good schnapps," Shesta tried to bring them back to reality and called Miroshka.

But Café Roma wasn't the be-all and end-all of the whole group. The general atmosphere was harsh. People were bitter and in despair. Most of the frustration was directed at Sime Spitzer and the Transport Administration. Nobody believed their promises, and some became depressed. The cold also contributed to the hardship. Not everyone could afford to sit at Café Roma. Most people sat in unheated places like the mill and the granary, or in wretched apartments in town. Food supplies were further limited. There were rumors that this was because of the situation on the Balkan front, which probably affected the regular supply of food to such a large number of people.

Once a week, I did kitchen duty at the mill. I felt a need to be part of the group. Mother also encouraged me in this, in case the Youth Aliyah program did take place. Clearly, it was important to maintain good relations with the group.

Olga Chaliti, who owned our house, holds rehearsals in her studio adjoining our apartment. When she saw me staring at the dancers, she invited me to come in and watch, and even said she'd invite me to their performance on the Christian festival of Saint Sava. On this day, everyone wears traditional clothes, and at local schools, there are ceremonies and plays in honor of the saint. One day, I went to see Trudeh, the Viennese dancer who'd astonished us all with a dance at our first Hanukkah on board the *Tzar Nikolai*. Here she was, helping Olga prepare the girls for the performance; she was also surprised to see me. I told her that we were living there, next door. But on the day of the performance, I saw that Teddy had written me down for kitchen duty, and I was uncomfortable about asking to change it because of a Christian holiday.

It was so cold mid-January that the water froze my fingers, and I had a hard time peeling potatoes. Mr. Herman, a short, energetic man who was in charge of the kitchen, scolded me for my slowness.

"It's because of the cold. My fingers are frozen."

"Ach! You're spoiled. It's obvious you come from an aristocratic home in Belgrade," he said half-jokingly.

"I forgot about that aristocratic home a long time ago," I responded. "It feels as if years have gone by since then."

"Luckily for you there's not much to peel today, but unlucky for everyone else. There won't be much to eat again today."

"Why? What happened?"

"Supplies haven't been coming in recently, and I see that it's getting worse. We'll work out something today too. It's been two weeks since we got any oil, and I can't fry a thing."

He disappeared among the large pots, and I saw him and Avreymel working hard, one of Avreymel's hands resting on his hip while the other slowly stirred a bubbling pot. He brought me the pot of soft potatoes, handed me a masher, and later called me to help with the meat balls.

"There's very little meat. We'll have to add more bread," he said, and sent me to the bread cupboard. "Bring ten loaves of yesterday's bread, please. It's on the bottom shelf."

I soaked the bread in water and crumbled it into a large bowl, the ground meat barely a quarter of the whole amount.

Before people came in to eat, Mr. Herman whispered to me, "Give sparingly…a spoon and a half of mashed potatoes and not many peas or carrots on each plate. No more, or there won't be enough for everybody."

When the time came to serve the food, I stood in an apron that fell to my knees. Those in line gave me beseeching looks for a little more of the tasteless mashed potatoes, another half a meatball, and I so wanted to give them more, but Herman's warning words rang in my ears.

"No more, or there'll be none left."

And heavy-hearted, I put one and a half spoons of mashed potatoes and one meatball on each plate, no more. Shesta came up, wrapped in blankets and a hat that almost covered his eyes, and held out his plate. His twisted smile expressed despair.

"Hey, boy, give me more. That's a helping for babies!" he said, continuing to stand there, holding out his plate.

"No vegetables have come in for two weeks now. There aren't enough supplies," I tried to explain, but he stayed there, plate in hand, as if rooted to the spot.

"Hey, what's going on over there? What's the holdup?" someone shouted from the end of the line, and others began rattling their plates in irritation.

I continued to refuse and suddenly felt something hot and sticky on my face. Shesta had smeared his mashed potatoes all over my face.

"There you are, insolent boy," he said angrily and grabbed the spoon from my hand.

Someone else, I think it was Mr. Roff, known as "the clean-hand president," an insult given him by the youngsters because of his exaggerated concern over cleanliness, shouted, "Bastard! Leave the pot alone, you parasite!"

But Shesta continued to scrape the bottom of the pot. Then Mr. Globerman, the man who'd slaughtered the calf in Kladovo, and who everyone feared, jumped in front of him.

"Get out of here at once, or I'll beat you to a pulp."

He came up close to Shesta; he was a head taller, although Shesta wasn't exactly short. Shesta rocked slightly on his feet, then shook off his blanket and tried to stand up to Mr. Globerman. But all at once, he realized he didn't stand a chance and left the place in shame.

I'd mashed up the remaining potatoes in the meantime and washed my face in the bowl of water Mr. Herman handed me. Despite the searing insult, I did not give up and continued to serve the food, in an attempt to ignore the indignity, feeling a burning desire to take revenge on Shesta. That bastard does nothing all day, every day, and then he comes for food; instead of saying thank you and sitting down quietly, he insults the people who prepared the food.

"I wouldn't have believed it; that lazy good-for-nothing who does nothing for anyone, but has the nerve to open his mouth," said Mother furiously, when she heard about the incident. "Emil, this cannot be ignored."

"But what's to be done? Do you want Hanne to call him out?" asked Father.

My parents continued to bicker sarcastically for a while without reaching any practical solution. Father ended the argument in good spirits and invited Mother to the theater that evening.

"We deserve a laugh, don't we?"

"Yes. We haven't been to a Fenit performance for a long time," said Mother. "We should go and see them again. I've heard they keep getting better and better."

"I'm also going today," I interrupted their conversation.

***

The dining hall of Hotel Paris was lit up and people were coming in from all over the city, among them German-speakers who were residents of Sabac and willing to pay the price of a ticket for a healthy laugh. Several city notables were also invited. When the mayor entered, he received a standing ovation.

The performance began with the tune "We're packing, we're unpacking," which had become the group signature tune. Freddie conducted the orchestra, and the choir joined in later on. When Richart and Yossi came on stage, the audience went wild. The skit dealt once again with the group's daily life and the anticipation of something good finally happening.

When the curtains open, the two actors are lying down with blankets up to their chins. Richart half sits up, leaning on his elbow, and looks over at Yossi, who is asleep.

Richart: "Yossi, Yossi, *nu*, are you already asleep?"

Yossi, still lying down, answers sleepily: "Leave me alone, Richart. I just fell asleep."

Richart sits up, his blanket over his knees: "And I've just woken up to the smell of roast duck and gravy. It's just come up from the warehouse dining room, and what's more, they're serving chicken soup there; it just slides down your throat, and there's compote and apple strudel for dessert. A really rich meal. Haven't eaten anything like it for over a year. And to end off the meal, a glass of hot mocha."

Yossi also gets up now: "What a pity. I didn't smell or taste it, not the soup or the roast."

Laughter comes from the audience.

Richart makes a dismissive gesture: "Never mind. Don't get too excited. It was only a dream. And now I want to go back to sleep."

Yossi is angry: "So go back to sleep. Who's bothering you?"

Both are quiet. Try to get some sleep.

Richart sits up again, leans on his elbow: "Yossi, Yossi, are you asleep yet?"

Loud laughter again, and someone shouts out, "Let him sleep, idiot."

Yossi, still lying down, is annoyed: "Leave me alone, Richart."

Richart: "The train whistle woke me up. It's a special train, just waiting for us, been at the platform for over an hour now. No one knew about it, no one heard. What do you know, Yossi? What do you know? A direct train to Prahovo. And everyone says there's a real big ship over there, just waiting to take us to Palestine. And I strolled around Tel Aviv in the summer sun in a smart hat and didn't even know it was a dream, and it's February today."

Yossi is alarmed: "Oh, God help me! I missed that transport too!"

The audience roars with laughter. Someone yells out, "Yossi, don't believe him!"

Richart again makes a dismissive gesture: "Don't worry, Yossi. It was just a dream."

Both of them lie quietly for a moment.

Yossi turns restlessly under the blanket: "Come on, let me sleep."

Richart again sits up, leaning on his elbow: "Are you asleep?"

Yossi, irritated: "What now?"

The sporadic laughter from the audience now becomes a rhythmic roar.

Richart describes peacefully: "I was in the Garden of Eden, and it wasn't a dream. Everything there is allowed, everything. You can enjoy yourself till dawn for only twenty dinars. And if that isn't enough, everyone gets gambling coupons too."

Yossi shouts: "Stop!"

They run off stage to the sound of applause and requests for an encore, coming back on stage to take a bow.

After the performance, the cold outside sent everyone home. I accompanied Inge to the infirmary. She preferred to sleep there when on duty rather than at the cold, noisy mill. When we got there, we found Dr. Bezalel, who was still reading *Death in Venice* by Thomas Mann.

"Read it?" he asked, closing the book.

"Yes," I responded. "I particularly like Thomas Mann."

"*Nu*, so what do you have to say about it?" he asked with curiosity.

"The resemblance to Mahler is so striking, it's impossible to ignore. My mother was a great admirer of Mahler, and thanks to her, I read that book."

"Yes, I didn't think of that, but now that you mention it… He wasn't called Gustav for nothing."

"There's a lot there that's taken from Mahler's biography."

"I find it curious that a young fellow like you would read a book about an aged hero, whose thoughts revolve around death."

344 | ESCAPING ON THE DANUBE RIVER

"I was actually captivated by the description of his thoughts on life. The beautiful young body of that young boy, I've forgotten his name."

"Tadzio, the Polish boy," said Dr. Bezalel. "The yearning for youth, for beauty, the desire to turn back time. When all is said and done, the body has laws of its own."

"See, you read that book as an adult from a doctor's point of view."

"True. One can't escape one's profession. Particularly that of a doctor."

"Ahem…" Inge cleared her throat to remind us of her presence. "You're off again," she said plaintively.

"Well, I'll leave you here," said the doctor, turning to Inge. "Ah, that woman from Sabac with the crying baby came again today. It turns out he's teething. I calmed her down and she went home. Good night!" said Dr. Bezalel and left.

"He talks and talks as if I didn't exist," complained Inge.

"But he started talking to me!" I tried to defend myself.

"You could have apologized and said you were with me now."

"I'm sorry, Inge," I said, drawing closer to her, but I felt her stiffen.

"Lately, you've been distant. You don't behave the way you did when we first met."

"But I love you," I said, trying to get her to look at me. "I always have, ever since we first met."

"So why don't you say so? You used to tell me you loved me every day. Every time we met, I'd feel how much you wanted to be with me."

"Maybe it's the tension here. This constant packing and unpacking, it can drive you mad."

"I'm afraid, Hanne, I'm afraid," she said.

"What are you afraid of, Inge? I'm here with you. We'll survive everything together, you'll see. We'll get to Palestine in the end, we'll have sweet children, and we will always love one another. Until death do us part."

"I'm afraid that when we get there, you'll leave me. You'll look for someone who is educated, someone you can talk to about Mahler and Thomas Mann. I'm too simple for you."

"No, Inge, never think that. You are the beauty in my life. Without you, I'd be miserable here, really miserable."

"So tell me again. I want to hear it again," she said, in tears.

I put my hands on her waist and drew her closer. Trembling, she rested her head on my shoulder.

Inge told me that Yost was admitted to the infirmary last Thursday with a severe infection of the digestive system, and that the doctor had imposed a strict diet. I hadn't spoken with Yost for a long time; in fact, I'd only visited him twice in all the time we'd been in Sabac. Once when he and his family still lived crowded together with other youngsters in the granary next to the mill, and again in the small, well-kept house they'd been given on the outskirts of Sabac. Max, his father, was very busy, as he'd been made responsible for professional changes at the group school. Consequently, Yost spent most of his time with his mother in a house far away from the center and with friends. When Inge told me he'd been hospitalized, I wanted to visit him.

I found him in good spirits, and sat down next to him on the bed, taking care not to get too close so I wouldn't be infected. Yost told me he'd missed a great many group activities because they lived so far from the center, but that it also had its advantages. Their home was close to the agricultural area, and he'd made friends with the neighboring farmer's son. He helped him feed the chickens, collect eggs, and he'd even ridden their donkey, which was fun.

Then he reached under the bed and brought out the wooden chess box I remembered from Kladovo. At first, I was worried about infection, but I couldn't resist his look of longing and gave in. He sat up, opened the box, and we began to set out the pieces. I found Yost a tough opponent this time. He wasn't the same player he'd been in Kladovo, when we were evenly matched. He'd played a lot with his father and had improved.

While playing, he proudly spoke of his approaching bar mitzvah ceremony and that he was already learning his *parashah*. Mr. Goldman had agreed to teach him now, although he'd only be called up to the Torah on the first of March.

"You'll come to my bar mitzvah, won't you?"

***

The following day, when I got back from my work at the farm and was sitting with Father and Pauli eating breakfast, Mr. Goldman suddenly appeared in a state of great excitement.

"This is it! It's finally come! Yesterday, I was instructed by the *Eretz Israel* office in Zagreb to fill out the forms they'd sent me and my wife and return them to the office as soon as possible." We all knew he'd invested enormous effort in obtaining immigration permits for himself and his wife.

"Good," said Father. "Your efforts have paid off. Never give up."

"Yes. My son in *Eretz* Israel takes good care of us. In his last letter, he says he and Zigi Shneider were even invited to a meeting with Henrietta Szold."

"Too bad I don't have anyone there to do the same for me."

"Make no mistake, it was no easy matter. It took a great many letters and meetings. But I knew it would all work out in the end. They asked us to have medical examinations. It sounds as if it will happen soon," he said, his face glowing with happiness.

"Well, good luck! You probably have a great deal to do now."

"Yes, I'm off to fill in the papers and then to the post office. They think I'm a nuisance there, but I don't care," he said, bundling up in his coat and putting on his wool hat.

"Do you want me to talk to Zigi about you too? Maybe he can use his connections with Henrietta Szold for you as well," he said, and left without waiting for an answer.

***

Every morning, on my way to the farm, I'd meet Mr. Goldman on his way to the post office to see if there was an answer waiting for him. A quick look at his furious face and pursed lips under his mustache was enough to know I shouldn't ask him about it. About ten days had passed since he'd sent off their questionnaires, and nothing had been returned to the post office for them.

In the middle of February, on a clear, extremely cold day, I was going past the post office as usual when I saw a crowd at the closed door and heard Rudi Lempel's loud, upset tones. "The Führer" was arguing with someone there. Curious, I went over and saw Mr. Gottesmann standing next to Lempel, both of them listening to Mr. Goldman, who was gesticulating as if he'd lost his mind. It turned out he'd just had a difficult telephone conversation with the *Eretz* Israel office in Zagreb.

"A scandal. An absolute scandal. Those lazy so-and-sos in Zagreb," he cried out in a broken voice.

"The office there must be in total chaos. I've always said papers should be sent with specific names on them," said Mr. Gottesmann. "They can do whatever they like with those papers if they aren't sent to specific people."

Rudi reinforced his words, "We need to have someone there. Someone who will supervise administration."

"I've been telling you all along that there's something wrong over there," raged Mr. Goldman. "How can Mr. Weinstein have received his immigration permit already when he filled in the forms after me? It turns out they haven't even sent Rivka's and my passports yet!"

"Impossible, they must have been sent," interrupted Rudi. "The question is whether they received letters about it."

"They say they received letters from the Jerusalem Executive Committee," Mr. Goldman now spoke more quietly.

"But letters from whom?" asked Mr. Gottesmann. "Do they know who sent them? The Jewish Agency? the Mossad L'Aliyah Bet? Or some Jewish Agency department?"

"No. They don't know exactly which Jewish Agency department. A catastrophic mess," said the distressed Mr. Goldman.

"It's not directed specifically at you," Rudi tried to soothe him.

"The question is whether the office in Zagreb can delay the process by passive or hostile action," said Mr. Goldman worriedly.

"That doesn't sound logical," said Mr. Gottesmann with his confident know-it-all tone. "They're just a conduit; whatever they receive they have to pass on."

"They've just told me over the telephone that they received a telegraph from Jerusalem informing them that immigration permits have been sent to someone who filled in the forms after me. How is this possible? Their passports are already on the way to Zagreb, whereas mine and Rivka's haven't been sent," he raged again, positive there was some deliberate malice here, some intervening hand.

"You're just getting yourself upset, making up stories and theories that upset you even more," said Rudi.

"Neither of you seems to understand what's going on here. This isn't a conspiracy at the Zagreb office. I think someone here is mixing up the immigration permits and giving them to someone else." He stopped to take a breath, "have you heard of Moishe Flashkis?"

"Of course," said Rudi. "He's one of the General Zionists who emigrated a year ago."

"Yes, and you know what? He was the one who speeded up Weinstein's immigration permits. I know. I also turned to him for help."

"I'll be happy to check it out for you in Zagreb. Give me a few days," said Rudi.

"And if the problem isn't in Zagreb," said Mr. Goldman. "Then I think I know who might sabotage my efforts here, and you all know who I mean."

My heart broke for the idealistic, Zionist Mr. Goldman, who so believed in Zionist Movement institutions and had now received a ringing slap in the face. The *Eretz* Israel office in Zagreb treated him with contempt, led him on, and didn't help him in his distress. I couldn't understand how come Mr. Goldman, with two sons and his friend Zigi Shneider in *Eretz* Israel, wasn't able to overcome institutional bureaucracy. I was uneasy about our situation, because Father had no connections in *Eretz* Israel. If this was what had happened to Mr. Goldman, with all that help from *Eretz* Israel, what would happen to us? When would we, if at all, get our immigration permits?

A few days later, Mr. Goldman again sat with Father in our kitchen, trying to resolve his situation and find a way out of the bureaucratic maze in which he was entangled. Father mainly listened, occasionally nodding his head. Mr. Goldman held his cup of tea in both hands, staring at the tablecloth, sadness and despair on his face. Mother came in every now and again to serve more tea.

"The hardest part is what's happening with the boys in *Eretz* Israel," he said, following a long silence during which only the sound of cups on saucers and sips of hot tea could be heard. "I expected more help from them, particularly Arieh, the eldest one. I understand that he's very busy actively building his future on the *kibbutz*, building the country. Ach… How good it is to be immersed in an ideal. That's how I was when I stopped identifying with Hungarian nationalism and became a Zionist. Ach… What I left behind there! What a comfortable life I led in Hungary! I left it all to emigrate to *Eretz* Israel, anticipating a certificate on a dubious luxury boat," he said with a sigh. "I even wrote about it in my last letter to Arieh. Afterward, I felt uncomfortable about pressuring him with my problems when he's in the throes of fulfillment."

"As for me, if you only knew what a good and pleasant life we led in Belgrade" Father mused. "That boat, all four hundred of us crowded on it, I used to rent a similar one for a private pleasure cruise with family and friends every Sunday."

"I saw you boarding at Vukovar," said Mr. Goldman. "You looked like a wealthy family. You had no idea what you were doing in all that dirt and crowdedness, and dressed in clothes more suited to the opera, too!"

"Don't remind me of the opera. We used to go at least once a month, and elegantly dressed too. Louisa, with her fox-fur collar and fancy hat, and me in my black frock coat and bow tie; we had a driver to take us to the opera house."

"But it was more than just a comfortable life," said Goldman. "I'm talking about life and action for an ideal. When I believed with all my heart in the ideal of Hungary for its citizens, I acted enthusiastically out of belief, no matter the location or conditions. Afterward, when I discovered Zionism, I acted out of a burning passion for the Zionist ideal, including the desire to leave everything and emigrate to *Eretz Israel*."

"I also see myself as a Zionist, but I only decided to leave when I saw Louisa breaking down, after anti-Semitism started in Vienna and Germany, after what happened to her grandfather on Kristallnacht. He was found at his store with both legs smashed."

"So you left out of fear, not so much because of an ideal. Many of my friends did so too."

"Well, there was also less work at the office," said Father. "At first, I didn't realize the reason. It was only later on that I understood it was because I was a Jew."

"My friend, let's get back to our affairs," said Goldman. "How do I find out exactly what is holding up Rivka's and my immigration permits?"

"You know what, let me tell you my position here," Father began his story. "Although we lived in Yugoslavia for thirty years, I don't have Yugoslavian citizenship to this day. In the Great War, I was an officer in the Austro-Hungarian army and was sent to fight on the Yugoslavian front. Although at the time it opened a door to the possibility of living and working in Yugoslavia, which was much cheaper than Hungary, and I lived there for all those years, I was refused citizenship because in the distant past, I'd fought against them. They don't understand that I had no choice in the matter. I was recruited and trained as an engineering officer in the south-east division's artillery regiment."

"So you still don't have a Yugoslavian passport? How will you get an immigration permit?"

"I have a Hungarian passport, and Louisa has a Czech passport because she was born in Pressburg, but I'm not a full citizen of the country in which I live. And moreover, the Hungarians are also angry because I moved to Yugoslavia and are threatening to cancel my Hungarian passport. Why do you think I chose illegal immigration?"

"So my situation could be worse," said Goldman. "I see there could be worse situations."

"Exactly," concluded Father, taking a sip of cold tea. "I promise you that in the end it will all work out. We just need to be patient. I also lose it sometimes, but it will come, you know that. I don't even have anyone in *Eretz* Israel like your Zigi who could talk to Henrietta Szold, and my children are here with me, and I have to take care of them, so what do you have to complain about?"

"I think I'll be on my way now," said Goldman. "Tomorrow is a new day. Let's wait and see."

"And that anger of yours, as long as you can't prove that someone in the Zagreb office is against you, even if you suspect him, it will only cause you grief."

"Thank you for your welcome," said Mr. Goldman, turning to leave. He peeped into the kitchen on his way out. "Madame Louisa, thank you for the hot tea," he said, and went on his way.

A day before Yost's bar mitzvah, he and his mother came especially to invite us. Yost and I sat talking under the tree, and Elli, his mother, went in to talk with Mother. He was very nervous and said he wasn't sure if his friends would come to the synagogue or the party afterward. Apart from me, he'd invited Chaim Shatzker, a boy his age from Vienna, who'd joined the transport with his mother.

Recently, there'd been a spate of rumors that about two hundred and fifty immigration permits for children and young people were on the way. But instead of being glad about the possibility of at last going to *Eretz* Israel as he'd dreamed of doing and meeting his beloved brother Grad on the *kibbutz*, Yost was very worried. He told me about his parents' great concerns. Ever since they'd heard about the children's transport that was about to leave, they couldn't sleep nights and argued constantly about the fate of their child, who was apparently also listed for an immigration permit.

"They're always arguing and forget that I'm in the middle and hear everything. Father supports the transport; he says my Aunt Ina and

Uncle Albert will take me in. I don't know them, but they'll take care of me until my parents come. Mother's reluctant; she says she doesn't feel comfortable about taking their help. They've helped enough with my brother, who lived with them for several months. And apart from that, she says it's dangerous to send a boy my age alone on a journey of several days through enemy countries. Father reminds her that I'm a bar mitzvah already, an age when you should be more independent, but Mother says that even if this is so, as far as she's concerned, I'm still a helpless boy. It is so annoying. I want to go. I don't mind traveling alone. The opposite. I want to get myself out of their bear hug. Look, Chaim Shatzker is my age exactly, and his mother has no doubts at all. She knows it's temporary and that she'll be joining him in two or three weeks' time. You have to help me," he begged. "Maybe they'll listen to you. Tell them you're older; you'll be responsible for me until we get to *Eretz* Israel. They know you, after all. You protected me once before."

I was in a very uncomfortable situation. My back came out in a cold sweat. I really wanted to help Yost. He was my protégé. I wanted to tell them, "Leave the boy alone. It'll be good for him to get out of here. I promise to protect him." But I knew I couldn't. They were his parents, and I couldn't interfere. When I told him I couldn't do it, he suggested I speak to my mother. She knew his mother and might be able to influence her.

We went into the house, and judging from the conversation issuing from my parents' bedroom, I understood that Ellie had confided in her. Mother understood Ellie. She told Father that if I were bar mitzvah age, she would also refuse to send me alone on such a dangerous journey. "In our case, if Hanne were going alone, he wouldn't have any family in *Eretz* Israel who could take him in and care for him until we arrived. With Pauli, it's different; he's older and far more independent."

I reflected that during the long months in Sabac and Kladovo I'd changed a great deal, so I felt insulted by Mother's comment. I might have been a spoiled little boy four years ago, but not now.

When Mother told Father the story, like Yost's father, he couldn't understand Elisheva's resistance.

"The boy has grown, Louie," said Father. "I was extremely independent at his age. They can't coddle him all his life. If they don't let him go, he will always be dependent on them."

The next day, we all went to the bar mitzvah. Mother had managed to unpack and iron our best clothes. Yost's parents greeted us at the door of the synagogue. They, too, were wearing their best clothes. Max wore a light, slightly creased festive jacket and a fine tie. Elisheva looked very elegant in a long dress.

Mother and Ellie went behind the curtain of the women's section on the other side of the synagogue. Pauli, Father, and I joined those already seated. Yost was already on the podium, dressed like a young man. He told me his mother had sewn those clothes for him according to his size and had begun to work as a seamstress for one of the men's stores in town. This work contributed to their family budget.

I saw how nervous Yost was on the podium with the prayer shawl on his shoulders. He stood between Mr. Goldman, who was ready to hear the Haftorah he'd been working on for a whole month, and Mr. Weis, who was also the *chazzan*. The scene reminded me of how I'd stood in Yost's place just four years previously, in the great synagogue, in front of a large and frightening audience; I'd forgotten the words of the Haftorah, remembered only the melody, and I'd lost my speech notes.

Yost did well. He read the verses clearly and confidently. Mr. Goldman's glowing face was proof of his satisfaction.

All the guests gathered in the only room of their modest apartment on the outskirts of town. It was beautifully arranged. Elisheva served a yeast cake she'd baked and lemon juice and sugar she'd prepared, and the ceremony was very dignified. Yost had nothing to be ashamed of, because apart from Chaim Shatzker, four other classmates came. All the children were talking about the approaching journey while Yost listened sadly; he already knew he wouldn't be going with them.

A few days after the bar mitzvah, a messenger from the *Eretz* Israel Zagreb office came to Sabac with the long-awaited papers: 244 immigration permits for *Aliyah* youth under the age of eighteen. He announced that all those entitled to a permit should be at the Sabac train station in two days' time, at seven in the morning, ready to board the train that would take them toward *Eretz* Israel.

Mother wept with joy. "Do you understand, Hanne? This is it. It's over!"

She hugged me, tears in her eyes, as if she and Father were irrelevant, as long as Pauli and I could get out of there. I didn't know whether to jump for joy or wipe away tears that refused to flow. The only thing bothering me was whether or not Inge was included on the list.

On a stormy, rainy evening, we gathered in the basement of the mill. We sat on wooden benches from the dining room to receive last instructions from group counselors regarding what to pack, the route, and most importantly of all, eligibility. We were divided into groups according to organization affiliation, and a leader was chosen for each group. I was with the Mizrahi group, together with Inge, who sat beside me. She whispered her great fear that she might not get an immigration permit. Although no one knew her real age, Inge, with her responsible role, and mature appearance, didn't look as if she belonged in a youth group, despite the fact that she was part of the Vienna Mizrahi youth group and attended lessons at our school, when time and work allowed it.

"Two hundred and forty-four immigration permits have arrived, about two hundred with specific names and the rest we'll fill in. Tonight, we will go over the registrations you filled in at Kladovo, and all those who have not yet turned eighteen will be added to the list," announced the messenger from Zagreb, who was dressed in a smart suit that was quite unsuitable for the occasion. He waved the package of immigration permits. "I assume you all filled in the forms at the end of last summer, including medical examinations."

"And what if there aren't enough immigration permits?" someone shouted.

"According to the lists you submitted, there are enough for everybody. Nevertheless, the British are making difficulties, especially for those from Germany or Austria, because they are considered enemy countries. However, with the generous help of Mrs. Michaelis-Stern from the main London Youth Aliyah office, and Mrs. Henrietta Szold, we managed to overcome that obstacle." The envoy cleared his throat and added, "Yes, I almost forgot Mr. Chaim Berlas, an envoy from the Istanbul Youth Aliyah office. It was he who brought the immigration permits to Zagreb. It wasn't easy, because the London Youth Aliyah office wanted to give preference to Youth Aliyah groups under their jurisdiction from before the war."

"But we belonged to Youth Aliyah before the war," called out Teddy, who was sitting with his group on benches at the front.

"I'm sorry, but because of the many postponements and loss of time we've suffered here, they relate to our youth groups as a refugee group, and not as groups that were organized even before the war. But it doesn't matter now, that's all behind us."

When Yokel gave us details of the route that included Bulgaria, sounds of disappointment rose in the group. We knew that Bulgaria had allowed Germany a foothold in their country, and we were concerned that our train would be stopped.

"There's another small detail holding up our departure—transit visas for the Bulgarian border. But I hope this will be arranged by tomorrow. Otherwise, we'd have left tomorrow morning. We have to go through Bulgaria, because that's the route of your train. From Bulgaria, you will travel to Greece, and from there to Turkey." Bata paused, and then continued, "From Istanbul, we will go in small groups along the Syrian border, and from there to Lebanon and *Eretz* Israel."

"Why aren't we traveling together?" someone asked.

"Because of the limitations imposed by the Turkish regime," answered the envoy. "We will send a group of about fifty boys and girls a day. You can walk around the city for a day or two, until the next group can set out. But on no account are you to walk about alone, only in groups."

Again he paused, as there was great excitement in the room. Exhilarated, Mother hugged me and Pauli again.

"So, ladies and gentlemen, that's it. I want you to finish packing by tomorrow evening, and the following day, at seven o'clock in the morning, everyone with an immigration permit must be at the Sabac train station."

"But we haven't yet received an immigration permit," someone called out, and an uproar ensued.

"Calm down! Calm down!" called Bata Gedalja. "Everyone allotted an immigration permit will receive it by tomorrow afternoon. Tomorrow morning, we will go over all the youth registrations, and those who qualify in terms of age and who do not yet have an immigration permit will be given one tomorrow. You have nothing to worry about."

***

After the meeting, Inge took me aside and whispered, "I must make sure I'm on the list. Fortunately, all the questionnaires and medical tests are at the infirmary. Please, let's go there now."

"And what will you do? How will you find out?"

"I have to make sure that I filled in my age properly. I told you that I took a year off my age. Now he says that those born after 1923 will receive immigration permits, so first of all I have to find out how I'm registered. Then we'll see."

"And what's my role? Do you want me to come into the doctor's office with you?" I asked, afraid she was giving me a role that would jeopardize me if we were caught.

"No, no," she reassured me. "You just stay outside and let me know if anyone comes. If you hear steps, knock twice on the door. I'll pretend

I just came in to check the sterile instruments."

I sat outside the doctor's room, and every passing second seemed like eternity. I imagined I heard approaching steps, but it was the storm making the shutters creak and groan. A loud rolling sound made my heart jump even after I understood it was only thunder. Finally, I realized that no one was likely to appear in such a storm or be out in such cold.

When Inge finally came out, the smile on her face said it all.

"All's well, Hanne." She embraced me and kissed my cheek. "In terms of age, everything's all right. I wrote March 1923, a bit borderline, perhaps. Let's hope there are enough immigration permits for all the youth, otherwise they might give one to someone younger than me by a few days. I saw Esther's name. She's very close to me in age."

"Who's Esther?"

"The girl who was here in isolation for a few days. She had a high fever and suspected jaundice."

"But what will happen if there are fewer immigration permits than eligible youth?" I asked with concern.

"It will be very bad for me, but the envoy from Zagreb said there are enough for all the youth."

"Let's hope so. I don't know what will happen if there aren't," I said, as if it were impossible that only one of us would go.

"I know, Hanne. It would be very hard, but we would get through it. Worst-case scenario, two or three weeks later, immigration permits will come for the remaining youth and even, finally, for everyone."

"You're optimistic," I told her. "Look how long it took to get two hundred and forty immigration permits, and you're talking about a couple of weeks?"

"Well, do you think worrying does any good?" she responded. "If I only saw the half-empty glass, I'd have gone mad a long time ago."

"I am worried. You forget that I'm leaving aging parents here."

"And what about Yost?" she asked. "Did you know his parents don't want him to go at all?"

"Yes. His mother's afraid to send him alone, although he does have an aunt in Palestine who could take care of him."

"I'm not judging them. I don't know what I'd do if I were a mother who had to send her child to an unknown future. Don't forget he's only a boy of thirteen."

I accompanied her back to the mill. The storm raged unabated with periodic bursts of rain that washed the street. We stood under a store entrance, waiting for the rain to ease up a bit. In the beam of light from the street lamp, the rain seemed to be diminishing to a drizzle. The pavement stones shone, and puddles formed in the road.

"When I think about our conditions here, we seemed to have gotten used to this refugee situation, as it's called," I said reflectively. "After all, we have a home, even a school, and I have you and my parents. So what's wrong with that?"

"What's wrong with it?" she protested. "Do you call this a life? Life here is temporary. I won't even mention the danger. But a human being should be affiliated with a home and a place where he can join his fate to that of his people. That's what I had in Germany and you in Belgrade, until all this horror began. A human being also has to fulfill himself. Work, study, get a profession…"

"That was a joke, Inge. I didn't really mean it," I remonstrated. "It's obvious that we have no home and almost no identity. I was just teasing, darling. But I see you aren't in the mood for jokes right now... It's hard for me to accept that Yost's parents have decided to keep him here with them...he wants to go so badly."

The rain had stopped, and we walked the rest of way at a fast pace, parting at the entrance to the mill, confident that the next day we'd know for certain that both of us were going.

When I got home, I found Mother sitting at the kitchen table, straining her eyes to darn a sock.

"Why so late, Hanne?" she asked, without raising her eyes from the torn sock. "There's a lot to do. You have to pack."

"Some of us stayed on after the envoy from Zagreb finished his explanations. We wanted to hear everyone's ideas about how to manage there. They're talking about a place called Atlit. Have you heard of it? Apparently, we'll be living there in tents at first."

"Yes, I heard them talking about it. The British don't want you there at all. Atlit is temporary; they'll probably send you to a *kibbutz* at some point."

"Mother, I don't know anything about *kibbutz*. I hope they prepare us for it."

"On the *kibbutz*, everything is shared. Everyone works together, and the income is also shared. They eat in a common dining room; they've prepared you for that anyway! Are you nervous?"

"Yes, I am. Mainly about what's waiting for me there, and about the fact that you and Father aren't coming with us."

"You have nothing to worry about, Hanne. We'll probably get there in two or three weeks, maybe a month. Everyone says you're our pioneers, and we will all probably get our immigration permits soon."

"And if you don't?" I insisted.

"Don't be such a pessimist. Why wouldn't we get them if the first group has?"

"But we waited so long for those two hundred and forty immigration permits to arrive! Who knows what will happen with the remaining eight hundred?"

"Enough, Hanne, that's enough. Stop filling your head with such dark thoughts," she said. "Better to see the positive in everything. I think you've been reading too much philosophy lately."

"Tomorrow, I'll get up early and go and say goodbye to Farmer Radoyevich. He also owes me last week's pay."

"Then go to bed and stop thinking so much," she said, getting up to kiss me. "Good night. Sweet dreams."

I tossed and turned, unable to fall asleep. In my mind, I saw a hot country where the sun burned, winter and summer. No lakes or forests, only barren hills. I saw myself sitting with Pauli and six friends in a hot tent in Atlit, no one caring about us or telling us what to do. Inge left behind with my parents and the other adults. Before we left, she'd comforted me—everything would be all right, and she'd be joining me in two weeks' time. The taste of her parting kiss was still on my lips, and her last words would be, "look after yourself, Hanne, and get things ready for us there."

Finally, I was tired of lying there fantasizing in my bed and got up to write. It was still dark outside when I put on my work clothes and coat with the fur hat to protect my ears from the cold. The street was quiet. Not even the neighborhood dogs barked at me as I went past the fence adjacent to our house. But as I passed the bakery, I could smell the rising dough and baking bread. I knocked on the window where fresh rolls would be sold later on, and Illyich, the baker, opened it with a welcoming face.

"Good morning, Hanne. The usual?" he asked.

"This is the last time, Illyich," I made a leaving sign with my hand. "We leave tomorrow."

"So this is it. You're leaving!" he said sadly. "I'm sorry." But he pulled himself together and said, "I'm sorry for us here in Sabac. You fit in so well here. I can't imagine you not being here."

"Tomorrow only the youth are leaving. The adults will remain here for another few weeks or a month, depending on when their immigration permits arrive."

"Then two rolls today. On the house," he said, taking a paper bag from the top shelf.

"Thank you very much! We've also felt good with all of you. Thank you for making us feel welcome here."

"The minute you got here, we realized you were humane and cultured people. Good luck to you!" he said, giving me the bag of rolls.

I did my usual chores for Radoyevich, and only when he appeared with a jug of boiling coffee did I tell him that I'd come to say goodbye to him. He was so moved that he spilt some coffee while pouring, and his hands shook.

"I knew this day would come," he said emotionally. "But I'm glad for you and your whole group that things are finally working out."

"Not everyone leaves tomorrow. Just us in the meantime, the young people. We received our immigration permits."

"I suppose the others will get theirs soon. A pity, we will miss you here."

I took a fresh roll from the bag and offered it to him.

"It's from Anji's bakery. They gave me two this morning, on the house."

He shook his head when he realized that this was my last day and worriedly felt about in his pocket.

"If I'd known, I'd have brought you your money now. Wait a moment. I'll go home and get it," he said. A few minutes later, he returned and gave me the notes, adding one.

"There you are; a little extra for the journey."

We parted with a firm handshake, and I saw him turn his head to wipe away a tear.

When I got back to the mill, there was already news of another postponement. *Another one?* I thought. *Just don't let this be a repeat of the usual nightmare we've gotten used to.*

"This time it's because of the Bulgarians," said the know-it-all Mr. Gottesmann. "They still haven't sent the transit visas for the border crossing," he stated. "And the train must go through Bulgaria. There's no other way."

They'd promised to send the visas today; the day was over, and they hadn't arrived. Everyone was on edge. We were packed and emotionally ready to leave, to board the train, and the waiting was excruciating.

Pauli and I sat at the kitchen table with our parents, talking about the coming journey.

"When you get to the *kibbutz*, you'll probably be able to send postcards. I beg you not to be lazy about it," said Mother, looking at Pauli. "Pauli, you tend not to relate to things like that," she said, a hint of reproof in her tone. "But know that it is really important now. This isn't summer camp in the mountains, when you didn't write at all," she said, looking at me too. "This is different. You're going to a new and unfamiliar place. It's not Slovenia; it's different weather, different people, another language…"

"But most of all, boys, be responsible and look after yourselves. You don't know anything about the place. Or what to be careful of…" Father started to say.

There was a sudden knock at the door. Mr. Goldman's face appeared in the opening.

"That's it. It's final," he said excitedly. "There's a list of those going on the mill notice board. Pauli and Hanne are on it. I checked."

"What about Inge? Is she also on the list?" I asked anxiously.

"Don't know," he answered. "Didn't notice."

I sensed he was hiding something.

"I'm going to see Inge," I said and left.

I ran all the way to the granary next to the mill. I'd probably see Inge there. Mr. Goldman's evasive answer worried me. My heart was beating frantically as I ran the length of Pop Luca Street that led to the mill. It was unthinkable that Mr. Goldman hadn't noticed. And what if she wasn't on the list? What if she was staying here alone? For how long would she stay? Who knew when the immigration permits would arrive? We'd waited so long. And what about Mother and Father? I'd forgotten about them altogether. After all, they'd also be staying here. As I approached, my breathing became heavier, and despite the cold, beads of sweat dripped down my back.

I threw open the door of the granary and ran to the northern area where Inge slept. Her bed was empty. Raisel and Esther were sitting on a nearby bed. There was an open suitcase on the floor, clothes and objects strewn about all over it. Esther folded a dress and laid it on the suitcase.

"Are you looking for Inge?" she asked composedly, without raising her head.

"Yes," I responded. "Do you know where she is? I see her suitcase is ready."

"Don't ask, Hanne," said Raisel. "She left here in a state after opening her suitcase and throwing everything on the floor."

And Esther added, "It's not like her. I've never seen her behave like that."

I didn't wait to hear the rest but ran in the direction of the infirmary, hoping to find her there. I had a bad premonition. It was clear to me that she'd had bad news, two words she herself used frequently. Her reaction worried me. I arrived panting at the infirmary and tried to open the door, but it was locked. I beat on it with my fist, but there was no answer. I tried to open it by force but to no avail. She was apparently not there. I started to walk about like a caged lion. Where could she be? I had a sudden thought—maybe she'd gone to talk to someone in charge of the transport. Sime Spitzer, perhaps, who'd come himself, especially for the event of the Youth Aliyah journey.

I went over there, and as I approached the closed door, I thought I heard her voice. I opened the door a crack and saw the committee representative sitting in his chair, Inge beside him. She was tense and upright, her foot anxiously tapping the floor and her fingers clasped anxiously together.

She noticed me and said, "You can't come in; you can see we're in the middle of a conversation."

"Excuse me," I gently closed the door.

I sat down on the stairs outside to wait for her. There was nothing I could do to help in there anyway. Tension mounted, and I bit my nails nervously, a habit I thought I'd overcome but that had recently returned. The door opened after a long time, and the elegant envoy came out with Inge, his arm around her trembling shoulders with a gentle fatherliness.

"It will be all right. These are just the first tidings of spring," he said, in an attempt to calm her. "And by the time spring arrives, everyone will get their immigration permits, and we will all finally be able to forget this nightmare."

Inge wiped away her tears as she came downstairs. She fell into my arms barely able to control her sobs.

"Let's go to the infirmary," she said in a strained voice. "I want us to talk quietly." And then she hissed through tight lips, "I don't want to go back to my bed and meet that Esther again. I can't deal with her, and I can't bear her."

Later, in the infirmary, sitting in the doctor's quiet room, she told me everything. How her dreams were dashed when she didn't find her name on the Youth Aliyah list. How she'd returned to the room in tears and found Esther and Raisel cheerfully packing and singing.

"You have no idea how angry I was with myself at that moment," she said, wiping away her tears with the back of her hand. "I should have been more alert, and made sure no one took my place at the last moment."

"But what could you have done?" I said. "Break into the infirmary to forge your name on an immigration permit?" I was trying to make her aware of how impossible it was.

"No. You have no idea, Hanne. I should have been on guard. Even here, at the entrance to the transport director's office, to make sure no one went in at night," she said angrily. "And you know what? That Esther, with her seemingly innocent smile and malicious eyes…" Inge was whispering now as if someone was listening. "I give so much of myself and my time to people here. Does anyone appreciate it? What do I get in return? Nothing. And then someone comes along, Esther perhaps, maybe someone else, and interferes with the papers."

She began to cry again in justified self-pity.

"And you know me," she said. "I don't do it for a prize. It's true that Dr. Bezalel respects me and pays me a few dinars each week, but that's not why I work here. You know me."

"Of course I do", I assured her. "You give of yourself to everyone here, far more than any regular infirmary nurse."

"So, am I asking too much? Do you think I care whether people respect what I do or not?" She was angry again. "But I resent being imposed on, exploited for my naïveté, resent people thinking 'She's naive. Let's give her immigration permit to someone else. She probably won't even feel it.' What do you think I was doing in the office of the Zagreb envoy? I was trying to convince him that someone did something unethical and that this should be rectified," she said. "And do you think it made any difference? He sat there like some big-shot director. What does he care? And there I was with tears boiling in my eyes, trying to persuade him. Showing him my age on the list, 'look, can you see I'm under eighteen?'"

"But what did he say?"

"Nothing. Sat there in his wide chair and looked at me with big calf eyes. Until I picked up the list and shoved it into his face. You arrived after it was all over. When I realized the time had come to beg and plead, what do you think he said?"

"I don't know."

"He said, 'Do you want me to go to someone else and take them off the list? What do you want? Should I go to Esther or Raisel and tell them there's been a mistake and you aren't on the list after all. Is that what you want?'" She looked at me helplessly. "What could I do? Tell me."

I was silent, because there was nothing to say.

After a long pause, she added, "But maybe it isn't such a terrible tragedy. I'll be joining you in a few weeks anyway, won't I?"

"You're right, that's absolutely true. I just so wanted us to get there and start our life there together."

"And I wanted that even more than you. It's the reason I did that whole performance for him, because I so badly wanted us to be together. And I was very angry at the *foile-shtick* that's happened here."

"But Inge, between you and me, you also tried to stretch things a bit. You changed your real age, didn't you?"

"I'll let you in on a secret, Hanne. I've never been sure of my real age. At some point in school, I wanted to be with the older children, and I told everyone I was born in 1923. And that's how it stayed on my documents. Who knows?"

Although I really wanted to leave together, the story about her wishing to be with the older girls didn't sound plausible to me, but I didn't want to argue with her, particularly not in her present mood.

"But you will come to the station on the morning we leave, won't you?" I asked. "They say almost the entire group will come to say goodbye."

"Depends on my mood. Anyway, they say there's a delay because of the transit visas for the Bulgaria crossing."

"As you wish," I answered morosely.

"Hanne, come. Don't be angry. I was just teasing you. What do you think? That I wouldn't come to say goodbye to you?" She held out her arms, "Come on. Come to me, my love. Let me kiss your lips." I couldn't resist and went to her. All the distance between us dissolved in a second and she drew me to her, holding me close as she put her head on my shoulder.

"Hanne, promise me. Really truly promise me."

"Promise you what? I can promise you in advance that…"

"Wait! You haven't heard what I mean," she continued to murmur into my shoulder.

"So what did you mean?" I asked sullenly.

"Be faithful to me. Always. Be mine alone. Just as I will be faithful only to you here. Although you gave me a ring three months ago, we aren't really engaged." We both burst out laughing, and she pressed her soft, warm lips to mine. I felt the sweetness of her lips pierce my body, setting it aflame.

But predictably, the following day, the third of March, we did not set off. "The transit visas for Bulgaria have not yet arrived," the experts explained.

***

It was only the following day, after another battle of nerves, which brought the routine of the entire group to a standstill, that we received the happy news: In two days' time, on the sixteenth of March, the first of three groups will leave. Everyone must report to the station at seven o'clock in the morning.

After several days of constant rain, which kept everyone indoors, that morning was washed and fresh, as if a new day had dawned. The clouds drifted away from each other, revealing a light blue sky in the east. The roofs of the town shone clean and bright in the first rays of the sun, and puddles on the railway station paving stones sparkled like precious stones. The station yard was crowded with people, even some who had no son, daughter, or close relative getting on the train but who just wanted to be part of the great experience. At long last, the dream they'd held onto for a year and a half was about to be fulfilled, even if only partially.

On the way to the station, I was filled with anxiety that Inge might not come to say goodbye. Pauli, who was in a good mood, needled me, saying that today should be a happy day for me, and there I am, walking very dejectedly, with my head down. He couldn't possibly have understood what was going on inside me at that moment. Sometimes, I think I'd have preferred to be like Pauli, someone for whom life passes without really penetrating or changing him. He always behaved as if life was wonderful if you only knew how to enjoy it. He always succeeded at everything he did. He'd also inherited Father's good hands. All I got was Mother's heart—so they always said about me. A sensitive, transparent heart, just like Mother.

We walked in the direction of the station, each of us holding the same small suitcase we had with us that morning at Vukovar, while waiting for the *Tzar Nikolai*.

Mother and Father walked beside us, but I could only think of Inge, fearing she wouldn't come. We had said our farewells the evening before, for the fourth time, perhaps, but my lips still stung with longing and the taste of her kisses.

We parted, feeling sure we'd be reunited soon, but something in her face reflected an acceptance of fate that seemed to drive a wedge between us.

When we got there, the long train was already waiting silently at the platform. I gazed at the windows: all the shutters were closed. *How would I see the landscape?* I asked myself. Terrible to travel for so many days behind closed shutters.

We waited there with the rest of the crowd. I stood on the tips of my toes, turning my head in all directions. Maybe Inge would still appear, for the last time, just before we boarded the train. Every moment brought new announcements about boarding time or the reason for the delay.

Mother hugged us every few minutes.

"Write and tell us how you're settling in," she said, hugging us again. "And dress warmly. It's cold now in Palestine."

Father stood upright as usual; he was clearly emotional. With his height and dignity, his long elegant coat very shabby and stained now, he stood out in the human landscape there. He took me and Pauli aside and warned us again about bad people we might encounter in every place.

"You may think that all people are good, but Hanne, don't be so naive," he said clapping me on the shoulder with his heavy hand. "You have no idea yet of the kind of people there are in this world."

"But Father," I tried to argue. "We've been living here among all kinds of people for a long time. Isn't that enough?"

He looked at me reproachfully. "No, Hanne, it certainly isn't enough. These are all our people here. Most of them have more or less the same goal and come from a similar background. That's not the issue."

"Parents and relatives, please stand back. In a few minutes, the immigration permits will be examined for the last time," announced Yokel in a loud voice. "We want to see only the youth group now."

Mother kissed me and Pauli with mixed joy and sadness.

"I miss you already," she said.

Father bent to hug us, and then they stepped back and we remained with the youth group and counselors.

All of a sudden, out of the crowd came Inge, running frantically toward me in her white nurse's uniform, heavy winter coat, and a scarf on her head. As she came closer, I saw the tension in her face. With shaking shoulders, she fell into my arms.

"I couldn't bear it anymore," she sobbed. "I knew you were here, and I suddenly thought I might not see you again, that maybe this would be the last time."

Putting my suitcase down on the paving stones, I clasped her firmly to me. For a moment, we ignored all the eyes probably staring at us, and I felt the taste of her lips on mine. And this might be the last time, I thought.

After a long moment, she pulled away from me and was immediately swallowed up in the crowd.

PART II

AMSTERDAM NURSING HOME, NEW YORK

Seven in the evening. Alan exited the underground at Broadway, at the corner of Ninety-Sixth. *Luckily, the express goes all the way from my downtown office to upper Broadway in twenty minutes*, he thought to himself as he shut his umbrella and tightened his woolen scarf. The wet street shone with pink and yellow reflections from the store lights.

He knew that Erica was waiting for him. This was his second visit to her at the nursing home since his daughter had told him about her. Nina spent two afternoons a week there as part of a good citizenship program.

His first meeting with Erica had been short. He told her how he'd gotten to her through Nina, and Erica told him how she'd been a battalion nurse and lost her right eye fighting with Čiča's Partisans in the winter of 1944.

His daughter Nina didn't immediately understand his enormous excitement when he learned that the blind old woman she took care of twice a week as part of a good citizenship program, wasn't "just" a Partisan hero who fought with Čiča's battalion, but was apparently the sole living survivor of the large group of *Ma'apilim* who'd remained in Sabac and not boarded the train to freedom.

Alan suddenly realized that while he'd been busy at work and seen Nina as a little girl who needed protection from the cruel, outside world, his daughter had grown, and he could now tell her things that in the past he'd tried to spare her. So he sat down with her in her room and told her grandfather's story, until Rachel called them to dinner.

He told her about the innocent, happy childhood in that luxurious home in Belgrade during the 1920s and 1930s, about the desperate attempt to reach *Eretz* Israel, illegally, sailing on three riverboats down the Danube River. He told her how a voyage meant to last a week or two turned into a traumatic journey, filled alternately with hope and frustration, and that ultimately took a year and a half. He promised to show her his father Hanne's diary of the journey. At dinner, Nina said she wanted to meet Erica again.

"Now that I understand she's almost family…" she said, tears rolling down her cheeks. "And why are we living here?" Nina suddenly asked. "After all, Grandfather went through all that suffering just to get to *Eretz* Israel, not America!"

"Look, Nina, maybe you're too young to understand, but…" he stammered awkwardly, remembering that he had no appropriate response to her question because he himself had been accompanied by that very conflict for years.

"Why do you think I'm too young, Dad? I'm fourteen now, and I've already written one good citizenship report and gotten a grade of excellence."

"Well, Israel is a very difficult country to live in; not everything is good there."

"But it's our country," she insisted. "We studied Herzl and Zionism just a few months ago. It did seem a little far away from me, but now that I've heard Grandfather's story, I feel connected."

"There are always wars going on over there," Rachel attempted to dampen Nina's enthusiasm.

"Dad, I want you to take me there, to see Grandfather's home. Please, Dad!"

"We'll think about it," responded Alan. "Not this year, but maybe next year."

***

Now, sitting beside Erica, Alan wondered about her family situation. Did she have any family in America? Maybe she was alone and had come to die here in this nursing home, without anyone to visit her. As if she could hear his thoughts, she began to speak.

"I also had a family," she said with a heavy sigh. "My husband died fourteen years ago, and my daughter lives in Michigan, but she comes to visit occasionally. How is that sweet Nina of yours doing? She's such a devoted little girl."

"She's great. Taking everything very seriously, as always."

"Her devotion touched my heart. I thought that generation was spoiled. They didn't go through what we did."

Alan pushed her wheelchair along the corridor to the large veranda overlooking the myriad lights dotting the steel cables stretched between the tall, illuminated columns of the bridge. This was the George Washington Bridge, a two-story engineering wonder suspended above the Hudson River between New Jersey and New York. He took care not to knock into corners as the corridor curved, and recalled pushing another wheelchair at Fliman Hospital in Haifa, and his father's unrelenting distress.

"No need to run, Alan," he'd bark. "No need to hurry anywhere anymore."

"Tell me again what you see, Alan," Erica asked. "You do it so well. Have you ever thought of being a writer?"

"Several times," he said. "But my job is very demanding, then marriage, and one baby, then another. You know how it goes. So, opposite us are the illuminated arches of the bridge, and they look close enough to touch with our fingers. To the west, beyond the highway along the Hudson, you can see the distant lights of New Jersey. Between them and the highway is the river. It's dark now, apart from a large cargo ship with a chimney decorated with lights. On the highway, you can see the red lights of cars speeding south, in the direction of the city center, to a theater or dinner at a fancy restaurant. The road is still wet; you can see reflections of colorful, dappled light in the puddle next to the pavement."

"It makes me think of the *Kraljica Marija* at night. It was always decorated as if for a party on the Danube. Rows and rows of lights hanging on deck and strung around the chimney. Every evening, we'd see that festive picture, the very opposite of our oppressive thoughts: For how long would we be stuck here? When would the signal be given for us to set out toward freedom?"

"I'm curious to hear about the railway platform in Sabac on the morning of departure."

"It was a rainy morning in the middle of March. Those about to board the train couldn't believe it was finally happening. Everyone was thinking about a brief parting, a month or two at the most, after which we'd all be reunited. Who knew what would happen just two weeks later? We had no idea that, in fact, we were parting forever," she said, tightening the woolen blanket around her body.

"You were very young, weren't you?"

"I was already nineteen, and anyway, fighting for one's life makes you older. I remember standing opposite the carriage of children who were twelve to thirteen, and the sight of those small hands waving from the windows is ingrained in my memory as if it were today. Afterward, they closed the shutters so no one would know it was a children's transport. When I think of that time in Sabac, and before that in Kladovo, I'm filled with nostalgia. We had many good experiences too, a busy social life, many cultural activities. The horror only began when the Germans arrived, and this happened not long after the parting at the train station."

"How well did you know Inge?"

RETALIATION, MARCH 1941

"Inge and I were good friends. we planned to escape together. I didn't know your father well, of course. But I remember a tall, good-looking fellow who'd sometimes come looking for her at the infirmary or the 'magazine,' as they called the long storage building near the mill. He was a little shy, withdrawn. He had a brother, didn't he?"

"Yes. His brother's name was Pauli. He was even taller."

"Then yes, the fellow with the sweet tuft of hair in front looked just like a movie star; all the girls were talking about the two good-looking boys from Belgrade. Pauli was a bit of a show-off and looked down his nose at everyone. I have a clear memory of him from sports day in Kladovo. He was such a star."

"I had another good girlfriend then, a young local girl from Sabac, Mara Yuvanovich; she was sensitive and very special, a girl my own age, bubbly and full of curiosity. Her father was the head of a school or responsible for education in Sabac. I even had time to teach her some German. She picked it up very quickly. We went through that period together, until the deportation to the camp on the Sava River. I couldn't go and visit her from there. Getting to Sabac was too dangerous by then.

"We were a close-knit group. Friedl, Inge, myself, and Ancel Dajč.

All the rest were locals. There was Mara, whom I told you about, and Milka, a lovely gypsy girl all the young boys were after. She had a wonderful voice, and she'd sing gypsy songs at the famous Café Roma. Her brother accompanied her on the violin, and Nicola, her boyfriend, on the accordion. People at the café were always moved by her. Ancel, Inge, and I sometimes went to Café Roma and loved hearing her sing. When Nicola played 'Csárdás,' the audience fell completely silent. Nicola also knew French and taught Milka French songs.

"Our entertainment team, who started with the amateur *schiffsreview* in Kladovo, continued with a spectacular performance in Sabac that now required a proper hall. Milka and Nicola were also invited to perform with them. All this took place before hell broke out in Sabac. At the beginning of April, when the Germans entered, everything was turned upside down at once.

"During the first days after the trains left with children and youth for *Eretz* Israel, there was an atmosphere of anticipation, that everything would be all right, that if one transport had left, then the next would not be long in coming. But this dream was to shatter very quickly."

"Was Ancel from your group or from Sabac?" asked Alan.

"He was one of our group. Ancel Dajč, a young fellow from Vienna. Mara and her friends called him Zoran. Our group called him Ancel. At first, we all called him 'the student,' because he studied law in Vienna. They say he was brilliant, and several major firms in the city took an interest in him. At the beginning of the journey, he was a frightened, silent boy, and he looked weak and delicate. In time, though, he grew up and became more confident. He was highly intelligent, and people looked to him for advice on issues like agreements with the locals to do with accommodation and work. He often said that the Germans should be taught a lesson, and if he had the strength, he'd do something."

* * *

One day, Mara told me they were going out on a retaliation mission at the Zorka Factory. I immediately asked to participate, and Ancel also joined us. Inge said she was afraid of provocations and wasn't coming. I was curious about how they intended to retaliate. Ancel said at every opportunity that the time had come to take even symbolic action against the Germans and their collaborators. But he was afraid at first that the police would catch us and that it would end badly. I reminded him that we couldn't just sit there talking. We had to take action. In the end, I persuaded him to join us.

It was a warm, sunny day at the end of March. The air was full of the scent of blossom. Ancel and I stood waiting on the road leading from the mill to the factory. Both sides of the road were dotted with acacia trees blooming with yellow flowers. Around the bend in the road came a group of young people from Sabac, among them Mara. "Come along," she called out. "It'll be fun!"

They had sticks and walked rapidly, their faces alight and their eyes shining with determination. We got to the building just before sunset. At first, I froze in my tracks, and I saw Ancel hesitating as well. Acts of destruction and revenge were not in our nature. But when the boy next to me picked up a stone and threw it at the window in front of him, I plucked up courage and threw stones at the glass windows.

The sound of glass breaking and the scattering shards increased our enthusiasm. Mara went from window to window with her stick, finishing off the windows that had only cracked.

We suddenly heard a whistle blow not far from us. "Police!" called our friends and immediately dropped everything and began to run in the direction of the cemetery. Afraid and panting, I ran after them, trying with all my might to keep up. But then I suddenly realized that Ancel wasn't beside me. I looked back but couldn't see him. My heart was beating fiercely. Of all people, Ancel, who was weak and awkward, had probably been caught. And it was all my fault. I'd persuaded him.

I hid in the cemetery, each of us lying behind a headstone. In the distance, we could hear the police shouting, alternately approaching and getting further away. Mara crawled over to me. She was panting, and her face was red with effort.

"What happened to Ancel?" she asked anxiously. "Didn't he get away?"

I answered that I was very worried about him. We lay there for a few minutes that seemed like an eternity. I was no longer worried about being caught. I just didn't want Ancel to pay the price. *God, please don't let him get caught*, I prayed.

Our local friends got up cautiously to make sure the coast was clear. I heard steps approaching, and Ancel appeared. His back was hunched, and he was looking anxiously around him.

"Ancel," I whispered from my hiding place.

He hurried over to lie beside me. He couldn't speak for effort and fear. A large weight rolled off my heart. I hugged him and whispered in his ear, "God heard me. I was so worried about you."

Later, we heard he'd run in a different direction, and thanks to him, the police went off in the wrong direction.

When we got to Mara's house, her mother was waiting anxiously outside. The rumor had spread.

"Were you also breaking windows at the factory?" she asked in alarm.

"What? Did they break windows there?" Mara asked innocently.

"They deserve it, those German pigs!" said a passerby who heard the conversation.

"You're finally understanding what we Jews are going through," yelled Ancel. "At least someone is doing something! All we do is keep our heads down all the time."

"That's all we need, another war!" moaned Mara's mother. "Come inside for dinner at once," she barked at her daughter.

Later, we sat in the infirmary with Inge. We listened to the radio and heard that there were similar uprisings all over Yugoslavia. "The freedom-loving people of Yugoslavia are taking their fate into their own hands and want to show this weak, traitorous government that we will not be another Austria. We will fight to the end!" intoned the Free Station of Belgrade. Inge tried to translate for us with the little Serbo-Croatian she'd learned from Hanne.

She had recovered and returned to her old self. After the parting at the railway station in Sabac, she was in a deep depression, and no one could rouse her. "It's just a matter of time now," everyone told her. "Be strong. We'll be on a train ourselves in two or three weeks."

One day, then another, and we all realized from the radio transmissions that it really was only a matter of time—not the time that would pass until we left Sabac in the direction of *Eretz* Israel, but the time it would take the Germans to arrive.

On the morning of the sixth of April, we woke to the excited voice of the announcer: "German planes have been bombing Belgrade since early this morning." I was filled with depressing thoughts. Who knew where this would lead? Leaving didn't seem so near, but we didn't lose hope yet.

Mara arrived and told us she was going with her parents to her uncles who lived in the village of Varenska, not far from Sabac, "until everything calms down."

Every five minutes, the radio in the infirmary announced what area had been bombed and which buildings were damaged. Our counselors gathered us together and told us not to scatter but stay close for instructions. This went on all that night and the next day. Convoys of refugees left Sabac on roads leading to surrounding villages like Varenska and even Ruma. There were rumors of large groups of armed Partisans organizing in the forests. Yanek and three other young men from our group tried to persuade me and Inge to go with them to join the Partisans.

Inge said she was not so afraid for herself but that she feared it would bring disaster to the people in the group. That's who she was, always concerned for others and least of all for herself. I, on the other hand, very much wanted to join. I was tired of doing nothing and being constantly humiliated. On the other hand, I wasn't sure the time had come yet. We had to find the right moment, the point of no return, because at that stage, we still hoped they were trying to get us out and that the *Aliyah* would take place, so I put off the idea. Also,

386 | Escaping on the Danube River

the Transport Administration warned us that those who joined the Partisans might not be able to find their way back.

∗∗∗

On the train home, Alan sat thinking about what Erica had told him. She had a great deal to tell, and her memories were filled with life and details of life. He must write them down. Maybe, one day, he'd put them all in a memorial pamphlet about heroes she'd mentioned. Maybe even a book. The problem was that until he had the time to write, many of the details might be forgotten. He must record her. Pity he hadn't done so that evening. Next time, he'd take a high-quality recording device with him. He'd keep it in his pocket so it wouldn't bother her.

The next day, during lunch hour, he went to the J. R. Electronics store on Fulton Street and bought a recording device, and that evening, he recorded all the details he could remember from their meeting the previous day.

The following day, he planned to meet with Erica again, but his secretary informed him that an important meeting had been set up for him in Chicago and there was a lot of material to prepare.

The meetings with Erica, her stories, all evoked in him an enormous curiosity and a hunger for information. Around five thirty, he began to reflect on the details of their previous meeting. He was amazed by the workings of long-term memory and the gaps in short-term memory. If he asked Erica what her doctor had said yesterday, she'd have to work hard to recall a few hesitant details. He was curious about her story of joining the Partisans and their escape. He felt himself drawn into it. Maybe he'd find out more about Inge and his grandparents.

He wondered when she'd made her decision to cross the lines. It was probably a conflict felt deeply by many of the group who remained. Erica called it the point of no return, one they had to be ready for. She probably arrived at that point, or she wouldn't be here today. Until now, he thought to himself, he hadn't heard of anyone who'd survived.

Maybe he'd be able to see her that evening after all. For a brief visit. He'd promised to read her another section from the project Nina had submitted. He'd prepare for the meeting in Chicago at home that night.

When he reached her room, he found her with sunken cheeks and covered up in bed.

"Just not my day," she said. "Another bad day. I seem to be sinking fast."

"What happened?" he asked in alarm.

"You wouldn't understand," she said to him. "You are still young and so very busy. And you have a family…"

"But that's what I'm always trying to do. Trying to understand life, and I don't think I'm doing too badly."

"I don't feel I belong anymore."

"Don't belong where? What do you mean?"

"Don't belong to this life. This time is so different from that of my youth. When we were on the boat and then in Kladovo, we were together, older people, younger people, there wasn't such a gap between us."

"Yes, times have changed," he agreed, adding, "Look, Erica, I want to ask you something." He drew closer, "Your story has so gripped me that I want to record it. I've brought a small recording device," he said, taking it out of his pocket to show her. "Would it bother you if I keep it in my pocket to record your story?"

"Not at all, but on one condition. That it stays between the two of us."

"For the time being, I'm not going to do anything with it. Although you did once ask me why I don't write, remember?"

"Yes, but not yet. I'm not ready."

"So where were we? You were saying there wasn't such a gap between older and younger people."

GERMAN SOLDIERS

"Less so for me, but Inge spent a lot of time with your family. She and Louisa had a special relationship. They were very close. Not only because of Hanne. Louisa was the mother she missed so much all that time. Inge would go to their apartment in Sabac and help with the cleaning, wash the floors, and so on. She was a very quick and practical girl. They spent a lot of time together, particularly after the young people left, and your grandfather, Emil, went off to Belgrade. Did you know that he left?"

"Yes, I have two letters he sent to *Eretz* Israel after Father and Pauli left."

***

He left three days before Passover, I think, and returned on Seder night. But the second day of the Seder was the day Sabac was most heavily bombed. We were all busy filling sandbags in the mill yard. We suddenly heard bombs whistling over our heads. And then we heard explosions and saw Miklos come running out of Emil and Louisa's home, which apparently took a direct hit. He was a single fellow, older than the youth group but younger than the adults with families. He was holding his head in his hands, running in the street and wailing hysterically.

"What's happened, Miklos?" we asked, and he said, "Direct hit. Go and save them, quickly."

"Call Inge. People may be injured! Call someone."

When we entered, we saw a cloud of smoke. The kitchen was completely destroyed. Through the smoke, it seemed as if nothing was wrong. We saw Emil and Louisa sitting at the table with cups of steaming tea, as if they didn't understand what all the fuss was about. We couldn't believe our eyes. Inge stood behind them, murmuring, "A miracle, it's a miracle."

They were unharmed, but the kitchen was ruined and shards of glass lay scattered on the floor. They told us they'd been sitting there with Miklos and the Birnbaum couple when suddenly they heard an approaching whistle followed by the sound of an explosion and all the glasses in the cabinet shattered.

The next morning, armored vehicles in German military colors were seen, and German soldiers in green uniforms and green helmets patrolled up and down the town on motorbikes making a deafening noise. It was then our people began to understand that we were trapped and that the transport would never reach its destination. Many of the young people planned to escape before it was too late. They tried to persuade me and Inge as well, but we felt the time wasn't right. And I didn't have the emotional stamina for it. I told myself that we hadn't yet reached the point of no return.

I wanted to find out what had happened to Café Roma where so many of the group used to spend time. It was hit at the back, and the roof had collapsed. When I approached, I heard the whistle of a German soldier, who barked at me, "Don't go any closer. The place is blocked."

Suddenly, I saw Mara. She ran up panting, "We are so lucky, Erica. Our house is still standing. It's unharmed. We are so lucky. All the adjacent buildings were hit. All the windows at Mignon, the clothing store, were shattered."

"I only came for a while," said Mara excitedly, adding, "Mother wouldn't let me come. I persuaded her, told her I just wanted to see what happened to our house, but I have to go back."

I offered to accompany her to the exit from the town.

When we passed the railway station, we saw a large crowd of people. An old woman was carrying a sack on her bent back.

"What have you got there?" asked Mara.

"Leave me alone," she answered crossly. "Everyone's taking stuff. What do you want from me?"

It was a shameful scene. People had broken into stores and were looting and taking everything they could lay hands on, sacks of rice or corn. Ripped sacks lay in the middle and on the sides of the street, and people gathered around, filling bags and pails or any available container.

We suddenly noticed an oil barrel on its side and a little girl's small sandaled feet sticking out. Her head and most of her body were inside the barrel. Mara hurried to pull her out by her legs. The child was holding onto a large jar and weeping bitterly.

"What will I tell my mother?" she yelled. "She told me to fill a jar with oil."

"But you could have drowned in that oil," Mara shouted back. "You should be thanking me for saving your life. Now go away at once."

The child obeyed.

A group of local women laden with loot walked ahead of us: bags of corn, flour, and bread. When we came to the mill on the road leading out of Sabac, a few of the young people from our group were standing there, looking pityingly at the looters. On the side of the road stood two sacks of flour.

"Take it, my friends. You'll be needing it." Mara pointed at the sacks. But they stood there proudly, without blinking an eye, not tempted by the food. With a small contemptuous smile, they said, "We will never descend to that level. Steal someone's goods? No matter how bad things get, we still have our pride."

After we'd gone past, Mara compared their youths with ours.

"See that? They can stoop so low just for a few bags of rice or a jar of oil; they're even willing to die for it. Your youths wouldn't dare humiliate themselves like that."

That evening, we heard shots. Soon after, the bodies of about twenty youths were brought in. They'd tried to escape under cover of darkness. We buried them. It was very sad. Eight were killed, some adults and Hechalutz youth, among them Karl, who was my age, a very talented young man. He was the one who'd tried to persuade me to join the escape. In a second, I understood why I'd postponed my decision. There was still something to lose.

***

That evening, when Alan got home, he went to his room, but instead of preparing material for the meeting in Chicago, he sat down to listen to the recording. Part of it sounded familiar. At first, he didn't understand why, and then he remembered the letters he'd found in his father's house before his death. He hadn't even had time to talk to him about what was in the large envelope with all those photographs and old documents. It was the letter Grandfather Emil had written from Belgrade to his sons in *Eretz* Israel. Alan looked feverishly in the drawer into which he'd thrust all the papers he'd brought back from his father's house after his death. He found the large envelope. Here they were. Exactly as he'd found them three years previously, three pages of closely written words:[23]

> Belgrade
> 14/5/1941
>
> Hello my dear children,
>
> On the third or fourth of April, we received a telegram from Mrs. Shteindler telling us you'd arrived in *Eretz* Israel. Praise the Lord.
>
> I was in Belgrade for two or three weeks because of our visas for *Eretz* Israel, although on Saturday the fifth of April, I was told to come on Monday for the visas. You probably also know what has happened in the meantime—on the

---

23   The letter is an original document (slightly adapted for the story) translated by Hanne (Shlomo) David from Serbo-Croatian to Hebrew, before the Kladovo survivors' gathering at Kibbutz Gan Shmuel in 1977.

first day of the bombing, I was at the Pops family's house. Do you remember Mr. Pops? He's the one Hanne was so afraid of when he was a child. Well, his house was in bad condition. We had to reinforce the cellar ceiling to prevent the building from collapsing, and that's how we passed the first and worst day of bombing in Belgrade. I spent the night there too. We were lucky no bombs fell in our vicinity.

The Topcider and Dedinje neighborhoods were left almost completely untouched. On Monday morning, a car went into town, and I took the opportunity to go and take a look around and see Belgrade after the bombing. The city looked terrible. Houses were destroyed and burned. There were cracks in the pavements, shards of glass everywhere, in the houses, cafés, and offices.

The worst thing was the silence that hung over the city. It was completely dead; here and there, someone could be seen with a small suitcase, leaving the city—and I finally decided to return to Sabac, because Mother was probably worried about me.

Trains and buses were no longer running, and a group of us decided to leave on foot through Valjevo in the direction of Avala, believing we'd find a ride to take us on to Sabac. I left with Olga Timotievich, Raiku Levy, Vladimir Pops's wife, and some others. We were nine in all.

In the meantime, the alarm and evacuation were so great it was impossible to find a car with any room, so we had no choice but to walk south, in the direction of Raila, forty kilometers from Belgrade. What saved us was a car stuck at the side of the road. The driver asked if one of us knew anything about engines. I know a little, so I looked inside and asked him to switch on the engine. I saw the gas pipe was blocked and helped him to fix it by an old method I knew. When the engine was finally working, I asked if he could give us a ride. He said he was going to Raila, so we got in the back and went with him. In Raila, we managed with difficulty to organize a cart that took us as far as Mladenovac. The following day, we got to Aranđelovac in the cart, where we had to wait two days to continue. We met many people we know there: Sime Spitzer, the Popses, and many others who'd escaped from Belgrade and waited there with us.

The next day, we traveled to Valjevo, and from there, by the last bus to Sabac. Throughout the journey, we heard sirens because of the German planes. The last came as we arrived in Sabac. It was Saturday night, the Seder night, Passover night. You can imagine my joy at being reunited with your mother again. I wasn't even sure I'd find her in Sabac, because we heard rumors about the division of the camp. With all the stories and tears of joy upon meeting, and also because Mother hadn't had time to prepare anything for Passover, we decided just to have the second Passover night, but that too did not take place.

On Saturday the twelfth, at six in the evening, the battle for Sabac began with a heavy bombardment. We had a feeling that something was brewing even before noon. There were frequent sirens and a lot of military traffic. Many Jews wanted to escape from Sabac, and Mother also wanted us to go, didn't matter where, as long as we left. I was opposed to leaving the apartment, because I believed we were better off behind the front line. At seven o'clock that evening, our building got a direct hit. We were sitting in the kitchen with the Birnbaums and Kramer Miklos, who whined more than anyone. Even though the kitchen was hit by shrapnel from a bomb, no one was hurt!

The bombardment went on all night. Bombs were exploding on all sides. By morning, the Germans were in Sabac. All the Jews who remained in Sabac were alive and healthy. About a hundred and fifty Jews had tried to escape, eight of whom were killed, among them Fritz Zimmermann, two young men from the Hechalutz youth, and five more whom I don't know. They were buried in Sabac.

I must end now.

Many kisses,
Father

They were having a difficult time with Nina. She decided to stop her dance lessons after studying for more than five years.

"I will never be a dancer," she said with tears in her eyes. "Better to donate the money for my lessons to some charity, or Keren Kayemeth LeIsrael," she added, and reminded Alan of his promise to consider a trip to Israel. "Two of my friends are going to visit family in Israel during the summer, so why can't we?"

Alan was overwhelmed with guilt. Maybe Nina was right. Was he just being stubborn and trying to avoid dealing with the decision to return to Israel? After all, he'd already privately decided it was time to deal with going back. It wasn't the right time for him, but maybe he could still send Nina to a good school in Israel so she could get the same Israeli education he had. Then he rejected the idea, telling himself that it wasn't the right time, he was busy at work, and now there was Erica in the nursing home. He felt himself drawn as if by magic to her memories of the war. He may not be able to restore Inge to his father, but some riddle was unravelling, and he hadn't been aware of his internal hunger for this information.

Erica was in a cheerful mood.

"My daughter is finally coming to visit tomorrow. I haven't seen her since Thanksgiving."

"Why so long?" he asked. "Is she that busy?"

"It's a long story. She's getting divorced now, for the second time. I don't think she really knows how to run her life. But I don't interfere. She must make her own choices."

"Does she have any children?" asked Alan.

"Yes, a daughter Nina's age and a son of seventeen."

"Don't they want to visit their grandmother?"

"They have their own lives to lead. They were here for Thanksgiving and stayed with her husband's parents."

Alan told her about his problems with Nina.

"Oh, Nina's another story altogether," she said. "That child is so sensitive to the suffering of others. She reminds me of Mara. I told you about her attitude to the looters who went past the train station, taking whatever they could, remember?"

Alan sat back in his chair and switched on the recorder.

"That's the last thing you told me last time."

"I didn't see her for many days after that. I consoled myself with the thought that her family might have returned to her uncle in the village. But I was also uneasy that maybe something bad happened to her, and I was afraid she'd never return."

YELLOW PATCH

Two weeks went by, and life went back to normal. The Germans imposed military law on the city, appointing Branko Petrovich, the bank clerk, no less, as mayor. Ever since they'd invaded Sabac, he'd become their lackey.

The atmosphere was unpleasant. A German soldier stood next to his motorbike at every street corner, and we had to move according to his orders. One of the young men tried to get smart. The German officer shot him with his revolver, and he was taken unconscious to the infirmary. Inge resuscitated him with great difficulty. A German officer who came into the infirmary noticed her devotion and ordered her to report the following day to an improvised hospital established at the Stana Milotovich Boarding School.

The next day brought me a pleasant surprise. Mara came home with her family and immediately came to see me, Friedl, and Inge, who'd just returned from the hospital. We were excited and shared our experiences. Mara told us that her father was very worried about her and her brother and didn't want them to leave the village. "There won't be any school," he said. "So why not stay with your uncle until the danger is past?" But Mara wasn't afraid and preferred to be closer to us, her friends, and to help if she could, rather than stay there and do nothing.

Inge told us that Louisa and Emil had gone with Mr. Birnbaum to Belgrade to get their immigration permits to *Eretz* Israel that were waiting at the Ministry of the Interior. I was surprised that they'd gone together to organize their papers, particularly as it was so dangerous to be in the streets. Just to get to Článek, they'd have to take a cart, then change; and there were bombings on the way and thieves, too, now. After all, he'd only just returned at Passover. Louisa told me they'd be back in two or three days because they'd left all their things in the apartment. But I sensed something else as well; it wasn't just about their immigration permits.

That afternoon, Friedl and I were on laundry duty. She was beginning to regret staying. Although she'd received an immigration permit and could have gone with the young people, she was afraid to leave her aging parents behind. Friedl and I always did laundry duty together at magazine 1, one of two long buildings beside the mill that had once served as granaries.

Hechalutz and Hashomer Hatzair youth stayed at the mill, and the others were divided into groups in two magazines, except for families and older people who rented rooms with Sabac residents. Two girls from each group were responsible for laundry duty—the whole process of sorting, washing in large tubs, hanging up the wet laundry to dry, and then resorting and folding.

I hummed quietly to myself, while Friedl probably wondered again, regretfully, why she hadn't boarded the train instead of being stuck there with her aging parents. She told me her boyfriend was waiting for her on a *kibbutz* in *Eretz* Israel. Suddenly, we heard the sound of rough steps in the corridor. Those were not the steps of one of our fellows, but hard boots on the concrete floor. We didn't have long to wonder, because we then heard loud shouts in German—orders urging all those still in the building to come out into the yard and stand in straight rows. We stopped folding laundry and ran outside.

An armed German soldier with a helmet on his head was hurrying us, yelling "*schnell, schnell.*"

Friedl became hysterical, stumbled as she ran, and fell to the ground. The soldier stood over her, shouting at her to get up. I saw her holding her knee in pain. I tried to explain to the soldier that she needed help getting up, and he raised his voice even louder, waving the baton in his hand. When we got there, we all stood in straight rows. The officer ordered the soldier to check the rooms, and once again, blood-curdling shouts were heard as the soldier ordered those still inside to get out fast. A few minutes later, the soldier appeared with old Pinchas Cohen, who was deaf. The soldier hurried him along, hitting him on the back with his baton.

"You," yelled the German officer at Pinchas Cohen. "Open the parcel and show everyone what's inside." He continued yelling and handed the parcel to Pinchas, who was trembling from head to foot and didn't understand what the officer wanted from him.

Ancel, a sensitive soul who never feared to express his opinion, strode up to the officer and asked him to take pity on Pinchas. He pleaded in perfect German. "He's deaf," he said, pointing at Pinchas. The officer, taken aback by the young man's temerity, took the parcel and handed it to Ancel.

"Open it!" he ordered.

Ancel opened the parcel and was terrified by the sight of its contents.

"Take one out and show it to everyone," the officer commanded.

Ancel took out a yellow patch with a black Star of David and the word "Jude" printed on it. Although we'd heard about the decrees in Germany, Poland, and Austria, we didn't believe that this status would be imposed on us as well.

The officer gave a stack of yellow badges to the first person in each line and ordered him to pass them along to the line behind. Heads bowed, the young men gave a yellow patch to each of us.

The officer wanted to demonstrate on Ancel's arm how and where the patch had to be. But Ancel, standing there with obvious reluctance, refused to present his arm to the officer, who began screaming at him, then grabbed him by the arm and threw him into the air as if he were an atonement rooster.

"Now stand there quietly and don't get in my way!" he screamed at him.

Drooping, Ancel stood still as another soldier pinned the patch to his sleeve and sent him back to the line.

"Pay attention everyone," shouted the officer. "From now on, that patch will be your sign of identity. You must wear it on your sleeve at all times, and everywhere you go." He waved a threatening finger, his face red with effort. "Any Jew found without a patch will be severely punished."

He went on to detail the rest of the restrictions.

"From now on, you are forbidden to be out in the streets after six in the evening and before seven in the morning. You may not shop at the market during the morning but only from eleven o'clock onward. Any Jew found in the market during fresh produce hours will be severely punished. The fresh produce is only for locals."

The officer finished and strode out into the street with his soldier.

As soon as the officer and his soldier had disappeared around the corner of the street, Ancel, still noticeably shocked by his humiliation, tore the patch from his arm and threw it to the ground. With tears of rage in his eyes, he stamped on it, shouting in anger, "Do the same, all of you. We aren't animals, and we aren't second-rate citizens."

That very evening, Friedl and I sewed the yellow patches with the word "Jude" onto our sleeves, and we helped some of the young men who had trouble doing it for themselves. Everyone took the decree very hard, and some reacted like Ancel and swore they wouldn't degrade themselves with the patch. I suggested to Ancel and Inge that we escape together to the forests and fight instead of sitting around lamenting. Ancel refused. He wasn't built for that kind of resistance. But Inge reacted differently. She felt compelled to resist. Everything she'd revered in German culture, the poetry and philosophy, was meaningless in the face of these inhuman decrees. My own determination to join the Resistance fighters was greatly reinforced. If any Resistance fighters had been there at that moment, I'd have left everything to join them.

***

That evening, while Alan was sitting listening to Erica's recording, he heard taps at his door.

"Alan? Why are you sitting in here with the door closed?" Rachel peeped around the door, surprised to see Alan's headphones.

"Is that what you've been doing for hours in your room?" she asked, surprised.

Alan let her listen to the recording for a few minutes, and told her he was recording the old woman Nina visited at the nursing home on Amsterdam Avenue.

As he listened to the story about the distribution of yellow badges in the mill yard, he remembered the second letter in which Grandfather Emil wrote about the distribution of yellow badges in Belgrade during his second visit after Passover. He opened the letter, and they read it together.

10/5/1941

My dear children,

We've decided to come to Belgrade together with Moshe Birnbaum and his wife. Moshe came to collect their papers, because they'd already received a visa to *Eretz* Israel and Syria, and we came to be at the center of things and see how life is here.

We left on the eighteenth of April in a cart going to Článek, and from there, in another cart to Ruma. From Ruma, we continued by train to Zemun, where we took a boat to Belgrade. We had a terrible night in Článek and again on the train to Zemun.

In Zemun, we heard about the April 19 decrees, requiring every Jew to report to the nearest police station to register, receive a yellow patch, and labor assignments. Anyone who doesn't report will be shot, according to the proclamation. Naturally, we reported at once to the police station in Zemun to get a yellow patch. The doctor and I were exempt from work for health reasons. Mother was also exempt. Women only work until the age of forty.

After a difficult journey, we arrived in Belgrade on the twentieth of April. It is fortunate that you two are already in *Eretz Israel*. In bombed Belgrade, we saw friends of yours who'd remained at school: Alphonso, Samito de Mayo, and Isaac as well, Hanne's good friend from Hashomer Hatzair. We even saw Pepi (Yosef Peretz) and Omer (Bihali). They clean the streets or work on demolished houses, loading bricks and taking out bodies. I met Michel and Alkalay, who do the same work, and they said it's emotionally very hard to deal with the bodies and the smell.

The Dorćol neighborhood was hit worst in the bombing of Belgrade. During the first days, there was no electricity, water, or sewage. The electricity is back on now almost everywhere, but water has to be fetched from faucets in the street or carts that allocate water. No home toilets can be used. There are mobile and field toilets in various places. What has happened to Jews in other countries is happening here too. They will have to emigrate. You'll find some of the details interesting: The Second Gymnasium for Boys, Hanne's school, was burned to the ground, only bare walls remain. But the Reali School is still standing. The Serbian King Hotel opposite was completely destroyed. The lovely bridges were also destroyed. In Croatia, they've already introduced the Nuremberg Laws. Here and in Zagreb, Jews and Serbs can only be out in the streets until six in the evening.

I must end now.
Hope you are both well.

Many kisses,
Father

**

Alan switched on the recorder again and listened to the rest of Erica's story.

**

In the days that followed, meal portions became smaller at the mill. There were constantly new food shortages because of the prohibition to go to the market before eleven o'clock in the morning. Fresh vegetables and bread had been unavailable for a long time. One day, I saw Max Tanenbaum, who was responsible for kitchen purchases, returning with his two helpers; he threw the empty bags on the ground and screamed from the bottom of his heart.

"This is unbearable. Today, there were no products left at that hour, and the little there was there wasn't worth buying." He hammered on the table with his fist, crying out, "Damn the Germans!"

As the days went by, the meal portions served at the mill shrank even further, and more and more people, who usually didn't complain, began to talk of possibly circumventing the decrees. Someone suggested going to market without the patch and dressed as a local to buy the necessary products. They also spoke about an organized uprising, and one day, when meeting with our Sabac friends, Mara suggested to Ancel that some of the young men should join the Partisans to fight the Germans.

A few days ago, an envoy had arrived in secret from a Partisan brigade in the nearby forests. He talked to the Sabac youth, and some were willing to join.

When Mara told me and Ancel, we saw this as a good idea at first, but later doubts arose. Ever since the humiliating incident that day at the mill, Ancel refused to wear the yellow patch on his arm and barely left the mill. Mara failed to persuade him.

"Look," she said. "Our young men are going to the forests where each one will get a rifle and lessons in how to shoot. It's very simple, so I've heard. If it wasn't for my mother, who is constantly anxious, I'd join too."

Ancel, guilty at being afraid, finally said, "Impossible. If they discover that someone is missing, they'll kill us all."

Mara asked, "But how will they know if someone is missing? Do they have name lists?"

"Of course they do. The committee gave them all the names of the group and they—"

"That's terrible," said Musha, who'd been spending a lot of time with Mara lately. "Why did the committee agree to do that?"

"The German officer threatened the head of the committee." Ancel sighed.

The decrees were increasing. Dr. Bezalel and another doctor who worked with him at the local infirmary in town were forced to stop their work and return to the mill. Dr. Bezalel was immediately taken to help at the German military hospital, where Inge was already working.

Yosef the carpenter, who made a good living working at the big carpentry shop not far from the mill, had to give up his work. In addition to his carpentry work, he made his famous wooden clogs at home, which quickly became a commercial success. Everyone wanted to wear Yosef the carpenter's wooden clogs, mainly because of their soft tread, which made no sound on the cobble stones. With the coming of summer, Yosef's special clogs could be seen almost everywhere in town. Even German soldiers bought them, emptying the stores to send them to their wives in Germany. One day, I saw two soldiers arguing over the last pair of clogs in one of the stores. It almost turned into a fight.

A few days after the evening curfew decree, a food rationing decree was announced, which further aggravated the hunger. Hunger wormed its way into people, causing uncharacteristic behavior. For instance, Vera, once a wealthy property owner in Vienna, put up her expensive fur coat for sale at the mill gate. She hoped to sell the fur to local wealthy people and buy food for herself and her ailing husband. But in the prevailing situation of distress and scarcity, Madame Vera was left holding her fur coat.

AN ATTEMPT TO ESCAPE, JUNE 1941

Alan sat in front of his computer screen and continued listening to Erica's voice on the recording machine. In his hand, he held his grandfather's last letter, which he'd copied into the computer file for Erica's story. He pressed Start on the recorder in order to continue typing up the story.

***

The evening curfew hour was particularly tough for young people. In the month of June, six in the evening seemed more like late afternoon, and by that time we already had to be inside our houses. We used to be able to walk around the town streets, but now they, too, were empty, though we could still smell the fragrance of flowers in the air. By evening, their perfume had faded and our hearts grew heavy.

Milka appeared that evening. Until then, she'd always been cheerful no matter what the situation; she'd find some light in every new decree and was always hopeful that things would get better. This was the first time I'd seen her incandescent with rage. With tears in her eyes, she told us how that morning all the gypsies had been summoned to City Hall and presented with yellow patches.

"Just like the Jews," she said, her gypsy eyes glaring with anger, adding, "Just without the word 'Jude.' We are also forbidden to go out after six in the evening." She spat on the floor and cursed coarsely. "Now we must sit inside like you and think about what's to be done."

Imposing a curfew on the gypsies created a sense of common misery between us. Every day, we'd meet at the mill or the infirmary to talk. Two days after the curfew was expanded to include the gypsies, they were forbidden to play in restaurants and cafés.

Trying to encourage us, Musha said, "You're not missing anything by not going out in the evening. Without the gypsy music, the cafés are almost deserted anyway. Take Café Roma, it was always so busy, and now it's almost empty in the evening." Three days later, we were sitting as usual in the infirmary, Inge, Friedl, and myself, when we were joined by Musha, Nicola, and Mara.

We were just saying that six weeks had gone by without our hearing from Louisa and Emil, when Miklos suddenly rushed in.

"I got back from Belgrade today. What a nightmare. I barely made it. I was told to report to the police station. So I went. At the station, I met Louisa," he breathed heavily. "She looked terrible. She's living with Sophie now, her maid, the one who worked for her when they still had their big house. She said she'd come to the police station to try and get Emil released. He's been in prison since their attempt to escape."

"What attempt to escape?" we asked. No one here had heard they'd tried to escape. We only knew they'd gone by cart to Belgrade right after Passover.

"Something terrible happened to them, really bad luck," said Miklos and clapped his hands. "I've brought a letter," he said, breaking the silence, and took an envelope out of his pocket. "It's for you, Inge. Louisa made me swear to give it to you."

Inge read in silence, occasionally wiping away a tear from the corners of her eyes. When she finished, she agreed to read it to us.[24]

22/5/1941

Dearest Inge,

My Inge, you have no idea of what we've been through since leaving Sabac by cart that day after Passover. It's a never-ending nightmare. I'm here alone now, trying to get Emil released from prison. The day we left with the Birnbaums, I told you we were going to Belgrade City Hall to find out what had happened to our immigration permits, but the story was a little different, and I didn't want it to get out before we left.

The last time Emil was in Belgrade, before Passover, he met Olga Timotievich and told her about our troubles in Kladovo and then in Sabac. Olga asked him why we'd waited so long to try and escape, and Emil told her about our problem with the immigration permits and how they'd strung us along with promises they didn't keep.

In short, she told Emil about a group that was organizing to

---

24 Hanne (Shlomo) David received this letter about a year after he arrived in *Eretz Israel*. Inge was able to send it with one of the group who managed to escape from Sabac to Switzerland, right before the July uprising, after which all exits were blocked.

escape to Hungary, as the Germans hadn't entered yet. Emil immediately remembered his two aunts in Budapest and thought it would be a good idea to go there. The problem is, though, that the Germans are everywhere, on the roads and side roads as well as in outlying villages, so this sort of plan was very risky.

Olga told him about a Serbian contact called Yanko who was willing to provide forged documents at a high price— eighty thousand dinars per person—in order to cross the border. The price included a ride to the border crossing in a truck that took calves for slaughter in a Hungarian village not far from the Yugoslavian border.

We went to visit this Yanko. Right from the beginning, he seemed a slimy character to me, someone interested only in money, not in people. You probably know what I mean. He came to meet us at the Sabac market with a carter's hat on his head, chewing tobacco and speaking coarsely. He didn't make a good impression on me from the start, and I said so to Emil. But Emil said that people who undertake things like that are naturally not people with whom you drink evening tea. That's what he said.

Yanko came to an agreement with Emil regarding eighty thousand dinars per person, and Emil went to his relative with whom he'd left the remaining money from the sale of our house on the hill. I once told you about her. She's a very wealthy woman. Her husband isn't Jewish and has a high government position. I'm trying to get her to help get Emil released.

After Emil gave Yanko the money, they agreed to meet the following day. He was to pick us up early in the morning from Sophie's house. She was my maid in the house on Dedinje Hill and has fond memories of the time she worked for me. She's such a good-hearted woman.

We left early in the morning, together with three other people we didn't know. It turned out that one of them knew Emil through a common friend who'd worked with him, and they reminisced together. We were relaxed and in a good mood, sure that money had bought our freedom and within two hours we'd cross the northern border near Schatzka, and at long last, we'd be in a safe country. We traveled for an hour and a half in the back of the truck, which was covered in canvas so we wouldn't be stopped on the way. We couldn't see a thing, could only guess where we were. The driver warned us it would be about a two-and-a-half-hour journey. As time passed, so our tension grew and we spoke less. We sat quietly, hoping that at the border they'd only look at the documents and let us pass. Part of the money we'd given Yanko was for his partner at the border crossing, so he'd look the other way. It didn't enter our minds that he'd want all the money for himself. Apparently, this is what happened. The villain took it all for himself and betrayed us.

It happened long before we got to the border. The truck

slowed suddenly and went off the road. We heard voices in German and understood that the worst had happened. Even as we sat there in the back, silent and trembling with fear, the canvas was thrown up. In the blinding sunlight, we saw the satisfied face of a German soldier who aimed his gun at us. He burst out laughing when he saw us sitting there in shock and called out, "Smart little Jews, surprised again, huh?" He ordered us to get down.

We were imprisoned. I was released after two weeks because of dysentery. They were apparently afraid I'd infect the rest of the prisoners. Emil is still in prison, and I'm doing all I can to get him released.

I don't think this nightmare will ever end. I hope that things aren't worse for you all in Sabac.

With love,

Louisa

P.S. I wrote this letter three weeks ago and hope to find a way to send it to Sabac.

***

On the subway train, on his way to the nursing home on Amsterdam Avenue, Alan was preoccupied with thoughts regarding his superficial connection with Israel and his rare visits there. Why should Nina suffer because he'd kept his distance from his country? Maybe the time had come to renew the connection, at least for his daughter's sake, since she'd suddenly developed an interest in it. Maybe he really should organize a family visit. Even if she wouldn't be able to see her grandfather. She'd only met him twice, when he'd come for a visit. The first time was when she was born, and the second was when she went into first grade. She was too small to understand where he'd come from. He felt a pang at not having taken her before to see his home on the *moshav* where he'd grown up. She should at least know where her father came from. For her family roots project, she'd been satisfied with stories and the many photographs he had. But it wasn't enough. The child had asked him. Maybe the whole family should go to Israel for the summer.

✳✳✳

When he got to Erica that evening, he found her once again in a melancholy mood.

"I'm waiting for the demon to take me as well," she said brokenly.

"Has something happened?" he asked in concern. "Who did the demon take?"

"The only friend I had left in this institution died yesterday," she said, crushed.

"The one I saw laughing here with you one evening over a bottle of schnapps?"

"Yes. Her name was Klara. She was also from Austria. She liked to drink and always kept a bottle in her room, hidden away from the keen eyes of the doctors. Especially after the cancer returned. In Sabac, that's what kept us going—the friendships between the transport group and the locals of our age—Mara, Musha, and the gypsies."

A SAD PARTING, JULY 1941

They were about to send us away from the town to a camp near the river. Although it wasn't far away, we knew we wouldn't be able to meet as usual. We sat there in the infirmary that evening, the three of us—Friedl, Inge, and myself. The evening hours were the hardest in terms of the curfew and not being able to go out or have people visit us. We sat talking about the move to the camp and agreed that the hardest part of the move would be the loss of local friends in Sabac. Despite the worsening situation of hunger and hardship, we'd found new friends here, and we'd miss them.

Inge told them that after she'd parted from Hanne four months previously, she'd found in Mara a true and supportive friend. Mara had invited her home on several occasions to meet her parents, who'd received her with generous warmth, as if she were one of the family.

I told Friedl and Inge about the get-together Musha and Mara were organizing for them the next day. A kind of farewell party. We'll meet at seven at the entrance to Mara's house, Musha told me, and asked us to bring Ancel, Rudi, and Yanko. All their friends will be there. Nicola will bring his violin, and Milka will sing songs for us to remember. Maybe Laza will bring his clarinet.

Inge, who always obeyed laws and regulations, immediately resisted.

"And what if the Germans come? We'll be breaking the curfew. They'll catch us all," she said in alarm.

I was also a bit uneasy at being caught, but I calmed everyone. "There's nothing to worry about. If the evil Germans come, we'll run into the yards." *Only Ancel might be a problem,* I thought to myself. He hadn't left the mill since he'd refused to wear the yellow patch on his sleeve.

But no tears, Mara made me promise, then ran back to help her mother in Mignon, the clothing store near Café Roma.

Everyone agreed to be there by seven o'clock, even Ancel. He was very fond of Nicola and carried away by his music. It was a pleasant summer evening, the smell of honeysuckle on the air from the fence near Mara's house. We all arrived at seven and sat on the bench. Or, rather, the girls sat down and the boys gathered firewood to make a fire. Nicola took out his violin and with trembling hands played the song "There, Faraway," which we all loved, and Milka sang the words in French. Then Laza took out the clarinet. Since the restrictions on gypsies, she, like Nicola and Milka, no longer appeared in the town cafés. Softly, she played "Sail on, French Ship," and Friedl and Inge sang along with her. Later, we sang "Hava Nagila, with a Glass of Wine," regretting that we didn't really have a glass of wine. Despite the hovering sadness of parting, we were happy and elated just to be sitting and singing together. When the fire died down and only the crackling of embers was heard, Mara asked to speak and read out a moving piece she'd written about us, the transport, who'd arrived in their forgotten, dusty, and culture-less town, bringing with us a refreshing spark of culture.

"Tomorrow, when you leave, the town will be suddenly empty. You'll go with bowed heads, but I know that each and every one of you are heroes in your own way," she said, the words catching in her throat. "Yosef, the carpenter, who goes on making furniture as if nothing was happening around him. Ancel, the student, serious before his time, and always hungry for knowledge. Inge, the wonderful nurse, who does sacred work even among our patients and wounded, and now the Germans need her help. With everything she's been through—and I've been with her at difficult moments, after her parting from her beloved—she's stayed optimistic and smiling. Just like hard-working Rudi, who always shows us what true happiness is, how we can be happy even under tough daily conditions and maintain a romantic spirit." She looked mischievously at him and said, "I understand that cupid works hard here. One morning, I saw a drawing of a heart on the mill wall, with an arrow, with the name Rudi and another name I can't remember. I thought to myself at that moment, how victorious love is, even in a place like this with all its terrible suffering."

Rudi sat silent, large tears rolling from his eyes. He, too, had parted from his girlfriend who'd boarded the train four months previously. Afterward, we all ran to hug Mara. We hugged the others goodbye, too, promising we'd meet again.

We knew we'd be walking two kilometers south along the banks of the Sava, and innocently believed that the distance would be difficult, but we didn't know there'd be a far graver problem—the strict guard kept over us by the Germans at the camp.

***

Early the next morning, truckloads of armed German soldiers came to the mill. They quickly jumped out. One of them, probably the commander, entered the mill with heavy steps and loudly ordered us to be outside with our suitcases and equipment within ten minutes. People came out with bowed heads, each one with a backpack or a knotted blanket containing all their belongings. We stood there in the cold, misty morning, the German commander's orders and shouts blending with fresh, pleasant memories of the previous evening around the fire and particularly Mara's moving words to us.

A few strong young men loaded tables, closets, and large kitchen pots onto the trucks. Other mill and granary residents, as well as those living in rented apartments in the town, stood in two rows, according to their group leader's instructions. Their shabby backpacks on their backs, they sullenly and reluctantly obeyed the German officer's order to start moving.

After less than an hour's walk along a path bordered with vegetation on the banks of the Sava, we arrived at the camp. It looked like an abandoned military camp with the remains of barracks. On each side of the main avenue, two more rows of long huts had been erected. They organized us according to our order in line, approximately forty people to a hut. Luckily, Friedl, Inge, and I were in the same hut, which was located next to the well. A large bucket, tied to a rope, stood at the opening.

***

That evening, on his way home on the subway train, Alan listened to his last meeting with Erica, realizing that he had a lot of material for a book. Erica's story complemented his father's diary, and he felt a strong need to do something with the material. He knew he should make time to write, but how? Working in a senior position at the bank was demanding. It would be hard to keep a low profile. No one there would agree to such a step.

At the next meeting, as Alan was wheeling Erica in her wheelchair, he told her that Rachel had asked him to spend more time at home. Erica understood Rachel.

"It's important for you to be at home. I can't understand the work culture here. You all work late in America. When I was young, people came home early to be with the family."

Alan explained that because of the urge to build a career, people commute long distances from the suburbs to work. Seventy years ago, in Belgrade, his grandfather Emil had motored every morning in his private car to his office in the city.

They sat on the veranda overlooking the other side of the building, and he described the squirrel on the lawn below, fruit in each tiny paw, industriously eating it.

"I so love nature," said Erica. "And today, I can't see it. The orange-colored trees in autumn and the heavy lilac blooms in spring. Today, my entire world is one color. It's only in my memory that I can feel those colors. Tell me more about Nina. I wasn't much older then than she is now."

"Her latest craze is going to nursing school. She wants to be a certified nurse in a hospital."

"That's wonderful," said Erica. "She reminds me so much of Inge.

Now she wants to be a nurse."

"With her grades, she could easily get into medical school and become a doctor. It's considered a more secure profession, with an appropriate salary. I'm afraid she'll be wasted," he said.

"Let her follow her heart. If she wants to help people, that's great. Not everything can be measured in money. You see the world through glasses of career and money. See what a wonderful daughter you have. I remember the talks we had with Inge in the infirmary. I talked a lot about ideals then. About helping others when all hell was breaking loose around us."

MAČVA BATHS, AUGUST 1941

Every morning, we three and a large group of young people and adults went to work at the German military hospital. It was situated in a building used as a dormitory for the teaching college, until the German occupation. Inge was already a veteran there. A German officer had seen her resuscitate someone and took her to work there as a nurse. We cleaned houses and offices, including the toilets of the garrison district headquarters. At the end of the workday, we returned to camp at Sava, a walk of about a kilometer. We younger ones walked at the head, followed by the adults, who dragged their legs with difficulty. In between walked armed German soldiers. How enraging it was to see armed, fully equipped soldiers with the words *Gott ist mit uns* (God is with us) on their belts when their hearts were made of stone as they shoved lagging adults with their rifle butts.

These were the hot, close days of August, and the walk along the Sava took us through swarms of mosquitoes and blackflies that made us itch and scratch until we drew blood. The days at the mill and granaries seemed like the Garden of Eden in contrast to life in the camp and hard labor. Some of the young people were made to carry sacks of wheat from the mill and granaries to ships anchored not far from there at Sava Dock, providing the German forces up the Sava with wheat. One day, Ancel came to the infirmary with a bleeding cut on his face. A soldier had struck him with the butt of his rifle.

Inge disinfected the cut, carefully taping the edges together, as only she knew how to do.

Ancel told her they were carrying sacks from the mill and loading them onto barges on the river. He looked pitiful, his back hunched and his shoulders weak. How could he possibly carry a sack of wheat on those shoulders?

"We walk part of the way through shallow water to the barges," he told Inge as she wound the bandage around his forehead. "And heaven help anyone who drops a sack into the water by mistake or, according to the Germans, on purpose. They could kill for that."

He related that he'd collapsed under the weight, and the sack had fallen into the water. He was sure it was the end of him. The German soldier guarding them attacked him, screaming that it was forbidden to load wet sacks into the hold of the ship. He was sure that Ancel had done it deliberately to spoil the entire shipment. He was mad with rage, aiming his gun at him.

At that moment, said Ancel, he saw pictures of his childhood in Vienna pass before his eyes; his mother the pianist, who wanted him to be a pianist like herself and who made sure he had piano lessons and took care of his delicate fingers, now gnarled and stiff with effort. He saw the rifle butt in front of his eyes, believed his end was near. The German soldier approached, threatening that if he didn't lift the sack out of the water and take it to the pile of spoiled sacks, he'd shoot him. He tried to get up and lift the water-logged sack, now even heavier, but couldn't, and then he felt the sudden blow of the rifle butt on his forehead.

"I saw stars," he said. "Yes, actual stars, as they say. It's not just an expression," he said, looking admiringly at Inge.

Inge and I looked at him with pain and compassion. Inge checked the bandage she'd just applied to make sure it wasn't loose.

"Enough humiliation. We have to do something," said Inge, voicing what we all felt.

The young men worked hard for two nights, removing the sacks from the granaries. Ancel, who was walking around with an elegant bandage around his forehead, managed to evade heavy labor the next day and joined the line of cleaners at the barracks. In the meantime, the food supply to the camp dwindled fast; it was now virtually impossible to get bread or fresh vegetables.

One evening, as we sat in the infirmary during curfew, we longingly remembered the summer days at Kladovo, when we'd swim in the Danube, even holding swimming competitions there. A pity we couldn't find a place to cool off now as we did last year in Kladovo. When she heard this, Inge told us that not far from the barracks, on the way to the Mačva Baths, which once served as a bathing spot for residents, were pools of clean water. One day, she'd heard a couple of soldiers talking about going there to bathe.

"Why shouldn't we go there?" I asked.

"It could be dangerous," answered Inge. "If we're caught there, it would be the end of us."

I suggested we go there when the German soldiers leave.

"We could at least try," I said. "Let's go and see the place. Maybe it's worth taking a risk."

We agreed to go the following day, after finishing our work at the

German barracks.

"We have to get cleaned up after that disgusting work," said Friedl. "Every time I get there, I don't understand how I can actually do that filthy job. At first, I used to vomit every morning."

The next day, toward evening, Friedl and I went to look for the pools hidden behind the Mačva Baths. We approached the place quiet as mice, hiding behind the huge leaves of river undergrowth. We could hear the soldiers laughing and chattering. We drew closer, until we could see them. They were very close to us. One of them was humming the German tune on all German lips at the time, that song of yearning, "Lili Marlene," which every lonely soldier at the front sang to his girl waiting for him at home. Now that Café Roma had become a dim beer hall, you'd hear drunken Germans singing it.

The soldiers sitting in the pool were well-fed and overweight, their upper bodies exposed to the summer sun, red as a steak before it's placed in the hot frying pan. Metal disks on chains around their necks jiggled on their hairy chests.

The pools with their clear, clean water were very tempting. We waited until the last soldier left the place. We wanted to jump in immediately but hurried back to the camp to tell our friends. We told them how close the Germans were; although they didn't see us, they were almost close enough to touch.

The next day, we went there to bathe. The water was very pleasant, and the spot hidden among the trees was magnificent, even more beautiful than the place we'd bathed in on the Danube. We didn't know then that we only had a few days left to enjoy the beauty of the place and the fresh water. It didn't occur to us that within days the horror would increase. At least we made good use of those days, when relative quiet reigned.

One day, when we came to our private pool, we were surprised to find familiar visitors. From a distance, we could already hear Milka's voice, and when we approached, we saw that Mara and her friends from Sabac were also there. We were overjoyed. Reunited, we told them what had happened since our farewell party at Mara's house.

On a cold and misty morning on the twenty-first of August, we woke to the sound of doors slamming, shouts in German, feet dragging, and voices pleading for their lives. From the door of the hut, Inge and I watched in shock. We had occasionally hidden behind the door to avoid attracting the soldiers' attention. In the square near the well, about ten meters away, the soldiers had gathered together about thirty young men from the first two huts. Their hands were tied, and the soldiers were giving them orders. Among them were Ancel and Heini from our group, who were both trembling with cold…or fear.

A few moments later, the group disappeared with the soldiers. We sat on one of the beds, frightened to death, trying to understand what had happened. Rumors started coming in about locals shot in their homes that night in Sabac. They talked of seven or nine deaths, among them the local doctor, Bora Tiric, whom soldiers took from his home in the middle of the night and shot in the back.

When we left for work at the Sabac barracks that morning, we were afraid of what we would find. We heard bodies were lying in the street, and our hearts hammered as we approached the town with its scents of dew-wet grass and morning coolness. At the well in the little market, we saw the first body, a man lying in a pool of blood. Not far away was the body of a young man who'd been shot. As we advanced toward the German barracks, two of our young men approached us. One of them was Richart, who had always made us laugh with his *schiffsreview* sketches about camp life. He looked humiliated and wretched. His back was bent under the weight of a young man's body. His feet were tied with a rope, a long trail of blood behind them. I tried to look away so as not to see this horror, and then I saw Ancel and Heini standing next to an electric power pole opposite the entrance to the bank. Threatened by the soldier facing them, they were forced to do the unthinkable—hang the body lying at their feet from the pole. Ancel tried with all his strength to wind the rope around the pole but couldn't do it. He looked from the soldier in front of him, gun ready, to the electric power pole, and back to the lifeless body lying at his feet, as if pretending to consider how to deal with such a horrifying task. The soldiers hurried us along to the barracks.

That evening, Ancel told us about the viciousness they'd experienced. He said that the day's events had made him lose any remaining will to live. He hadn't recovered from the horror he'd been forced to carry out that morning.

"I feel dead," he said. "Hanging a dead man's body from an electric power pole is an unspeakably barbaric act."

I saw no point in raising the issue of resistance or escape. He seemed to have lost any remaining will to fight. Partisans probably wouldn't be interested in him. But Inge and I became even more determined.

The following morning, as we were going past the square, we saw a town garbage cart moving slowly, a bare, blood-stained foot sticking out. On top was another body, its hand outstretched as if asking for help. Alongside the cart walked some of our young men with shovels in their hands. The procession made its way slowly to the old graveyard, where the bodies would be buried in a common grave.

That evening, Ancel told us that what had happened two days previously was in retribution for Partisans' actions. Eleven locals were killed—Dr. Tiric and Dr. Bata Cohen and nine farmers. On the evening of August 22, unexpected visitors arrived at the camp. They were almost destitute, with only the few belongings they were allowed to bring. These were Sabac's local Jews, about sixty men and women who were in a painful physical and emotional state. They'd managed to live a rather normal life in the town and had evaded our fate until then. They were put in the fifth hut, which had been almost empty until then. We talked to some of them, and it turned out that the soldiers had robbed them of their property, and they'd even had to pay a ransom for their lives. Melamed, the tailor, arrived in a state of total exhaustion and blindness, suffering from pain in every part of his body, having been cruelly abused. He was taken to the infirmary in Sabac, where Dr. Rousseau tried in vain to lessen his pain.

DEATH AT THE BARRIER, SEPTEMBER 1941

When Alan got to Erica's room, he was surprised to find her bed empty. He hurried to find the nurse. When she saw his worried look, she reassured him.

"Don't worry. She's been taken for an ultrasound. The machine is only free in the evenings. But good that you came—no need to wait," she said. "Could you answer a few questions for me?"

"I'm not family," said Alan. "Just writing a book about her. I don't understand. Don't you have any details about her?"

"Of course we do, but I wanted to ask some more questions. I thought you were the son she spoke of."

"I didn't know she had a son."

"I must have made a mistake. I'm sorry. Come back tomorrow, all right?"

That night, he listened to recordings he'd typed out and even began to see how he could organize them.

The following day, he returned to ask after her. He found her in her usual place next to her bed, ready to go for a walk. In reference to the previous day's test, she said only that there'd been concern over a possible tumor, but that everything was fine.

"What does 'everything's fine' actually mean?" quipped Erica.

"What's there to check? If the time has come to go, then that's all there is to it. One has to know when to leave. This is a time for young people."

"Why talk about death?" said Alan. "Look at you. I wish many more people your age were in your position."

"Now, that's enough! Looks to me as if I won't be allowed to go in peace. Tell me, did I ever tell you about Nada? I met her at a field hospital near Münster. What a brave young woman."

"You're brave too," said Alan, pressing Record.

"Not brave enough," she said. "My actions were always based on convenience, even when I finally escaped."

***

Friedl, myself, and a few other girls were sent to sew and iron soldiers' uniforms. At least we didn't have to walk every morning to the German soldiers' filthy barracks, or crouch over tubs of soapy water, constantly scrubbing and rubbing at their bedclothes. When I saw Chava's hands, she was from the Mizrahi hut, they were red and chapped so badly, the flesh was almost exposed, and I realized that we were fortunate. One day, Chava said she didn't have the strength to wash clothes anymore, that the soap made her hands peel, and one of the soldiers beat her. Inge joined us for a day one week after she persuaded her superiors that she should occasionally spend one day in camp in order to help the increasing number of soldiers there.

The washing was done mainly near the river bank. Soldiers on guard duty would sometimes walk away to the teapots they got from the military kitchen. I thought that if I had the courage, I'd try to run.

You would have to exploit the time the soldiers took to get to the pots. I even discovered a place in the fence that seemed hidden behind some trees. Once, when I went with Inge to the toilet, we crouched in our cubicles and I told her quietly that we ought to think about how to escape. I thought the no-return point had come, and if we waited any longer, we wouldn't be able to escape, or worse still, we'd die there.

A few days later, at the beginning of September, close to noon, several rounds were fired from a machine gun. Inge, who was working with us that day in the sewing hall, hurried in the direction of the fence. It was clear to us all that someone had tried to escape. I stayed glued to my seat. I didn't want to see the horrors I'd witnessed two weeks before. But it quickly became apparent that I wouldn't be able to avoid the terrible scenes of death. Inge and three men ran toward the fence. They returned in alarm within a few minutes and told us that two of the washer women, Rita and Chava, had been shot by guards stationed at a low point of the fence. Chava's body was wrapped in blankets and brought to our hut. Inge murmured that nothing could be done to help her. She was sprayed with bullets, her hands still grasping the barbed wire.

***

Fear of reprisals increased as a result of the escape attempt, and in the meantime, we heard rumors of special reprisal squads who'd arrived from France. When we heard machine-gun fire on the northern border of Sabac, in the direction of Bara, we realized they were already here. For two days, we heard non-stop firing in the Mačva area. They indiscriminately shot farmers, women, and children. We sat shivering with terror in our huts, but not for long. Even as we sat huddled in fear, the thud of boots on the asphalt was heard outside. The camp paths and square quickly filled up with scores of soldiers in green uniforms, square backpacks on their backs, as if they'd all been manufactured by one machine. Among them, several *Volksdeutsche* were rushing about with black swastikas on white sleeves, as well as about five Jewish prisoners who did their work faithfully. They took us from the huts under pretext of a headcount. An order was given to take a pile of logs from the fence to build another hut. They chose a group of about ten young men and ordered them to run with the logs on their shoulders to the entrance gate about a hundred and fifty meters away and back again—one log between every two men. And then they sent another group of men on the same mission. Ancel and Yanek were in the third group. My heart ached for Ancel, whose shoulders were so frail they couldn't carry the heavy log, and every time he tried to raise it, he fell to the ground. The soldier opposite him gave him a cruel look and aimed the rifle at him. Yanek suddenly volunteered to help him. He was from the Hashomer Hatzair group, a large man known to be one of the strongest men in the transport, with the softest, most sensitive heart. He easily raised the log, but the German soldier stubbornly demanded that Yanek put the log on Ancel's shoulder.

Ancel collapsed under the burden, and the soldier forbade Yanek to help him. Yanek swiftly turned toward the soldier and hit him hard on the elbow. The soldier collapsed with a cry.

Two soldiers standing not far away hurried to seize Yanek. He fought them bravely until a revolver shot was heard and he fell. A

German officer had shot him once in the chest.

The torture went on for hours. We girls were given cleaning tasks in the yards between the huts and in the toilets. The men were made to run to and fro with logs on their shoulders, while German soldiers threatened them with guns and batons.

Later, the men from Sabac arrived with the gypsies, all of them marching in the direction of our camp. They joined the Jewish men there, who were made to run at the head of the line, followed by the gypsies and local men. To make things even harder, the Germans added various loads onto the backs of the Jews; heavy backpacks, they didn't know what was in them. Ancel, among those running at the head, collapsed under the heavy load and was forced to get up and continue. He glanced fearfully at the German soldier standing over him, tried to get up, but fell again. The German kicked him and he fell, the heavy backpack forcing him to the ground. The soldier hit him in the face with his rifle butt. Blood covered his face. Among the Jews and locals from Sabac were others who collapsed and fell like Ancel. Others continued at a walk. The bloody march continued for twenty-three kilometers as far as Jarak; constantly in the background, they could hear machine guns firing from Bara.

***

Alan arrived for his meeting with Erica and was surprised to find her in a good mood. She even asked him to read to her from a volume of poems on her cabinet. On its faded jacket were the words *Wandering,*

Hermann Hesse,[25] 1941.

"Instead of my talking all the time and you recording me, today I want to indulge myself a little and listen to my favorite poems."

"No problem. Today is your special day. You decide and I'll do whatever you say."

"In that case, please open the book at page 116 and read the entire poem," she handed him the crumbling book.

Alan read the English translation of the poem:

> *As every flower fades and as all youth*
> *Departs, so life at every stage,*
> *So every virtue, so our grasp of truth,*
> *Blooms in its day and may not last forever.*
> *Since life may summon us at every age*
> *Be ready, heart, for parting, new endeavor,*
> *Be ready bravely and without remorse*
> *To find new light that old ties cannot give.*
> *In all beginnings dwells a magic force*
> *For guarding us and helping us to live.*
> *Serenely let us move to distant places*
> *And let no sentiments of home detain us.*

"Isn't that wonderful?" she asked at the end of the first stanza. "Do you

---

25 Hermann Hesse (1877–1962) was a writer, poet, and German philosopher who won the Nobel Prize in Literature. Because of his resistance to the Nazis, he emigrated to Switzerland in 1943, where he died. The poem which is cited in the next lines is Stages from the book Wandering.

have any idea how often I was in that situation of dying and rebirth?"
she mused. "But today, I know there won't be another stage of rebirth
for me. I'm beyond old age now. Look at me. It isn't right that I should
have to stay here and see this crazy world of yours. Do something."

"Is it so bad that you don't want to live?"

"Really, Alan, someone in my position no longer enjoys very much.
This is not living."

After he finished and closed the book, she asked him to take her to
the veranda and tell her if there was anything interesting there. At first,
everything looked the same, but then he saw a blue bird standing by
itself on a branch where a pair of bright blue songbirds usually stood,
and which he described to Erica. They're always together, on the same
bare branch, like a pair of lovers. But today only one of them is there.
Alan told Erica about the pair that had apparently been separated.

"Maybe she found a male bird who sings more beautifully," he said.

But she was more optimistic.

"Maybe they finished building the nest, and now she's sitting on her
eggs. He's probably watching the nest to make sure she isn't in danger.
It reminds me of the time I was a lookout for a Partisan unit. I'd often
watch headquarters to make sure no enemy soldiers were nearby, putting us at risk."

"Last time you began telling me about Nada," he reminded her. "Do
you want to continue? You said it wasn't time yet. Maybe the time has
come," he said and switched on the recorder.

ESCAPE, SEPTEMBER 1941

Toward the end of September, we heard rumors that the Partisans were very close and planning to take Sabac. Preparations for the Partisan attack were in full swing. The mayor supplied sand that was piled up at the entrances to buildings, and we were sent to fill sacks with sand for raised walls at the entrances.

Inge and I had already decided that if the Partisans entered the town, we'd find a way to join them. In the morning, I arranged with Inge to meet her at the entrance to Mara's house at five thirty that evening. Inge went as usual to work at the hospital in the seminar building, and I volunteered to go out with the men to clean the barracks. I told Friedl we wouldn't be returning, so she'd understand we were trying to escape and wouldn't tell anyone. After work, we were on our way back to the camp when shooting came from the direction of Bara. A commotion broke out, and the German guards ran for cover. I took the opportunity. As the firing increased and everyone hid behind the sack barriers, I ran alongside the barrier. I realized that I was very close to Mara's house; I remembered its location—Sixteen Karlova. I ran, panting all the way, counting the entrances that were barely recognizable behind the sand barriers. I got to number fourteen; *it's the next house*, I said to myself. Mara let me in quickly, asking in alarm, "What are you doing here? They'll catch you. The minute the firing stops, the guards will come after you like madmen. They won't give up on anyone."

We stood there for a few minutes, hiding behind the sand barrier. The sounds of firing only increased. Suddenly, we heard explosions. Maybe they were really close now. Mara suggested I hide in her house that night. I told her Inge would be coming later on. Mara said she'd hide us in the attic, but that we were responsible for our own safety. I told her about our plan to join the Partisans if they reached the town, that we'd look for an opportunity to offer our help, and if they agreed, we'd escape with them to the forest under cover of the upheaval. Mara looked at me with respect, saying I was doing something very brave, but she wouldn't do it. The plan seemed like a fantasy to her.

She took me up to the attic, and we sat there on a mattress. There was no bed there, because the wooden ceiling was very low. I told her how in the movement in Vienna, and later on at the ice dock at Kladovo, I learned a bit about self-protection and survival, and now it was time to act. I was emotionally ready for anything. Even losing my life in order to put an end to the daily humiliation and pain. Mara said she understood. But she had to take care of her little brother and her parents, and she wouldn't dream of leaving them in all this unrest.

At five thirty, three consecutive knocks followed by one more were heard at the door.

"That's our signal," I said. "It's Inge."

Mara went down to let her in and she entered, red-faced and panting.

"What happened? Did they discover you?" I asked with concern.

"No," she said. "I ran between the bullets. They say the Partisans are really close."

The three of us sat on the mattress. Mara asked what our plan was, because clearly, we couldn't hide there for long.

"As soon as the Partisans arrive, we'll join them," I said.

"That could be tonight, or tomorrow morning," said Inge. "I can help them with the wounded. They probably need someone like me."

"And I'll say I know how to throw a grenade, which is true. We were taught. They even brought a practice grenade," I said.

"They're not real Partisans," said Mara. "The Partisans are still getting organized. Those are Četnici Partisans, Serbian nationalists, who've been wandering Serbia since the last war. They're very cruel. And they hate the communists most of all. They'll want to kill them no matter the price. But right now, it doesn't matter. The most important thing is for someone to liberate the town. What's happening now is no life." She sighed deeply. "Just look at what's happened to my beloved town. Now it's become a war zone, and residents who used to be happy and welcoming stay off the streets, and all the houses are surrounded by barbed wire and sand sacks," she said sadly.

"Lucky you came," she said, meaning the Viennese transport Jews. "Lucky you came and managed in such a short time to contribute so much to that joy of life, with all your operettas in the lobby of Hotel Paris and the wonderful sounds of Freddie's saxophone, or Little Fritz's harmonica. And all the readers that suddenly visited the library, raising morale and bringing a sense of openness to the town. And see what's happened since that damned invasion. The whole town is full of soldiers in uniform, and they walk about the fences and walls of sand sacks with eyes full of hatred. I miss the train station we once saw as a link to the big world, and now that too goes nowhere."

We listened to Mara, silent and nodding.

"It's sad for us, too, to see the town full of German soldiers," said Inge. "But it hurts me more to see my young friends losing their best years in such a hard life of humiliation and contempt, and every passing day means having to be grateful you're still alive."

Mara suddenly reminded us that they hadn't celebrated the Mala Gospojina Festival in September as they usually did, with a festive meal of beans and a pot of sheep ribs, with apple strudel for dessert, and other tasty delicacies. I remembered my mother's hot apple strudel fragrant with cinnamon. Now we could only dream of such things. There hadn't been a fair that year either. The Sabac Fair was famous throughout the region. Carts of sheep and piglets came from all over to the main square, and the shrieks of pigs could be heard from far away.

Mara continued to yearn and reminisce, and only late that night did she go down to sleep with her parents and little brother.

I didn't really sleep that night. Echoes of explosions constantly drew nearer. At dawn, the sound of an explosion was heard very nearby. I got up in alarm, but Inge and Mara continued to sleep. Mara's parents and little brother went down to the cellar for greater safety. Outside were sounds of shooting and German soldiers running. I didn't know if they were in pursuit or running away, because I could also hear Serbian-Croatian voices. I was thirsty and hungry. I hadn't eaten anything since the previous afternoon. Finally, when I saw that no one was coming up, I went quietly down into the kitchen; tiptoeing to the sink, I gently opened the faucet, bent, and drank deeply, taking care not to make any swallowing sounds. There were two slices of bread on the table—one for me and one for Inge. I began to go back upstairs, careful to make no sound. At that moment, the sound of a machine gun was heard, a long ominous rattle. Inge woke up.

At noon, Musha came running over. Mara cautiously opened the door. Musha came in agitatedly and told them that the Germans had entered their home and taken her brother away. She'd run after them, screaming to let him go, but they'd aimed a gun at her and she'd panicked and fled. On the way, she'd seen Nicola and Laza being led away with other gypsies. They were all terrified. Nicola's head, usually held high, the joker of the group, was now bowed. Finally, a truck arrived and they were loaded on.

Musha also told us she'd heard that reinforcements of hundreds of German soldiers were being sent in from nearby Člának. Mara was afraid and told her parents to go back downstairs, that she would prepare some sandwiches. I helped her and made one for myself.

I waited impatiently for my fateful moment, the arrival of the Partisans who'd liberate us. Would I manage to join them or not? And what could I offer them? Nothing at that moment. I didn't even have a weapon.

In the meantime, the attackers' firing grew less. Mara's parents came upstairs again that evening. They thought maybe the danger had passed and decided to sleep in their beds that night. I returned to my hiding place and must have fallen asleep.

Toward morning, loud kicks and shouts in German were heard at the door. The German reinforcements appeared to have arrived. I lay terrified, my whole body trembling. Instead of the Partisans, German soldiers had arrived. My plan had failed, I thought. I lay beside Inge, and we clung soundlessly to one another. Burying our heads in the pillow, we barely breathed.

A tremendous noise was heard as someone broke down the door. The soldiers burst into the house and took Mara's father by force. The father, dressed only in his underwear, was begging for his life and trying to protect his face from the threat of blows from the soldier's baton. Zanek, Mara's brother, who was still in bed and in his pajamas, was taken by force by another soldier, his hands bent behind his back. Inge and I peeped out through the curtain covering the attic window. We saw Mara running after them and screaming, "Leave him alone. He's still a child. He hasn't done anything."

But the soldiers ignored her screams and took her brother and father out into the cold, mist-covered street. They stood there with other men and many boys in their underwear or pajamas, their teeth chattering. They were given the order to move, and the entire line made its way toward the school.

We continued to hide until after the Germans had gone. At noon, we heard the sound of nearby drums. Mara explained that this meant there was a decree from the municipality. She translated for us, "All men from the ages of fourteen to seventy must leave their houses with enough food for two days. Anyone caught in his house two hours after this decree will be shot."

Immediately afterward, we heard a nearby explosion, and shortly after that, machine-gun fire, and shouts in Serbo-Croatian. "We're coming in! Partisans!" A moment later, they were inside the house and sounds of firing were heard.

"Come on," Inge pulled my hand. "Let's offer to help."

We quickly went down. There, we found two young men who were armed, with helmets on their heads, but not green like the Germans. They were so busy they didn't even notice us, until Inge tapped one on his shoulder and said in halting Serbo-Croatian that we wanted to help them.

"Get back," he yelled. "You could get hurt."

Shots were suddenly fired in our direction. The two Partisans took cover behind the sand sacks and held their fire a moment. We heard running outside. The thuds on the asphalt identified them as German soldiers. A moment later we saw them. Two soldiers stood carefully examining the new position they'd taken. In the time it took to look for the source of the fire, one of the Partisans shot a quick round at them. One fell, and the other immediately turned and fired indiscriminately. We felt the bullets go past us and hid behind the sand sacks. Suddenly, one of the young men fell with a shout. The second returned long bursts of fire, and then everything went quiet. Inge knelt beside the wounded man and skillfully examined his leg. He groaned in pain. Drops of sweat gathered on his forehead. She rolled up his trousers. Blood poured from his shattered leg. Inge took my hand, clenched it, and placed it on his groin. "Press hard inward," she ordered. "It will stop the bleeding." She took a strip of black rubber from her first-aid bag that was always with her and began to wind it around his thigh, above the bleeding wound. Once she'd tied it tight enough, she ordered me to release the pressure slowly and got up to go to the sink.

At that moment, Mara arrived with tears in her eyes. "They took

Father and Zanek," she said, shrinking back when she saw the wounded man. Inge just had time to fill a glass of water for him and hold it to his lips before the firing started again. The second man, who'd stayed hidden all that time behind the sand sacks, knelt beside his friend, stroked his face, and said to us, "Look after Pavel. He's my best friend. I'm going to run forward so as not to lose the other fighters."

This was the moment I'd been waiting for. The time had come.

"I'm coming with you," I said at once. "I'll take Pavel's rifle. I know how to use one."

"No, not the gun. But take two grenades. Do you know how to use a grenade?" he asked, quickly opening his friend's weapon belt.

"You go," said Inge. "Can't leave someone who's wounded."

Armed with two grenades, I joined the Partisan, whose name was Peter, and together we slipped away among the bullets.

"The goal is City Hall. You know how to do it?" he asked, as he scanned our new position.

"Of course," I said confidently. "Follow me."

I never saw Inge again. That first week, I thought she'd come after me, but I quickly realized her devotion would never let her leave.

***

Alan had a very pressured week at work. Rachel was busy with the renovation of the kitchen, and whenever she could, she took him with her to various related craftsmen. He was stressed with work, and Rachel was frustrated by his lack of involvement in the home and family. He spent the small hours of the night going through Erica's recordings.

"I'll just finish getting all the material together," he told his wife one day, when she protested. "It's really important. I have to hurry. She isn't well, and apart from that, she needs me. Most of the time, she has nobody, and at least I'm there two hours a week."

When he arrived on Monday at the usual hour, standing next to her bed he saw a woman with a little girl. Erica's daughter was glad to see him and thanked him for his visits from the bottom of her heart.

"I wish I could come more often," he said. "But I have work and family, which limits me."

"It's very hard for me too," she responded. "I live far away and have to fly, and it's so expensive. I'll just say goodbye to Mother. Will you walk me to the elevator?"

"Bye, Grandma," her granddaughter approached and kissed Erica. "Feel better."

Alan accompanied her daughter and granddaughter to the elevator.

"You know that her situation has grown worse?" she said. "The hospital called me to say I should come and see her."

"If it was so bad, they'd have moved her from here by now."

"They explained to me about the markers that indicate the progression of the illness," she said, pressing the elevator button.

"I'm sorry to hear that. But sometimes, you know, even despite the progression, she might live for another year or more."

"Anyway, you are truly an angel. What you are doing is sacred work. I am so grateful," she said as the elevator arrived.

When he got back to Erica's room, she made a dismissive gesture with her hand.

"Oy, children, children…" She sighed.

"What's so bad about children?" he asked her.

"Just as well I don't have to rely on them. Life has taught me not to rely on anyone."

"What about friends?" He turned on the recorder and let her continue her story.

THE RAILWAY BRIDGE, OCTOBER 1941

Once we'd taken up position at City Hall, we tried to locate the source of the shooting, and at that point, the German reinforcements arrived. Scores of armed combat troops poured into town, on their backs were square backpacks with the swastika. We realized that the battle was lost and tried to retreat. Each time a small Partisan unit made an attempt to escape among the walls and retreat, Peter and I covered them, firing from the City Hall veranda. When the Germans surrounded City Hall, we decided to retreat and try and join the base regiment.

At first, I didn't realize what I'd gotten myself into. I thought I'd joined Tito's Partisans, until I recalled what Mara told us about Četnici Partisans. When we reached the regiment's base in the forest, I understood that they were indeed Četnici Partisans, who were collaborating with the Partisans. It didn't bother me. Peter treated me well and took care of all my needs. I didn't believe we'd get to the base. We joined up with ten other fighters who'd escaped from Sabac when the German reinforcements arrived.

The walk was very hard. I didn't have comfortable shoes and was wearing the refugee clothing we'd worn at camp in Sabac; I looked like a ragdoll. When we reached the base, Peter brought me some clothes. Navigating to the base wasn't easy. Fortunately, we had Goran with us; he had a map, and we all followed him. On the way, we avoided German ambushes. When darkness fell, we took shelter under a bridge and continued walking early the next morning. After a day's hike, we came, exhausted, to the regiment. Peter was immediately called to make his report to the intelligence officer. I was sent to do a shift in one of the improvised hospital tents at the edge of the camp. There, I met Jelka Shavnich[26] for the first time. She was in charge of instructing us in methods of first aid. She'd arrived as a nurse only a week before me. Jelka was abundantly motivated. She was raised in Hashomer Hatzair in Zagreb and joined Tito's Partisans at the end of August. The regiment was in the process of getting organized and was joined by young people who'd heard about Čiča's heroism. He was a fighter who became a legend in his own time. We very quickly became good friends. She filled the empty space Inge had left but was far more idealistic than Inge. As a communist, she was very resentful of Četnici Partisans. We spoke intimately, and she told me a great deal about herself and her childhood in Zagreb.

Peter met me the following day when I was in the middle of a mouth-to-mouth resuscitation lesson with Jelka. He enthusiastically told me about an ambush planned for two days' time near Valjevo and asked if I wanted to go along.

He also told me about his meeting with regiment commander Čiča,

---

26 A daring fighter and nurse who saved many people. She fought in Čiča's regiment and was killed in March 1942 when a Četnici group surprised the regiment camp. Characteristically, Jelka grabbed her gun in one hand and her first-aid bag in the other and ran to the wounded. While helping them, she was hit in the shoulder and stomach.

known as the "old man from the Romanian mountains,"[27] the stories of his heroism well-known among the Partisans.

"No bullet could touch him," enthused Peter. "This evening, he wants to get all the regiment fighters together to report our achievements and future plans."

I told him I preferred to participate in smaller operations until I felt more experienced as a nurse. Jelka impressed me with her composure and the knowledge she passed on to us. To this day, I remember her quick hands sewing up a deep cut with the skill of any surgeon I met here later on in my work at Mount Sinai Hospital. Not even the whistle of nearby bullets disturbed her. After several days of instruction, I became her assistant. But I didn't have much time to get organized. I participated in all kinds of small operations not far from the camp.

The high point was the blowing up of the bridge of the train from Nis to Belgrade, planned for the end of October. We were seven fighters and the regiment commander himself. It was then I saw what a hero he really was. The evening before, he called us to his tent and explained the details of the operation. The cargo train carrying food and equipment for the German army in the north would go over the bridge just after four in the morning, but we would get there three hours before in order to quietly prepare the bomb.

He showed us the travel route on a map, using a sharpened stick to

---

27 Slaviša Vajner Čiča, born in 1903, son of a poor Jewish family, was the popular commander of a Romanian Partisan unit, a member of the Yugoslavian Communist Party, and a hero of the Bosnian uprising. He was killed in the struggle against the Germans in 1942. Vajner Čiča, a legend in his lifetime, was declared national hero of the Yugoslavian people in November 1944.

point out the starting point, Nis in the south, and the twisting route in the direction of Belgrade and from there to Slovenia. We had to sabotage the track, destroy the carriages and engine, disconnect telegraph and telephone lines, and of course, kill as many of the German enemy as we could.

The excitement was enormous. It was the first time I'd participated in an operation of this kind. The night was quiet and cold, and apart from the barking of a dog in a nearby village, there was complete silence. We walked quietly in the direction of the bridge. I carried the first-aid bag, two grenades, and a revolver. I feared unexpected fire, but most of all, my first test as a nurse under fire. Would I be able to do my job if the life of a young man was my responsibility? Would I be nervous; would my hands tremble if I had to stop the flow of blood? We were filled with pride and the desire for revenge.

It was then we caught the gypsy in the forest. He told us everything with terrified eyes. At first, we thought he was making up the story. How could we believe that they'd lined up fifty people and shot them in the back of the neck? And then fifty more, and fifty more after that. All this took place at Zasavica, not far from the camp at Sabac, where we lived together with the Jews from Sabac. We swore to avenge the blood of our brothers, crying to us from the earth and igniting the spirit of battle in us. All the gypsy knew was that German soldiers had come to the Senjak camp near Sabac and taken about a hundred gypsies for burial work.

We sat around him, and Čiča managed to get the whole horrifying story from him. I didn't connect the murder with our group at all. The gypsy told us that many gypsies were at the slaughter. I didn't know what happened to Ancel, Inge, Friedl, and our other friends. Were they among the murdered?

Early in the morning, the German soldiers had woken them with shouts, hurrying them to work. They didn't yet understand what kind of work, because they sometimes went out to do agricultural work for farmers in the area. It was only when they got to the maize field that they were told it was digging work. They were ordered to dig a long, wide ditch without knowing what it was for.

In the meantime, trucks with Jewish and gypsy prisoners arrived from the camp on the Sava. They were taken off the trucks, put in three lines, and made to join in the work. When the ditch was longer than two hundred meters, the soldiers shouted at them to widen it to two meters and make it deeper. A German officer walked up and down above them all the time, occasionally looking with dissatisfaction at the ditch. When the ditch was two and a half meters deep, he ordered the soldiers to drive stakes into the mounds of earth on one side of the ditch, at a distance of four meters from each other.

At this point, the gypsies from the Senjak camp were ordered to go and wait by the trucks. When they were some distance away, the soldiers led the Jewish and gypsy prisoners from the camp up to the ditch. Their hands were tied behind their backs, and they were positioned with their legs slightly apart, each one opposite a stake exactly between their legs, their faces to the yawning ditch underneath them. Once the prisoners were in a straight line, the shooters were called to stand behind them. The order "fire" was answered by a burst of gunfire, and the line of prisoners collapsed to the earth. The gypsies at the trucks were then called to continue their labor and throw the bodies into the ditch.

It was only a few days later that we got the terrible news. Almost all the men from the Kladovo transport and many gypsies were executed above the ditch dug by friends of the gypsy they'd caught. The murder was in retaliation for the killing of twenty-one German soldiers ambushed by Serbian Partisans near the town of Topola.[28] This was immediately followed by a decree whereby, for every German soldier killed, a hundred Jews would be killed as punishment.

Cold swept through my warm clothes. The gypsy's story about the three days of slaughter tormented me. I was ready to explode the grenade on my body in order to avenge the deaths of my people. But we had to complete our operation quietly and cause as many losses as possible for the other side and send that train into the gaping abyss under the bridge. We made our way stealthily through the terraced vegetation that smelled of fungus and leaves. Suddenly, in the pale moonlight, I saw the shining train tracks twisting below us like a river. But the bridge was still some distance away. The first-aid bag weighed heavily on my shoulders, swaying on my hips. We climbed up a steep hill, and I breathed deeply with the effort. When we reached the top, we saw the deep valley from the other side and the bridge on its huge pillars connecting our hill with the next. One of the young men participating in the operation was Lazo from Belgrade, who'd been trained as a saboteur. He showed incredible courage. We crouched

---

28 Ambush at Topola. On October 2, the Partisans won a victory against Wehrmacht soldiers near the town Topola, far away from Sabac. Twenty-one soldiers were killed by Partisan fire. This stinging failure persuaded the German General Böhme to order Turner, head of the German Administration in Serbia, to hand over 2,100 Jewish prisoners from the camps at Sabac and Belgrade for reprisal actions in response to the blow they'd received.

down quietly, waiting for Lazo and the commander to finish preparing the bomb and leave for the appointed place to set it on the bridge. Unease and fear filled my mind. What if the train came early and crossed the bridge while they were still on it? They'd have nowhere to run; the bridge was narrow. What if we were all seen by a German patrol guarding the bridge? Čiča and Lazo laid the bomb and returned with the electric cable to our hiding place behind the hills. Iche, a nice young man from Hashomer Hatzair in Belgrade, crawled on his stomach up to the track and placed his ear to the ground to hear if the train was near. He lay there listening for about a minute and then stood up. "It'll be here any minute."

Like a serpent with an eye of fire, the train zigzagged through the valley toward us. We heard its snorts and saw the smoke rising from its chimney into the pale night sky. And now it was passing above us as we lay motionless, waiting for the last of the carriages to gain the bridge, and then an explosion was heard, and an enormous jet of fire rose into the sky. A series of further explosions was heard, probably from explosives on the train, and the carriages fell into the valley like a toy train, some still attached to each other, hanging for a moment between sky and earth. Screams of alarm and fear were heard, and then the groans of the wounded. None of our people were hurt. The commander looked through the binoculars and commented, "A huge success. Everything collapsed. No need to open fire."

***

When Alan returned home on the train that evening, he was consumed by Erica's story about the slaughter at the maize field. He continued to envision the picture of the Jews, old people in city clothes, as described by the gypsy caught by the Partisans. How they stood on the edge of the ditch, when German soldiers, who'd gone by with a blanket collecting all their valuables just a moment before, had shot them. Did they know these were their last moments? Did they realize that in a second they'd drop dead into the ditch in front of them?

BETH ISRAEL, JANUARY 2002

On Monday morning, a day before their usual meeting, Alan received a call from the hospital. Erica had been transferred to the oncology ward at Beth Israel Hospital. Her condition had deteriorated. He left the office early that day and hurried to the hospital. When he asked the nurse at reception where Erica was, he suddenly remembered that he didn't know her surname. Fortunately, the nurse helped him.

"Mrs. Grinberg, she's at the end of the corridor on the left. Are you her son?"

Again, he felt uncomfortable, and, fearing they might not let him see her, he almost answered in the affirmative.

"No, but I am very close to her," he said after a brief pause. "She hasn't any family in town."

"That's all right, just don't stay too long. She's just had a treatment."

"What treatment?" he asked worriedly.

"Chemotherapy. It leaves her very weak. Didn't you know?"

"She didn't say a word to me," he said, embarrassed by her not telling him. "How long has she known?"

"Several months now."

When he sat down next to her and saw the IV in her arm, he realized that she probably didn't have long to live. He was suddenly anxious at the thought she might not have time to tell him the story of her war from the Partisan lines. He was angry with himself for being bothered by that now—her story instead of her condition, and he looked at her with concern.

"Hi, Alan," her voice was peaceful when she opened her kind eyes.

"Hi, Erica. How are you?" he asked, continuing, "This how you treat a friend, by not telling me?"

"What's there to tell?" She played innocent, "Old woman with cancer. That's the whole story."

"Yes. But don't you think you could have told me? I feel close to you, a member of the family, and here you are, hiding something so serious from me."

He remembered he shouldn't be upsetting her, that she was weak after the treatment.

"I didn't want to make an issue of it."

The nurse came in to check the drip.

"Your friend is a brave and rather odd woman," said the nurse quietly, so that Erica wouldn't hear. "Better you let her rest today. It's best you talk to her two days after her treatment."

"What about your daughter? Is she not coming?" he asked.

"She doesn't know I'm here," said Erica. "No point in adding to her burden."

When he left, he promised to come the following day.

On his way home at rush hour, he stood crowded with everyone else on the train, hoping that on Forty-Second Street, many of them would get off and he'd be able to sit comfortably. He promised himself that the next day he'd talk to Erica about the idea of writing a book about the whole affair. He had to confide in her. After all, he'd promised not to do anything without her consent. He had to get her consent, while she was still lucid.

The next day, she looked a lot better. When she heard about the idea of his writing a book, her only regret was that she'd not be able to read it.

"And you won't be able to read it to me," she said. "Because you won't have anyone to read to. But I would like to say that your visits have given me great pleasure. At least I'll know that I am leaving a good world with people like you and Nina in it."

"So you are okay with my publishing your story!"

"Your curiosity made me revive that period in my mind. I summed up a period of my life that is considered beautiful in terms of age—but for me and my generation in Europe, it was traumatic."

"I hoped to hear about my family, and I did, but I was also given the fascinating and sad story of everything that happened in Sabac and the heroism of the Partisans."

"Yes. I'm sorry I couldn't give you more details about your family. Only about Inge, and she, too, went in the end, like all the women, on the death march to Sajmište. As you know, no one came back from Sajmište to tell the story."

"Is there no written material about what happened there? A diary? Letters?"

"You know, come to think of it… I remember now that there were letters…"

"What letters?"

He pressed Record and Erica continued her story in her steady, calm voice.

***

Around June, a Partisan from Belgrade joined us. She worked as a nurse at the Christian hospital there, and she told us about two friends who'd received letters from a common friend at Sajmište. Her friend was also a nurse. Her name was Hilda, Hilda Dajč, I think. What was incredible was that she wasn't forced to go there. She volunteered, went willingly. Her father was highly respected in the community, and the Germans wanted him to be their liaison person with the Jews. That's why they didn't send the family to Sajmište like the rest of the Jewish families in December 1941.

They didn't yet know what was going to happen there, but Hilda Dajč wanted to go and help her people in that terrible place. But after she left, the noose only tightened, until the way out was blocked.

The friend from Belgrade, I've forgotten her name, joined us in June, after Jelka was killed in our terrible battle with the Četnics, and we urgently needed another nurse for the regiment. We became friends. She told me that some of Hilda's letters got through to her at great risk. At first, she sent a letter when she arrived—the Germans weren't yet reluctant to allow letters out. But from January to February 1942, when they started to implement their plan to destroy the camp, anyone caught with a letter was hanged. Hilda made a huge effort to tell her close friends what happened to her. They were studying at Belgrade University. Find those letters. She probably mentions people's names, including Inge, because they apparently worked in the same infirmary.

PART III

SAJMIŠTE

Belgrade, February 2002

Two months had gone by since Erica's death. Alan had listened to her story for months and now knew it as well as he knew his father's story. He felt close to her, as if he were part of her family. Her death left a great void in his heart. He and Nina were at the funeral, together with her daughter and some other close friends. Not many attended. Most of her acquaintances and friends had already died.

Throughout this time, her voice echoed in his mind, telling him to look for Hilda Dajč's letters.

He approached the Holocaust Archives in Belgrade, but the impression he got from their response was that he could expect nothing from them.

He contacted the Holocaust Museum in Belgrade. He wrote, telling them he was looking for material on Belgrade Jewry during the war, between the years 1941 and 1942. Apparently, they did not give out information over the phone or by mail to strangers, and he would have to go to the archives himself. He spoke to a pleasant, kind employee called Barbara, who called back with the news that she had information on Hilda Dajč, but that he would have to come to the archives and sign papers before he could see it.

Alan's heart beat hard as he mounted the steps. He was about to meet Barbara in her office. She had done so much for him, without even knowing him. She was glad to help and promised to give him access to any material she had. Recently, Alan hadn't been able to take leave, and so he used the long weekend of their wedding anniversary in February. Rachel had planned a little holiday that weekend. She didn't understand why it was so urgent for him to travel to Belgrade when at long last they had an opportunity to spend some time together, skiing in Denver with friends. But work constraints enabled him to go to Belgrade only on these dates.

When he reached Belgrade after a stop in Zurich, the city seemed to him to have stood still. Seven years had gone by since the Dayton Agreement, but in his mind, he could hear the Allied planes diving to bomb again. As the taxi drove through the main streets of the city, he saw walls damaged by machine-gun fire. The wide streets seemed abandoned. There were so few cars, and these were from the seventies and eighties, which gave the place the appearance of a city living in the past, or which had lost its will to live.

Barbara was small and plump, very different from how he'd imagined her in their phone conversations. After a few polite words about the flight and the journey, she took him to the coffee corner and made them both coffee.

The archives were beautifully organized, and a caring and responsible hand was clearly evident. They paced the length of walls heavy with documents, while Barbara explained to which periods and geo-graphical regions they all belonged. When they reached the year 1942, the Jewish camp at the Sajmište exhibition grounds, Alan's heart was beating very fast. Together, they examined documents and photo-graphs. Almost six thousand Jews and gypsies were murdered there in the three months between March and May of 1942, said Barbara, showing him a picture of the Saurer *polizei*. There were two of them. The names of the drivers were also known: Getz and Majer. Just as he was despairing at the sheer quantity of documents on the Sajmište wall, Alan was surprised to find a notebook that looked rather like a school exercise book. The binding was stained, nothing was written on it, and the pages were gnawed at the corners. Inside the notebook, in gothic letters, was the name:

Inge Müller

Block 14A

February–April 1942

Next to the notebook, he found a file with the following:

Hilda Dajč

Letters to Nada and Marianna

BLOCK 14 A, FEBRUARY–APRIL 1942

February 10

I'm sitting on my rickety wooden bunk in the corner of Block 14 A, on a thin layer of damp straw to soften the hard, wooden surface. Luckily for me, my bunk is in the corner, so I have a little more privacy than the other girls. It's two thirty at night. I've just finished my night shift. All day on my feet and a night shift too. I share my shifts with my good friend Hilda, and Matilda, our pharmacist. Every night, something unexpected happens; no night goes by without drama. Sometimes it's anxiety or the night fears of women or children. How could there not be after all the terrible things we went through on the way here? Just that interminable walk through muddy snow, our worn-out shoes soaked in icy water, was enough to drive you mad. How much can a human being take?

That march finally persuaded me that there is no limit to the body's endurance. And today, I am even more certain that women have more stamina than men.

Tonight, I was called to Block 7. Someone was screaming there as if she was being slaughtered. I could hear her screaming before I even got there.

"Emily!" She was waving her arms frantically in all directions. "Give

Emily back! Give her back!"

I gave her some valerian I had in my bag. After a few moments, she calmed down a little and stopping screaming.

I was afraid she might harm herself. Later, her friend told me she'd been forced to leave Emily, her baby, to die of cold in the snow, while a German soldier stood there, shouting at her to hurry, "*Las, las.*" Emily was only a year and half, blue and almost frozen. She thought she could return later on to take her, and even left her the wool blanket she'd hastily packed the day before when they set out on the march from Ruma.

We arrived at camp Sajmište near the city. Hanne had told me about his favorite city, and I can see the shining lights across the Danube. That's where he spent his beautiful childhood days with his mother and father, Louisa and Emil. I can actually imagine him there. Our world seems so close, but in fact it's very distant from the life that goes on across the river. Sometimes we seem to be on another planet, another one of Hanne's frequent terms. If we'd known where the march was headed, many of us would have jumped into the freezing Sava to die there, rather than reach this terrible camp. Ever since the young people left Sabac on the train, we've been condemned to endless atrocities. Who knows what will happen? What's certain now is that there's not a single spark of light at the end of the tunnel.

The journey here began on January 26. Early that morning, we heard the Germans shouting in the camp on the bank of the Sava, "*schnell, schnell,*" hurrying us along. They ordered us to take our few belongings and led us along the bridge above the Sava in the direction of Člának train station. The sun hadn't risen yet; we walked under gray January skies, and a fine rain stung our faces. At Člának, we were loaded into a train of dilapidated cattle cars. We were so exhausted from the march through the snow, we didn't have the strength to climb onto the train. Beside me was a woman with a small girl who was afraid to climb on. One of the soldiers barked at her, yelling and pushing her with his rifle butt. I couldn't control myself and shouted at him, "Shame on you. Don't you have a mother too?"

He didn't look at me, just continued to push the mother and her child. I tugged at his arm with what strength I had left. Only then did he turn and strike me hard in the face. Afterward, when I was inside the car, I heard about the mother of the baby who'd been forced to throw him inside like some object.

The cars traveled slowly to Ruma, where we got down and began the exhausting march on foot to Zemun, a march I thought would never end. A procession of women in black or gray moving through the white snow. Some with babies in their arms, some with small children holding their hands, their eyes staring forward in despair, oblivious to the shouts of the soldiers. The cold penetrated our thin layers of clothing, and a thin wool blanket hastily taken that morning or a worn-out coat were of no help. There are only women and children on this march. The men were left behind, in the long ditch in the Sajmište maize field. They were left tangled together, a pile of gypsies and Jews.

I have to stop writing now; my eyes are closing. Tomorrow we get up early, and I have to report to the infirmary at seven thirty in the morning.

February 15

The cold wind gives no respite. It comes in through the broken window, whistling and banging at the window frame in the wall. The cold gets into every corner, causing us to suffer even during the little rest time we have. However, the huge, terribly crowded building we live in without partitions, all the windows open to the wind, is still less crowded than Block 3, where most prisoners live in less than a meter per person.

There are very few men in the camp. Only the lucky ones got here for various reasons, unlike those captured in the hunt for hostages, who were made to stand over open ditches, to be shot in the neck by a firing squad. Every morning, they are taken out to labor that perhaps makes them curse the fact they're alive and weren't made to stand over ditches in front of a firing squad.

The buildings here were once used for international exhibitions and fairs organized by Sajmište in 1937, and each block was named after the country that exhibited there. Block 14, for example, is also known as the English Pavilion. And Block 3, where most of the prisoners are housed, is also known as the German Pavilion. Between five hundred and a thousand women are crowded in there. It's a huge place, and not every woman has her own bunk. Block 9 is also called the Turkish Pavilion. Ironically, this is where the showers are located, if you can call those openings in the ceiling showers. Now, with the daily rise in the numbers of the dead, the Turkish Pavilion serves as a storage space for the bodies until they can be taken for burial across the Sava to Belgrade, labor that frequently falls to us. Our block, Block 12, is adjacent to the hospital building and the pharmacy. It holds fifty beds, and is usually full. The latrines are outside for hygienic reasons. We all work around the clock. The Germans make us work at every kind of imaginable labor. Fortunately, I am in the infirmary all day. My workday begins at seven thirty each morning and ends at nine o'clock at night. I'm lying on the mattress now, exhausted, but I have to write this journal. Who would believe me otherwise?

We are two nurses here under the direction of Matilda, the pharmacist. She isn't from our transport group. She's one of those who've been here since December, when the camp was established, like Hilda Dajč. She has good ideas about how to pass the time and how to keep warm. Today is the weekly day for making tea with milk. She asked us to light all the kerosene burners in the infirmary. We have twelve of them. I stand over the pot of milk mixed with tea, stirring and stirring, my eyes tearing from the smoke. That's how I keep warm. My friend Hilda stands over the second pot. She also got here in December, but unlike the others, she volunteered to come. We talk a lot, and she tells me about herself. She was born in Vienna, but her parents left long before the *Anschluss*. They moved to Belgrade because her father, Emil, an engineer, had an opportunity to open a flourishing business there. This reminds me of Hanne's family. His father, also Emil, came from Budapest to Belgrade for economic reasons as well.

In Belgrade, Hilda went to the city school, where she excelled in all subjects, but her soul was mainly drawn to literature. She came to architecture after her father explained to her that literature is for the soul, and in order to make a living, she needs to study something practical. She believed that architecture was the closest profession to art. She managed to complete her first year with honors.

The Germans invaded Belgrade when she was in the middle of her second year. Her yearning for literature never left her, and she stayed in touch with art and literature students. She told me about the literary society named after the adored Bosnian poet, Aleksa Šantić,[29] which says it all. Hilda was the editor of the newspaper and had her own column. She's an inspired, idealistic girl with a tendency to excessive emotion. I can't understand how she can bear the horror of this place.

Hilda told me how she got here. No one forced her to come. It never occurred to me that anyone would willingly volunteer to come to such a hell. Her father was the liaison between the Jewish community and the occupying regime, so at first, they didn't touch her family.

In April, at the beginning of the occupation, she was working as a volunteer at the Jewish hospital established in Visokog Stevana Street after the terrible bombing attacks by the Germans. There were scores of wounded, and the Jewish community initiated this with the permission of the local German office. The hospital was run by Dr. Bucič Pijade, a very special person in his own right. He greatly admired Hilda, who had come there without much knowledge and devotedly and responsibly learned everything on her own.

In December, the Germans ordered all women to report to 23 Washington Street, and Hilda joined them.

"I went with the women and children. I thought there'd be a need for someone who could give first aid, and they'd probably open an infirmary. I'm willing to do anything to help the unfortunate, and so

---

29 Aleksa Šantić (1868–1924) was a Bosnian poet from Serbia, beloved throughout Yugoslavia.

here I am. Dr. Pijade tried to persuade me to stay at the hospital, but I knew my place was here, with the most wretched of all."

That's what Hilda told me with her characteristic naïveté and irresistible, winning smile.

"My parents begged me to stay at home. 'Why would you go rushing off there to volunteer? Who knows what dangers are waiting for you? In a few months, all this will be over, and the university will open again.' But I told them I'm not needed at home. I'm needed at the camp. I acted in accordance with my conscience, and I'm at peace with that. I see, too, that they were wrong. Not only is the situation bad, it's getting worse by the day."

But our situation is better than that of the gypsy prisoners. It's even worse there. Hilda and I were called to take care of the gypsy children who suffered from lice. We cut their hair. I've never seen anything like it. Afterward, we rubbed kerosene into their heads; my skin is still burning right up to the elbows. It was terrible. There were about twenty children in that state, and who knows what will happen tomorrow? It's contagious.

When we got back to the camp, mealtime was over—if you can call sauerkraut with watery soup a meal—so we didn't eat. This meal is served once a day, in the morning or the evening, and there isn't enough for everyone. We are all becoming skeletal. I've noticed that the less we eat, the less we feel the hunger, which was very hard in the beginning.

That evening, they told us we'd eat only bread and tea with milk. Luckily, we'd prepared tea that morning, as we hadn't eaten a thing for lunch. We made do that evening with a piece of bread each and tea with milk.

Soon, the block supervisor will come to do the head count. Each block has five hundred women living crowded together. The girl who is responsible for us is young, like all women in authority here, sixteen to twenty-three years old, and all of them seem born to the role. Interesting that they all come from Banat. That lot always knows how to manage. There are almost a hundred policewomen like that, all of them actually doing the Germans' job in the camp.

February 16

Two thirty in the morning. I'm doing another shift at the infirmary. I only do a shift every four nights now. That's something too! The sound of raindrops on the tin roof is mixed with a symphony of coughs coming from the sickroom.

I no longer get upset by the work I do. Today, I did something I'm used to now, although it is actually horrifying. Hilda and I laid out the bodies collected over the past two days in the yard of the Turkish Pavilion. Twenty-seven bodies. We placed them one on top of the other in a pile, like medication cartons in the storeroom. There was already another pile there of the same height.

Tonight, when I return to the block, I weep like a little girl. The women around me don't understand why a young woman who heroically works with bodies and disease just has to cry. But I'm not only crying because of the work, although one of the bodies was that of a little girl I knew. Children are the hardest. It breaks my heart to see them here. A child comes into the world and this is all he knows. He doesn't know any other life. At least I experienced something else once. I'm crying because of the futility, suffering, and loss of humanity here. No one knows when it will all end, just as no one knows why we are imprisoned here. They should just tell us what they intend to do with us.

Shoot us in the neck, as they did yesterday to the four women who tried to steal bread? Or maybe hang the lot of us, as they hanged those who accompanied patients a week ago and tried to smuggle out a letter Hilda had written to her friend Marianna at the Christian hospital in the city. I couldn't calm Hilda. Her eyes were a sea of tears. She cried as if she was about to be executed. She didn't understand that a bitter end awaits her, too, and said that she didn't care if she were hanged instead of those who'd tried to do her a favor. She's afraid to write now. I see the light in her eyes when she receives a letter from Nada or Marianna. Suddenly, she's someone else for an entire day. Her eyes are veiled with tears of happiness. I recall her receiving a letter once while making milk tea. She dropped everything with cries of joy.

Today, after we'd finished with the bodies, she whispered a secret to me.

"You're the only one I'm telling. Tomorrow, I'm accompanying patients. I've also added patients who aren't really terminal, as we've been ordered to do, just to get out of here. I'm going to meet Marianna, my good friend from university days, at a café near the hospital gates."

"How will she know you're coming and wait for you?" I asked in order to check Hilda's plan.

"Don't worry. From her last letter, I understand she's at home with her parents. I'll ask someone who works there to call her from home, tell her to meet me at the café near the gate. Luckily, they give us a half-hour break at this café. It'll be all right, Inge," she tried to soothe me. "Just cooperate with me and tell them they're terminal patients.

They can check the register at the infirmary where they're listed. But ignore the list, because those I registered are not really terminal. It's just between us," she whispered.

Naturally, I agreed. I'd do anything for Hilda. She suffers like everyone else here. Just the fact that she came of her own free will is troubling. However, her parents and little brother, Hans, arrived a month after her in the last transport of privileged Belgrade Jews. But she could have remained in Belgrade with her parents, like Marianna, or tried to escape like Jennie Lebel[30] and not come here at all.

She has moments of regret. She arrived when the camp just opened, armed with Dr. Pijade's promise to open a branch of the city hospital here and a strong desire to help the unfortunate. Today, she says she hates them. That's what she said. She's surrounded by women who behave like animals, who constantly talk about bowel movements and digestive juices in their mouths when they taste a morsel of cheese or a piece of bread.

"Inge, look what's happened to us here. The hardest thing isn't the icy winds that blow through broken windows into your very bones. And it isn't the hunger either. It's the people who watch every motion of your jaws while you chew, as if you'd stolen the last piece of bread out of their mouths."

February 17

Yesterday afternoon, an unconscious woman was brought to the infirmary. Her eyes were closed and her mouth slightly open. The two

---

30 Jennie Lebel (1928–2009) was a journalist from Belgrade.

women who brought her in looked tough and stocky.

"She collapsed while cleaning the officers' quarters."

"Who are you?" I asked, although they looked to me to be Banat women.

"We were guarding the cleaners," the older one answered. "And we were told us to bring her to the infirmary at once."

"Why is she so wet?" Hilda asked.

"She fainted, so we threw water on her face and gave her a few slaps. It didn't help."

I immediately realized it was a panic attack. They laid her down on one of the beds, and I told them they could go. I remained alone with Hilda. I began to massage the woman's temples and asked Hilda to raise her feet, and she set them gently on a stool I'd placed on the bed. Slowly, she opened her eyes. She had a strange look about her, and I realized it was connected with her hysterical state. When she opened her eyes, she seemed familiar. A woman in her fifties, head shaven, and so thin that her legs and arms had barely any flesh and looked like match sticks. Many of the camp women were in bad shape, but I'd never seen such thinness before.

And yet, the look in her eyes reminded me of someone. I thought of Mara's grandmother, a woman I knew in Sabac before coming here. But it couldn't be. She was in her sixties with silver hair in a bun on her head, very different from this woman with her shaven head and wild eyes. In the meantime, Hilda said her breathing was returning to normal. She removed the stool and laid the woman's legs, knees up, on the bed. I tried to encourage her to talk, and when she opened her mouth, only a few broken words in Serbo-Croatian came out, which I recognized from my time with Hanne, and then, in a flash, I realized it was his mother, Louisa. She looked at me expressionlessly, and I called her by name. "Louisa, Louisa."

She tried to raise her head but fell back. Again she tried, and again she failed. I continued to massage her temples and call her name, and then she finally focused on me and called out, "Inge! What am I doing here? What are you doing here? Are we in Sabac?"

In my most soothing voice, I explained that she was at Sajmište and I was at Sajmište, a nurse again. She gave me a brief look, lay back, and said in German, "That's impossible, impossible. I must be dreaming."

I told her, "It's no dream, and I'm here to help."

Hilda was surprised and asked, "Do you know her? Where is she from? I heard her speaking in Serbo-Croatian."

"Yes. She's from Belgrade. I told you that everyone in our transport was from Austria and Germany, but there was one family from Belgrade. She's my boyfriend's mother; he managed to get an immigration permit and left with the youth group on the train."

As we talked, Louise continued to recover.

"What's their name?" asked Hilda.

"David. This is Louisa, and her husband's name is Emil."

"Good heavens!" Hilda cried out in astonishment. "I also knew her. What a small world. Louisa David? I can't believe it!"

"Yes, it's her. You can ask her yourself in a while."

"Hilda!" Louisa suddenly cried out, to our surprise. "You're here too!"

She tried to sit up and talk to us. Hilda brought water and held it to Louisa's mouth for her to drink carefully. With our help, she sat up a little, murmuring all the time in a mixture of Serbo-Croatian and German.

"How did you get here, Hilda, my poor child? What have they done to you?"

"I'm fine, Madame Louisa. I came voluntarily. It's a long story."

Louisa sat up a little more, shaking her head in disbelief.

"Weren't you at Aleksa Šantić's Literary Society?" she asked.

"Yes," responded Hilda. "And I came to your house once. You lived on Dedinje Hill, right? You had a huge house."

"Ah, yes. That house seems unreal to me now, like a memory from another world," said Louisa.

"You invited me and two friends to an evening of Aleksa's poetry. Nada is considered an expert on his poetry."

"It's hard to believe I'm actually meeting you here, in this terrible place. And you, Inge, you saved me when we boarded the boat. I will never forget it. You were a life-saver for me, and later in Kladovo as well."

"I only did what anyone would have done, nothing special," I answered her.

"Don't underestimate your own worth. I can't believe I'm meeting you here. Did you get the letter I sent with Miklos?"

February 17, Night

It is ten o'clock at night. Tonight, Hilda is on duty. She replaces me every two nights, so I have more time to sleep. The wind is wailing, banging on ripped-out windows and letting in cold that freezes the bones. Today, we had sauerkraut again for the afternoon meal, the seventh time in the last two weeks. Everyone knows the exact cycle of sauerkraut, and they talk about food all the time. Hilda told me she can't bear these discussions. They apparently don't have anything else to give us, except sauerkraut or gray potatoes. The women are getting thinner, and who knows how they'll be able to do their work in the sewing workshop or cleaning soldiers' quarters and the latrines when the food portions are so poor.

I try to sleep, but again and again I see pictures of their attempt to escape as Louisa described; how the Serbian driver, who had already received the money they'd scraped together, betrayed them to the Germans.

That afternoon, I met Hilda when she returned from her meeting. The minute I saw the ambulance come in, I knew she'd returned, and I was looking forward to hearing her experiences. She looked like a different person.

"You have no idea," she said. "What all that does for me."

"As soon as we crossed the bridge over the frozen Sava, I sent someone to tell Marianna that I'd be at the café. It's lucky the soldiers accompanying us allow this break after we've handed over patients to the emergency room. To get a little taste of the world I knew, even if it's only for a moment—and then back to our hell behind the fences. She came twenty minutes later. This was our third meeting at the café. She was groomed and fashionably dressed, as always. I sat there with a cup of tea that I was too excited to drink. We held hands, and Marianna looked at me in my gray prison clothes with tears in her eyes. I tried to comfort her and paint a less harsh picture, but she said she was afraid she wouldn't be able to see me soon—I was all skin and bone. I wasn't plump before, but now… We've gotten used to our skeletal bodies here, but to someone from the outside, who used to know us, it looks terrible.

"Marianna told me that all of Aleksa's activities had been stopped. The university was closed, and she sat home with her parents, bored and wanting it all to end. When I told her about you and what you've gone through, with sailing and the endless wait on the Danube, she recalled that in December 1939, on a trip along the Danube with her parents, they anchored in Vukovar and saw three ships in port. They even transferred food to one of the ships. When they asked who was on the ships, they were told that they were Jews from Austria and Germany who were waiting for immigration permits for Palestine. What a small world.

"Marianna asked if I still think volunteering for the camp was the right thing to do. I told her that I wanted to help where I knew I was needed. But I couldn't have imagined where all this was going. I tried to soften the picture, but Marianna is smart. She understood. I told the story you've already heard, how as a small girl in Vienna I had a recurring nightmare of being buried alive. It was after I understood, or thought I understood, what death meant, when my parents returned from my grandfather's funeral. I understood he was in a grave now. Outside, snow was falling, and I didn't understand how my mother could have left him alone in his grave when outside it was cold and snowing. Today, I feel as if I've been buried alive. And our life behind the fence is like being buried underground.

"And then, so it wouldn't sound so dark, I told her about the rumors of our perhaps being transferred to a labor camp in Poland, where conditions are better."

February 24

I've been working in the office of SS-Untersturmführer Herbert Andorfer for a week now. He saw me one day at the infirmary and decided he wanted me in his office. His aide recently had to return to Germany. This was last Wednesday. I was on night shift in the infirmary. It was after midnight, the sounds of groaning had finally calmed down, and I had time to organize the medication cabinet. I heard the familiar sound of boots on the paving stones. I had no doubt as to whom those boots belonged. He appeared with his two aides, tall and trim in his ironed uniform. Both held their guns in their hands, and he held a thin cane and seemed somewhat perturbed. I immediately saw the dark circles under his eyes.

"How can I help you?" I asked.

He asked his aides to wait outside.

"I've been told there are two highly professional nurses at the camp infirmary who can help me."

"What's wrong? At a guess, you are suffering from insomnia."

"How did you know?" he asked in surprise. "Is it written on my forehead?"

"More or less," I answered. "It's written in the dark circles under your eyes."

"It's been going on for quite some time," he said. "I wake up in the middle of the night and can't fall asleep again…"

"Do you want a sleeping pill?"

"Yes, I do. What do you have that could help?"

I wanted to tell him it was hardly surprising that he couldn't sleep. With all the atrocities going on in the camp, he'd need heavy armor to block his heart and mind, but instead I went to the medication cabinet and put a few pills in a small packet.

"Here you are," I held it out to him. "There are five pills here. But you need to be careful. No more than one at a time."

He took it, put it in his ironed pocket, and bowed his thanks.

"No need to thank me. Just be careful, those pills are narcotics."

And then he sat down, crossed one leg over the other, resting his stick on the floor.

"My name is Herbert. I'm camp Untersturmführer Herbert Andorfer," he introduced himself.

"I'm Inge. Inge Müller."

"I wish to offer you an opportunity it would be hard to refuse," he said. "My aide returned to Germany two days ago. He has family problems. His wife has been hospitalized in a psychiatric unit."

"What does this have to do with me?" I asked.

"It's simple. I hear how well you speak German and see how practical you are, and I thought you might take his place."

"That's out of the question," I said. "How can I leave the infirmary? It would be a crime."

"It wouldn't be a problem," he said. "I'll find you a replacement from among the Banat women."

"Just like that? It's that simple to replace me?"

"Yes, it won't be a problem. You'll just have to train her for a couple of days."

"I don't know…"

"You'll be able to eat properly. You won't freeze in this huge football stadium of a place."

"I'll see. I'll need to think about it."

"Tomorrow, an aide will come to fetch you. Think about it tonight."

He got up, put his stick under his arm, clicked his heels together, turned to the door, and left with his two aides, the sounds of their boots filling the building space.

That entire night was devoted to the bombshell thrown by Untersturmführer Herbert Andorfer. Why would I go with him? But not really with him, just to his office. So what? Be his aide? The enemy's aide? I might be able to save myself that way. How can I do this to the group? Although we aren't really a group now. We're all here together, all the women and children of Belgrade, Banat, and surrounding places. What connects me to the Banat women we all hate? Many of them have turned into camp policewomen, collaborators. Is that what I'll become, too? A collaborator?

No. I'll never be like them. They treat us brutally. I'll just sit in an office and organize papers. Maybe it isn't so bad. Maybe I'll even find a way to help my friends in the group. I'd especially like to help poor Hilda. She so regrets having volunteered to come here. Now, when it's too late for regrets, she understands she made a mistake. But who could have known? Maybe it would be a mistake to refuse Commander Andorfer. Maybe I should learn from Hilda's mistake, because who knows what will be? All she wanted was to help others, and now she's buried here, like her childhood nightmare, buried alive and screaming from the grave, her mouth full of earth and no one to hear her. That's how she feels today—buried alive. So why shouldn't I take what he's offering me now?

In fact, I have a wonderful idea: I'll suggest that Hilda go to

Andorfer's office instead of me. She came here voluntarily, and maybe it will compensate for her suffering. That's it. I'm at peace now. I'll talk to her about it tomorrow. If she agrees, I'll tell Andorfer's aide there's someone else here who speaks German just as well as I do, so why shouldn't he take her in my place? In this way, I comforted myself until morning.

The following morning, while making beds, I told Hilda about the offer I'd received. I suggested she go in my place, and maybe she'd manage to get herself freed to go home to Belgrade, which is so close by.

"Are you suggesting that I leave Jewish patients to sit in the office of a German officer?" she asked angrily. "How could you even think such a thing?"

"Because I see your suffering here and want to help you."

"That's not help. After all, I did come here voluntarily, to relieve the suffering of the unfortunate."

"But you've told me how much you suffer, how you hate the people who watch you eat as if you'd stolen the food right out of their mouths."

"Yes, things are terrible for me here, but I wouldn't degrade myself to that extent."

One of the soldiers suddenly rushed in.

"A nurse is needed, urgently! Someone's tried to kill herself in Block 10 A. She's critical." I grabbed my first-aid bag and we both ran to Block 10 A.

"Quick! Quick!" someone urged us from the doorway. "She's losing a lot of blood."

The scene was horrific. Hilda pulled a tourniquet from the bag while I made a temporary tourniquet by pressing my fist into the hollow of the shoulder. Quick and practical, Hilda didn't say a word as she worked. Once she'd stopped the blood and tied the tourniquet, she asked for a stretcher to be brought from the infirmary. Someone standing beside us started shouting.

"No, no, you should have let her die. She's right. Her little son died two days ago. She has nothing to live for. Leave her alone. We should all have done the same. It's a pity to make such an effort." Her words provoked the women standing there watching us.

In the meantime, I took out the IV bag and needle. Although her veins were sunken in for lack of blood, Hilda managed to insert the needle into a vein, but very little blood came out, which meant we hadn't inserted the needle in the right place. We were thinking about changing the place, but when we connected the tube, the color red appeared at the juncture of the needle, and we realized that the infusion would soon begin to drip. She was in her forties and had decided there was no point to this existence. She's probably right, but we aren't here to resolve philosophical problems but to save a life. It's just not possible to start asking every patient if in fact they'd prefer or deserve to die. It's hard for me to save a woman who doesn't want to live.

We took her to the infirmary and laid her down on one of the beds we'd made up that morning. She began to revive and murmur the odd word, finally bursting into sobs we were unable to calm. Maybe she was glad to be alive, and maybe she was actually disappointed to find she was still alive in this terrible, anguished camp where the concept of life has lost all meaning.

When we were once more alone, Hilda told me she in all conscience couldn't work in that commander's office.

"But everyone is built differently," she added. "And each person has to think about how to save him or herself, not only how to save others. I reached that insight after many internal debates," she said with a piercing look into my eyes.

"You're right," I responded. "Maybe the time has come to save my own skin. Though I also experience internal debate. My heart tells me not to go, but my head tells me I should act in my own interests. Maybe that's where the solution lies."

"If you choose to leave here, there's a chance you'll be saved from something we don't know about yet but that's waiting for us."

"On the other hand, there's our friendship, and I'd hate to lose that," I said.

"*Wunderbar*!" Hilda cried out. "Do you think I don't feel the same? You're my best friend in the camp. Almost like Marianna and Nada. But they are free outside. It's different."

"We'll stay friends even if I go. After all, I won't be leaving the camp. We talk as if tomorrow I'll be getting a free pass out of here while you have to stay."

"Do what you think is right. You have my blessing. All I want is for you to be free and happy."

March 15

Night again. I always write at night. I've been in Untersturmführer Herbert Andorfer's office for almost three weeks now. From now on, I will call him Commander Andorfer. I have my own corner here, and I'm spared the constant noise of the crowd of women in Block 14 A. And the cold and blowing wind don't bother me anymore either. Because of the broken windows, I felt as if I were living in a house without walls. I arranged with Hilda to do night shifts twice a week. In this way, I quieted my conscience a little. But my mood remained as low as ever.

The painful scenes at the infirmary continue to haunt me even after my shift. Even the relatively simple cases of facial frost bite, which cause deep skin peeling that distorts the face, are unbearable for me.

In the morning, I clean the camp administration offices, including the toilets. Afterward, I am free to take care of Commander Andorfer's office. He introduced me to the typewriter, and after several exercises during the first two days, I learned how to use it, daily improving my typing speed. He doesn't give me everything to type up, only things that have to do with the daily running of the camp. In this way, I found out that Commander Andorfer was furious at the neglect of the infirmary building in the Nikolai Spasič Pavilion. He demanded more beds and the installation of inside toilets with running water. He was concerned by the food portions coming from Belgrade and demanded that Belgrade food suppliers increase the portions so that the prisoners could carry out their tasks in the sewing rooms, and the men, whose numbers were decreasing daily, could work in the camp metal and carpenter workshops. In the matter of the pharmacy and medication supply, he asked me and Matilda for advice. She's the main pharmacist in the camp, and he wanted to know which medications were lacking, and wrote urgent requests to Belgrade and Berlin.

Herbert Andorfer turned out to be a completely different person behind his tough exterior and the menacing person he is. I noticed this when he came to the infirmary to ask for sleeping tablets. I thought that for a man like him, who does the things he does, it would be a miracle if he could sleep at night. If he needed sleeping tablets, clearly his actions during the day would make it difficult for him to rest at night.

I will never forget my first encounter with him. He came to the camp to replace Edgar Enge, who was inexperienced and did not find favor with his superiors in Berlin. Following his sudden replacement, we discovered that he became Andorfer's subordinate.

That day, a young gypsy woman, her baby in her arms, attempted to escape. Commander Andorfer took out his revolver and shot the woman and her baby. Then he continued his daily routine as if nothing had happened, merely shouting that the soldier who was derelict in his duty should be court-martialed. The bound soldier was taken aside somewhere and supposedly shot. The three bodies were added to the daily number at the Turkish Pavilion.

On the very first day, when I was cleaning his room, I was surprised to see a book of Schiller's poems on the shelf above his head. *Strange*, I thought. *The murderer reads poetry. Doesn't seem like him.*

That day, he asked me where I came from and where I'd gone to school. He completely ignored the fact that I was a Jewess. He didn't ask, and I didn't volunteer the information. I looked Aryan in every way. But on another occasion, he surprised me, saying, "I saw the little book you keep hidden next to your bed."

"I didn't know you were prying into my things," I was amazed. The blood rushed into my face.

"You're lovely when you blush like that." He added, "You have nothing to worry about. I already knew about you."

I am also curious, and more than once hastily glanced at the papers on his desk. This is how, a week ago, I discovered the request he'd filled out for a transfer from the camp. I discovered that he was only thirty-three, had already been awarded the Iron Cross for bravery, and that he had a wife and two daughters in Düsseldorf.

He justified his request for a transfer thus:

"Although I do my best to carry out my role here at the camp," he wrote. "I feel that my training as an observation officer and professional gunner is going to waste running a labor camp for Jews and gypsies, most of whom are no longer really useful. My job is administrative, not combat, which I would prefer in order to better serve Germany and the Führer." I hastily read the letter and returned it to its place under the leather upholstery on his desk, just the lower corner peeping out.

One day, I found a curious document, which I didn't really understand. A letter placed next to the typewriter that didn't look particularly secret. It was addressed to the Commander of Sajmište, Untersturmführer Herbert Andorfer, from the Head of the Gestapo in Berlin, Heinrich Müller.

I read that the Head of the Gestapo was happy to inform Commander Andorfer of the arrival of Z. Pol. No. 71463.

"At your own convenience," was written. "You can now end your important job for the Führer and Germany with all possible speed and greater efficiency, and without any physical harm." At first, I thought it was about a horse called Z. Pol. No. 71463. A gift, perhaps, from the

Gestapo for doing a good job. After all, he did tell me once that horses were his favorite hobby. But something about it didn't feel right to me. It can't be a horse. It can only be something far more terrible. The words written there were, "You can now end your important job for the Führer and Germany with all possible speed and greater efficiency, and without any physical harm."

You don't need a horse for that; you need a tool of destruction. My heart beat fast and my hands trembled. I returned the letter to the envelope and tried to go back to cleaning, but at that moment the door opened, and Herbert Andorfer entered. He noticed my distress and asked, "Why are you so pale? Is something wrong?"

"No, no, nothing."

I must have stammered. He offered me a glass of water.

"You look faint. Maybe you need to rest in your room. I'll bring you a glass of water."

I sat in my room and thought about the meaning of Z. Pol. No. 71463—it was probably something dreadful. That night, I couldn't sleep. I was tormented by the words "Z. Pol. No. 71463" and how Andorfer would swiftly and efficiently end his role in Sajmište Camp. What did the words "end your job efficiently" mean? Finish at the camp? Or perhaps finish off the people here, or transfer them to another place? Terrible thoughts began to rush through my mind concerning this Z. Pol. No. 71463. I have to confide in my friends in the block.

At the time, there were a lot of rumors going around about transferring the female prisoners to a labor camp in the north, where conditions were far more comfortable. Directions for facilitating this were also given, which Commander Andorfer asked me to type out. Between eighty and a hundred people would be divided into groups each time. Those in the group would be permitted to take their personal belongings to the new place, which was more spacious and comfortable. Every day, prisoners would be allowed to check the notice board to see who was on the next day's list.

I persuaded myself it was probably a term for a large truck that could transfer between eighty and a hundred men or women at a time, to a better place, as they say, somewhere in the north, and I calmed down.

March 16

I met Louisa today. We'd met occasionally, by chance, in line for the evening meal, or on our way to our various jobs. She'd worked in the sewing shop like many other women, but as her eyesight was failing, she was given work that didn't strain her eyes as much. At each meeting, she managed to tell me a little more about what had happened to her and Emil after they left Sabac, tried to escape, and been caught. But today, she particularly asked to speak to me.

We met this morning, she on her way to the sewing shop, and I on my way to the office of Commander Andorfer. She was surprised to hear that I'd gone to work for the German.

"We'll talk this evening," I said. "I haven't left altogether, you know."

"How could I know? I haven't been to the infirmary for two weeks."

"Yes," I answered. "I'm still doing shifts at the infirmary."

I ended the conversation and quickened my steps.

That evening, she appeared as promised. She'd tied a scarf around her shorn head.

"I've gotten used to having no hair," she said, when she saw me glancing at the scarf.

"At first, I found it very strange. And then I got used to it," she said, sitting down opposite me. "When Hilda told me you were working in the German's office, I couldn't believe it." She spoke, looking directly into my eyes. "'Is this the Inge I knew?' I asked myself. 'What does it mean? That innocent, idealistic girl suddenly prefers the comfort and ease of the commander's office? The same commander who is responsible for all the terrible things happening here?'"

Louisa's harsh words caused me great discomfort. I answered that I hadn't just given in. I didn't have a choice, I tried to explain, telling her about the evening Commander Andorfer came to the infirmary, about his suggestion that initially hadn't attracted me at all. I also told her about my conversation with Hilda the following day, how she'd had strong reservations but after going through further difficult experiences, she gave me her blessing.

Louisa had trouble believing it. She said it was hard for her to understand how a girl with values and moral judgment could take such a step, lean on the tyrant who deprives us of life.

"It isn't right, no matter how you look at it," she said. "It simply goes against everything I believe in, and I thought you and Hilda believed in the same things. All the values we were raised on."

I tried to explain that we were living in a completely different reality. The world I grew up in was being destroyed in front of our very eyes. Hilda had also said so. This is not a world we've ever known. Here, people are simply trying to survive. Hilda was shocked by her exposure to the animal sides of women who were once just like her mother and her mother's friends.

"What would you do instead of me?" I asked. "Wouldn't you consider trying to save your own life? Or enjoy a little comfort?"

Louisa answered vehemently that she wouldn't do it even if her life depended on it.

And then I told her about the other reason. How I thought I might manage to find out what they were planning to do to us and tell the other women prisoners. Which is what happened with the letter I found about Z. Pol. No. 71463.

How I'd been trying for days to make my friends in Block 14 A understand the implications of this seemingly innocent name. I tried to find out what she thought. Should we do something, perhaps? Organize an uprising or escape?

Louisa gave a bitter laugh and said that, in her experience, the chances of escape were so small that even talking about it was a waste of time.

"And anyway," she said. "We will never know what happened to those who have already gone on the truck, if they really did transfer them to another, safer place, or to a firing squad in the forest. I've already survived one escape attempt. Even those I trusted had no hesitation in betraying me. Emil made very thorough plans in advance. Checked in different places, with various people, and even on the evening before our departure, he was uneasy and had doubts. Maybe this man really only wants our money. Maybe he isn't really trustworthy. Emil was very anxious and tried to organize everything, think of everything, every detail. He knew how long the journey would take. He knew the route, and who would be waiting for us on the other side. That's Emil, as you know." A transparent tear rolled down her cheek. She was quiet for a few seconds, adding, "And when the blow fell, he was so surprised. He told me that his experience with cards should have taught him how to read faces. He blamed himself all the way back to Belgrade; we sat, hands bound behind our backs, like criminals caught for some dreadful crime."

She told me that after she was imprisoned at the Banjica camp, he wrote her what he'd really thought about on the way, as they sat bound there in the truck. He wrote her that he was sure they'd be taken to some distant spot in the forest and shot, as he'd heard happened in other similar situations.

"He didn't say so, because he wanted to encourage me. We sat close to one another all the way. We couldn't even embrace because our hands were bound, and he only told me what he was planning to do when we arrived, that we had to go on trying to organize immigration permits, so I wouldn't think about the worst of all. But now, I'm worried, Inge. They took him to an even worse place, the Topovske Šupe concentration camp, as punishment for trying to attack a German officer. They're taken from that camp to the firing ditches."

"How do you know all this? Did he write to you about it?" I asked.

"No, I know it from letters that Dr. Bucič Pijade managed to send to his wife. She told me that Sime Spitzer was also interned there. The same Sime who was responsible for our transport, which didn't take place, and whom everyone hated when we were in Kladovo. He was arrested in September, on the day they arrested most of the men in Belgrade, and taken to Banjica. He was badly tortured there by SS officers, especially by a Dr. Jung."

"We couldn't see what they did to him," Dr. Pijade wrote in his letter. "Until one day, Emil saw the camp doctor, Dr. Jung, hitting Sime with a baton on his arms and back. He couldn't stay silent and stood between Sime and the German officer, using his large body as a shield against the German officer, holding his hands and pulling at the baton. In seconds, two SS soldiers appeared, handcuffed Emil, and threw him into a cell. Sime Spitzer was shot that day by Dr. Jung, and Emil was transferred to Topovske Šupe as punishment, and from there, groups are regularly taken out for execution."

In the meantime, Dr. Pijade was made director of the hospital at the Banjica internment camp.

Louisa remembered that Dr. Pijade had visited their home once in Dedinje, and she greatly appreciated his qualities. He wasn't only a superb doctor, but also had a poetic heart. He was interested in poetry and literature and came to one of the literary evenings at her home. She recalled, too, that he'd taken Hilda Dajč under his wing when he ran the Jewish hospital on Visokog Stevana Street and taught her the basic rules of medicine.

Dr. Pijade's wife had shown the letters to Louisa to encourage her.

"Although in his first letter, he comforted everyone. He wrote there was nothing to worry about," said Louisa. "Because everyone was fine, including Emil and the rest of them. But later on, in his second letter, he did tell how Emil had tried to protect Spitzer, how he was thrown into a cell, and transferred. We haven't heard from Emil since then. I didn't know what had happened to him for a long time, and in my heart, I believed the worst until finally the last letter arrived."

The doctor's wife was living with a friend in the city center, next door to the house where the David family had lived before leaving Belgrade for *Eretz* Israel, not far from Topovske Šupe camp. She knew he was there but couldn't do anything to help him. She spoke of her tension and anxiety when she heard that at Topovske Šupe they executed Jewish prisoners in retaliation for Partisan military successes: fifty Jews for every German killed and twenty for every German wounded.

"My heart sank every time they announced a Partisan success," she said. "When everyone rejoiced in the German misfortunes, I cringed. On the day Partisans killed twenty-one Wehrmacht people near Topola, in an attack considered a major success at the time, I shuddered, positive they'd execute Emil."

Two days later, the commander of the Jewish department in the Belgrade office called her to his office. At first, she was very alarmed, thinking they were going to arrest her as well, but she was surprised to find that they'd called her in to give her a letter Emil had written. He didn't complain, although he described the place in very frightening terms. Every morning, after a restless sleep on a concrete floor in a huge hall, they stood in line for a lukewarm coffee-like beverage and a small piece of bread for breakfast. A slice of bread for a prisoner is a hundred and fifty grams per day. Immediately after the meal, they go out to work at different jobs in the city and surrounding areas, and at work, they are given a bland soup for lunch. At the end of the letter, Emil asked Louisa to try and speak to the commander of the Jewish department at the police station who supervised the camp.

That very same day, Louisa personally appealed to the police commander to act on Emil's behalf for his release. But she understood from him that there was no chance. He said that every day, more Jewish prisoners were brought to the camp. By the end of September, about one thousand men had been arrested and incarcerated in the city of Smederevo.

The police commander allayed her concerns, saying she had nothing to worry about, because conditions there were better than at Banjica and that the internal management of the camp was in the hands of Jewish prisoners.

"When I compare their situation there with this situation here, at Sajmište," she said. "I realize that conditions here are far worse. But what most disturbed me, even more than the food, were the sleeping conditions on a concrete floor without mattresses. You know Emil. He writes that he is busy now making beds for each of the five hundred prisoners in the camp. At least he's employed from morning until evening."

March 18

Today was a long day. It began with the discovery of another letter and ended with a depressing meeting at the infirmary with Hilda.

Until today, I felt quite calm about Z. Pol. No. 71463. I even managed to smile at my first foolish thoughts about the horse to be given to Andorfer. But today, I discovered another letter, and again, I was worried. In it, I read that this Z. Pol. No. 71463 requested by Harald Turner, head of the military government in Serbia, would reach the Jewish hospital yard in Visokog Stevana Street on March 20. The vehicle came with an experienced team of two men, Getz and Majer, who knew how to operate the machine and had tried it successfully at the Polish border.

The letter also said that a message had been sent to Untersturm-führer Emanuel Schäfer, head of the security police in Belgrade, to concentrate all Jewish staff members in the hospital yard as well. About seven hundred Jews would be present at the hospital on the day of the operation, including patients and medical staff. But secrecy was an important condition for the success of the operation. The day before, people would be informed that the truck would arrive to take them to their new quarters.

Again, I was alarmed, and a cold sweat broke out on my skin. I thought about Hilda, who had worked at that hospital, where she'd received her training before coming here. Her friends still worked there. I must speak to her about the letter. Hilda didn't know anything. Two weeks before, she'd received a letter from her friend at the Jewish hospital in town saying that everything was improving and that they'd received new equipment.

That afternoon, Commander Andorfer stormed into the office and ordered me to write a letter to the medical team at the Jewish hospital. He apparently didn't know I'd seen the letter he'd left on the table. He walked up and down the room in an effort to find the right words for the instruction to transfer the medical staff to their new quarters, a three-and-a-half-hour journey away.

In the same breath, he told me he couldn't bear his work at the camp any longer, and that he'd applied for a transfer to the front, his rightful place, he said, not playing around ordering food or beds for the hospital.

"I wasn't trained as an observer and tank commander for that," he said angrily. "But the commanders in Berlin don't want to hear it," he pounded on the door frame. "I hoped they'd transfer me before that damned Saurer *polizei* gets here, but I see there's no chance of that."

It was the first time I'd heard the precise name: the Saurer *polizei*.

"Why is it so important to you to leave before the Saurer *polizei* gets here? What's so terrible about it?" I asked innocently, in an attempt to understand the purpose of the Saurer.

"Don't you understand?" he said angrily. "Do you have any idea of the pandemonium there'll be here every day until we get everyone to the new camp?" He began to count on his fingers. "One, prepare flyers and lists of those leaving on that particular day so they can get ready. Two, make sure that only those leaving are ready to get onto the Saurer in the morning. Three, supervise them getting onto the Saurer. After all, everyone wants to get away from here. Four, in order to hasten the transfer, we may have to operate the Saurer twice a day. I have to make sure that's possible."

Again, I felt a rising hope that we would leave here. Commander Andorfer is very pedantic and leaves no loose ends untied. But I still had to talk to Hilda.

"We'll start from the hospital on Visokog Stevana Street. The Saurer will get there in two days' time, and the medical staff should get to the new place before the patients. So they will be the first to go." He took a piece of paper out of an envelope in his drawer, which apparently included a list of the hospital staff.

"Untersturmführer Emanuel Schäfer sent me the list yesterday; he's concentrated all the medical staff at the hospital. Here, can you see how orderly it is? But it requires a lot of work."

By the time we'd finished preparing the announcement regarding the transfer of eighty-four hospital staff and thirty-three seriously ill patients, it was late. Commander Andorfer called his deputy, Edgar Enge, and told him to send it by messenger to the hospital at once.

Knowing I had a shift at the infirmary that night, I decided to try and rest a while before going to the Nikolai Spasič Pavilion. But I couldn't sleep. Again, uneasy thoughts about the truth of the transfer rose up. Although Commander Andorfer had tried to calm me, painting a persuasive picture of the orderly preparation of prisoners to be transferred, I still suspected him of deliberately misrepresenting the truth.

That evening, I sat in the infirmary with Hilda. She repeated her hope that they'd all reach a better place as promised, but she also understood that her method of communication with the outside world would end now. She'd often used the opportunity to take patients to the hospital in order to exchange letters with her friends. She said she must get there the following day to meet with Marianna, or at least pass on a last letter to Nada before they left.

I knew how important the outside world was to her, but not the extent, not that it was her life's blood. With tears in her eyes, Hilda told me that her connection with her friends on the other side was the only thing that gave her the strength to go on living. Knowing that there was another life across the Sava, even if she was no longer part of it. Just knowing there was a world there, a world that went on almost like the one she used to know, gave her the strength to survive.

Only now did I notice how thin she'd become since I'd gone to

Commander Andorfer's office. The bones stood out in her elbows and hand joints, and the tight skin looked almost transparent. Her cheeks were sunken and her skin cracked from the cold and wind. Her almond-shaped brown eyes, once beautiful and full of life, were dull now and sunken deep in their dark eye sockets.

The severing of her link with her friends seemed like a death sentence for her.

When I told her of my concern that the transfer was merely a cover-up, she didn't relate to it seriously.

"But Hilda," I said. "It's possible they are taking everyone to their death. We have to do something."

"Nothing matters to me anymore. As far as I'm concerned, they can take me to my death."

March 30

Again, it is late at night, and I am sitting writing in my room. I did another night shift at the infirmary last night. Hilda isn't feeling well. Since the evacuation of the hospital on Visokog Stevana Street, she's getting weaker every day. She is even thinner now, barely eats a morsel, and is apathetic to everything happening around her.

The day after I told her about the letter with its instructions concerning the hospital evacuation, she tried to organize the transfer of a group of gravely ill patients from the infirmary to the hospital, as a ruse to hand over another letter to her friends and meet with Dr. Pijade, her favorite doctor, who'd trained her as a nurse before she came here, but this time her request was denied. She was told that the Jewish hospital had been evacuated and that all the staff and patients had been transferred to a new more spacious and comfortable camp. Hilda pleaded with Commander Andorfer to allow patients to go there, at least for tests. He responded saying that soon we would also be sent to a new camp. But Hilda was distraught. She met me with tears in her eyes and said she didn't believe a word Commander Andorfer said.

"They're all liars. Murderers. I know it."

Yesterday, late in the evening, two soldiers entered the infirmary. Short and squat, they resembled each other. Their uniforms weren't ironed and clean like that of Commander Andorfer and his deputy, but rough, thick work clothes. One introduced himself as Majer, Sergeant Majer, and the other, who sat down heavily on a chair and showed me a large blister on the back of his hand, introduced himself as Getz.

"It's a burn, see? Got it this afternoon."

They didn't have to introduce themselves. I immediately recognized them. They were the two drivers of the Saurer *polizei*. They were always together, most of the time standing and smoking next to the Saurer, their enormous truck. A week ago, once they'd finished their work at the hospital, the Saurer had also begun to transfer prisoners from our camp to the new place everyone was talking about.

One day, when looking for Commander Andorfer, who had an important call to take, I found him standing smoking in their company, next to the Saurer. One of them was leaning with his back to the wheel, the other leaning against the side of the vehicle. Now here they were, in front of me. When I asked Getz how he'd gotten the blister, he hesitated. I didn't understand why it was hard for him to tell me if boiling water had splashed on him as he made coffee or tea or whether he'd touched some hot instrument. When I insisted, he said he'd been hurt by the exhaust fumes of the Saurer, the chimney-like pipe that rose behind the driver's seat. I didn't ask how he'd gotten his hand near the exhaust pipe, only explained there might be danger of infection.

After I finished taking care of him, Majer asked me if I had any pills for his headache.

"I've had very bad headaches recently," he said. "It happens every time I'm on my way back to camp."

I asked him if he'd suffered from headaches in the past, and when he said he hadn't, I suggested he come to see the doctor the next day.

"No," he said. "I don't have a single free moment during the day. I'm very busy."

I asked him if he traveled with the cabin windows open.

"Of course not," he responded. "How can anyone travel with windows open in this cold?"

I suggested that if he left a window slightly open, his headaches might disappear. But nonetheless, I gave in and handed him several dipyrone pills from the medicine cabinet. They both thanked me and went heavily on their way.

I seem to be the only one who doesn't believe the story that Commander Andorfer is spreading around the camp. The other women are all praying their turn will come. It isn't surprising; it's impossible to imagine worse conditions than the ones we live in. Although I have better conditions now, I don't believe there is anything baser than inhumanity. Hunger and cold turn people into animals, make them think only of food and a corner where they will suffer less from wind and frost.

Every day, I type up a notice formulated by Commander Andorfer, with a new list of prisoners and explicit instructions for reporting, including permission to take personal belongings, primarily hygiene items, and some warm clothes, to pack them into a small bundle that won't take up unnecessary space on the truck. Commander Andorfer even made sure to emphasize the travel time—three hours and forty minutes—so they'd know what to expect.

Every morning, I see the women standing in line, each with a small, well-packed bundle in her hands, waiting at the English Pavilion to get onto the Saurer. Getz and Majer stand next to the driver's cabin, with a morning coffee in one hand and a cigarette between their teeth, watching the women standing patiently waiting for the signal to be given. Then one of them walks toward the rear of the vehicle and, with a loud grinding of hinges, opens the rear doors and pulls down the folding steps to make it easier for older women and small children to get into the passenger cabin.

To sweeten the journey for small children, Getz and Majer walk along the line handing out candies to children. On Sunday, when there wasn't a transport, I saw them walking through the camp and handing out candies to children, probably to gain their favor. Maybe they felt the children were afraid of them, although they don't look any more frightening than any other German soldier. The opposite. They're two round people with good, smiling faces. The way they passed among the young children who were playing in the pavilion yards, handing out candies and stroking their heads, reminded me of The Pied Piper of Hamelin. But there was no pipe here to attract victims, except for the candies from the hands of Getz and Majer, who tried very hard to appear as kind uncles.

April 6

A few days ago, I returned to Block 14. The final days were unbearable. I ran away from Commander Andorfer's office when I was absolutely sure that the formidable Saurer *polizei* was nothing but a "souls killer." I heard the policewomen from Banat talking about it among themselves one day. I tried to talk to the young women in Pavilion 14, some of whom had been on the transport from Vienna—they were already assimilated with the Serbo-Croatian women who'd been brought here—no one wanted to listen to such a possibility. They're all waiting for their turn to get out of this hell.

But I didn't leave, only because I realized that Commander Andorfer had managed to create a false impression of going toward freedom, when in fact he was carrying out systematic murder. I knew I couldn't spend even one more day in his presence, knowing what he was doing every day. What also persuaded me to return to Block 14 was Hilda's state. She was sinking rapidly and no longer able to work at the infirmary. One day, I found her lying exhausted on her bunk, smelling of vomit. I took her wrist and barely found a pulse. I brought her a glass of water and managed to get a few words out of her. All she said was that nothing mattered anymore. She had nothing to live for. She'd parted from her family the day before, and Max, her little brother, promised to wait for her in the new camp. Her father and mother seemed to accept their fate. They no longer cared where they were taken. They quietly packed their things in a small bundle and waited for the following day.

I went to the infirmary and asked the nurse if we could take a stretcher to Block 14. Together, we brought Hilda to the hospital adjoining the infirmary.

I sat beside her and put my hand on her forehead. She was burning. I brought more water and a cloth and tried to cool her face. She recovered somewhat and told me she probably wouldn't come back to nurse and that in the present state of things she preferred death to life. She hadn't anyone to live for, and living just for herself had never been a sufficiently important goal. The world of art, poetry, and literature that had once been worth living for had exploded in front of her eyes.

I raised her head a little so she could sip some water, and she continued.

"What's left of that beautiful world?" she asked faintly. "What's left of this world that only gets more brutal? There is no value to life, the sublime, beauty. Maybe that's what the world is like. Maybe I and others like me have been naive, because what is happening here exposes all its ugliness," she said, after sipping more water. "Not only the murderers, us too, the victims, we've become animals. There is nothing to distinguish between us and a herd of calves in a pen." Tears fell from her eyes, "I wanted a different world. I strove to heal the world through literature, poetry, philosophy. That's why we founded the Aleksa Šantić Literary Society. The three of us[31] burned with desire for a better world, but we were naive. We didn't see the deterioration of the world or where it was headed."

I continued to sit beside her, knowing I would not be returning to Commander Andorfer's office. It was only when I looked out the window and saw a line of people walking from the pavilions to the

31 Nada, Marianna, and Hilda founded Aleksa Šantić's Literary Society.

kitchen that I realized it was time for the evening meal. I told Hilda I was going to get her something to eat, and she responded that she had no appetite and feared she'd just vomit it up again. I persuaded her to try even some dry bread in her mouth. I covered her up to her emaciated neck with the stained blanket and told her I would try and find something for her to eat and went outside, a lump rising in my throat as I took in for the first time that I was about to lose my good friend, the only one left to me here in the camp.

April 20

The camp is emptying fast. Every day, sometimes twice a day, the monstrous Saurer goes on its way with another cargo of women and children. Getz and Majer stand at the rear opening to the truck, checking the names of those getting in. Majer gives candies to the children to sweeten the journey. Commander Andorfer, his eternal stick under his armpit, marches up and down, making sure that everything is going as planned. I follow those departing with a pang. I'd realized by then that I couldn't change the minds of the people who remained, all of whom believed the truck would take them to a better place.

Once all the prisoners are in the truck, Getz and Majer close the door with a loud screech, get into the driver's cabin, and start to move slowly toward the camp gate. Shortly afterward, an accompanying vehicle sets out, a small military truck with a driver and a soldier in front, and behind, two armed soldiers and five prisoners from the men's block. No one asks why an accompanying vehicle is necessary or what role the prisoners play.

The two nurses, the pharmacist, and I were informed that we would not be leaving in a hurry. The same went for the kitchen staff and other services. We were being left for last.

I parted from Louisa two days ago. She came to tell me she was leaving the camp the following day. I didn't want to arouse her anxiety, and we talked of other things. She seemed indifferent to her fate, praising me for my brave decision to leave Commander Andorfer's comfortable office to be among friends. She spoke a lot about her longing for Emil, not knowing what had happened to him, hoping he wasn't suffering too much.

She'd heard from the children while in Belgrade. They feel well and are living on an Akiba Movement *kibbutz* in the center of the country. I told her I'd written to Hanne and wanted to know if he'd received the letter. She said she had no contact with him or Pauli; better they don't know what is happening to us here. I asked if he was working in agriculture as he'd dreamed of doing when we were in Kladovo.

Louisa suddenly remembered her daughter Klarie, and her eyes filled with tears. I went to hug her. She said I reminded her of her Klarie, and ever since our first encounter on the *Tzar Nikolai*, she'd seen me as a beloved daughter.

Before we parted, she also said goodbye to Hilda, whom she'd occasionally nursed after we moved her to the infirmary.

***

A week has passed since Hilda Dajč left us. Her last days were difficult. I hope that after a certain point, at least, she stopped suffering. The last time I asked to weigh her, she weighed thirty-four kilograms.

She died of exhaustion. I tried but failed to persuade her to eat. Toward the end, she refused to drink. The doctor said it was malnutrition linked to depression. Every day, more of her hair fell out and her skin became flaky. She could no longer get out of bed, and I had to help her to the toilet. It was hard to rouse her, and when she spoke, it was only about her friends Nada and Marianna, and she asked when she'd be able to go and visit them. Two days before her death, she said she was ashamed to go out and meet Marianna in the state she was in, and asked me to wash her and dress her in pretty clothes that would hide how pale and thin she was. On the last day, I sat beside her all day, holding her frail hand. She no longer spoke, just stared vacantly at the ceiling.

Later on, I could no longer bear it and left the room. When the pharmacist told me she'd died, I thought, *she's been released from her suffering.* I asked other friends to remove her body to the Turkish Pavilion, a job I'd done so often with Hilda.

The day after Louisa's visit to the infirmary, I went to part from her for the last time. She stood there with the whole group getting into the Saurer *polizei* that would take them to their destination. We fell into each other's arms and I let my tears flow down my cheeks. Afterward, when she'd gotten into the truck, I waved my hand in farewell and turned back to the infirmary.

BELGRADE–NEW YORK, APRIL 2002

After Alan returned to New York, he was once again busy with his daily routine. But the photographs of the Sajmište camp and his experiences reading Inge's journal gave him no rest. At home with his wife and daughters, at work, and primarily on the long train ride to work, the pictures constantly rose in his mind.

When he finished reading the journal, Barbara had to bring him back to reality. She reminded him that he still hadn't seen Hilda Dajč's letters, four letters that tell the heroic story of a young girl who'd sacrificed her life to take care of her people who were suffering in the camp. Barbara suggested he postpone reading the letters until the next day. And he promised himself that if he did write the book, he would make a place for her.

Barbara suggested he rest at the hotel that evening because it was late and this had been a difficult experience for him. The next day, he could return and read the letters and even go and see Sajmište if he wanted to.

The following day, after a quick breakfast at the hotel, he hurried off to meet Barbara at the museum. She was already waiting for him beside a large man with a graying black beard. He was wearing a photographer's vest with many pockets, a big black bag on his shoulder.

Barbara introduced him. "This is Peter, a professional photographer and site guide from Belgrade. He will take you through Sajmište."

Peter turned out to be well versed in the history of Belgrade's Jews. His father, a Jew living in Vienna, separated from his Christian mother, raised him, and made sure he studied at good schools in Belgrade and then in Vienna. Peter knew Sajmište camp very well. He showed Alan the pavilions that still stood in silent witness of the inferno.

"That's the Turkish Pavilion," Peter pointed it out and they went inside. "And this is where the showers were."

Afterward, they passed by a large building with a square chimney. Peter pointed at it and said that this was the hospital with fifty crowded beds for patients before they were transferred by ambulance to the other side of the Sava River.

Peter knew Hilda's story and could speak of her trips by ambulance to meetings at the café adjacent to the hospital. He promised they'd go past the Jewish hospital on Visokog Stevana Street on their way back to the museum. Next to the hospital building, he pointed out a large block.

"That's the American Pavilion," he said. "Or, as it is called here, Block 14." Alan felt a strong shiver as they entered the pavilion and he saw the huge spaces.

"Wooden bunks were crowded in here; several hundred women lived in this building together."

Despite it being a pleasant spring day, Alan felt the cold wind blowing through Block 14, through broken windows, which had been fixed in the meantime, and he could almost see Inge sitting on a thin layer of straw on her bunk, writing in her journal.

When he returned with Peter to the museum, the three of them went out to lunch together at a nearby restaurant. Barbara told them she'd been able to discover details about Hilda's two friends, Nada and Marianna. Both were still alive and living in Belgrade.

"Marianna Petrovich is eighty-three today. Her name is Marianna Kasanin, and she lives at Number Four Šmogorska Street. When we get back to the office, we can call her," promised Barbara.

Peter took him to visit Marianna. She'd just returned from the hospital, after breaking her left hip when she fell in the shower. She lived on the third floor in a building without an elevator. Now, she was confined to her home but received them with a wide smile, and suggested they help themselves to the cake her son had brought her yesterday. He was a man of about sixty and was helping her at the moment. Alan was surprised to hear that she had not set foot outside Yugoslavian borders since the war. Marianna distinctly remembered the secret meetings with Hilda at the café next to the Jewish hospital on Visokog Stevana Street. She clearly recalled waiting for the messenger from the hospital who would ask her to come at once to the café where Hilda was waiting, while German soldiers marched beneath her window. She remembered how Hilda's physical and psychological state deteriorated from visit to visit. At the last meeting, she already feared for her life and spoke about how she hated being near screeching women, how all they cared about was the taste of the first piece of meat in their mouths after they left the hell of the camp.

***

That evening, Alan flew back to New York. The visit to Belgrade, particularly the journal he'd found there, had greatly moved him. He knew now what he'd do when he got home. Although he did need to calm down first, get back into the routine of family and work, but it was now clear to him that he would write a book about the Kladovo Affair and dedicate it to his father. He suddenly felt all the weight of his lengthy estrangement from his father, and a profound sense of what he'd missed rose up in him. Why had he waited until his father was on his deathbed to find out what had happened to the love of his life?

As the plane circled over New York and he saw the skyscrapers on the skyline of Manhattan, he recalled his promise to Nina. The very next day, he would call the travel agent and book four tickets to Israel. He would also ask his sister Bracha to book them into a B&B on the *moshav* for a few days. He'd take both his daughters and Rachel to see the house he'd grown up in, the house his father had lived in for most of his days in Israel, most of his life in fact, after leaving the comfort and abundance of Belgrade to spend a year and a half with his parents and his brother as refugees on the Danube, on their way to *Eretz* Israel.

He thought to himself that maybe, as a result of this visit, he, too, would start thinking about returning to Israel, leaving behind all the comfort and abundance of America.

They at least deserve what he had received. Maybe he'd even start looking for a job on this visit to Israel. Although working in Israel felt odd to him. But he had to take the first step. After all, he'd promised Nina. And as she liked to remind him, promises are made to be kept.

The voice of the flight attendant informing them that they'd shortly be landing in New York recalls him to reality. The temperature in New York is seventy-two degrees Fahrenheit, and a fine rain is falling. Not yet summer.

EPILOGUE

Hanne David, known as Shlomo in Israel, fulfilled his dream of working the land in *Eretz* Israel and maintained this ideal to the end of his life. He was able to establish an agricultural farm on a *moshav* in the Galilee, work there, and raise a family who were his pride and joy.

The freedom train with its shuttered windows that set out from the Sabac railway station that morning in the middle of March 1941 arrived in Atlit after a journey of almost two weeks, during which they'd stopped in Constantinople for three days.

Hanne/Shlomo stayed a few days in Atlit before going as part of Aliyat Yeladim to an Akiba training spot in Hadera. There, he met Lotte Hertz (Varda today), born in a small village near Köln in Germany. After Kristallnacht, when she was fourteen, Lotte was sent alone to *Eretz* Israel on an Aliyat Yeladim transport. She met young Shlomo from Atlit in the Hadera group that was organizing to join Kibbutz Beit Yehoshua. They fell in love and married there in 1945, living and working on Kibbutz Beit Yehoshua until 1949. The founders of the *kibbutz* were Akiba activists. In 1949, the couple moved to Bustan Hagalil, a *moshav* in the north. Varda was a nurse by profession and known to be devoted. She was much loved on the *moshav*. She worked there as a nurse until her retirement. The couple had three children.

Inge (Henny) Müller, born in Germany, was Hanne's girlfriend during the group's long wait at Kladovo. She died at Sajmište in May 1942, on one of the Saurer *polizei* ("soul destroying") death journeys. She worked devotedly at the infirmary in the camp until her last hours and never believed that the journey would take her anywhere good.

Pauli David, later Abraham, arrived in Atlit on the freedom train from Sabac with his brother, Hanne. From there, he went to a training spot in Hadera. He was sent by the Akiba Movement to work as a counselor in town. At this time, he met his future wife, Esther, born in Vienna. The couple lived on Kibbutz Beit Yehoshua until 1949, when they moved to the Agricultural High School in Pardes Hanna. Faithful to his path as an educator and counselor of coming generations, Abraham devoted thirty-two years to this institution in the field of counseling, teaching, and education. In time, he completed his academic studies in Torah teaching and became a teacher of Torah at the same school.

Louisa David (Alkalay family) escaped with her husband Emil from Sabac to Belgrade at the end of the summer of 1941. When they were caught trying to cross the border into Hungary, she was taken with all the other women from Belgrade and its surroundings to Sajmište, where she died on one of the Saurer *polizei* death journeys, between March and May 1942.

Emil David, together with other Jewish prisoners held at Topovske Šupe, was taken to the killing fields not far from Belgrade. From this internment camp and from Seniak, near Sabac, the Kladovo group was held as hostages for retributions carried out by the Germans in response to their people being killed by Serbian Partisans. He was murdered by firing squad as he stood, bound, at the edge of a ditch, guarded by the SS.

Yost Pomerantz died with his mother, Elisheva, at Sajmište on one of the Saurer *polizei* death journeys between March and May 1942. They were on the march to Sajmište in the framework of the women's march. Max Pomerantz, his father, was murdered by firing squad at the death ditches, together with the rest of the Jewish men and gypsies held at the Seniak camp near Sabac.

Hilda Dajč was born in Vienna, raised and educated in Belgrade. She died at Sajmište, apparently at the end of April 1942. It isn't clear whether she died from exhaustion and malnutrition or in the Saurer *polizei*. She sacrificed her life to help others.

Jacob (Ya'akov) Langnese was born in Berlin in 1923, son of a religious Jewish family with six children, all of whom were murdered in the Holocaust. Jacob joined the transport as part of the BAHAD Movement, a religious youth movement once known as Hechalutz Hamizrachi. He, too, reached Atlit on the freedom train from Sabac in April 1941. From Atlit, he went to Mikveh, Israel, where he joined the army and served in the air force until he retired. In 1953, he married Emma Shimoni, and the couple had four children.

Shimon Spitzer, known as Sime, tried passionately to save the group. But his efforts paled in the face of historical events, natural disasters, and human frailty. He was cruelly murdered by a Gestapo doctor at the Banjica camp near Belgrade.

Naftali Bata Gedalja was born in Yugoslavia in 1906. He was active in community committees before the transport. He served as commander of the transport on the ships and then in Kladovo, where he alternated with his replacement, Elli Haimbach. He played a most significant role in the leadership of the transport. He was appointed by Sime Spitzer, and they worked closely together.

After the failure of the transport, he remained in Yugoslavia, helping Jews make *Aliyah* to Israel both from Yugoslavia and neighboring countries. He himself made *Aliyah* only in 1951, when he realized that his mission was complete. He came with his second wife and her mother (his first wife perished at Sajmište), and settled in the neighborhood of Kyriat Yovel, Jerusalem. He worked as a clerk in the Bureau of Statistics for the Ministry of Trade and Industry until his retirement. At the same time, he published articles about the Kladovo Affair and other issues related to Yugoslavian Jewry. One of these articles was titled "Two Princes and a Queen," which inspired the title of this book.

Naftali Bata Gedalja died in 1989. To commemorate his work, there is a Square in his name in the Hagiva Hatzarfatit neighborhood of Jerusalem.

The Darien. In the framework of Sime Spitzer's efforts to find a ship that would wait for the Kladovo group on the Black Sea and take them to *Eretz* Israel, a Mossad agent, Shmarya Tsameret, found the *Darien* in May 1940, at the Port of Piraeus. Italy entered the war in June that year, effectively putting a spoke in the wheel, and fearing the predictable fate of passenger ships sailing the Mediterranean, the heads of the Mossad postponed the voyage.

At the end of June, the heads of the Mossad and the Hagana, among them Eliyahu Golomb and David Hacohen, decided to hand over the *Darien* to their allies (David Hacohen and Yehuda Arazi), who cooperated with the British. The reason given by Chaim Weizmann at the time was that joint espionage actions with the British would enable the promotion of other actions against the British, such as *Aliyah Bet*.

It was only in September that the Mossad again turned their attention to the *Aliyah* of the Kladovo refugees, but by then conditions had changed for the worst. You could say that removing the *Darien* from the jurisdiction of Mossad activists and *Aliyah Bet*, and placing it under the jurisdiction of the group cooperating with the British, prevented the *Aliyah* of the Kladovo group in the summer of 1940.

The men from the Kladovo group who remained in Sabac after March 1941 were murdered in October 1941, within a space of three days. They were methodically slaughtered by SS firing squads, by order of General Franz Böhme. The shooting was recorded by a company of soldiers whose role was to record and document the actions of the German unit operating there. The picture appears at the Yad Vashem Museum in Jerusalem, and at the Topography of Terror Museum in Berlin. The killing was carried out in Farmer Ivanowich's corn field, above ditches dug by Jewish prisoners and the gypsies themselves, under the threat of SS guns. The farm was near Zasavica, a village on the banks of the Sava.

The women from the Kladovo group were taken from the camp near Sabac on the infamous women's march that left on January 10, 1942, for nearby Člának. From there, they were brought to Ruma on a cattle train. From Ruma, they continued through the frozen snow, exhausted, their shoes in tatters, as far as Zemun on the outskirts of Belgrade, a distance of about thirty kilometers. Among them were mothers with babes in arms, some forced to leave them in the snow, in the hope they'd be able to return for them.

All the women perished at the Sajmište camp in the recurring journeys of the Saurer *polizei*, the soul killer, carried out between March and May 1942.

The Kladovo group consisted of 1,140 men, women, and children who were attempting to reach *Eretz* Israel before the appalling wave of terror sweeping Europe drowned them too. The door was closed in their faces and they were lost.

Only two hundred and fifty youth were saved from this hell—those fortunate enough to be the right age to board the freedom train that left Sabac for Atlit, via Bulgaria, Greece, Constantinople, and Beirut.

The Kladovo Affair continued to trouble the waters many years later in *Eretz* Israel. These were the political waters of the leaders of the Jewish Agency and the Mossad L'Aliyah Bet, who tried to evade accountability for the complications that brought about the searing failure to bring the group safely to *Eretz* Israel.

Ingram Content Group UK Ltd.
Milton Keynes UK
UKHW022212240723
425713UK00005B/77

9 789655 751437